Smoke
and
Ashes

ALSO BY ABIR MUKHERJEE

A Rising Man
A Necessary Evil

Smoke and Ashes

A Novel

ABIR MUKHERJEE

PEGASUS BOOKS

NEW YORK LONDON

SMOKE AND ASHES

Pegasus Books, Ltd.
148 West 37th Street, 13th Floor
New York, NY 10018

First Pegasus Books hardcover edition March 2019

ISBN: 978-1-64313-014-9

10 9 8 7 6 5 4 3 2 1

Printed in the United States of America
Distributed by W. W. Norton & Company, Inc.

For Mum,
Hope this makes up for not being a doctor.

Forget not, that thou art born as a sacrifice upon the altar of the Motherland.
Swami Vivekananda

ONE

21 December 1921

It's not unusual to find a corpse in a funeral parlour. It's just rare for them to walk in the door under their own steam. It was a riddle worth savouring, but I didn't have the time, seeing as I was running for my life.

A shot rang out and a bullet flew past, hitting nothing more offensive than rooftop laundry. My pursuers – fellow officers of the Imperial Police Force – were firing blindly into the night. That didn't mean they mightn't get lucky with their next round, and while I wasn't afraid of dying, *'shot in the backside while trying to escape'* wasn't exactly the epitaph I wanted on my tombstone.

And so I ran, opium-fogged, across the rooftops of a sleeping Chinatown, slipping on loose terracotta tiles, sending them smashing to the ground and clambering from one roof to the next before finally finding shelter in a shallow crawlspace beneath the ledge of a low wall which separated one building from its neighbour.

The officers drew closer, and I tried to still my breathing as they called out to one another, their voices swallowed by the darkness. The sound suggested they'd separated, now possibly some distance from each other. That was good. It meant they were groping around as aimlessly in the dark as I was, and that for now my best chance of escape lay in staying still and silent.

Being caught would lead to some rather awkward questions which I preferred not to have to answer: such as what I happened to be doing in Tangra in the dead of night, smelling of opium and covered in someone else's blood. There was also the small matter of the sickle-shaped blade in my hand. That too would be difficult to explain.

I shivered as the sweat and the blood evaporated. December was cold, at least by Calcutta standards.

Snatches of conversation drifted over. It didn't sound like their hearts were in it. I didn't blame them. They were as likely to stagger off the edge of a roof as they were to stumble across me; and given the events of the last few months, I doubted their morale would be particularly high. Why risk a broken neck chasing shadows along rooftops, when no one was going to thank them for it? I willed them to turn back, but they doggedly kept at it, tapping in the blackness with rifle butts and lathis like blind men crossing a road.

One set of taps grew louder, a rhythmic presence drawing ever closer. I considered my options, or I would have done, had I been able to think of any. Running was out of the question – the man was armed and sounded so close now that, even in the dark, he'd have little difficulty in shooting me. Taking him on was also a non-starter. I had the blade but I was hardly going to use it on a fellow officer, and, in any case, with three of his colleagues in close proximity, the odds of eluding them were shrinking faster than a poppy at sunset.

The tone of the tapping changed, taking on an echoing hollowness as it struck the thin concrete of the ledge above my head. The man must have been standing directly above me. He too noticed the change in tenor and stopped in his tracks. He knocked at the ledge with his rifle, then jumped down. I closed my eyes in anticipation of the inevitable, but then a voice called out. One that I recognised.

'All right, lads, that's enough. Back inside.'

The boots turned towards the command, and for the longest of seconds stood rooted before finally climbing back onto the ledge. They began to move off and I breathed out, then ran a hand, still sticky with blood, over my face.

The voices receded and the rooftops returned to silence. Minutes passed and from the street below came shouts – English, Bengali, Chinese – and the sound of lorries starting up. I stayed where I was, shivering in the confines of the crawlspace, and tried to make sense of it all.

The night had started quite normally, though *normal* is, admittedly, a relative term. At any rate, tonight seemed no different from any other night that I visited one of the opium dens which pockmarked Chinatown. From my lodgings in Premchand Boral Street, I'd made my way south to Tangra by one of many circuitous routes, to a den I was fairly sure I hadn't visited for at least a month. This one was in the basement of a row of sagging tenements, entered via a dank stairwell at the back of a funeral parlour that reeked of formaldehyde and the proximity of death. It was one of my favourites, not for the quality of the opium, which was as bad as anywhere else in the city – one part opium to three parts God knew what – but because of the faintly Gothic aura the place exuded. Calcutta opium is best smoked ten feet below the corpses of half a dozen dead men.

I'd arrived sometime after midnight and the doorman had seemed surprised to see me. I didn't blame him, though it wasn't the shakes that unnerved him – he would have seen many a punter coming through the door with those symptoms. Rather it was the colour of my skin. Seeing an Englishman in Tangra wouldn't have been all that remarkable a year ago, but a lot had happened in the last twelve months. These days, with the police force stretched thin outside of the meticulously manicured confines of White

Town, sahibs were hard to find in Calcutta after dark. Fortunately, though, in this part of town economics still trumped issues of race and politics, and upon sight of the fan of rupee notes I clutched in my hand, I was admitted without fuss or fanfare and accompanied down to the cellar.

The first drag of the first pipe was a deliverance, like the breaking of a fever. With the second pipe, the shaking stopped, and with the third, the nerves steadied. I called for a fourth. If the first three had been a medicinal requisite, the next would be for pleasure, setting me on my way to what the Bengalis called *nirbōn* – nirvana. My head rested on a pillow of white porcelain as the velvet veil enveloped my senses. That's when the trouble started.

From a thousand miles away came sounds: jagged and incomprehensible, growing louder and piercing the fog of my stupor. I screwed my eyelids shut against them, until a woman, one of the girls who rolled the O and prepared the pipes, was shaking me like a rag doll.

'Sahib! You must go now!'

I opened my eyes and her heavily powdered face floated into focus.

'You must go, sahib. Police raid!'

Her lips were painted blood red, and for some seconds the sight of them held my attention more than anything she might be saying. It was the sound of crashing furniture and porcelain smashing on a hard floor somewhere close by that finally began to break the spell. That and the hard slap across the face she gave me.

'Sahib!'

I shook my head as she slapped me again.

'Police here, sahib!'

The words registered. I tried to stand on legs shaky like a newborn calf. Taking my arm, she pulled me towards a darkened passageway at the far side of the room, away from the oncoming commotion.

She stopped at the threshold and gestured with her free hand. 'Go, sahib. Stairs at end. Up to back way.'

I turned to look at her. She was little more than a girl. 'What's your name?' I asked.

'No time, sahib,' she said, turning back towards the room. 'Go. Now!'

I did as she ordered and staggered into the blackness, as behind me I heard her trying to rouse another punter from temporary oblivion. I groped blindly, feeling my way along walls slick with moisture, the stone floor slippery underfoot and the air fetid with the ammonia stench of stale urine. In the distance a blue light illuminated a narrow, sagging staircase. My head spinning, I made for it. Sounds echoed down the corridor: orders shouted in English. Then a woman's scream.

I didn't look back.

Instead I lurched on towards the stairs and looked up. The exit was barred by a hatch, a little light falling in thin shafts between it and the floorboards. Hauling myself up the steps, I reached the top, pushed the hatch and cursed as the thing refused to budge. I shivered as a wave of fear swept over me. Wiping the sweat from my eyes, I tried to focus on the hatch's outline. There seemed no sign of a lock, at least not on this side. I took a breath and tried again, this time charging it with my shoulder. The hatch shifted a few inches, then fell back heavily. There was something on top of it. Something weighty. Behind me, the voices grew louder. Summoning what strength I had left, I charged the hatch one more time. It burst open, and suddenly I was flying through the air, momentum carrying me upward into a ruin of a room, its ceiling half gone and open to the moonlight. I landed hard on the floor, in a pool of something wet. Pulling myself up, I quickly shut the hatch and looked to weigh it down with whatever had been on top of it. Strangely there was nothing close by. Other than a body.

I stared at it. Not in shock – or anything else for that matter. Morphia deadens the senses, and I probably had enough of the stuff coursing through me to becalm a bull elephant. It was a man – or what was left of him. Chinese, judging by his cheekbones. The rest of his face, though, was a mess. His eyes had been gouged out and left on the floor beside him, and an old scar ran down the left side, from his hairline to his jaw. Then there was the small matter of the knife stuck in his chest.

Wooden crates, the type that tea is packed in, stood stacked next to a wall, their metal studs glinting in the blue light. I stumbled over to them and made to topple the topmost to the ground. Whatever was in it weighed half a ton. Nevertheless, I managed to shift it, inch by inch, until it overhung the crate beneath and gravity did the rest. It landed with a thud; the wood of one side cracked but remained thankfully intact. Lodging my feet against the wall, I steadily pushed it over the top of the hatch then slumped beside it in the hope that I'd bought myself a little time. I looked over at the dead man, lying there on his back, with the knife sticking out from his sternum like the lever of a Bell fruit machine. I assumed he was dead. That was a good thing. For me, if not for him. Then I heard his breathing – shallow, ragged and bloody – and I cursed. Any time I wasted tending to him diminished what little chance I had of escape. Judging by the amount of blood on the floor, he was already beyond saving, and there was little I could do, especially with Calcutta's finest raiding the place. Explaining to them exactly what I was doing, covered in the blood of a critically wounded Chinaman, wasn't a prospect I relished. Besides, the Chinese were a law unto themselves. What they did to each other was none of my business.

Still…

Taking a breath, I crawled over to him. Making sure not to disturb the knife, I undid the buttons on his shirt and, retrieving a handkerchief from my trouser pocket, wiped the blood from his chest. There were two wounds as far as I could tell: the one in which the knife was stuck, and another, almost identical mark on the right side of his chest, but there could have been more. In the half-light and in my condition, he could have been missing an arm and I might not have noticed.

He tried to stir.

'Who did this?' I asked.

He turned his head towards me and tried to speak, but only managed a bloody gurgling.

'Your lung's punctured,' I said. 'Try not to move.'

It was sound advice. He should have heeded it. Instead he reached for the knife and pulled at it. I should have stopped him. The knife fell to the floor. Grabbing the handkerchief, I pressed down on the wound, trying to staunch a weak stream of blood, but knowing, even as I did so, that it was in vain. When you've seen the life ebb away from as many men as I have, you get a sense for these things, and within seconds he was gone. I leaned forward, put my ear to his mouth and listened for a breath, but there was nothing.

Behind me, someone was trying the hatch. Instinctively I picked up the knife and spun round. There were voices on the stairs below. It sounded like at least two of them were pushing against the trap-door, but the crate was doing its job and the hatch hardly budged. Nevertheless, I doubted they'd give up.

I turned and looked for an escape route. There were two doors. I chose one and ran through, into a courtyard bordered on three sides by the walls of two- and three-storey buildings. The fourth side, though, consisted of a single-storey wall topped with shards of broken glass. In its centre was a wooden door, which I assumed led

7

to an alleyway. I was about to make for it when I stopped. This was a police raid – there were probably half a dozen armed officers on the other side, waiting to nab anyone looking to escape.

Instead I headed for a stone staircase that ran up one of the walls and onto the roof. One of the officers must have spotted me from a window as, moments later, a door on the roof burst open and officers were shouting for me to halt.

Declining the invitation, I'd run for it, and as I lay in that crawl-space, shivering, it was heartening to know I'd made at least one correct decision that night.

My thoughts returned to the dead Chinaman and to the raid itself. The fact was, there shouldn't have been one. With the city on the edge of anarchy and a mass of resignations among the native officers, resources were stretched to breaking point. The force simply lacked the manpower for fripperies such as raids on opium dens.

What's more, none had been planned. Of that I was certain. I knew because I made a point of stopping by Vice Division's offices on days when I was considering a trip to Chinatown. I'd even made a friend of its commanding officer, a man called Callaghan whose voice I'd heard earlier, calling his men back. Indeed I'd bought him many a drink, just so I'd always know when he and his men were planning an evening's excursion. On nights when a raid was on the cards, he was generally too busy to chat, and the atmosphere in the department would be electric. I'd popped by earlier in the day and the place had been dead, with Callaghan himself more than happy to indulge me.

And yet here I was, hiding from him and a lorry-load of his officers.

TWO

I waited.

Twenty minutes, which felt longer; staying there till the voices and the noises stopped. Eventually, my head began to clear and I crawled out and slowly stood up. Going back to check on the corpse was out of the question. Callaghan and his goons might have gone, but they'd have left men behind to secure the place, luckless local constables from the closest police thana, most likely. I didn't envy them. More than one native copper had had his throat slit in the dark in Tangra.

No, my first task was to get rid of the knife. I still wasn't sure why I'd picked it up. It certainly hadn't been through any urge to preserve evidence. The attacker's fingerprints might have been on it, but now so were mine. Maybe it had something to do with the shape of the thing: a blade, more bent than curved, about ten or eleven inches long, like the kind the Gurkha regiments had carried during the war, only with an ornamental hilt that was wrapped in black leather and inlaid with the image of a small silver dragon.

The smart thing to do would be to throw it in the Hooghly. Only the river was several miles away, I was covered in blood and I wasn't going to get far in my current garb. What I needed was a change of clothes. I set off across the rooftops scouring the vista until I found what I was looking for. Moving silently, I covered the distance in a matter of minutes, and was soon rifling through the articles on a washing line like a housewife examining the wares at Chukerbutty's Fine Clothing Emporium on Bow Bazaar. Hindus have a fixation with ritual cleanliness, not just of their bodies but their clothes too. That preoccupation seemed to have infected all of the town's other non-white residents too, and at any given time, half of Black Town seemed submerged in a sea of drying laundry. Picking out a shirt, I quietly slipped off my own and wrapped it around the knife. The shirt from the line was old, faded and a size too small, but I buttoned it as best I could and rolled up the sleeves. To complete the ensemble, I stole a black shawl, which the locals called a *chador*, and wrapped it round my head and shoulders like an old woman, then continued over the rooftops until I found a place low enough to jump down to the street. From there I headed north to the Circular Canal where, weighing down the knife and my shirt with a brick, I deposited the package in the black waters below, like a Hindu devotee making an offering to the gods. Then I set off west, stopping at a tube-well to wash my hands and face, before continuing the mile or so to the all-night tonga rank at Sealdah station.

As I walked, my head buzzed with only one thought. I had to find out why the raid had taken place. It couldn't be coincidence that a man had been murdered as Vice Division, without warning, launched its first raid in months on a den, just at the time that I happened to be there.

The clock in College Square read a quarter past three, and I was back in Premchand Boral Street soon after. I was early. Most nights it was at least 4 a.m. by the time I made it home from Tangra. I'd have laughed at the irony if it wasn't for the dead man I'd left lying back there.

Trudging up the stairs to my lodgings, I slipped the key into the lock. The apartment was in darkness. Nevertheless, I had to tread carefully. I shared my lodgings with a junior officer, Surrender-not Banerjee, and he was a light sleeper. His real name wasn't Surrender-not, but Surendranath. It meant king of the gods apparently, and like the names of many of the kings I remembered from my history classes, its proper pronunciation was beyond me and most of the other British officers at Lal Bazar. A senior officer had rechristened him Surrender-not. That man was dead now, but the name had stuck.

He knew of my opium habit, of course. We'd never discussed it but the boy wasn't an idiot, and in the early days he'd couched his concern in vague, open-ended questions as to my health, all framed with the sort of disappointed look a mother might give you when you came home from having been in a fight. Not that it had changed anything, and these days, he'd given up the questions, though I still encountered the stares from time to time.

The more pressing issue was our manservant, Sandesh. He too slept in the apartment, though generally on a mat under the dining table. He was supposed to sleep in the kitchen but claimed it was too large and that high ceilings gave him insomnia. Waking him was not normally a concern, for even if he *did* care as to where I was going most nights, he was mindful enough of his station never to voice an opinion on it. Nevertheless, seeing me wandering in dressed like a Spanish fishwife might just challenge even his monumental indifference.

I crept along the hallway to my room and once inside, locked the door. Light from a crescent moon bled in through the open window and fell like a veil on the furniture. The darkness felt like protection and, dispensing with the lamp, I removed the chador and pulled a crumpled pack of Capstan and a box of matches from my trouser pocket. I extracted a cigarette, lit it with shaking hands and took a long, steady pull.

In one corner stood my almirah, the large wooden wardrobe that was a fixture of most Calcutta bedrooms. With a mirrored panel inlaid in one of its two doors, the thing was unremarkable, save for the lockable steel compartment inside, which occupied a quarter of it and contained the few valuable possessions I owned, together with a larger number of more questionable ones. Placing the fag end in the old tin ashtray which sat on my desk, I stripped out of the borrowed shirt and, together with the chador, bundled it into the almirah's steel compartment before locking it again. The clothes would need to be burned, but for now this was the best place for them. With the evidence concealed, I sank onto the bed and covered my face with my hands as, on the desk, the cigarette burned down to nothing.

THREE

22 December 1921

The cup of tea on the bedside table was stone cold. Sandesh, as was his habit, had placed it there, probably several hours earlier. I extricated myself from the mosquito net, picked up the cup and threw the contents out of the window, waiting for the gratifying splash as the stuff hit the concrete courtyard below.

It was likely to be the closest I came to festive cheer. Christmas in Calcutta was an odd affair. While freezing for the natives, it was still never bleak enough for anyone who'd grown up in true British winters, and though the carol singers from the local churches, with their *hosannas* and *hallelujahs*, did their best to remind you of the joy of the coming of Our Lord and Saviour, Christmas with palm trees in place of spruce and Norwegian pine just wasn't the same.

Christmas aside though, the city had grown on me. Maybe it had something to do with the fact that, in its own way, Calcutta was as flawed and dysfunctional as I was: a city built in the middle of a fetid Bengal swamp, populated by misfits all struggling to survive against the odds.

Surrender-not was long gone by the time I'd washed, dressed and made it through to the dining table. He'd always been an early riser, but these days I'd rather formed the impression that he left early in order to avoid having to talk to me. Sandesh entered and wordlessly placed breakfast and a copy of the day's *Englishman* in front of me. From the creases on the paper's front page, it looked as though Surrender-not had already gone through it. I pushed it to one side and began to pick at a lukewarm omelette liberally sprinkled with chopped green chillies. I'd little appetite for food these days, and, thanks to Mr Gandhi's antics, even less for the news. The country was a powder keg, and had been so ever since the Mahatma, as his followers liked to call him, had asked Indians to rise up in a frenzy of non-violent non-cooperation, and promised that if they did so, he'd deliver independence before the year was out.

Of course, Indians are gluttons for mysticism, and the sight of the man in his little dhoti was enough to persuade them to do just that. Millions of them – not just the parlour-room revolutionaries of Bombay, Calcutta and Delhi, but the ordinary folk, the farmers, peasants and factory workers from ten thousand towns and villages across the length and breadth of the country – had heeded his calls to boycott British products, resign from government posts and generally cause a bloody nuisance. You had to hand it to the little man; he'd taken the Congress Party from a talking shop of lawyers and turned it into a movement of the people. Co-opting the masses – that had been the Mahatma's masterstroke. He'd told them that they mattered, and they revered him for it.

The Bengalis of Calcutta, always eager to stick two fingers up to the British, had taken it upon themselves to lead the charge – not that there was much charging to be done, seeing as how the Mahatma's preferred modus operandi was to get his followers to sit down and refuse to move. What's more, as a means of protest, it seemed almost tailor-made for the Bengali psyche, which was predisposed to causing maximum inconvenience while doing as little as possible. Striking was in their blood, so much so that you'd be forgiven for thinking that many of them only turned up to work so that they could then go on strike.

Not so long ago, our city had been the capital of British India. If we'd hoped that moving the centre of power to Delhi might lessen the capacity of Calcutta's native population to cause trouble, we'd been sorely mistaken. They'd reacted to the Mahatma's call with their usual zeal. Students had walked out of universities and schools, civil servants had resigned and government institutions were picketed. Most worrying, though, were the resignations from the ranks of the police force. It had started inconsequentially – a few native officers handing in their badges on principle soon after Gandhi's call – but later, with the mass arrests and jailing of protesters, and amid mounting pressure from families and communities, the flow had increased steadily.

The situation in the city had gradually worsened. One might have expected law and order to improve, given the emphasis on peaceful protest, but the Mahatma had unleashed forces that he couldn't control. Not all of those fired up by his words seemed quite as keen on non-violence as he was. As the months had passed, passions had risen, and there had been sporadic attacks on whites, Anglo-Indians, Christians, Parsees, Chinese and just about anyone else suspected of being less than euphoric about the prospect of an independent India. And the Imperial Police Force didn't have the manpower to protect everyone, even *if* we had wished to. For that was our dirty secret. The fact was that the powers that be rather welcomed the attacks. Anything that punched a hole in the Mahatma's sainted aura was seen as a positive, and attacks by his followers were the perfect pretext for a crackdown. The plan might have made sense on paper – indeed the viceroy and his coterie in Delhi seemed to approve, but they might as well have been sitting in London or, for that matter, on the moon, given how far removed they were from the realities of what was transpiring on the streets. With tempers fraught and jails full to bursting, such a crackdown didn't seem quite so sensible on the streets of Calcutta.

Word had it that the viceroy, never the most steadfast of men, favoured a compromise, but a number of stiff telegrams from Downing Street, and no doubt a few stiff gins too, had served to bolster his resolve, and in the end he hadn't yielded an inch to native demands. Now there were barely ten days to go before Gandhi's year was up, and with the discipline of even his most ardent supporters wavering, the hope in high places was that if we could weather the storm for another fortnight, the Mahatma's whole peaceful protest movement might collapse, taking his credibility with it.

But then had come the news that His Majesty's government in London had, in its wisdom, decided that the way to strengthen the bonds of empire was to send us His Royal Highness Prince Edward, the Prince of Wales, on a month-long royal tour. The effect, of course, had been electric, though more on the natives than on the city's loyal British subjects. The protests, which had been dying down, suddenly erupted with renewed vigour, as Congress leaders called for a complete boycott of the visit.

The prince had arrived in Bombay some weeks earlier and was greeted by brass bands and a full-scale riot. Calcutta, on the other hand, had remained stubbornly peaceful as the city awaited his visit. This had caused anguish verging on panic in some quarters – because that peace hadn't been enforced by the brave officers of the Imperial Police Force, or the army for that matter, but instead by a different presence, the khaki-clad members of Gandhi's Congress Volunteer Force. Young, earnest, idealistic men, they'd been tasked by the Mahatma with ensuring that non-violent protest remained just that: non-violent; and yet the sight of them directing people like some vigilante militia sent a chill down my spine. 1921 had proved to be a vintage year for uniformed mobs. In Italy, Mussolini's blackshirts were going from strength to strength, and their brown-shirted brothers in Germany were making a nuisance of themselves too. Our home-grown Congress Volunteers might profess non-violence, but I distrusted any civilian organisation which felt the need to bedeck their members in quasi-military uniforms – and that included the Boy Scouts.

The Volunteers had been charged by Congress with enforcing Gandhi's call for a general strike – a total shutdown of shops, businesses and civilian administration – to protest the prince's visit. At the same time, the viceroy had ordered us to arrest anyone seeking to compromise the efficient operations of the government. Everyone knew there was a showdown coming, and at police headquarters at Lal Bazar, plans were being drawn up to deal with the worst.

As for the prince, right now he was processing his merry way across the country and was due to arrive in Calcutta in three days' time – on Christmas morning no less.

We couldn't have handed Mr Gandhi a better Christmas present if we'd tried.

Sandesh entered the room and placed a fresh cup of tea on the dining table. I picked it up and pushed politics from my mind. In their stead, my thoughts returned to the previous night. My escape had been fortuitous, owing more to a Chinese girl's quick thinking than skill on my part. It still felt like a dream, and maybe some of the memories were just that – opium-induced figments of my subconscious. *Pipe dreams* they were called, but the corpse had been real enough. Of that I was sure.

The dead man had probably been a foot soldier of one of the opium gangs which were forever fighting for control over Chinatown: the Green Gang or the Red Gang, most likely. They were the biggest players in the Chinese opium trade after all. Both were based in Shanghai, and Calcutta – the gate through which their opium flowed – was a prize they were both willing to shed blood for. In the past, we'd managed to keep a lid on their feud, but now, with our numbers depleted, other matters took precedence, and the gangs had been quick to capitalise, fighting with each other for the right to fill the void we'd left.

As to the man's identity, it would be up to someone in my department to find that out – at least technically. Legally, we had a duty to investigate every murder which occurred within our jurisdiction. In practice though, if the victim wasn't white or, God forbid, a high-profile native, the initial inquiry was often perfunctory, a form-filling exercise before the case was farmed out to a local thana and forgotten about.

Still, I wondered on whose desk the case would initially fall. There was even a chance it would land on my own as, by luck or design, I wasn't exactly rushed off my feet at the moment. And if it didn't, I'd make damn sure to keep tabs on any inquiry, not because I was worried about it leading to me – once I'd burned the clothes there would be nothing linking me to the scene – but because the whole business had been disturbing.

I drained the last of the tea and headed for the door. Outside, Calcutta assailed the senses as it always did: a cocktail of primary colours, pungent aromas and the cacophony of life in a city of a million souls packed into a space too small for a tenth of their number.

I made it to my desk at Lal Bazar by half past ten. My timekeeping of late had been less than impeccable, but not to the extent that it had been commented upon by other officers – not to my face at least. It's true, Surrender-not had made some rather cryptic references to things he'd heard, but I wasn't sure what he'd meant. When it came to imparting information, he could be as opaque in his pronouncements as the Oracle at Delphi. Either way, the views of my fellow detectives didn't trouble me. Only one man's opinion mattered, and, according to the note on my desk, it appeared he wanted to see me. Urgently.

I composed myself, then headed out of my office and, collecting Surrender-not on my way, made for the stairs up to the top floor and the office of Lord Taggart, the commissioner of police for Bengal.

———

'C. R. Das. What do you know about him?'

It wasn't the question I'd been expecting. I was seated in Lord Taggart's office, across the desk from him. Surrender-not sat on the chair next to me.

'Sir?'

The commissioner shook his head. He looked tired. All of Calcutta's policemen did these days.

'Come now, Sam. You must know the name. Or have you been asleep for the last year?'

Of course I knew the name. Everyone in India did.

'Gandhi's chief rabble-rouser in Bengal,' I said. 'His face is in the papers most days.'

The answer hardly seemed to placate the commissioner.

'That's it, is it? The sum total of your knowledge of the biggest thorn in my side?'

'I tend to keep my nose out of politics, sir. But if you suspect Mr Das has killed someone, I'll be sure to acquaint myself more closely with him.'

Taggart eyed me suspiciously. We had a history of working together which dated back to the war. As such he afforded me slightly more leeway than he did most others, but there was a limit to his tolerance.

He let the comment pass and turned to Surrender-not. 'Maybe Sergeant Banerjee can help you out?'

Surrender-not looked like he was having trouble staying on his seat. He often found it hard not to show off his knowledge and I half expected his hand to shoot into the air like an overenthusiastic schoolboy.

'Chitta-Ranjan Das,' he replied. 'Advocate at the High Court, and reputed to be one of the finest legal minds in India. A supporter of the Home Rule movement, he first came to prominence about fifteen years ago when he defended the poet Aurobindo Ghosh in the Alipore Bomb Conspiracy trial when no other advocate was willing to take the case. Das got him acquitted. After that, his fame spread and he became one of the most successful barristers in Calcutta. As the captain mentioned, he is now Gandhi's chief lieutenant in Bengal, responsible for organising the non-cooperation movement and the Congress Volunteers throughout the province. The people love him. As with the Mahatma, they've given Das an honorific title: they call him the Deshbandhu. It means "friend of the nation".'

'Yes,' replied Lord Taggart bitterly. 'Well, he's no friend of ours, and neither are his blasted Volunteers.'

Surrender-not was making me look bad. I shot him a glance implying as much and received nothing but a shrug from him in return.

Taggart turned his attention to me. 'As you know, Sam, His Royal Highness the Prince of Wales is due to arrive on Sunday, and both Delhi and London are anxious that his visit to our fair city be a success.'

The prince had something of an American film star about him. Maybe it was his charm, or the natural confidence that came from the knowledge that you were born to rule one-sixth of the globe; or maybe it was just the well-cut, very expensive suits he wore, but whatever it was, crowds the world over seemed to flock to the man to bask in his reflected glory, and the British government was more than happy to capitalise on it, sending him on goodwill visits to all corners of the empire.

But Calcutta wasn't Cape Town and I wondered if the mandarins in London or Delhi really knew what a tall order it would be
for the prince to do any good here. If it was tranquillity you were
looking for, Calcutta was about as good a choice as the Second
Battle of the Marne. I'd met him once, Prince Edward Albert
Saxe-Coburg Windsor, or whatever his name was, back in the
trenches in '16. Then, as now, they'd sent him on a morale-boosting
tour, though it eluded me how a handshake from a prince who'd
never have to experience the horrors of war was supposed to raise
the morale of men whose lives consisted of little more than waiting
for the machine-gun bullet with their name on it. He couldn't have
been much more than a boy then. I remember the smooth face and
the uniform which seemed a size too large for him. He didn't lack
courage though. Rumour had it he'd volunteered for the Front in '15
but the king and the government had dismissed it out of hand.

'To that end,' Taggart continued, 'the viceroy has decided to
designate the Congress Volunteers a proscribed organisation; and
not before time. They will be banned as of tomorrow. And that's
where you come in, Sam. I want you to deliver that message personally to Das. Tell him to consider it fair warning.

'As for the prince, I'm rather hoping he won't be in much of a
mood to dawdle in our fair city. Word has it he finds Indians rather
odious and just wants to get back to the arms of his mistress in
London. Nevertheless, on no account are we to allow any stunts or
other actions to occur which could cause embarrassment to His
Royal Highness or to His Majesty's government.'

'And you think Das is planning some *stunt*?' I asked.

Taggart picked up a silver pen and tapped it on his desk. 'I've no
doubt that's exactly what he's doing. What you need to find out is
what specifically he is planning, and then persuade him not to do it.'

'We could always arrest him,' I ventured. It seemed like the
obvious solution, assuming we had anywhere to put him.

Taggart shook his head. 'That's what he wants us to do. If we arrest him on a charge of sedition, we make a martyr out of him and suddenly another ten thousand flock to his cause. Besides, the London and foreign press will be in town covering the prince's visit. The viceroy is rather keen that we avoid any adverse reaction. A general strike is one thing – I can live with pictures of empty streets – but an angry mob protesting the arrest of Bengal's most beloved son is quite another.'

'I'm not sure I understand what you expect of us, sir,' I said. 'In any case, surely this is a matter for our military intelligence friends at Section H? Or have they given up trying to crush political sedition?'

'I doubt they've given up, Sam,' he replied. 'It's more likely they just don't know quite what to do. It's one thing tackling a few hundred bomb-throwing terrorists. Dealing with a national mass movement led by a saint whose strategy is to smile at you before he orders his followers to sit down, block the streets and pretend to pray, isn't something they're particularly adept at dealing with. And to be honest, I can't say I'm surprised. The whole thing's damned unsporting.' He placed the pen back on the desk. 'No,' he continued, 'I fear that we'll need more than the sledgehammer that is Section H to crack this particular nut. And that's where you come in, Sam. You spent time in Special Branch in London, infiltrating Irish nationalists.'

'That was a long time ago,' I said, 'before the war. And anyway, following an Irishman around London is hardly the same thing as dealing with an Indian in Calcutta. For a start, I'm the wrong colour to infiltrate much of anything out here, unless it's the bar at the Bengal Club. How am I supposed to get close to Das?'

'Don't be obtuse, Sam,' he sighed. 'I'm not asking you to infiltrate his bloody inner circle. What I want is for you to meet him, deliver the viceroy's ultimatum and warn him off. Then report back to me with your assessment of the man. You've dealt with his sort before. You know how their minds work. Gauge what he's up to.'

'And why would he tell me anything?' I asked.

'Because.' Taggart smiled. 'I understand that our Mr Das is a close family friend of Sergeant Banerjee here.'

FOUR

'You kept that one quiet,' I said, taking a seat behind my desk.

Across from me, Surrender-not shifted on his chair.

'All the trouble we've had over the last year – the strikes, the resignations, the attacks – you didn't think to mention that the man behind it all was a chum of yours?'

The sergeant dropped his gaze to the floor. 'I very much doubt he'd consider me a *chum*. He's my father's friend,' he replied. 'It's been years since I've seen Uncle Das socially.'

'*Uncle* Das?' I teased. In the past, I might have assumed that *uncle* meant an actual familial connection, but you didn't have to be around Indians for very long to realise that they referred to almost every acquaintance as uncle, or aunt, or grandfather or big brother. Everyone was a *kakū*, or a *masi* or a *dada*, as though all three hundred million of them were one big extended unhappy family.

'Well, if he's your uncle, we should be able to sort out this whole business by lunchtime.'

'You know he's not my *real* uncle,' said Surrender-not. 'And even if he were, I doubt that would help very much. Not given my current standing within the family.'

That much was true. The boy had made more than his fair share of sacrifices in order to continue doing this job that he loved. He'd battled his own conscience and burned bridges with his kith and kin, and while I hadn't exactly been keeping tabs, I doubted he'd seen his parents since Kali Puja, the festival of the goddess Kali, over a year ago.

I should have apologised, but of course I didn't. I doubted he even expected me to. There were so many things I needed to apologise to him for, one more hardly made a difference.

'He and my father were at Lincoln's Inn together,' he continued. 'They were called to the Bar within a year of each other. When I was a child, he and his family would often visit our home, especially at *puja* time. In fact' – he laughed sourly – 'I expect he has been inside my family home more recently that I have.'

'What else can you tell me about him?'

'What do you want to know?'

'What we're up against. What sort of a man is he?'

'The type you hate – a Bengali who knows the law.'

'I don't *hate* them,' I said, 'not *all* of them anyway, I just prefer dealing with people who appreciate the job we do.'

He smiled sardonically. 'I doubt there are many of *them* left in the country, sir.'

'Do you have anything useful to contribute?' I asked.

'Yes, sir, absolutely,' he replied. 'Das is the scion of a prominent Bengali family and one of the wealthiest barristers in Calcutta. At least he was.'

'Was?'

'After he met Gandhi, he donated it all to the independence movement. Even his house. He's an ardent believer in the Mahatma's creed of non-violence. He was the one who first advocated the boycott of Western clothes, which is ironic as he used to be famous for his tailor-made Parisian suits, before he burned them all and took to wearing only homespun Indian cloth.'

The man sounded like a fanatic.

'Anything else?' I asked.

'He has a wife and three children,' he ventured.

I had the feeling he was holding back.

'Do you think he's planning something?'

'In his place, wouldn't you?'

'Get me his file,' I said.

'Yes, sir.' He nodded. He rose and headed for the door.

'And find out where he is,' I said. 'We're going to pay the Deshbandhu a visit this afternoon.'

———

A few minutes later, once I was sure Surrender-not was safely back at his desk, I left the office on a journey of my own.

Across the courtyard lay an annexe, on the second floor of which was Vice Division. I walked up and into a rather barren room. The morning after a raid, the room should have been as busy as Waterloo station at rush hour. Instead it was dead. A couple of secretaries sat whispering in a corner and a few junior officers cooled their heels while the fans on the ceiling creaked round at half-speed. I'd become such a regular visitor that no one paid me much notice as I walked through the room to the cabin at the end, knocked and stuck my head round the door.

Inspector Callaghan was poring over some document, pen in hand. He was a stocky, earnest-looking man, with a head of thick red hair, glasses and that peculiarly pale, Celtic complexion that went as red as a lobster at the first hint of sun. He also had a mortal fear of foreign food that, when taken in conjunction with his pallor, made you wonder exactly what it was that had persuaded him to leave Britain in the first place, let alone settle in Calcutta. Still, he was an affable chap and I liked him. What had started off as an attempt to inveigle myself into his confidence had turned into a friendship, of sorts, and it would have been a shame if one of his men had shot me the previous night, as I imagine he might never have forgiven himself.

He looked up. 'Oh, it's you, Wyndham,' he said, placing the pen on his desk. 'What can I do for you?'

'Lunch?'

He shook his head. 'You know I don't eat lunch.'

It was true. He'd told me before. Lunch played havoc with his digestion. He blamed it on a long-standing stomach ulcer. That no doctor had ever been able to find it only made him more certain that it was there, and while all medication had proved useless, a few glasses of Guinness generally acted as a palliative.

'Of the liquid variety?'

He glanced at his watch. 'It's not even noon.'

I entered his office and sat down in the chair across the desk from him.

'I'm having a rough day.'

He peered at me over the ridge of his spectacles. 'Yes, well, you certainly don't look your best.'

'So how about it?' I persisted.

'Can't, I'm afraid,' he said apologetically. He picked up the pen and tapped it on the document in front of him. 'Too much to do.'

I feigned incredulity. 'Come on,' I said. 'You've been sitting on your backside, twiddling your thumbs for months. I can't even remember the last time you launched a raid. When was it – June?'

A hint of a smile brightened his face. 'It was last night, if you must know. Big one too. Down in Tangra.'

'Really?' I said. 'You kept that quiet.'

'There's a reason for that,' he confided. 'I only found out myself about an hour beforehand. All very hush-hush. Ordered by Lord Taggart himself at the request of Section H apparently.'

'Section H? What were they after?'

Callaghan glanced over at the open door behind me. 'Close the door,' he said conspiratorially. I leaned over and pushed it shut.

'Seems they'd received a tip-off that some Green Gang kingpin by the name of Fen Wang was in from Shanghai, and that he'd be in Tangra last night.'

'And was he?'

Callaghan shrugged. 'Well, if he was, he'd left by the time we got there.'

'Any arrests?'

'Just the usual dross – a few local Chinese and a Belgian who should have known better. We passed their names on to Dawson at Section H, but he just ordered us to release them. I expect they were only interested in Fen Wang.'

Callaghan sounded bored. There was no mention that a man had been murdered on the scene. Surely that was worthy of note?

'Anything of interest to CID?' I asked.

He stared at me intensely. 'Are you feeling all right, Wyndham?'

'Fine,' I said defensively.

'Are you looking for work? It's not like you to volunteer your services. You're sure you're not ill?'

'Just trying to be helpful,' I said. 'I'm at a bit of a loose end.'

'Yes,' he sighed. 'So I'd heard. Look, old man, I'm afraid I've got nothing for you. Last night was a washout.'

'Fair enough,' I said, and rose to go.

'And, Wyndham,' he called from behind me. 'We'll have that drink soon, all right?'

———

I left him, walked out of the office and slowly back down the stairs. At the foot, I leaned against the wall and pulled out my packet of cigarettes. Lighting one, I tried to make sense of Callaghan's story. Last night's raid had apparently been ordered by Section H on the pretext of a tip-off about a Chinese gangster being in town. But Section H were charged with monitoring Indian political subversives. Since when had they started worrying about Chinese drug runners? And if this Fen Wang was so important, why leave the raid to the police and not carry it out themselves? It was true that since Gandhi's calls for soldiers to resign their commissions, the military had experienced a spike in the level of native troops going absent without leave, but I couldn't believe they'd suffered losses any worse than we in the police had.

The reason for the raid, though, was only part of the conundrum. There was also the question of what had happened to the corpse of the murdered man. Why hadn't Callaghan mentioned it? Had his men simply failed to find it? The opium den and the premises above it were a warren of small rooms, nooks and crevices. Was it possible his officers hadn't searched the place thoroughly? That seemed unlikely, given that they were hunting for a specific person, and the effort they'd put into chasing me.

I supposed someone might have moved the body in the minutes between my leaving him and the police searching the room. If so, who, and where to?

None of the circumstances made much sense, and then a more disturbing possibility came to mind. Maybe there never had been a body. I'd been groggy with O. Maybe I imagined the whole thing?

But I'd held the murder weapon in my hand. The dead man's blood had been on my shirt and on my hands. Alas, the knife and my shirt were now at the bottom of the Circular Canal, and my hands were washed clean. There were of course the borrowed shirt and chador locked away in my almirah, but they proved nothing. The truth was I had no physical evidence that anything had ever occurred.

I took a long, hard pull on the cigarette and tried to put the thought out of my mind. The man *had* been real, I told myself. The obvious explanation was that Callaghan was lying to me. His men must have found the body, it was probably that of Fen Wang, and Section H had ordered him to keep quiet about it. That had to be it. Everything else was just paranoia.

———

There was a thick file waiting for me on my desk. The name *C. R. Das* was typed on the tab, and on top of it, a note in Surrender-not's hand. He'd managed to track down Das. The Deshbandhu, it appeared, would be at the High Court that afternoon.

FIVE

Surrender-not and I were seated in the back of a police Wolseley, going nowhere. The car was pointed in the direction of the Strand Road, but we hadn't moved in almost ten minutes. In the distance, the whitewashed tower of the High Court glinted in the afternoon sun.

'You're sure he's in there?' I asked.

'We wouldn't be stuck in traffic if he wasn't,' replied Surrender-not.

Around us, horns blared and tempers flared. I opened the door and jumped out. Some yards away stood a forlorn-looking native traffic constable, made conspicuous by his red fez and the umbrella affixed to a harness and his belt, leaving his hands free to direct vehicles – not that he was doing much directing, seeing as all the streets in the vicinity were gridlocked.

'What's going on?' I said, walking up to him.

He shook his head in that curious Indian fashion. 'Road is blocked, sir. Demonstration occurring at court building.'

I thanked him and returned to the car. Surrender-not was standing there, waiting patiently.

'We'll go on foot from here,' I said.

———

The High Court was a neo-Gothic palace of a building, tucked between the town hall, the river and the cricket pitch at Eden Gardens. They said it was modelled on the Cloth Hall in Ypres. I'd passed through Ypres during the war, but couldn't remember anything that looked like this particular building. That wasn't so surprising. I hadn't exactly been there sightseeing, and there was always the possibility that we, the Germans, the French, or a combination of all of us, had by then shelled it to smithereens.

The cause of the chaos on the street soon became apparent. Halfway along Esplanade Row, two dozen or so men in white caps and dhotis were seated in the middle of the road, shouting slogans and waving placards calling for the usual things – the release of political prisoners, Home Rule for India and, for good measure, the restoration of the Sultan of Turkey as the defender of the Mohammedan holy places. The last one might have seemed odd, but it was Gandhi's idea, and it had been bloody clever. By tacking on that final demand to his calls for independence, the little man had done something no one else had managed to do in the best part of a thousand years: he'd won over the millions of Mohammedans and united them in common cause with the Hindus. That was a rather unfortunate development, at least as far as the viceroy and the India Office were concerned. After all, a key plank of the government's refusal to grant independence was that we couldn't just leave the minorities of India, especially the Mohammedans, to live under the tyranny of the Hindus. But it was a difficult argument to make when they were all joining hands and playing nicely with one another.

A crowd of a few hundred natives, marshalled by a phalanx of Congress Volunteers, had also gathered on the pavements, blocking our route to the courthouse. At the front, on a raised platform and flanked by two more khaki-uniformed Volunteers, stood a young, bespectacled Bengali, with a moon face and neatly parted, prematurely thinning, black hair. Dressed in a white dhoti and kurta, and wrapped in a heavy white chador, against the cold, he was addressing the crowd.

'Any idea who that is?' I asked.

'His name's Bose,' replied Surrender-not. 'Subhash Bose, recently returned from England. His father sent him there to sit for the Civil Service entrance examinations. Word is, he passed in the top division, then promptly declined his commission and came back to Calcutta to join the independence movement.'

Suddenly, the name came back to me.

'Not the chap that the *Statesman* ran a piece on the other week?' I asked.

'That's correct, sir.'

'Congress's Gain is the Government's Loss' – that had been the title, or something *like* that, at any rate.

'They say Das has taken quite a shine to him,' Surrender-not continued. 'Made him head of the Congress Volunteers in Bengal.'

'Friend of yours, is he?'

'That depends,' he demurred. 'When we were younger, maybe. These days I doubt he'd think so. An acquaintance perhaps. His father too is an advocate.'

'Do you know *everyone* on the other side?' I asked, exasperated.

Surrender-not shrugged. 'Only the lawyers.'

Bose thrust his fist in the air and continued to whip up a storm. After two and a half years in Calcutta, my Bengali wasn't bad – I knew enough to order almost any drink in several dialects – but it wasn't quite up to the standard necessary to decipher a political diatribe in full flow.

'What's he saying?'

'The usual thing. The need to stand firm in the face of British aggression.'

A roar went up from the crowd and, encouraged by Bose, they took up a chant. Though it was the largest demonstration I'd witnessed in a while, neither their numbers nor their fervour were a patch on those of the crowds that had come out earlier in the year. It had been a long, gruelling struggle for both sides and it seemed that not even the Prince of Wales's imminent arrival could enflame passions to the extent that they'd been aroused earlier.

About twenty feet away stood a couple of constables, who looked on warily but made no effort to intervene. That was sensible. For a start, there was little they could do, and if they did try, there was always the risk that a stray shoe would come innocently flying out of the non-violent crowd and smack them in the face. Still, this was the heart of White Town and the powers that be couldn't let such a blatant challenge to British authority go unanswered even if they'd wanted to. The God-fearing readers of the *Statesman* and the *Englishman* would have choked on their kedgeree, and those of the *Daily Mail* in London might require a dose of smelling salts. Sure enough, moments later came the wail of sirens and the booming cadence of a Home Counties accent amplified through a bullhorn, ordering the stationary traffic to clear a path. Two police trucks drew up and disgorged a detachment of lathi-wielding native constables onto the flagstones. The English officer, a haggard-looking chap I knew by sight, though not by name, descended from the cab of the lead truck and prepared to address the crowd.

The constables lined up and the officer raised the bullhorn to his mouth. 'This gathering is proscribed under the articles of the Anarchical and Revolutionary Crimes Act 1919. Disperse at once or you shall be arrested.'

There was a tired formality to his voice. Indeed, there was a staleness to the whole spectacle. Both sides had danced this two-step so many times by now that everyone knew their respective roles. The protesters linked arms and continued chanting their slogans like some time-honoured religious liturgy.

After waiting a matter of minutes, the officer took to the megaphone once more. 'This is your final warning. Clear the road immediately.'

Those words, when uttered by a policeman, might be presumed to carry the weight of a threat, but in India, in this year, they were positively welcomed by those on the receiving end.

At a nod from the officer, the constables divided into two units, one turning towards the crowd on the pavements, the other making for the demonstrators blocking the road. Ushered by his lieutenants, Bose descended from the platform and I lost sight of him.

'We should go,' said Surrender-not, as the first of the crowd on the pavements began to disperse. I didn't disagree. The show was over and most of the others would soon follow them, leaving only the real zealots, and the ones seated in the road, to court arrest.

We pushed our way through the thinning crowd as the constables moved in and began the task of manhandling the remaining demonstrators off the road and into the waiting wagons. Behind us, the air filled with the cries of the wounded as a hail of blows from bamboo lathis rained down on the bones of the demonstrators. Some of the onlookers hurled insults at the policemen, but they were soon brought into line, not by the constables lined up in front of them, but by Bose's Congress Volunteers.

We continued through the knot of protesters and into the open street beyond.

The gates to the High Court compound were manned by a platoon of armed soldiers who pored over our identification papers as though they were an exam syllabus. Once happy, they waved us through into grounds which resembled the courtyards of an Oxford college, with black-robed barristers ambling the lawns in quiet conversation, oblivious to the events occurring a few hundred yards down the road.

'I understand Mr Das is defending a case in court number 3,' said Surrender-not.

'Any idea what it's about?'

'No, sir, but the court generally breaks for lunch around now, so we shouldn't have long to wait.'

We took a seat on a worn wooden bench in the corridor outside court 3. We'd been here many times before; sat in the same place and watched the same harried-looking officers of the court scuttle past, heads bowed and briefs clutched close to their chests, as we awaited the call to enter and give evidence.

The minutes ticked by but the door to court 3 remained resolutely shut. What opened instead was a door at the far end of the corridor, and into the hallway stepped a patrician-looking Indian dressed in a three-piece pinstripe suit and the black robes and grey wig of a barrister. He came down the hallway towards us, trailing two juniors, each weighed down by bundles of files, behind him.

The man looked remarkably familiar and I was about to point him out to Surrender-not, when the man spotted us and his expression changed. It was an expression that resembled one I'd seen many times before.

'Is that your –'

'Yes,' said Surrender-not. 'That's my father.'

Before he could continue, I stood up and began walking. 'Come on,' I said. 'You'd better introduce me to your dear pater.'

'I'm not sure this is such a good idea, sir,' he said as he struggled after me.

'Nonsense,' I said. 'You should have done it ages ago.'

'Father,' said Surrender-not as we drew level with the man and his aides, 'may I introduce Captain Wyndham, my superior officer.' He turned to me. 'Captain Wyndham, this is my father, Mr Sasadhar Banerjee, barrister-at-law.'

'How do you do,' I said.

Banerjee senior removed his spectacles and smiled. 'Likewise, Captain,' he said, stowing his glasses in his breast pocket and offering me a hand. 'So you are the Englishman responsible for filling my son's head with imperialist nonsense.'

'I just teach him about police work, sir,' I said. 'The imperialist nonsense I leave to the viceroy. And to be frank, your son's a credit to the force, and to his family,' I continued, sounding like a form master relaying the progress of a prize pupil.

Banerjee senior nodded sagely. 'It is gratifying to hear that Suren is acquitting himself appropriately,' he said. 'However, I and his uncles would have preferred it if he had chosen an alternative profession.'

'The country needs detectives, sir,' I said, echoing something that Surrender-not had said to me the day I'd first met him, 'whether it be the British or Indians in charge.'

'The country needs doctors too, Captain,' he replied, 'and a doctor has the advantage of doing good while avoiding the moral dilemma of aiding and abetting an alien, occupying power.'

'*Baba*, please,' said Surrender-not. 'This is not the time for such a discussion.'

'Your son upholds the system of laws in this country,' I said to the barrister. 'One might say you do the same, sir.'

'I defend those fighting against injustice,' he replied.

'And your son fights for justice for the families of those victims who have no one else to fight for them.'

The old man pondered this for a moment. 'Tell me, Captain. When was the last time you and he investigated the murder of an ordinary Indian?'

I sidestepped the question. 'I can tell you, sir, that your son's actions have saved the lives of Indians as well as Englishmen. I can think of no finer officer that I have served with.'

Behind us, the doors to court 3 opened. 'It seems we shall have to continue this discussion another time,' I said, much to Surrender-not's relief. 'I'm afraid we have some business to attend to.'

Having made our excuses, we headed back towards court 3, from which a scrum of journalists and other more principled members of the public were exiting. There was, of course, no jury. There hadn't been one since 1908, at least not for political crimes, on account of the difficulty of finding *twelve good men and true* in this country of three hundred million souls. Indeed, the presence of the press and the public was somewhat of a surprise, as the authorities were within their powers to hold all such trials in secret. I surmised that whatever was going on inside, the government was more than happy to have it publicised.

Surrender-not and I stood back as the courtroom emptied and Das, accompanied by a bookish-looking junior counsel, strode out. The man whom Surrender-not had called a towering figure in Indian legal circles was about five feet six inches tall and dressed, like the protesters outside, in a white dhoti and kurta which in these august halls seemed as out of place as a pinstripe suit in a paddy field. He was in his fifties, according to his file, though he possessed the soft, youthful features of a much younger man. It was something I'd noticed before in Bengalis. They aged in a different fashion from other people. Their faces stayed young while their stomachs grew ever larger, so that it was easier to assess a man's age not by the grey in his hair but by the girth of his belly.

Das's eyes lit up as he saw Surrender-not. Cutting short the conversation with his aide, he raised his arms towards the sergeant.

'Suren, my boy!' He beamed. 'What brings you here?' His smile disappeared as he descended into a fit of coughing which almost doubled him over. Both his aide and Surrender-not made to help him as he raised a handkerchief to his mouth. Das held his free hand out to stop them. The coughing subsided and he righted himself, eyes watering from the strain.

Surrender-not fiddled with his cuffs. 'Das *kakū*,' he said. 'May I introduce Captain Wyndham? He comes bearing a message from the commissioner of police, Lord Taggart.'

Das turned to me and held out a hand. 'Your reputation precedes you, Captain. It is a pleasure to finally meet you.'

'As does yours, sir,' I said, taking his hand, 'though I'm surprised you should have heard of me.'

'Of course,' he said, smiling affably. 'Suren's father has on more than one occasion mentioned the devilish English officer who has so perniciously convinced his son not to resign his post. However, I shall not hold it against you. So what is it that our esteemed commissioner of police wishes to tell me?'

Despite the chill, I felt myself sweating. Taking a handkerchief from my pocket, I wiped some perspiration from my forehead. 'Maybe we should take a stroll?' I said.

'Consider it a friendly warning,' I said as we ambled along a cloistered corridor and out onto a palm-lined path through the court gardens. 'As of tomorrow, the government will issue an order outlawing all Volunteer organisations. Anyone gathering in paramilitary uniform or similar dress will be subject to summary arrest.'

Das's face darkened as he pondered my words. 'It may be a warning,' he said eventually, 'and I appreciate the advance notice, but there is nothing friendly about it. Our Volunteers help to maintain order. You've no idea how much discipline is required to maintain the "non" in non-violence. The Volunteers stop the people's passions from spiralling out of control.'

'I doubt the viceroy sees it quite in the same terms,' I said. 'I understand the order comes directly from him. Besides, maintaining order is the job of the police. It's what Sergeant Banerjee and I get paid to do.'

Das gave a small chuckle. 'Of course, Captain. But you must admit that the Volunteers have helped you significantly in that regard over the course of the last few months. Especially when your own numbers have been so stretched.'

If our numbers were stretched, it was because of the protests he led and the resignations from the force that he and Gandhi had called for. He was turning the facts on their head. But then he *was* a lawyer after all.

'I hope you will comply with the order,' I said.

'Do you expect me to?'

I doubted he expected an answer.

'I'm leading a non-cooperation movement,' he continued. 'I'd hardly be doing a very good job of it if I were to start cooperating.' He patted me softly on the shoulder. 'Let me ask you a question, Captain. Should I follow an edict which I believe to be unjust? If our roles were reversed, would you do so?'

I hated this new breed of pacifist Indian revolutionary. So often they acted like we were all just good friends who happened to disagree about something, and that once the issue was resolved – obviously in their favour – we'd go back to taking tea and being the best of chums. It made punching them in the face morally difficult. Give me an old-fashioned terrorist any day. At least you knew where you stood with them. They might try to murder you, but at least they had the decency not to engage you in debate first.

'I'm not one for politics, sir,' I said. 'I just do my duty.'

'Your duty to whom, Captain? To your emperor across the seas or to the people of this city? Ridding Calcutta of the stabilising influence of the Volunteers is a dangerous game. Without them, what's to stop the protests getting out of hand? Or maybe that is what His Excellency the Viceroy is hoping for? Mobs rampaging through the streets, just in time for the arrival of the Prince of Wales and the cameras of the international press corps. That would play very well for him in the court of public opinion.'

'I'd remind you, sir, that it was Mr Gandhi, and not the government, who unleashed these forces and called for the police to resign en masse,' I replied. 'In any case, whatever the viceroy may or may not want, I'm sure the commissioner wishes to avoid any needless provocation or misunderstanding.'

We walked past the guards at the compound gates and out onto the street. Waiting there was the young man, Bose, who'd addressed the demonstrators. He'd somehow avoided arrest and now stood leaning against a tree, smoking a cigarette, no doubt waiting for Das, though he seemed surprised to see him walking out with us. Nevertheless he stubbed out his cigarette, flicked the butt into the drain and made his way over.

Das turned to Surrender-not. 'I take it I don't need to introduce you to Subhash.'

Before the sergeant could respond, Bose was already shaking his hand. 'Well, well,' he said. 'If it isn't Surendranath-*da*. I thought I saw your face earlier. Don't tell me you've finally decided to join the struggle?'

'Not quite yet, Subhash-*babu*,' Surrender-not replied. 'May I introduce my superior officer, Captain Wyndham.'

The young Indian turned to me and held out his hand. 'Bose,' he said, 'Subhash Bose. I'm pleased to meet you, Captain.'

'You won't be so pleased when you hear what the captain has come to tell us,' interjected Das. 'As of tomorrow, the Congress Volunteers are a proscribed organisation; you, my friend, will be subject to summary arrest.'

'How nice,' said Bose acidly. 'I suppose it's about time. I've been back in Calcutta for months now and it seems they've arrested everyone *but* me. Frankly it's getting rather embarrassing. I do wonder where they'd put me, though. I understand all the jails in India are bursting at the seams.'

'There's always Burma,' I said.

Das at least found the comment amusing, and he burst into a laugh which soon descended into another fit of coughing. Bose put his hand on the older man's elbow to steady him.

'I must apologise,' said Das, once the fit had passed. 'As you can see, Captain, the cold weather is playing havoc with me.'

Beside me, Surrender-not shifted nervously. 'If I may make one request, *kakū*,' he said. 'Do what you must, but please don't court arrest. Your health is not what it used to be, and neither Calcutta Central Jail nor Mandalay Prison are places from which men return stronger.'

Das put his hand on Surrender-not's shoulder. 'A man cannot cheat his destiny, Suren. If it is my fate to be arrested, then so be it.' Surrender-not made to object, but the Deshbandhu continued. 'Yet I shall take your request under advisement, on condition that you too heed some advice. Go and see your parents. Your mother misses you – and your father, he is as stubborn as you, but I know him, he feels your absence just as sharply.'

SIX

'And what did he have to say?'

Taggart stood with his back to us, hands clasped behind him, staring out of the window of his office onto the city below.

'He said "*thank you*",' I replied.

'That's it?' Taggart turned to face us.

'More or less. He also requested we pass on his best wishes to you.'

The commissioner failed to suppress a jaundiced smile. 'I'll bet he did. And he didn't say anything else?'

'He thinks outlawing the Volunteers is a dangerous move, sir,' said Surrender-not.

'Oh, does he now, Sergeant?' said Taggart. 'And why would that be?'

'He's worried that without their presence the demonstrations might spiral out of control. He's not sure we have the manpower to keep the peace.'

It might have been a fair point, but I still baulked at the thought of law and order being maintained by anyone other than the police.

Taggart walked back to his chair behind the desk and sat down.

'The gall of that man. I expect he'd love to show the world that we don't have the ability to maintain calm in this town. If it wasn't for his antics, there'd be no danger to the peace in the first place.'

'I fear he doesn't quite see it that way, sir,' said Surrender-not.

'No,' said Taggart, 'of course he doesn't. The question is, will he comply?'

Surrender-not and I exchanged a glance.

'I doubt it, sir,' I said.

'Well, he'd better,' said Taggart. 'For all our sakes.'

———

The meeting with Taggart had ended somewhat abruptly, with the commissioner again suggesting that I draw upon my experience in Special Branch in London and military intelligence in wartime France to figure out exactly what Das planned to do next and then make sure he didn't do it. I could have pointed out that divination wasn't exactly a skill I'd picked up in either Scotland Yard or the trenches, and that trailing burly Irishmen or tracking down German spies afforded little insight into the innermost thoughts of a wily old Indian lawyer in bad health, but it wouldn't have made a difference. In his current mood, Taggart would only have dismissed it as a convenient excuse.

And so, having been tasked with the impossible, Surrender-not and I had retreated to my office to lick our wounds and figure out how best to achieve it. Blame, like water, always flows downwards, and just as Taggart had taken out his frustrations on me, I took out mine on Surrender-not.

'I don't care what you have to do,' I said. 'Call in whatever favours you're owed, speak to whoever you need to, from your father to Das's washerwoman if need be, just find out what he's planning.'

Surrender-not's expression wasn't dissimilar to the one I'd given Taggart when faced with the same ridiculous order. Nevertheless, he made some notes in his little yellow notepad and then excused himself.

My head was pounding. I checked my watch. It was only just gone 3 p.m. These days, a half-day's work seemed about all I was good for.

I settled back into my chair and tried to concentrate on work. Figuring out Das's plans might be beyond me, but I could at least try to determine what had happened to the body of the Chinaman I'd left at the opium den.

I'd made scant progress when the telephone rang. I expected it to be Surrender-not, calling to tell me he'd worked out Das's next move, or, more likely, to ask a stupid question.

I picked up the receiver.

'Sam?'

It was a woman's voice; one that I hadn't heard in a few months.

'Annie?' I replied. 'To what do I owe the pleasure?'

'I'm not bothering you, am I . . . ?' Her voice trailed off.

'Not at all,' I said. 'Is everything all right?'

For a detective, it wasn't the most astute of questions. Something had to be wrong. She wouldn't have called otherwise. For a moment, the only response was static. Then she answered.

'Something's happened, Sam.'

Half an hour later I was in Alipore, among the boulevards and bungalows of White Town. In this part of Calcutta you'd be hard pressed to tell that most of the city had been in turmoil for the best part of a year. Maybe the grass of some lawns was half an inch longer than usual, or the paint on a mansion or two hadn't been retouched after the monsoon deluge back in August, but it was only to be expected. These days, with so many natives on strike, it wasn't always easy to find the right workmen for the job. Of course it had been worse earlier in the year, when every native and his dog seemed to have heeded the Mahatma's message and gone on strike.

A *hartal* they called it. But it seemed that *hartals* were subject to Newton's laws. For every action there was a reaction. For every flower bed that went untended, a workman went unpaid and his family edged closer to penury and starvation. Strikes, like warfare, are campaigns of attrition, and in the end, an empty belly trumps politics. Over time the workmen, the malis, the durwans, the rail-waymen and most of the others had drifted back to their posts, and behind their well-tended hedgerows the houses of Alipore sparkled in the winter sun once more.

The driver stopped on the road outside Annie's home. The iron gates were locked shut and beside them sat her durwan, a greasy little fellow with the appearance of an overfed cherub and the work ethic of a sloth. It usually took a stream of invective or a natural disaster to prise him out of his well-worn chair at any speed faster than a snail's pace, but today he was up from his seat like a tubby greyhound out of the traps. Taking a key from a ring on his belt, he quickly unlocked the gates, flung them open and waved us into a gravel driveway the length of the Suez Canal, at the end of which stood Annie's house. With its green shutters and pink bougainvil-lea climbing the whitewashed walls, it would normally have been considered picturesque, but not today. Not with its front door daubed with red paint.

I jumped out before the car came to a halt and made for the steps to the entrance. The door was opened by Annie's maid, Anju, a slight woman with a pronounced stoop and an expression that suggested she had the cares of the world on her back. I'd met her before, quite a few times in fact, when I was a more regular visitor to the house. She generally greeted me with a cautious smile, a *pranam* and a few mumbled words, but there were other things on her mind today.

'Captain Wyndham, sahib,' she said, before launching into a flow of Bengali so rapid it was beyond me. Sensing my incomprehension, she stopped abruptly, then, all but taking my hand, she gestured for me to follow. 'Come,' she said breathlessly, 'memsahib is this way.'

I accompanied her through the hall. The place smelled of gardenias. Annie liked gardenias. There was generally a bunch or two scattered around the place, and it struck me that I could have done myself a favour by bringing a bouquet along too – not that this was a social call. The maid stopped at the open door to the drawing room and looked up at me, hopefully. I wasn't sure what the look meant.

'Please wait. I call memsahib.'

I walked past her into the room. It hadn't changed much since my last visit. The same few photographs of family sat on a walnut table in front of a brocade sofa, the kind favoured by people in Calcutta who possessed that rare combination of both money and good taste. On either side of the picture window stood the two large statues of the Hindu god Shiva, the creator and protector of the universe, standing on a lotus flower, performing his celestial dance inside a ring of fire. You'd have been forgiven for thinking that they were identical, but a closer look would reveal subtle disparities. The god's expressions and his poses were dissimilar. Annie had once explained the difference to me.

'The first is Shiva in his benign state,' she'd said, 'the creator dancing the universe into existence. The other is his angrier form.'

'The destroyer?' I'd asked.

She'd hesitated. 'In a way, but not like our God destroying the world as in the book of Revelation. Hindus believe in reincarnation, not just of the soul but of the universe. Shiva pulls down the old so that it can be renewed. He destroys so that he can create again.'

I had hoped it might be a metaphor for our relationship. There certainly was a pattern to it. More than once, things had blossomed between us, but circumstances always seemed to conspire against us. It was possible those circumstances were orchestrated by the gods; more likely they were precipitated by my actions.

It's true that I'd once suspected her of withholding information about the death of her former employer from me. I may even have broached the subject with her, but the way she told it, I'd practically accused her of stabbing the man herself. The truth was I'd done no such thing. I'd merely considered it.

There had been an *entente* of sorts a year later, but even that cordiality floundered, partly on the rocks of my opium habit. At the time, I could go several days without the need for a hit and could even keep up a decent air of respectability during daylight hours. But there was no hiding the nocturnal excursions, and in Calcutta there were only two reasons why a man would go out so late and so regularly, and neither of them was particularly palatable. She'd noticed them and confronted me, and I'd denied it all. I'd told her it was police work – and she'd believed not a word of it. That was six months ago and I'd seen her only intermittently since. At first I'd hoped she might reconsider, but that was never likely. She looked like a princess and had a bank balance to match, thanks to the careful investment of cash she'd received from someone else I'd once suspected of murder. I might have been wrong on both counts, but surely it's right and proper for a detective to have a healthy sense of suspicion.

From the day I'd met her, I'd known she was something special. She wasn't perfect; she wasn't even English for that matter; but she was intelligent, and tough, and in a society that valued breeding over ability she was a misfit. Like me, she was a survivor, and she was pretty good at it, probably because she'd had to fight for everything her whole life. As such, I couldn't blame her for grasping any opportunity for advancement that came her way. The point was, these days she was never short of admirers, even with her part-Indian blood. I had no problem with that, nor with her using them to get what she wanted. Of course I'd felt our relationship had been different, and while in my darker hours I might have suspected I was no different from the rest of those men trapped in her orbit, I could still accept that. My real fear, though, was that one of these days she'd meet some man and see in him more than a means to an end.

Word had it, of late, that she'd been seen around town on the arm of an American businessman recently arrived from some place no one had ever heard of called Wisconsin; no one save for Surrender-not of course, who was a veritable walking atlas, and who said it was cold there; colder, at any rate, than anywhere sane men had reason to be. That was good. I doubted the man would survive a Bengal summer. With luck he might even melt.

'Sam?'

I turned to find Annie at the entrance to the room.

It didn't matter that I'd been expecting her, seeing her standing there like a Greek goddess was still like a punch to the stomach.

She looked perplexed.

'I didn't expect you to come yourself,' she said as she entered. 'Sending a constable would have been fine.'

I didn't believe a word of it. If she'd wanted a constable, she'd have telephoned the local thana – an officer would have been here in five minutes. Instead she'd called me at police headquarters.

'It's no trouble,' I said. 'What happened?'

'You saw the door?' There was a brittleness to her tone.

'It was hard to miss.'

'Well, take a look at this,' she said, leading the way into the hall. I followed her to the dining room at the rear of the house. The window had been smashed, and on the floor, amid the glittering shards, sat a brick.

I knelt down and made a show of examining it. People expect a detective to examine things. It went with the badge, and like some performing monkey, I felt almost enthusiastic about obliging her. If it had been a new brick, I might have had something to go on. Maybe there was construction work going on nearby and someone might have taken it, but this one was old and worn – like most of Calcutta. It was just a brick: reddish-orange and no different to any other of the thousands you could find strewn all over the more dilapidated parts of town.

'And this came through the window?' I said, straightening up.

It was a stupid question, but I got an odd satisfaction from asking it. She stared at me as though I was an idiot.

'No, Sam. It came in the post. Of course it came through the window.'

'When did it happen?'

'About an hour ago. Maybe ten minutes before I called you.'

Attacks on properties in White Town were as rare as a hot day in the Hebrides, and an attack in broad daylight was unheard of.

'Did you see the perpetrators?'

She shook her head. 'The room was empty. It was the noise which alerted Anju. She arrived to see two men running away towards the trees.' Annie pointed to the far end of the garden.

I looked out. The trees were a hundred yards away.

'Indians?' I asked.

'She thought so.'

'Did she recognise them?'

'No,' she said, with an air of resignation. 'There are so many new faces around these days …' Her voice trailed off, but there was no need to finish the sentence. Das had called for a one-day general strike earlier in the year, and many of Alipore's workmen and gardeners had heeded his request. Certain sahibs had taken the actions of their staff as a personal insult and sacked them the next day, replacing them with new men who knew on which side their roti was buttered.

'What about that durwan of yours?' I asked. 'Isn't he supposed to patrol the grounds?'

'He was at the front gate,' she said. 'He only does his rounds after dark.'

'And he didn't see anything?'

'No.'

'Not even someone throwing a bucket of paint at the front door?'

'Apparently not.'

I supposed it was possible. It was a fair distance between the gate and the house, and her durwan couldn't have been much less vigilant had he been dead.

'You know,' I said, 'for all the good he does, you might just as well employ a scarecrow. It'd be cheaper.'

She sighed. 'And then who would feed his family, Sam?'

I let the matter drop. If she wanted to act as patron saint to every native in Calcutta, that was her business, but it hadn't stopped a couple of them lobbing a brick through her window.

'Have you received any threats?' I asked.

'No,' she said, 'but the neighbourhood is panicky. A Parsee doctor and his wife who live nearby had their garden room set alight a few nights ago.'

'What about you?' I continued. 'Any idea why someone would wish to target your house?'

She shot me that look again, the one that made it clear that she wasn't exactly in awe of my deductive skills.

'Isn't it obvious?'

Anglo-Indians were a soft target. Attacks on them were up all across town. They'd always had it tough – viewed with distaste by us and with distrust by the Indians – but things had worsened considerably since the summer. The reason was the railways. They were the government's Achilles heel. Without them, the country would be paralysed and the authorities would have been forced to compromise. But after some initial disruption, the trains were up and running again within a week. The natives blamed the Anglo-Indians. After all, people thought they ran the railways. They didn't, of course. While it was true that many railway jobs were reserved for them, the top posts were all held by British men. Nevertheless, the Anglo-Indians made convenient scapegoats. It was always easier to blame sabotage on a minority than admit that maybe not all Indians were behind the Mahatma's call to drop arms.

If Das was right, and the banning of the Volunteers from the streets *did* lead to more attacks, it didn't take a genius to work out who the first targets would be.

'It might be better if you moved out of the house for a few days,' I said. 'Just until tempers cool.'

'And where would you have me go, Sam?'

There was an edge to her voice.

'A hotel.' I shrugged. 'The Great Eastern, maybe?' The thought brought back memories. It was the first place I'd taken her to dinner. But that was over two years ago. We were different people then.

'I'm not going to be driven from my own home,' she said, and her tone made clear there was no point in debating the matter. Instead I nodded and followed her back into the hallway.

I gave the rest of the place a quick once-over, checking the external doors and windows, and offered to post a constable at the door, which was rash, given we were short of men and that I had no authority to do so in the first place, but it wasn't the first time I'd shot my mouth off in an attempt to impress her.

Declining the offer, she accompanied me back to the front door, just as several workmen arrived with tools and wooden boards to temporarily barricade the broken window.

I turned to face her, still unsure why she'd called me out here in the first place. Part of me felt she might not know herself. Maybe, confronted with danger, she'd done it on instinct and was now regretting it. Judging by the look on her face, that was a distinct possibility.

'You're sure you'll be all right, here?'

'I'll be fine, Sam,' she said. It sounded like she meant it. 'I was just a bit shaken by everything. I shouldn't have troubled you.'

'I could come back later,' I said, 'and stay over ... if you're concerned?' The words were out of my mouth before I even realised.

She gave a mirthless laugh. 'Would that be all night, Sam, or just till two in the morning?'

SEVEN

I left Annie's place as the fog descended, both in the streets and in my head. As ever, the stillness of dusk was punctuated by the sound of crickets. My limbs ached and even the exertion of climbing into the waiting car was energy-sapping. I slumped into the back seat and pulled the door shut.

'Lal Bazar, sir?' asked the driver.

'No,' I said, 'Premchand Boral Street.'

It was going to be another uncommonly cold night. Lately, the mercury had dropped as low as forty and for the natives, that must have felt like the Arctic. On a night like this, in the poorer parts of Black Town, some of those without a roof or a fire wouldn't make it through to morning.

To them, winter was nothing but a perilous time of the year. Indeed, to most of the city's denizens, Christmas was an alien festival, planted in their soil by zealous missionaries and celebrated by the British and some misguided converts from other parts of the country – South Indians mainly – who'd settled here. Not that they necessarily resented it. The Hindus of Bengal could be a pragmatic people, and many of them had no problem accepting Jesus as another deity in the universal pantheon of gods and holy men, especially since we British had decreed his birthday as a holiday.

Still, the festivities were half-hearted at best, and that was fine with me. I preferred not to be reminded of the ghosts of Christmas past. The few happy memories I had of the festive period were of the days I'd spent with my wife, Sarah. She'd died four years ago, and like a man scared of his own shadow, I'd spent every Christmas since running away, first into a bottle, and then to Calcutta; because looking back at the past was like picking at the scab of an unhealed wound.

If there had been joy in my life since then, it had come from Annie Grant. The irony was that, while I ran from my memories, my inability to move forward – to consign my time with Sarah to the past – had probably crushed any prospect of a future with Annie.

The hibiscus fragrance of Alipore soon gave way to the stench of sewage as we approached the Tolly Canal, the boundary between the well-heeled suburb and the centre of town. The driver seemed to being doing his damnedest to drive through every pothole on the route back and my head pounded, as though the goddess Kali herself was hammering at it, hoping to add mine to the garland of skulls around her neck.

Dusk had settled by the time the car stopped outside my lodgings. Premchand Boral Street wasn't the most salubrious of locales, but the rent was cheap and, more importantly, the landlord had no objection to a white man sharing lodgings with a native. The street was quiet at this hour. Most of the girls didn't do much business before eight, and even then things only got rowdy after ten. Before that, it was the refined clientele, the salarymen with their starched dhotis and their neatly oiled and parted hair, stopping off on their way home for their regular appointments with a box of sweetmeats in hand and a smile on their face.

I made it up the stairs and turned the key in the lock. The hallway was in darkness. It meant Surrender-not was still out, but of course Sandesh would be in, probably in the kitchen, cooking by candlelight. It wasn't that he was frugal – he just didn't trust electricity.

'Sandesh.' My voice echoed off the walls.

'*Hā*, sahib.'

The reply came not from the kitchen but the living room. From the scraping of the furniture, I surmised he'd been having a nap under the dining table. There came the scratching of a match, a flaring, then the soft glow of a hurricane lamp as he padded into the hallway.

'Switch on some lights,' I said, 'and bring me my tonic.'

'*Hā*, sahib.' He nodded, pressing the switch in the hall, before heading off to the kitchen. I entered the living room, took off my jacket and threw it over the back of a chair, then made for the drinks cabinet.

Minutes later I was on the veranda, a tumbler of Glenfarclas in my hand, seated on a wicker chair about as comfortable as a bag of rocks. With a shaking hand I lifted the heavy glass to my lips as, from behind me, Sandesh came out and wordlessly placed an enamel cup and a small brass pot and spoon on the table beside me, then retreated back inside. The cup was filled with a greyish, pulpy liquid that made Ganges water taste like ambrosia. But I wasn't complaining. Not about that, nor the spoonful of clarified butter I'd take from the brass pot as a chaser.

The concoction had been prescribed by a quack called Chatter-jee, whose consulting room consisted of a cabin little larger than a priest's confessional booth in an unhygienic alley off Dharmatolla Street. He called himself a doctor of homeopathic medicine, and judging by the number of certificates hanging on the wall behind him, he seemed well qualified in his field.

I'd been sceptical of course, but as they say – needs must and all that. My cravings had reached the stage where the symptoms were becoming impossible to hide, even from myself. Going to a European doctor, even one of the Armenian chaps who practised over Barabazar way, was out of the question, seeing as how the confidentiality clause of the Hippocratic oath only seemed to sporadically apply in Calcutta. Besides, when it came to combating opium addiction, Western medicine appeared to have little in its armoury other than electroshock therapy, which sounded about as much fun as being bled by leeches.

So it had to be an Indian doctor, and it had to be secret. Even being caught making enquiries could cause trouble. But I was a detective with over a decade's experience in covert surveillance. Tracking down people was what I did. From the outset I felt my chances of finding an appropriate physician were good; and they improved considerably when I saw Dr Chatterjee's advertisement in the classified section of the *Statesman*.

Dr Hariprashad Chatterjee
Practitioner of Ayurvedic and Homeopathic Medicines
Remedies for infection, addiction, constipation, marital dysfunction ...

One Tuesday evening in November, I'd made the trip to the doctor's consulting cabin to confess my sins. Chatterjee turned out to be a thin man in thick glasses, a dhoti, and a half-sleeve shirt, ink-stained around the breast pocket where a pen had leaked.

He listened without comment as I haltingly explained my problem and betrayed no surprise at seeing a white man come to seek his services. He gave the matter the attention it deserved, nodding gravely every now and then until my words dried up.

'*Hā*,' he said finally. '*Afeem* addiction is most serious *bāpaar*. Efficacious treatment is long-drawn, intensive affair. Most unsavoury to Western sentiments ...'

'But there *is* a treatment?' I said.

'Of course there is treatment!' He bridled. 'You are aware of Ayurveda?'

'Vaguely.'

Surrender-not was an advocate of Ayurvedic medicine, but like so much else about native practices, I'd found it hopelessly impenetrable, wrapped in the fog and folklore of Indian mysticism.

'*Cleansing*,' continued Chatterjee, the pupils of his eyes magnified through the thick lenses of his glasses. 'Cure involves cleansing. Of full body and spirit. You will need to travel to ashram of Devraha Swami in Assam.'

'And he's good, this swami?'

Chatterjee smiled. 'Most definitely! Devraha Swami is over 270 years old.'

'You've met him?'

'No. But I send him many patients. Process takes twenty-five days. There will be much expulsion of poisons from the body. You will need to examine your stools most carefully.'

It sounded lovely.

The problem, as ever, was time. In the current circumstances, the chances of Lord Taggart granting me twenty-five days' leave to visit an ashram in Assam were as high as Kaiser Wilhelm being awarded the French Legion of Honour.

'Is there nothing else?' I asked. 'Pills perhaps?'

The glasses on Chatterjee's face swayed as he shook his head. 'I am sorry, no. Not if you want full cure.'

I slumped back in my chair.

'But,' said the doctor, 'there is one temporary measure. *Kerdū*. In English it is called, I think, ash gourd. It is not cure, but its juices can alleviate symptoms of *afeem* sickness.'

Suddenly I felt like a man who'd been pardoned on his way to the gallows.

Chatterjee scrawled the details on a flimsy sheet of paper.

'Take one half *kerdü*. Mash into pulp and drink with one teaspoon ghee. Take when symptoms are becoming too great.'

I'd been sceptical, but it wasn't as though I had much of a choice, at least not until I could find the time for a month's vomiting and stool examination. So I'd tried it, hesitantly at first, and surprisingly it seemed to work. I found that, after a draught of the concoction, the aches would abate for a day or so, plugging the gap between the severest onset of my symptoms and the next visit to a den in the dead of night.

I set down the tumbler of whisky, reached for the enamel cup and steeled myself. The stuff tasted foul and I drank it down in two gulps, then took a spoonful of the clarified butter from the pot and swallowed it while trying not to retch. I knew from experience that the brew would need a while to take effect, so I did the decent thing and picked up the whisky, sat back, sipped and waited.

My thoughts returned to the events of the previous night. A raid, scheduled at the behest of Section H, in secrecy and at the last minute. A dead man whose body seemed to have gone undetected – or at least unremarked – even though the place was crawling with policemen.

But corpses didn't just disappear, not without the aid of a high-explosive shell, and as none had fallen on the opium den, it stood to reason that the body of the missing Chinaman must still be there … assuming, that is, I hadn't imagined the whole thing.

There was only one way to be sure. I got up, grabbed my jacket and headed out into the fog and hailed a taxi.

The streets were dead. On winter nights like this, Calcutta took on a ghostly quality, the veil between the living and the dead, indistinct at the best of times, now became positively porous. A rickshaw appeared out of the gloom, its driver wrapped up against the night in jumper, muffler and woollen cap, as though off to pick up Captain Scott at the South Pole.

The journey to Tangra was punctuated by the rickshaw-wallah's hacking cough, each eruption accompanied by a curse and an apology.

'Sorry, sahib. Bad coughing. Too cold.'

It was the same every winter. As soon as the temperature fell below fifty, half the city fell ill, and talk of pneumonia and chest infections soon vied for conversational space with those perennial Bengali obsessions: politics and bowel movements.

I alighted a few streets distant and walked the rest of the way back to the opium den. From the front, the building looked like any other in this part of town: barred and shuttered windows set in a facade of stained, cracked plaster and crumbling brickwork. A wooden hoarding was nailed to the wall above the padlocked door, its Chinese characters painted in fading red.

A solitary, scarf-clad constable stood outside next to a hurricane lamp, stamping his feet in an attempt to drum up some bodily heat. He looked barely twenty and twitchy, and at the sound of my footsteps, he snatched up his rifle.

'Who goes there?' he challenged, with as much conviction as a priest in a brothel.

He relaxed when he saw I was a sahib, and even more so when I pulled out my warrant card.

'What's your name, Constable?' I asked.

'Mitra, sir. From Tangra thana.'

I lied and told him I was from Vice Division. 'I need access to the premises,' I said.

'Yes, sir,' he said, fishing a ring of keys from his pocket. Finding the correct one, he turned and stooped over the padlock. It clicked open and the chain it fastened fell rattling to the ground. Mitra pushed it out of the way with the side of his boot, then held the door open. Borrowing his lamp, I stepped inside and into darkness.

It smelled different from the previous night. The aroma of formaldehyde and opium had gone, replaced by something else – something faint which I couldn't quite define but which reminded me of the trenches. I took the stairs down to the basement, along the corridor to the room where, less than twenty-four hours earlier, I'd lain comatose on a flimsy charpoy, surrounded by half a dozen other opium fiends. The room was empty now, mute like the antechamber of a pharaoh's tomb. Yet the ghosts of last night were still there: a broken chair, an upturned cot, an opium tray languishing in the corner like an afterthought; all bearing silent testament to what had transpired.

In the gloom, I stepped on a bamboo opium pipe, cracking it underfoot. I kicked it to one side and watched it roll into the shadows. I kept going, out of the room and into the corridor which the oriental girl had shepherded me to, then up the stairs, through the hatch and into the room where I'd found the dying man.

The room was empty. That was hardly a surprise. Short-staffed or not, the boys of Vice Division would hardly have missed a body lying in the middle of the floor. I knelt down and ran a finger over the tiled floor. There was no trace of blood. In fact there was little trace of anything. Was it possible that after my escape, with Callaghan's men crawling all over the scene, someone had moved the body and washed the floor? It sounded absurd – and yet it must have happened. The alternative was that I'd imagined the whole thing.

I shook my head. I couldn't start doubting myself. That way lay madness.

'Get a hold of yourself, Wyndham,' I whispered.

The dead man had been no pipe dream. I remembered him vividly: remembered putting my ear to his mouth and checking his breathing; remembered his blood on my shirt and on my hands; remembered the strange bent blade. But what proof did I have?

It was better to concentrate on the concrete. I was a detective. I dealt in evidence and if I currently didn't have any, I'd just bloody well have to find some. Retreating to the corridor, I once more knelt down and ran a finger over the floor. This time it came up coated in dust.

I returned to the room and walked over to where I thought the body had lain. Taking out my penknife and dropping to my knees, I flipped open the small blade and stuck it into the gap between two of the tiles, scraping it along the brittle cement of the join before bringing it up and examining it. The tip was coated in dirt and a dark powdery residue. I continued to scrape, further along the join between more of the tiles. Again the blade came up covered with the same dark brownish residue.

I wiped the blade on my shirtsleeve and stood up. The body might have been moved and the floor mopped, but the job had been rushed. Blood had seeped into the cracks between the floor tiles and dried.

The question was, who had cleaned up and what had they done with the body? I doubted it had been Callaghan's men. He'd told me to my face that they'd found nothing of interest for CID, and he wasn't the sort to lie, at least not convincingly.

That left Section H, the local police, or the Chinese.

I guessed the Chinese had either run or been arrested. Whichever it was, I doubted any of them would have been around long enough to hide a dead body and mop a floor. As for the local police, why would they bother to cover up a murder?

That left Section H.

If anyone had a reason to hide a dead body, it was probably them. The raid had been carried out at their behest. Maybe the dead man *was* the elusive Fen Wang, the Green Gang mobster from

Shanghai. The murder of a Chinese citizen in Calcutta, a drug lord at that, could well be the sort of thing they'd wish to hush up.

Storing my penknife, I walked slowly back to the front of the funeral parlour. Mitra was still there, rifle in hand, and looking as nervous as a baby.

'At ease, Constable,' I said, reaching into my pocket and fishing out a couple of crumpled cigarettes. I stuck one in the corner of my mouth, the way I'd expect a vice officer to, and offered him the other. His shoulders relaxed and he smiled and accepted it gratefully. I made a show of looking for a light.

'You wouldn't have a match, would you?'

His face brightened. Lowering his rifle, he searched his tunic pocket and extracted a matchbox, then took out a match and struck it against the emery. A halo of yellow light illuminated the dark, pitted skin of his face. Cupping the flame with his free hand, he lit my cigarette and then his own. I thanked him with a nod, and he responded with a look that suggested I'd just given him a medal.

'How long have you been on duty, Mitra?' I asked.

'Since 6 p.m., sir.'

A shift on watch tended to be six hours, though these days they could be longer. Either way, it meant that his relief wouldn't be here till at least midnight – still several hours away.

I took a pull on the cigarette and exhaled.

'Were you here last night?'

'Yes, sir,' he replied, 'from three o'clock to seven in the morning.'

That would probably have made him the first sentry on duty after Callaghan's men had got back into their trucks and left.

'Did anyone go in or out during your shift?'

He shook his head. 'No, sir. No civilians. Only a few officers who came at around 5 a.m. Just before dawn.'

'How many officers?' I asked.

'Two.'

'Sahibs?'

He stared, as though surprised by the question.

'Yes, sir. One officer, and one junior. But I am thinking they were not from Vice Division.'

'You saw their papers? What division were they from?'

He shook his head in the manner Indians do when they have bad news to impart. 'I saw the papers, sir, but I did not inspect them closely.'

That was normal. It was enough that the officer was a sahib. No other accreditation would have been necessary.

'So how did you know they weren't Vice?'

'Their uniforms, sir. They were khaki.'

'Of course.' I smiled. Calcutta coppers' uniforms were white, even those of the constables from Vice Division. Only police from outside the city boundaries wore khaki. 'Well deduced,' I said. 'We could use a man like you at Lal Bazar.'

Mitra beamed.

But there was one government organisation in town that did wear khaki uniforms: the military.

'Any idea what they wanted?' I asked. It was a long shot. The officers of Section H weren't in the habit of explaining themselves to anyone, let alone some native constable standing shivering in the cold of a winter's night in Tangra.

'Regretfully no, sir.'

'No matter,' I said. 'How long did they stay?'

Mitra took a pull of his cigarette. 'One hour, maybe slightly more.'

'And did they take anything with them when they left?'

'I don't believe so, sir. Nothing that couldn't be concealed in their pockets, at least.'

'And did they or anyone else come back?'

'Not during my watch, sir.'

'What about afterwards? Who took over from you? Another officer from the Tangra thana?'

Mitra nodded. 'Constable Grewal. He was here from ten o'clock this morning, before I once more came on shift at six. He did not mention any activity.'

'I want you to speak to him again,' I said. 'Ask him if anyone entered the premises on his watch, and find out if anything was taken away. Get as much detail as you can. You have a notepad and pencil?'

'Yes, sir,' he replied.

'Good,' I said. 'Take this down.' I gave him the number for the central switchboard at Lal Bazar and was about to tell him to ask for me, when I thought better of it. Maybe it was paranoia, but I decided to be careful. I'd already told him I worked for Vice Division. And anyway, when it came to dealing with Section H, a degree of healthy paranoia was not necessarily a bad thing.

'Ask to be put through to the pit,' I said. It was the open area where the native officers from several departments had their desks. 'Then ask the desk sergeant for Banerjee. You can leave a message with him.'

There were half a dozen Banerjees at Lal Bazar. I reckoned that should anyone take interest in the constable's call, Surrender-not could always claim that it had been intended for a different Banerjee and had come through to him by mistake.

'One last thing,' I said. 'The two sahibs who came last night. Was one of them smoking a pipe?'

Mitra pondered the question. 'I don't think so … Wait …' He smiled. 'When they were leaving. As they got back into their car. The junior was driving and the senior officer sat in the rear. I believe he lit a pipe as they drove off.'

That sounded like Major Dawson, one of Section H's senior officers. He hardly went anywhere without his pipe. As though he fancied himself as some sort of subtropical Sherlock Holmes.

The possibility that Dawson had turned up here, hours after the initial raid, reinforced my conviction that there was more to last night than just a fruitless search for a Chinese drug lord. The Section H officer would hardly have ventured all the way down here just to take a tour of an empty opium den. He must have come to see something, and my guess was that he'd come to identify the corpse of the dead man. That in turn suggested the body was still here somewhere – at least it had been when Dawson had visited, and from what Constable Mitra had said, it didn't seem likely that anyone had removed it since then.

So where was it?

I walked into the street, turned and looked up at the funeral parlour. Two blackened storeys high with barred windows, a faded sign above the door and a basement that linked through to the opium den. And then it struck me. The answer was staring me in the face.

I stubbed the butt of my cigarette out against the wall and rushed back inside. The best place to hide anything was always in plain sight. And what better place to stash a corpse than in the midst of other dead bodies. I made for the stairs down to the basement in search of the mortuary room. It didn't take long to find: I just followed the stench of formaldehyde and putrefaction.

It was a dark, low-vaulted room with a row of metal cabinets built into one wall. Reaching for a handkerchief, I held it to my face and pulled the handle of the first cabinet and gently rolled it out. There was a body inside, placed in head first, so I that had to pull the whole drawer out to see the chest and face. The cadaver wasn't my missing Chinaman. It was Chinese, but this one appeared to have died from natural causes rather than stab wounds to the chest. Closing it, I tried a second cabinet, which turned out to be empty. The third held the body of an old Chinese lady. The smell was becoming unbearable, and with a growing sense of dread, I pulled open the fourth and final one. I knew as soon as I saw the bloodstained shirt. Still, I checked the man's face to make sure. The scar was there; the eyes were not. It was good to know I hadn't imagined it.

Closing the drawer, I turned and made my way back up the stairs and out the front entrance. I thanked Mitra, and told him not to worry about asking any more questions of his colleague, Constable Grewal. I gave him another cigarette for his trouble, then headed off, to all intents in the direction of the main road and a tonga rank.

As I walked, I tried to piece it all together. Two British men in military uniform, one of them probably Major Dawson, had turned up some time after Callaghan's men had left. They'd stayed an hour at the scene before leaving, taking little if anything with them. In that time, they must have moved the body down to the mortuary in the funeral parlour and stashed it in an empty drawer. If they were Section H operatives, that suggested that someone in Callaghan's team had tipped them off. Maybe Callaghan himself had called them in. He'd already told me the raid had been called at short notice. Maybe Section H were behind it all along. The questions now were: why had they hidden the body and what did they intend to do with it?

I might have pondered the matter further if I hadn't found myself passing a familiar *gullee*. Some way down it was an opium den I hadn't visited in a while. It sat next to a shebeen run by Piet, a Dutchman the size of an oak tree, where the clientele was as rough as the liquor. Piet had washed up in Calcutta one summer and, like jetsam stranded on a beach at high tide, he'd been here ever since. I liked the man. He didn't ask questions, just served you a drink and left you alone. I might even have ventured in if I'd had the time. Instead I walked straight past Piet's place and headed for the opium den.

EIGHT

23 December 1921

The tea was lukewarm, which was a surprise. Either I'd woken earlier than usual or Sandesh had been tardy brewing it. My watch had stopped, so I couldn't be sure which, but it was probably the former as Sandesh wasn't one to vary his routine.

I got up, dressed and emptied the teacup out of the window, then stepped into the hall to the scent of boiled eggs.

'Good morning, sahib.' Sandesh brushed past me on his way to the living room with a glass of lime juice in his hand. I followed him. Surrender-not was at the dining table, studying the *Englishman* and dipping a triangle of toast into his egg. His eyes still fixed on his paper, he nodded as Sandesh placed the glass on the table in front of him.

Sharing lodgings with a junior officer, especially a native, wasn't exactly common practice among the officers of the Imperial Police Force, and my decision to do just that had been met with bewilderment in some quarters and consternation in others, but it hadn't deterred me. Indeed, the thought that my actions were met with horror by certain people was, I found, rather appealing. But there were practical reasons for it too: just as there was no point in learning about Paris from a German if there was a Frenchman around, the best way to understand Calcutta and its people was from one of its native sons – and Surrender-not, despite his

Cambridge education and cut-glass accent, was still Calcutta born and bred and able to offer me insights that a whole faculty of professors of orientalism couldn't. Then there was the fact that he'd saved my life, which was more than any English officer had done in Calcutta.

'Morning,' I said.

He looked up, startled, as though he hadn't seen me in months. Maybe he hadn't at this hour.

He made to rise. 'Good morning.'

I took a seat opposite him while Sandesh hovered behind me, savouring the novelty of seeing me up this early. 'Anything interesting in the paper?'

He tapped the headline on the front page. 'The viceroy's order banning the Congress Volunteers. It takes up three columns – and the editorial.'

I told Sandesh to bring me toast and coffee, then turned to Surrender-not. 'And what does the editor of the *Englishman* have to say about it?'

The *Englishman* was generally most strident in its denunciation of Das and the Congress-wallahs. Indeed, it was the sort of rag that would have accused John Calvin of being soft on Roman Catholics. I didn't much care for it, but Surrender-not liked it, though the irony of that seemed to escape him. Given the paper's strain of hard-line, uncompromising, empire-first rhetoric, which branded almost all natives as indolent, insidious or, worst of all, ungrateful, his reading of it seemed to me to be a rather unique form of self-flagellation.

'They think common sense is prevailing. And not a moment too soon, apparently. Here,' he said, passing me the paper, 'see for yourself.'

Sure enough, under the headline 'Taking back control', the editorial applauded the government's firm stance, criticised the police for being lackadaisical in their dealings with the agitators, and called for the toughest measures to be taken not just against those flouting the new rule but also *against those who by their actions close down the free flow of trade and commerce that is the city's lifeblood.*

The paper had long been an advocate of more active police and physical intervention against the demonstrators, and I had the impression that only the sight of us breaking bones and smashing heads would satisfy them. After all, there was nothing lackadaisical about a lathi charge.

'Why do you read this drivel?' I asked.

He looked perplexed. 'Would you prefer I confined myself to only reading things I agreed with?'

'Yes,' I said, tossing the paper onto the table as Sandesh arrived with the toast. 'At least over breakfast. Reading that rubbish first thing in the morning is bound to give you indigestion.'

I was right, as it turned out.

Ninety minutes later Surrender-not and I were back at Lal Bazar, in Taggart's office on the top floor, seated opposite him like two schoolboys summoned to the principal's office. The commissioner looked like he'd slept worse than I had – which was quite impressive in its own way. He had only one subject on his mind, and one name on his lips.

'Das,' he said, picking up a sheet of paper from the acreage of his desk. 'He's sent me a letter, thanking me for the advance notice of the new ordinance, but he regrets that, unfortunately, his conscience dictates he cannot accede to my request as it would endanger the lives of innocent civilians. *His conscience*, for crying out loud!' The vein in the commissioner's temple throbbed. 'Anyone would think *he* was in charge of security in this city.'

'Did he say what he plans to do?' I asked.

Taggart stared at me. 'If you'd care to remember, Captain, that's what I charged you with eliciting. Fortunately, Mr Das has been kind enough to tell me himself in his bloody letter. A mass demonstration protesting the order, scheduled for four o'clock this afternoon.'

'On the Maidan?'

'Don't be naive, Sam. Holding his damn rally in the middle of the park would hardly cause the inconvenience he wants. He's far too wily for that.'

'Where then?'

'See for yourself,' he said, tossing the letter across the table.

I picked it up and read. The words were written in neat, public-school handwriting with Das's flourish of a signature at the bottom.

'Howrah Bridge.'

'Exactly,' said Taggart. 'Or rather, the approaches to it. It would seem our friend Das would make a rather fine tactical officer.'

The Indian had indeed chosen his ground well. Calcutta was a strategic oddity in that it was situated on the wrong side of the Hooghly River from most of India. It had probably made sense when the city was just a vulnerable little trading post, at the mercy of Moguls and their local satraps, but these days it was a damn nuisance. Choked both day and night, the bridge was the city's lifeline; its artery across the river and its connection to the main rail terminus at Howrah.

'Clever,' I said. 'It won't take many people blocking the approaches on the Strand Road to bring the city's trade to a halt.'

'And all but cut us off from the rest of the country,' added Surrender-not.

'I'm not about to let that happen,' said Taggart, rising from his chair. He walked over to the windows and I sensed something precipitous was coming. 'I won't have this city held to ransom,' he continued. 'Not by the likes of a jumped-up Middle Temple lawyer, and certainly not two days before the arrival of the next king-emperor. That bridge must stay open, gentlemen. I want you to inform Mr Das of that.'

He might have been addressing both of us, but his gaze was fixed firmly on Surrender-not.

'Tell him that I've no issue with arresting him, his family and every one of his supporters to a man, if he tries to test me. Let him know I'll call out the army if I have to.'

Surrender-not swallowed hard and looked like he half wished the ground would open up and swallow him.

'With respect, sir,' I said, 'I fear that's what he wants. He's goading us. He's been at this game for nearly a year now, and the people are getting tired of it. His supporters are demoralised. He needs something big to stir their passions, and he's gambling that our arresting him would do just that. Any overreaction on our part would just play into his hands.'

Surrender-not stirred beside me. 'If I may, sir, there is another factor to consider. Das's health. He's not a young man. Should we arrest him and his health takes a turn for the worse, or, God forbid, he should pass away, the outpouring of anger would be such that it would take the army to quell it, probably at the loss of a significant number of lives.'

He had a point. Das was one of the most respected men in Bengal. The ramifications of him dying in our custody didn't bear thinking about.

'I must concur with the sergeant,' I said. 'The last thing we should do is risk making a martyr of him.'

Taggart returned to his desk and slumped into his seat, looking even wearier than he did a few minutes earlier. 'You have a better idea?' he said, rubbing a hand across his chin.

'Possibly,' I said. 'Perhaps we should let him know that we'll arrest everyone *except* him. It won't look too good for *"the friend of the nation*" if everyone he's exhorting to disobey the law gets carted away while he remains free. They'll think he's happy to see others suffer at his behest while facing no privations himself. Like those leaflets the Boche dropped over French trenches during the war saying the British were willing to fight to the last Frenchman.'

Taggart shook his head. 'No. I want him to know there'll be personal consequences for his actions. Tell him we'll arrest him *and* everyone else.'

NINE

Calcutta was a city divided in more ways than one. To the north, there was Black Town, home to the native population; to the south, White Town for the British; and in the middle, a grey, amorphous area full of Chinese, Armenians, Jews, Parsees, Anglo-Indians and anyone else who didn't fit in. There was no law demarking the city, no barriers or walls; the segregation was just one of those things that seemed to have evolved while no one was paying attention. There were oddities of course, the odd Anglo-Indian in Alipore or a couple of Englishman in Bow Bazar, but for the most part, the rule held.

The exception was Bhowanipore. While much of the Bengali elite resided around Shyam Bazar, a sizeable number had decided that it would be jolly to build their mansions in the south of the city. Not just anywhere in the south, but a stone's throw from lily-white Alipore. The walls were as high, and the houses as big, but where those of Alipore were set back from the road and hidden from view – as though the buildings, like their residents, were different from their surroundings – the mansions of Bhowanipore stood tall, their columned facades looming high over the road-sides. I doubted it was coincidence that some of Bhowanipore's finest houses were those visible from across the canal in Alipore. In a city where the natives were second-class citizens, the suburb's architecture was a political statement. Bhowanipore was two fingers raised towards the British. And Bhowanipore was where Das lived.

Surrender-not and I sat in the back of a police Wolseley as it drove down Russa Road in the hazy winter sunshine. The sergeant had seemed on edge ever since we'd left Lord Taggart's office.

'Come on, spit it out,' I said.

He turned to face me. 'What?'

'What's the matter?' I asked. 'You've spent the whole journey looking like someone stole your sweets.'

He vacillated for a moment.

'Don't make me pull rank,' I pressed.

'The commissioner's orders,' he said finally. 'I can't help but feel he thinks I have some pull with Das, when the truth is quite the opposite.'

'He *is* a family friend of yours,' I said.

'He's a friend of my family – which is something quite different to being a friend of mine. He's no more likely to listen to me than he is to listen to you; probably less so, given I'm an Indian who ...'

He didn't finish the sentence. He didn't need to. He was a native who'd sided with the British, at least in the eyes of Das and his cohorts. It didn't matter that, in his way, Surrender-not was as patriotic as any of them. He'd done what he believed was right – stayed at his post and continued to do his job. But he'd paid a heavy price for it.

The car stopped outside the gates to Das's residence.

'His house looks even bigger than your father's,' I said to Surrender-not as a manservant dressed in a white kurta opened the gates.

'Yes.' The sergeant smiled, as the car edged forward once more. 'But our house in Darjeeling is larger and better situated than Das's.'

'Of course it is,' I said drily.

The driver halted at the foot of a set of marble steps leading up to a column-studded veranda and we exited the car.

'We're here to see Mr Das,' I said to the manservant, who'd come running over.

'*Hā*, sahib,' he said. 'Do you have an appointment?'

'We're the police,' I said. 'We don't need an appointment.'

The man's face fell, yet he answered with good grace.

'If you'll kindly follow me.'

He led us through a high-ceilinged hallway dominated by an iceberg-sized chandelier to a drawing room which opened out onto a courtyard that could have doubled as a football pitch.

Surrender-not made himself at home on one of the sofas while I prowled the room. For a man who agitated for Indian independence, Das's drawing room was surprisingly Western, decorated in the style one would expect of a highly paid Lincoln's Inn lawyer, with French furniture, a gilt-framed mirror and portraits of several stern-faced native men on the walls.

It all seemed rather ostentatious for a man who now wore only homespun clothes, and yet, as Surrender-not had pointed out, Das had bequeathed this house and all its chattels to the Congress Party and the cause of independence. His conversion from advocate to acolyte seemed as sudden and wholehearted as that of St Paul on the road to Damascus, the only difference being that his new-found leader called himself Mahatma rather than Messiah.

The door opened and in stepped a rather striking middle-aged Indian woman in a plain blue sari.

Her eyes fell on Surrender-not and her face lit up.

'Suren, my dear. It has been far too long. How are you?'

Surrender-not rose from the sofa. 'I'm fine, *kaki-ma*,' he stammered, as she walked over and took him by the hand.

'Your parents are well?' she asked.

Surrender-not sidestepped the question. 'Allow me to introduce my superior, Captain Wyndham,' he said.

The woman smiled then placed her palms together in *pranam*.

'Captain Wyndham,' continued Surrender-not, 'I have the pleasure of introducing, Mr Das's wife, Mrs Basanti Das.'

'The pleasure is mine,' I said.

She was taller than I'd expected, and carried herself with a certain elegance that one associated with women who wore expensive jewellery. Save for a few bangles though, Mrs Das was bereft of such adornment. In this, it seemed, she followed her husband's example.

'You will excuse my husband,' she said, looking me in the eye with a confidence few native women displayed upon first meeting. 'He is concluding a meeting and will join you shortly. In the meantime, please sit. Would you care for some tea?'

It wasn't a question. In Bengal, even more than in Britain, tea was a given, a fact of life as constant as the air you breathed. She pressed a brass button on the wall, summoning a maid in a plain white sari, who, having received the briefest of instructions, nodded and retreated once more.

Mrs Das took a seat on the sofa opposite. She turned to Surrender-not. 'I take it this is not a social call, Suren? Your uncle mentioned you came to see him at the courthouse yesterday.'

Surrender-not cleared his throat. 'You must speak to him, *kaki-ma*. He listens to you. Convince him to call off the demonstrations.'

The lady smiled and shook her head. 'I could never ask him to do that.'

Surrender-not ran a hand through his hair. 'The authorities are becoming nervous, *kaki-ma*. Their only concern is that this visit by the Prince of Wales passes off without incident. They need to show a peaceful Calcutta to the world's press.'

The bangles on her wrist clinked against one another as she took his hand. 'But Calcutta *is* peaceful, Suren. The demonstrations are peaceful. What your authorities want, I think, is not a peaceful, but a *docile* populace, and that is something they will not obtain. If anything, now is the time to redouble the protests,' she said. 'It proves your uncle's tactics are working. In their desperation, the British will concede to his demands.'

'No, *kaki-ma*, they will not,' said Surrender-not forcefully. 'They will crack down and they will spare no one. They will arrest him and throw him in a jail somewhere, possibly hundreds of miles from here. Maybe even outside India. What good can he do anyone by languishing in prison in Mandalay? And you know the toll that the struggle has taken on his health. He is not a young man any more. I fear that prison would break him.'

A shadow of doubt flickered across the woman's face as the door opened. Both she and Surrender-not turned to it expectantly, but instead of Das, it was merely the maid returning with tea and Bengali sweetmeats. She set them down on the table in front of her mistress and began to pour.

'What do you wish me to do?' said Mrs Das. 'Your *kakū* will not listen to me. In matters like this, he won't listen to anyone, save for the Mahatma, and of late, not even him.'

Anguish etched itself like a rictus mask on Surrender-not's face and it struck me just how much he'd aged over the last twelve months. The idealistic, self-effacing young man I'd first met over two years ago had grown up quickly, forced to bridge the divide between the love of his family and community and the love for his job and his personal belief that he continued to do what was right and moral. It had proved impossible to square that circle, and, to the extent that he was all but excommunicated from his kith and kin, he was, ironically, as alone in this city as I was.

They say no man is an island, but the truth is that some of us are forced to be, fashioned by fate and circumstances beyond our control. I was one, and I feared Surrender-not was fast heading that way too.

The maid set out the teacups in front of us. Mrs Das picked one up and sipped. 'If you want to change his mind, talk to Subhash.'

'That young fellow Bose?' I asked. 'But he's positively looking forward to being arrested.'

'He may be,' she replied, 'but he worships my husband. His desire to keep him from harm will outweigh any wish to court arrest on his own part.'

'Who is going to be arrested?' said a familiar voice, as the door opened once more. Surrender-not and I stood as Das walked in, smiling like an imp and dressed in a dhoti and a grey-flecked chador. Looking at him, it was hard to believe he was anything more than a kindly old uncle, rather than the de facto leader of millions throughout the province. Behind him came Bose, who appeared altogether more earnest, in the way that only the young and untested can. It was how Surrender-not used to look when I'd first met him; how I used to look before the war beat all of that nonsense out of me.

'Captain Wyndham has come to ask you to call off the protests,' said Mrs Das as her husband walked over. 'Maybe you should listen to what he has to say.'

The glint faded from Das's eye. He gently squeezed her hand and then gestured for us to sit.

'You will excuse me, gentlemen,' said Basanti Das. Making her apologies and leaving her tea unfinished, she made for the door. Das took the seat vacated by his wife, while Bose continued to stand, taking up position some feet behind the old lawyer.

'So, Captain Wyndham,' said Das. 'Have you come bearing another missive from Lord Taggart?'

'I'm here on the commissioner's behalf, sir, to ask you to call off your protest at the bridge this afternoon, and to warn you that any attempt to close down the free movement of traffic will be met with the utmost severity under the law.'

Das listened politely. 'Thank you, Captain. Please inform the commissioner that I would be most happy to accede to his request, provided he rescinds the order banning the Congress Volunteers by noon today.'

'There's no possibility of that, *kakū*,' said Surrender-not. 'The order comes from Delhi.'

'Nevertheless,' I added, 'we shall pass on your request.'

'Then we find ourselves at an impasse,' said Das. 'Unless you can think of any alternatives?'

'Perhaps,' ventured Surrender-not, 'you could move the demonstration to another location? One that would allow you to air your grievances without provoking such a forceful reaction. The Maidan, maybe?'

Behind Das, Bose snorted. Das held up a silencing hand.

'Of course, we *could* move it, Suren, but that would precisely deny the purpose of non-violent non-cooperation. It is our *job* to provoke a reaction. Otherwise, what would be the point? We cannot lash out, and we cannot allow the government to simply ignore us, carrying on as usual.'

There was a certain absurdity to it all. Here we were, Das and I, in the drawing room of a south Calcutta mansion, taking tea and calmly issuing demands at each other, in the full knowledge that neither of us had room to compromise and avert a cataclysm that would no doubt lead to violence, mass arrests and possibly deaths in a few short hours. It was like heading towards a precipice in a car with the brakes cut. We both knew what was coming, there was still time to jump out, but neither of us had the ability to take action.

Das took a handkerchief from within the folds of his dhoti, held it to his mouth and coughed.

Beside me, Surrender-not was becoming agitated. Balling one hand into a fist, he slapped it into the palm of the other. 'If you go ahead, *kakū*, there will be arrests on a scale greater than we have seen since the start of the year. Fathers dragged from their families, sons locked up and deported. Do you want that on your conscience?' he asked. 'Hasn't there been enough hardship already?'

'All struggles involve hardship, Suren,' he replied benignly. 'It is only through such sacrifice that we shall create a new and worthy India.'

I'd seen more than enough hardship and sacrifice in the trenches to know it was all nonsense, of course, but the old man seemed to believe it. I suppose he had to. How else was he to justify the suffering that so many had endured by heeding the Mahatma's call?

'Please think of your health, *kakū*,' implored Surrender-not. 'A jail is no place for you.'

Das raised his index finger. 'I'm not so sure, Suren. Maybe imprisonment in a British jail is the most powerful message I could send.'

Surrender-not turned to Bose in desperation. 'Please talk to him, Subhash *babu*. What good will it do anyone if he should die in prison?'

Bose breathed in sharply but said nothing.

'Gentlemen,' said Das, making to stand. There seemed to be a new-found steel to his voice. 'If there is nothing further, you will excuse me. Today is going to be a particularly busy day. Perhaps for all of us.'

I thanked him for his time and made for the door.

'And, Captain,' he said from behind. 'Please pass on my best wishes to Lord Taggart.'

We stepped out into winter sunshine and walked back to the waiting car. The driver stood leaning against the car, a cigarette in his hand and a distant expression on his face. On seeing us, he jolted upright and threw the butt to the ground before composing himself and opening the rear door with all the gravitas of a foot-man at the viceroy's palace.

As he did so, a native police *peon*, in white uniform and red fez, came wobbling along the street on his bicycle and stopped close by. Leaning the cycle against a tree, he walked over and saluted.

'Captain Wyndham, sir? A message from Lal Bazar.'

TEN

We drove at speed along what was blithely titled the Grand Trunk Road, a stretch of tarmac so pitted with potholes that you'd be forgiven for thinking it had been on the receiving end of a Boche artillery barrage. The sun was high though, shining through a grey haze, making it pleasant weather for an Englishman but still perishing for an Indian.

We'd left Das's house and headed straight for the bridge at Howrah, crossing it and heading north, away from the city. To our right, the river was visible through breaks in the trees, cutting its way like a gash across the flat plain of Bengal. Our destination – the township of Rishra – lay about ten miles upriver, where the jungle gave way to smokestacks and the sort of dark satanic mills that Blake would have happily burned down had they been back in England. According to the note the *peon* had delivered, there had been a murder in the township which the local police must have deemed above their pay grade and so had called Lal Bazar. That suggested the victim was British, or at least European. Someone must have informed Lord Taggart, as I couldn't imagine anyone else assigning the case to Surrender-not and me.

The car slowed and weaved its way around another sinkhole like a drunkard negotiating his way home after last orders, and soon the first chimneys poked their heads through the jungle canopy of palm and palengra, punching fists of black smoke up into a soot-stained sky.

Dilapidated native dwellings of exposed brick and bamboo began to dot the roadside as we drove past the hole-in-the-wall shops, tea shacks with their clientele of shiftless, listless old men, pariah dogs, itinerant cows and all the other detritus of small-town Indian life. The native dwellings gave way to the high-walled compounds of phosphate factories and jute mills, their ramparts impregnated with shards of broken glass to deter the mischievous and the mendacious.

The driver brought the car to a halt and barked a request for directions from a thin native who happened to be walking past with a bicycle in tow. The man responded with a nonchalance bordering on the insolent, pointing further down the road and slurring a few indistinguishable words in Bengali. With no more than a nod of acknowledgement, our driver put the car into gear and moved off, before taking a left and continuing down a narrow lane and stopping outside a squat structure with maroon-washed walls and a hand-painted sign above its entrance with the words 'Rishra Police Station' and the emblem of the Imperial Police Force emblazoned on it.

Surrender-not and I got out and headed for the open door.

The interior was no different to countless other flyblown provincial police stations, which is to say it was dimly lit and manned by an apathetic constable for whom the energy expended in straightening up and coming to attention seemed above and beyond the call of duty.

'Who's the officer in charge?' I asked.

The man scratched at the folds under his chin. 'Sergeant Lamont, sahib,' he said. 'He is not here though.'

'Where can I find him?'

The man leaned over a counter awash with files, and opened his eyes wide. 'Lamont sahib is being at Shanti-*da*'s Medical Clinic,' he whispered. 'He is seeing to one *dead* body.'

'The body was found there?' asked Surrender-not.

The constable's brow furrowed in consternation. 'No, sir.'

'So it's been moved from the scene of the crime?'

He nodded emphatically. 'Most absolutely.'

Surrender-not and I exchanged a glance.

'Where's the clinic?' I asked.

'Very close, sahib. On Kalitala Lane, near the pond. You know Gaur-*da*'s shop? Near to that.'

Once more I looked to Surrender-not who sighed and then let fly a stream of choice Bengali invective at the constable. Two minutes later, and with the demeanour of a whipped dog, he was leading us at a trot down a mud alley to the door of a whitewashed building with a faded red cross and some words in native script painted on a sign beside the door.

As we approached, a British officer in a khaki police uniform and cap stepped out and was about to light a cigarette when he noticed us. He quickly returned the fag to its packet, stepped off the veranda and walked over.

'Sergeant Lamont?'

'At your service, sir,' he said with a nod before holding out a hand.

He looked in his late twenties and was in good shape, a fact confirmed by the strength of his handshake.

'Wyndham,' I said. 'From CID at Lal Bazar. And this is Sergeant Banerjee.'

'I'm glad you're here,' he said. 'We don't deal with too many murders in this part of the world.' His accent was Scots. It stood to reason. Rishra was a stone's throw away from Serampore, and Serampore was practically run by our tartan brethren.

'Where's the body?' I asked.

Lamont gestured behind him. 'Inside.'

'You moved it from the crime scene?'

'We had to. Orders from Serampore. It was attracting a fair bit of attention. The folk round here are a militant sort, Captain. This is the type of thing that could lead to trouble.'

It seemed to me that a murder probably already fitted the definition of *trouble* but there was little purpose in pointing that out.

'Any idea as to the victim's identity?'

'Aye.' Lamont gave an almost imperceptible nod. 'A woman by the name of Ruth Fernandes.'

'Foreign?' I asked. That might explain why Lal Bazar had been called.

'That depends,' said Lamont.

'On what?'

'Your definition of *foreign*.'

Lamont led us inside, through a cramped waiting room with empty wooden benches around two walls, through a doorway covered with a fabric curtain and into an anteroom, at the end of which stood a door guarded by a constable.

'There's no hospital in Rishra,' he said, as the constable stood to one side. 'The nearest one's in Serampore, but it was felt best to bring the body here.'

'Why do I get the impression, Sergeant, that Serampore isn't keen on handling this investigation?' I asked.

'It's no' that, sir. It's just, you know ... what with the political situation an' all.'

Covered by a white sheet, the body lay on a metal table in the centre of the room which was beginning to smell rather unsavoury. Lamont lifted the top of the sheet, lowering it to reveal the face of a native woman; or rather what was left of it. I took a step back and felt like I'd just been coshed over the head. The eyes were missing, gouged out in the same manner as the dead man down in Tangra, leaving in their stead two bloodied hollows. On her lips an encrustation of blood. Walking over, I steeled myself and reached for the sheet. I pulled it lower, revealing the upper half of her torso. Rather than a sari, the woman wore a blood-smeared blouse. On her chest were the marks from two stab wounds, one on either side. I stepped back and steadied myself against a chair as the room started to spin.

Two murders, ten miles and twenty-four hours apart, both exhibiting identical injuries, which in themselves were hardly commonplace, and yet the only person who could testify to the similarities was me. There were just too many coincidences for comfort.

'Are you all right, sir?' asked Banerjee.

'I'm fine,' I said.

Lamont seemed amused. 'I'd have thought you CID boys would be used to seeing this sort of thing.'

I proceeded to tear him off a strip, mainly to hide the torrent of thoughts rushing through my head.

'You think there's something funny about seeing a woman carved up, sonny?' I said.

'No, sir,' he stammered, 'I only –'

'Let me tell you, Sergeant. I pray I *never* get used to seeing it.'

They say that opium addiction and paranoia go hand in hand, and maybe that was why the first thought that went through my head was that someone was toying with me. Of all the detectives in Lal Bazar, why was it that *I* had been called out to investigate the death of this native woman?

Lamont mumbled an apology which I barely listened to.

'Why are *we* here?'

The question seemed to take Lamont by surprise.

'Sorry?'

'This woman's a native,' I said, 'not a European, despite her name. This is a matter for the Serampore police, not Calcutta.'

'You'll see, sir,' he said.

He walked over to a small metal trolley on which sat a tray containing, I presumed, the dead woman's possessions. He picked up something, turned and held it aloft. A small golden crucifix glinted in the light.

'She might no' be European,' he continued, 'but she was from Goa, and that makes her technically Portuguese. And she's a Christian.'

Beside me, Banerjee let out a whistle.

The Portuguese used to control quite a bit of territory on the western coast of India. Now all they really had left was Goa, a speck of land which they and their priests administered in a manner which, to my eyes at least, appeared rather distasteful, converting as many of the locals to Catholicism as they could.

'Standing orders,' continued Lamont, 'are that all matters which may be linked to the current tensions be escalated to Lal Bazar.'

'Did anyone request me or the sergeant specifically?' I asked.

Lamont shrugged. 'I wouldn't think so, sir. The details were telephoned through to Lal Bazar. I expect the decision to send you was taken there.'

I walked over to the table to get a better look at the body. In addition to the wounds to her head and chest, I noticed that a finger on her left hand was bent backwards, as though recently broken.

'Look at this,' I said to Surrender-not.

He examined the mutilated finger. 'Curious.'

'What else do we know about her?' I asked.

Lamont consulted a small notebook which he pulled from his pocket. 'Ruth Fernandes, a nurse, aged thirty-four, married to George Fernandes, an engineer at the Hastings Jute Mill here in Rishra.'

'Where did she work? At this clinic? Or at the hospital in Serampore?'

Lamont shook his head. 'Neither. She was a nurse at the military hospital across the river in Barrackpore.'

'Has anyone contacted her employers?'

'Not yet, sir.'

That she worked for the military could complicate matters. One whiff of her murder and there was a fair chance military intelligence would swoop in and take over the case. That might actually be in my best interests, but for the moment, I wanted to keep my options open.

'Right,' I said. 'Let's keep it that way for now. Any idea why someone would want to kill her?'

'We ruled out the obvious motives – she wasn't robbed and she wasn't ... interfered with.' He pointed to the body. 'Her undergarments were intact and untouched. That's why we assumed it might be related to the current tensions. The bastards keep talking about non-violence, but this is the reality: attacks on anyone who might not agree with them.'

'Why do you say that?' asked Banerjee.

The question took Lamont by surprise. 'What?'

'Why do you assume she was against the independence movement?'

'Well, she worked for the military, she was a Christian, and she wasn't a local. I'd imagine that would be reason enough to make her a target for a lot of these vigilantes.'

I looked closely at the corpse. There was a slight discoloration around the sides of her neck. It could have been bruising, but it was often hard to tell on dark skin. I lifted her right arm and turned it over, revealing the lighter skin on the inside of the wrist. There was more discoloration there, and this time I was sure it was bruised.

'Have you requested a post-mortem?'

'I thought it best to wait for you,' said Lamont.

'Contact Dr Lamb,' said Surrender-not. 'He's the pathologist at the Medical College Hospital in Calcutta.'

Lamont wrote the name in his notebook.

'I want the body moved there as soon as possible,' I said. 'And how does a Goanese woman find herself in the middle of Bengal in the first place?' The question was rhetorical, but Lamont saw fit to answer.

'As I said, her husband's an engineer at one of the local jute works. He probably got a job here and then sent for her. That's the normal practice with a lot of these folk.'

'And where's he, now?'

'We sent him home. He reported her missing this morning. Collapsed in shock when we brought him here to identify the body. Poor bugger.'

'I'll need to speak to him, and any other eyewitnesses. Who found the body, by the way?'

'And where?' added Surrender-not.

'She was found face down in a ditch, a few hundred yards from the ghat where the boatmen operate. We interviewed them. One of them remembers bringing her across at around 5 a.m.'

'And was he the one who found her?'

Lamont gave a laugh of sorts and shook his head. 'No. That was someone else. A holy woman the locals call Mataji. It means Reverend Mother apparently, though she's like no nun you'll have seen before. She's back at the thana if you'd like to talk to her.'

ELEVEN

Lamont was right. The woman in front of us hardly looked like a Mother Superior. For a start she was smoking a chillum pipe, and from the smell, the contents weren't tobacco.

Mataji was sitting cross-legged on the floor of Lamont's office, despite there being three perfectly good chairs in the room. She was younger than I'd expected, probably in her forties, with a shock of long, black unkempt hair, and was dressed in a saffron-coloured cotton sari. Her forehead was smeared with ash and around her neck hung a string of beads fashioned from bone into the shape of small skulls.

'She's a *sadhvi*,' said Surrender-not, as we sat opposite her. 'An itinerant holy woman. Like your Christian hermit priests, she's turned her back on this world to focus solely on the path to God.'

From the look of her eyes, I doubted she was able to focus on anything at the present time. She just sat there grinning at us, and especially at Surrender-not.

'Does she speak English?' I asked Lamont.

'I speak English,' interjected the woman. 'French also.'

'Then maybe you could start by telling me your name.'

'I have many names. Which one do you want?'

'How about the one your parents gave you.'

'They named me Mala.'

'And you found the body?'

'*Hā.*' She nodded. 'In the *gullee* that runs down to the river. Across the open ground between the ferry ghat and the factories.'

'What time was this?'

'Today.'

'Can you be more specific? What time exactly?'

She shook her head as though the question were meaningless. 'Time-fime I don't know. Maybe three–four hours ago?'

'And how did you come across it?'

'*Hāin?*'

'How did you find the body? Was it visible from the road?'

'No not visible.'

'Then how did you know it was there?'

'The birds told me.'

'The birds?'

'*Hā.*' She nodded definitively, then stared at me, and I felt a chill between my shoulder blades. She turned to Surrender-not and muttered something in Bengali.

'What did she say?' I asked.

Surrender-not had one eye on Lamont. 'Nothing, sir,' he said hurriedly. 'Only that she was attracted to the spot by vultures. She says she is in tune with the world.'

'Did you see anyone else in the vicinity?'

The *sadhvi* closed her eyes and rolled her head around her shoulders. 'No one important. Just a few women going down to the dhobi ghat with their washing.'

'No one else? Anyone suspicious?'

She opened her eyes. 'Only that sahib sergeant-wallah,' she said, gesturing at Lamont. 'And now, you.'

'Where were you off to at such an early hour?' asked Surrender-not.

The woman's brow creased. 'Off to? Off to?'

'Where were you going?'

'Going? I was going to look for God. Instead I found evil.'

We'd soon exhausted the font of wisdom that was Mala the holy woman. I turned to Surrender-not as Lamont escorted her from the room.

'What did you make of that?'

'I suppose her story makes sense. She saw the vultures and that attracted her to the body. I didn't get the impression she was lying.'

I didn't either, but the experience had left me unsettled.

'And what did she really say to you, just then?'

'When?'

'When she looked at me. You claimed she'd said she was in tune with the world.'

Surrender-not hesitated. 'She said she can tell when creation is out of balance ... and when people are, too.'

'Is something bothering you, sir?' asked Surrender-not.

We'd left the thana and were now following one of Lamont's constables through a maze of alleyways that ran between a shanty town of mud-brick dwellings stretching from the factories beside the river to the railway line, the best part of half a mile inland, and which housed the myriad native workers employed in Rishra's mills and machine shops.

'I was wondering how a hermit woman comes to learn English.'

'And French,' added Surrender-not.

'And French.'

'She's probably a widow,' he replied. 'Upper caste, I would imagine. Educated in English from an early age. Probably married off at an early age too. It's likely she turned to the path of the *sadhvi* when her husband died. It's not all that uncommon. Quite a few women do it. There's a certain stigma in our society associated with young widows. Becoming one is akin to being a social outcast, so why not go the whole hog and follow the path to God?'

'Why not indeed,' I replied.

We entered a *gullee* of squat, single-storey houses, with sagging red-tiled roofs and walls covered in cakes of cow dung set out to dry in the winter sun. The constable stopped outside one. Its walls were painted a faded blue and the crooked roof was missing a tile or two. There was no window, just a small doorway left open to let the light in. Surrender-not knocked on the open door, and without waiting for a response, bowed his head and entered.

As my eyes adjusted to the gloom, I heard the sound of children. Three of them, none older than ten, and the youngest, a toddler in nothing but a vest, sat on the large bed that took up much of the room. An old Indian woman, wearing a faded, patterned dress, was busy keeping the youngest one occupied, quietly reciting a rhyme while playing with the child's fingers. She stopped and looked up as we entered. The room itself was sparsely furnished. Beside the bed was a rough-hewn almirah, and in one corner a wooden table and chairs, unusual in a dwelling like this, as most Bengalis of this class ate cross-legged on the floor. On one of the chairs sat a man who seemed oblivious to our presence.

'Mr Fernandes?'

He snapped out of his reverie.

'George Fernandes?'

The man nodded.

'You speak English?'

'Yes.' His voice was little more than a whisper.

'I'm Captain Wyndham and this is Sergeant Banerjee. We're from Lal Bazar. We'd like to ask you some questions, if we may?'

'Lal Bazar?' he asked.

'Police headquarters in Calcutta.'

'I do not know what more I can tell you. Already I have spoken everything to Sergeant Lamont. He will tell you –'

'I've been placed in charge of the case,' I interjected. 'Maybe we could speak to you without the children present?'

It took a moment for the request to register.

Finally he gestured to the old woman and pointed to a door at the far end. The woman rose and, gathering the toddler in her arms, shepherded the other children out of the room and into what I presumed was the part of the dwelling where the meals were prepared.

'Our condolences on your loss,' said Surrender-not.

Fernandes nodded an acknowledgement. 'Please. Ask your questions.'

'We understand that you were the one who reported her missing?'

'That is correct. She did not return home. I became concerned.'

The man stared blankly past us, at a calendar on the wall with a picture of the Virgin Mary, who in turn gazed benignly at her son hanging on a cross on the wall opposite.

'When did you realise she was missing?'

Fernandes rubbed a hand across his forehead. 'She was doing night duty ... She is a nurse at the hospital in Barrackpore. Her shift is finishing at six o'clock ... then normally she is taking boat and is returning home by half past seven. I am employed here at the Hastings Mill only.' With a finger, he gestured vaguely in the direction of the door. 'My shift is starting at half past eight ... When my wife is still not returning by then, I am beginning to worry ... I go out to search for her ... down to the river but she is not there ... So I wait at the ghat ... for the boatman. He was returning from other side ... I am thinking maybe she is delayed with some urgent patient and she is now coming on this boat ...

But when boatman comes, he is telling me she had come across much earlier ... This is when I went to police.'

The hesitancy in his account, the measured delay, may have been shock, or possibly a lack of fluency in the English language. Or maybe it was something more.

'And what time was that?'

'Nine o'clock. I am waiting at the station not more than one hour, when they tell me she is found.'

A tear ran down the skin of one cheek before he wiped it away with the heel of his palm.

'Have you any idea why someone might wish to attack her?'

'No.'

'Maybe because she worked for the army?'

Fernandes stared at the floor and shook his head. 'It is true she is working for the British, but she is a nurse. She is everyone's friend. She is bringing medicines for the children of the *para*. Everyone is fond of her.'

'What about you?' said Surrender-not. 'Is there anyone who may have wished harm to you?'

'Me?' He gave a broken sigh. 'I don't know. So many people are angry these days.'

'Anyone in particular?'

'No.'

'What about at your place of employment? Have the workers come out on strike?'

'It is a jute mill. The workers are always happy to go on strike. But they are returning to work over two months now.'

'And did you take part in the strike?'

'I cannot,' he said. 'I have family to support. *Mā* requires medication. If I am losing my income, we could not afford to pay for them.'

'How does a Goanese come to be working in a jute mill in the middle of Bengal?' I asked.

Fernandes gave the thinnest of smiles. 'Once more due to the strikes. Almost ten years ago, the men of both Hastings Mill and Wellington Mill went on strike. Not just workers but engineers who maintained the machinery also. The sahibs sacked many people. But it is simple to replace manual workers. Harder to replace engineers. Englishmen are too expensive and Bengalis are too hot-headed, so mill owners advertised in Bombay and Delhi. I was working in Bombay. I saw advertisement in paper, made application and was called for interview. They offered me a position, so I came to Bengal and sent for family some time later. My wife had been nurse in clinic in Goa, and quickly she is finding position at hospital in Barrackpore.'

'You identified your wife's body, I believe?' I asked.

'Yes.'

'Have you any idea why someone would inflict those particular injuries on her?'

Fernandes fell silent, then began to sob gently. 'Who would do such a terrible thing to her?'

It was a good question.

We kept up the interview for another ten minutes or so, but it quickly became apparent that he had nothing more of use to tell us. I offered my condolences once more, then left him to his grief.

Back in the lane, I fished out my Capstans and extracted the last two cigarettes from the pack. I passed one to Surrender-not and stuck the other in my mouth, then crushed the empty carton and dropped it into the gutter that ran down the middle of the alley. Surrender-not pulled out a lighter and lit us both.

'What did you make of that?' I asked.

Surrender-not shrugged. 'Obviously, the man was in some distress.'

'Obviously,' I agreed without conviction.

The sergeant sensed my ambivalence.

'You think he might have something to do with it?'

'I don't think anything,' I said. 'Not yet anyway. All we know is that it wasn't robbery and it wasn't rape. That rules out most reasons for a random attack.'

'What about Jack the Ripper?' he asked. 'He didn't rape or rob his victims, just mutilated them.'

The sergeant had a fascination about the Ripper murders, a fascination that I'd exacerbated by telling him I'd known some of the officers who'd worked on the case. Since then, and despite me explaining more than once that I'd joined the force years after the murders, he still seemed to think I was some sort of expert on the subject.

I shook my head. 'Not the same,' I said. 'His victims were all prostitutes.'

That didn't seem to dissuade him. 'Maybe our killer has something against nurses?'

Of course he had no way of knowing, as I did, about the dead man in Tangra.

'I doubt it,' I said. 'Everyone loves nurses.'

We walked out of the slum and back towards the thana, the sweet tobacco smoke helping to mask both the stench of the place and also my fraying nerves. It wasn't just the usual cravings that were beginning to bite, it was also the feeling that someone was toying with me: the first raid in months on an opium den occurs just when I happen to be there; a murder which no one reports and where the body disappears; and now this poor woman turns up dead, bearing the same wounds as the dead Chinaman. And out of all the detectives in Lal Bazar, the case just happens to fall to me. I had trouble accepting the notion that I'd simply become embroiled in a series of random events – wrong time, wrong place. Could it all just be coincidence? And if not, then what was the point of it? Why involve me?

It was tempting to chalk the whole thing up to paranoia, and a better man might have questioned my suspicions – as better men had done in the past. But most of them were dead now, while I and my neuroses were still here.

———

Back at Rishra thana, the Scot, Sergeant Lamont, was behind his desk, finishing a telephone call.

'Captain Wyndham,' he said, replacing the receiver on its hook, 'I've made arrangements for the transfer of Ruth Fernandes's body to the Medical College Hospital as per your instructions, and I've left a message for Dr Lamb regarding the post-mortem.'

'Good,' I said. 'Let's hope the old man can add something to our inquiries. Has a first information report been filed?'

'A missing persons report was done when George Fernandes came in this morning. Did you get much out of him, by the way?'

'Not much, other than his wife was loved by all. He seems to be in shock.'

'So what now?'

'Now …' I said, 'now we go and pay our very own Charon a visit.'

Lamont's brow creased. 'Excuse me?'

'We're going to see the ferryman tasked with carrying the dead over the River Hooghly to Hades.'

———

The river was peaceful this far upstream, more peaceful than at Calcutta at any rate. Most of the larger vessels and ocean-going merchantmen never made it up this far, leaving the water to the barges that carried the jute downriver and the myriad smaller craft that had plied goods and people along and across the Hooghly since time began.

A few small boats were tied to a rotting wooden jetty. Others sat temporarily marooned in the soft mud of the riverbank, awaiting rebirth on the incoming tide. Several boatmen, barefoot and clad in little more than vests and lungis, were seated at a tea stall, engaged in vociferous discussion and enveloped in a haze of grey bidi smoke. Their conversation died as we approached, their voices ceasing as abruptly as a falling guillotine, replaced by the watchful glances of men who knew better than to talk to strangers.

I held back as Surrender-not went over to question them. From where I stood, their replies seemed slow and sullen, but eventually Surrender-not returned.

'The boatman who ferried Mrs Fernandes over this morning is called Kanai Biswas. He's not here at the moment – apparently he's taking some goods across to Khardah – but he should return soon.'

So we waited. Surrender-not went back and purchased two *bhārs* of sweet tea and rejoined me as I sat on the ledge of a low wall and took in the surroundings.

A *dinghi-nauka*, with its rounded hull and pointed bow, and from which we'd derived the word *dinghy*, sat rising and falling on the ebbing waves, its ebony-hued owner busy in its stern tending to a net with the care of a seamstress with her sewing. I presumed he'd be catching hilsa, that silvery freshwater fish so beloved of Bengalis, but which seemed to me to be nothing more than a million small bones wrapped in scales.

The leaves on the coconut palms that lined the bank shivered in the early-afternoon breeze. Surrender-not anxiously checked his watch.

'Keep calm, Sergeant,' I said. 'Das's protest doesn't start till four. We've still got time to get back to town.'

'Yes, sir,' he replied without much conviction.

Eventually a boat, what the locals called a *chandi-nauka*, began to draw near. It was little more than a large wooden canoe, with a deck of loose planks and a burlap hood over its middle. At the stern, his weight pressing down on the long wooden steering pole, was a boatman in a loose, dirty blue turban, vest and checked lungi. He looked as lean and gnarled as the boles of banyan wood which occasionally floated past.

As it approached the ghat, the man jumped off into the waist-high water and began to push the vessel aground. A couple of the men at the tea stall walked over to help pull it to shore. One of them gestured in our direction. The boatman straightened his back and looked over, wiping the spray from his face.

On drier ground, he bent over and wrung the water out of his lungi, then made for the tea stall. Surrender-not and I got up and walked over as he settled himself at one of the worn wooden benches with a *bhār* of tea.

'Kanai Biswas?' said Surrender-not.

The man took a sip of his tea and looked up. His eyes were little more than dark pits set in the leathery skin of a face pockmarked with greying stubble.

'*Hā.*'

'Tell him we'd like to ask him some questions about the woman he transported this morning,' I said.

Surrender-not translated. The man's response was brief.

'He says he's already told the local police all he knows.'

'In that case, ask him what he charges for the trip to Barrackpore.'

Surrender-not looked at me quizzically but then did as requested.

'*Du'i tākā,*' said the man.

'Two rupees –'

'*Prati ta.*'

'Each,' completed Surrender-not. 'It's extortion. He's trying to fleece us because you're a sahib.'

'Tell him we'll pay him five – for the journey, *and* a few answers.'

The man agreed, and while he finished his tea, I sent Surrender-not back to the road with a message for our driver, ordering him to return to Lal Bazar without us.

Five minutes later, we embarked from the jetty into the small boat. Kanai Biswas leaned on his steering paddle and pushed the boat out into the current. Between his position at the stern and where we sat was a small area covered by the burlap hood, in which sat some of his possessions: a reed mat, a water bottle, and a small shrine to the goddesses Kali and Durga. Surrender-not positioned himself on the portside of the boat, midway between Biswas and me.

'Ask him how long it'll take,' I said, sitting back on a bench of loose boards.

'*Bís minit prāi.*'

'Twenty minutes, give or take.'

I dropped one hand into the cold waters of the Hooghly and left it there. It was odd. From the banks, the river appeared almost bracken in colour, but close up it was much greener. The tide was with us, and all Biswas had to do was guide the boat in the right direction with the steering pole.

'I expect this is similar to your university days,' I said to Surrender-not. 'Punting on the Cam. Maybe you could give Mr Biswas here some tips.'

'Hardly,' replied the sergeant. 'You could almost leap across the Cam in a single bound.'

It was a fair point. Though not quite as wide as it was in Calcutta, the river here still seemed about a mile across.

'In that case, make yourself useful and ask him some questions about Ruth Fernandes.'

Surrender-not launched into a series of questions, the boatman replying with little more than monosyllabic grunts.

'He says he knew her quite well. She was a regular customer apparently. A kind-hearted woman, even though she was a non-Bengali … and a Christian. He would take her most days, whether she was on the day or night shift.'

'When does he clock off?'

'He doesn't. He lives on the boat and moors at either Rishra or Khardah in the evenings. He says this morning was unusual in that she was early.'

'How early?'

'He thinks about an hour or so. She normally arrives at the Barrackpore jetty when the sun is rising from behind the trees. This morning, she was there at first light. He says he's normally in midstream when the shift whistle at the Wellington Jute Mill goes off. That's probably seven o'clock. This morning, he was already on his way back with passengers when he heard it.'

'Was anyone else on the boat with her?'

Surrender-not asked the question. The man shook his head and muttered another solitary syllable in reply.

'She was alone,' said Surrender-not.

'Does he know why she was early?'

'He says it's not his place to ask.'

'Ask him if she seemed any different this morning. Was she at all anxious?'

'He says he couldn't tell. She was sitting where you are now, with her back to him, and he was at his position at the rear.'

Behind me, I heard the boatman clear his throat. Something he said caught Surrender-not's attention. The sergeant's demeanour changed suddenly and he fired off a volley of questions in rapid succession.

'What is it?' I asked. 'What's he saying?'

'He says he did notice something odd.'

I sat upright. 'What?'

'He says that when they arrived at the jetty in Rishra, there was a man loitering at the roadside. He says he appeared to be waiting for her.'

'Can he describe the man?'

'Short black hair ... middle-aged, maybe in his forties. He says he can't say much else. He didn't get a good look. It was dark and the man was a distance away, but it wasn't someone he'd seen before, at least not a local.'

'Might it have been the husband, George Fernandes?' I asked.

Surrender-not put the question to the boatman.

'He says he knows what Fernandes's husband looks like and it wasn't him. But he says the man wasn't Bengali – he was dressed in a chador, but wore trousers rather than a dhoti. He says he looked "Eastern". Assamese possibly.'

That wasn't so unusual. Assam bordered Bengal and there were plenty of Assamese in Calcutta, drawn to the city in search of paid work.

'Why does he think our man was waiting for Nurse Fernandes?'

Surrender-not translated the question.

'When she disembarked, she took the path to the right, towards him, rather than the normal route towards her home.'

I joined the dots. Nurse Fernandes had left work earlier than usual and caught the ferry back to Rishra, possibly to meet a man whom she might have known, but whom the boatman didn't think was a local. A few hours later she was dead, her face sliced up like a Picasso painting.

If she *did* know the man waiting for her at the riverbank, it suggested some sort of romantic assignation, and that, in turn, suggested two potential suspects: the man she was meeting; or the man she was married to.

By now we were in midstream, heading upriver, and the features of the opposite bank were coming into focus. The Barrackpore side of the river looked very different to Rishra. Gone were the warehouses and the mills with their smokestacks, and in their place, a regiment of neat, white, officers' bungalows of the military cantonment, with gardens leading down to the water's edge.

'Barrackpore was where the mutiny of 1857 started,' said Surrender-not.

'I thought it started up near Lucknow,' I replied. 'Something to do with tales of rifle cartridges greased in cow and pig fat?'

'That's true, but the first shot was fired here, a few months earlier, by a sepoy called Mangal Pandey. They hanged him of course, and disbanded his regiment.'

Barrackpore didn't seem the sort of place where revolutions started. Indeed, it looked like the most British place in all of India. The viceroy had a palace here, though it had hardly been used since the capital had moved to Delhi.

We approached the jetty, and with a pull on his oar, Biswas deftly brought the boat around so that it lined up neatly with the pier. I checked my watch. It was almost two o'clock. The protest at the bridge began at four. That didn't leave much time for what I needed to do in Barrackpore. Especially not if I wanted to get home for a dose of *kerdū* pulp prior to Das's demonstration.

TWELVE

A row of bicycle rickshaws was lined up on the roadside. Surrender-not and I walked up the shallow bank and commandeered a couple.

'Where to, sahib?' asked the rickshaw-wallah.

It was obvious communication wouldn't be a problem. If any rickshaw-men in the country were likely to speak good English, it was the well-drilled wallahs who serviced the military cantonment of Barrackpore.

'The hospital,' I said, 'and be quick about it.'

It turned out he didn't need to pedal too hard, as the hospital was only two streets away. We could have walked it in under five minutes but I've yet to meet a rickshaw-wallah who'd pass up a fare rather than tell you your destination was just around the corner.

We alighted as a detachment of Sikhs in olive-green uniforms and turbans marched past in time to oaths shouted by their sergeant. It was hardly a surprise to find these men from the Punjab here, a thousand miles from their homeland. The regiments billeted here tended to be from far away: Jats, Pathans and the like. It was a well-known fact that native troops were more willing to do our bidding when they were far from home. And that's what we did: moved them away from their native place, to somewhere they wouldn't have any ties; Sikhs to Bengal and Gurkhas to the Punjab, just so they'd be less tempted to side with the locals in the event of any disturbance. As for Bengalis, I had no idea where we sent them.

———

The hospital was a nondescript three-storey building set behind neat lawns bisected by a palm-lined path. A veranda ran the length of its whitewashed frontage and its windows were framed with green shutters. As hospitals went, it was nicer than any that I'd seen during the war, and as if to emphasise the point, the few recuperating servicemen taking exercise in the grounds all sported the correct number of limbs and lacked the bloodied bandages I remembered from my time being ministered to by the army. Still, that had been almost five years ago, and the world, outside of Bengal at least, had been a lot more insane then.

Surrender-not rang the bell at the front desk in a lobby that looked to have been polished to within an inch of its life, and an Indian duty nurse in a blue uniform appeared.

'Who's in charge of this facility?' I asked, with possibly less politeness than would have been ideal. I put that down to opium withdrawal.

'The senior medical officer is Colonel McGuire.'

'And where can I find him?'

The question seemed to throw her. 'The colonel?'

'I presume he's here.'

'Yes, but he doesn't see people without an appointment.'

I took out my warrant card and held it under her nose. 'He'll speak to the police.'

———

Minutes later we were being escorted up a flight of stairs by McGuire's personal assistant, a pretty nurse with a French accent and, I imagined, the sort of bedside manner that made you want to take your time recuperating. Her name was Rouvel – at least that's what it said on the identification badge pinned to her uniform.

I fought back the urge to ask her what a nice girl like her was doing in a place like this. I'd been in Bengal long enough to know that wasn't a question everyone appreciated. The place drew misfits like a magnet and many of them, myself included, weren't overly keen on divulging their history. Indeed, I'd wager more people came to Calcutta to forget their past than joined the French Foreign Legion. More importantly though, I was sure she'd have heard that line before, and you don't impress a girl by repeating what the last sap probably said to her. Not that the line I came up with was any better.

'You're a long way from home, Nurse Rouvel,' I said.

'Not really,' she replied. 'Home is only fifteen miles away.'

Beside me Surrender-not tried to stifle a laugh.

'But you sound French,' I said.

'I *am* French. I grew up in Chandernagore. You have not heard of it?'

Of course I'd heard of Chandernagore. It was a French settlement twenty-five miles up the Hooghly from Calcutta. Even after several centuries of Anglo-French hostility, including the small matter of the Napoleonic Wars, the town was still sovereign French territory – baguettes and all.

We followed her along a corridor that smelled of iodine, with a row of wards on one side and a view of the cantonment on the other. McGuire's office was at the far end.

'The colonel is finishing his rounds,' said Rouvel as she showed us in. 'Please take a seat and he will be with you shortly.'

The colonel's office was what you'd expect of a doctor who was also a military officer. Medical tomes arranged in regimental fashion, by colour and size, graced a bookshelf on one wall, while another was dominated by framed photographs, mainly of groups of officers and men – the kind of photographs that were popular during the war – mementos of a shared camaraderie; but more importantly in a time when death was indiscriminate and sudden, they were a record, in the event that the worst should happen, that you had actually lived – that you were more than just a name carved on a memorial to the fallen.

In the centre of the room was a large, leather-topped desk on which sat several buff-coloured card folders weighed down by a glass paperweight, and a framed photograph of a stern-faced woman doing a rather good imitation of Queen Victoria looking unamused, and another beside it of a young man in military garb. Behind the desk, a window looked out onto a building which, from the size of it, I presumed was the old viceroy's palace. Either that or the cantonment's commanding officer lived in a style akin to a Venetian doge.

The door opened and in strode an officer with blond hair, ruddy, handsome features and a white lab coat draped over an officer's uniform.

'Colonel McGuire?' I asked, turning my attention away from the photographs on the wall.

'That's right,' he replied. 'How can I help you?'

'My name's Wyndham, of the Imperial Police Force,' I said, stretching out a hand, 'and this is Sergeant Banerjee. I'm afraid we have some unfortunate news regarding one of your staff.'

I told him about the murder of Ruth Fernandes as he seated himself behind his desk and mopped at his brow with a handkerchief. It wasn't particularly warm, but the news had brought a sweat to his temples.

'Terrible,' he mumbled, not once but twice. 'Sister Fernandes had been with us a long time. Since before the war, I think. I saw her only yesterday.' He shook his head in disbelief, as though doing so might change the fact of her death.

'When you last saw her, did she seem anxious at all?'

McGuire puffed out his cheeks. He picked up a pen from his desk and began rolling it between his fingers. 'I don't believe so, but then I only saw her for a moment. You'd be better speaking to Sister Rouvel – Nurse Fernandes reported to her.'

'We'll make sure to,' I said. 'We believe Nurse Fernandes left her shift early this morning. Have you any idea why that might be?'

'Again, that's a question better put to Miss Rouvel. And to be frank, I'm not certain what more help I can be to you.'

'Mrs Fernandes was last seen alighting from a ferryboat at the jetty in Rishra in the early hours of this morning,' I said. 'We have reason to believe she was there to meet a man described as being of "Eastern" appearance, Assamese or Nepalese, possibly in his forties. You wouldn't happen to know anyone who might fit that description?'

The question seemed to unsettle him.

'You think this man killed Nurse Fernandes?'

I'd no desire to tell him anything I didn't need to.

'It's possible,' I said, though if it had been a romantic assignation, my gut told me that the husband was the more likely killer. Not that that necessarily ruled him out. Indeed, a love affair gone sour was as much a motive for murder as anything else I could think of. But the chances of either a jilted lover or a cuckolded husband deciding to carve his revenge into her face in exactly the same manner as had been done to a suspected drug lord murdered in Chinatown thirty hours earlier were pretty slim. Whatever the truth, I couldn't be sure of anything until we questioned him.

'At this stage, though, we simply wish to talk to the man,' I said. 'Rule him out of our inquiries. Is there anyone on your staff who might fit the description?'

McGuire set down the pen, removed his spectacles and began to wipe the lenses with the same handkerchief he'd used on his forehead. 'I don't think we have any Assamese staff here,' he said, 'but I'll ask Miss Rouvel to confirm that. As for Nepalese, there's presently a whole regiment of Gurkhas billeted in the cantonment.'

I'd fought alongside Gurkhas during the war. They were hard bastards, descended from Nepalese hill tribesmen that had fought the British Army to a standstill in 1812. We couldn't beat them, so we'd asked them to join us, paying them to enlist in the British Army. They were some of the fiercest soldiers in the world, with a disregard for death that was either heroic or foolhardy depending on your point of view. They'd fought at the heart of some of the bloodiest battles of the Great War, and as a British officer I'd been thankful they were on our side.

McGuire impatiently checked his watch. 'Is there anything else, gentlemen? I have an appointment in Calcutta this afternoon. I shall need to leave soon if I'm not to be late.'

He made to rise.

'There is one other thing you could help with, sir,' said Surrender-not. 'Could you furnish us with a copy of Nurse Fernandes's service record?'

McGuire stared at him.

'It's routine procedure,' he continued. 'We like to build up as detailed a picture of the victim as we can.'

'I'll have to check with my superiors,' replied McGuire. 'It's not standard practice to hand out military records to civilian authorities. Anyway, shouldn't this be a matter for the military police? After all, she was employed by the army, and worked in a military facility.'

'She was a civilian,' I interjected, 'and she wasn't killed in the military cantonment but in a civilian area on the other side of the river. That makes it a matter for the police. I take it I don't need to remind you that this is an inquiry into the murder of one of your own staff. Now we'd appreciate your cooperation and the chance to review Nurse Fernandes's service record.'

The colonel hesitated. 'As I say, I'll have to clear it with my superiors, but I'll see what I can do. In the meantime, I suppose we'd better break the news to Miss Rouvel.'

With that he rose and headed for the door, opened it and called out. 'Sister Rouvel, could you come in here please?'

'Mathilde,' he said as she entered the room, 'these gentlemen have informed me of some terrible news. Please take a seat.'

Surrender-not rose from his chair and offered it to her. She sat down, too bewildered to ask any questions.

'Sister Rouvel,' I said, 'I'm afraid that your colleague, Ruth Fernandes, was found dead this morning, not far from her home.'

The girl raised a hand to her mouth.

'She was attacked by person or persons unknown, shortly after leaving her place of work and crossing the river to Rishra.'

Rouvel shook her head. '*C'est pas possible*. I saw her only a few hours ago.'

McGuire put a comforting hand on her shoulder, causing the girl to stiffen almost imperceptibly. 'Now now, Mathilde. We all need to be strong at a time like this. The officers have a few questions which I want you to answer. Can you do that?'

Rouvel nodded and stared into the middle distance.

McGuire turned to me. 'I really must go now, Captain. Please feel free to stay here and ask Sister Rouvel your questions.'

I stood, shook his hand and thanked him for his time and for the use of his office. As McGuire closed the door behind him, I walked over to the window, leaned on the ledge and resumed my questions.

'Miss Rouvel,' I said gently, 'would you like a glass of water?'

She snapped out of her trance and focused on me. 'Thank you, no. That won't be necessary.'

'How was Nurse Fernandes's state of mind when you last saw her? Did she seem agitated at all? Excited or nervous maybe?'

Rouvel fiddled with her hands. 'The last time I saw her, she looked tired. But then she'd been under strain for much of the last week.'

'Was there something troubling her?'

'I don't know.' She shrugged. 'Possibly, but I could not tell you what it was.'

'We understand Nurse Fernandes finished her shift early, possibly around 4 a.m. That seems rather strange. Was it something you were aware of?'

'There's nothing strange about it, Captain,' she replied. 'She'd sought my permission to leave early. She said she had an appointment in Calcutta at eight o'clock this morning. She needed to take her mother-in-law to a clinic there. I believe the lady required a specialist.'

Alarm bells sounded in my head. According to George Fernandes, he had only gone looking for his wife at half past eight, shortly after the time at which she'd usually return home. If she was due to take her mother-in-law to Calcutta for an 8 a.m. appointment, surely he'd have started searching much sooner? Someone was lying, though whether it was George Fernandes spinning me a yarn, or Ruth Fernandes lying to Mathilde Rouvel, or even Rouvel lying to me, was a matter of conjecture. It was, I supposed, possibly all three.

In an effort to conceal my thoughts, I turned away and stared out of the window. Below me, I saw Colonel McGuire exit the building. I watched as he turned left, heading along the path to the riverbank in what seemed like inordinate haste. I followed his progress as far as I could, until he turned a corner and disappeared.

I turned back to Rouvel.

'Did Nurse Fernandes say which clinic she was visiting?'

'I didn't think to ask.'

'Couldn't she have brought her mother-in-law here? Why go all the way to Calcutta when I expect you have the finest facilities right here?'

Rouvel shook her head. 'She couldn't have brought her here. The hospital is only for military personnel and the families of officers stationed at the cantonment.'

'There's no exception for a close family member of a long-standing member of staff?'

'No, Captain. At least, not for Indians.'

Rouvel turned her gaze to the floor. 'I should inform the other nurses,' she said. 'Is there anything else I can help you with?'

'We'd like to see Nurse Fernandes's service record, if we may,' I said.

'Of course, but I'll need Colonel McGuire's permission before I can release it to you.'

I considered telling her that McGuire had already cleared it. In her current state of distraction, there was a good chance she'd have taken me at my word. Respectable people are conditioned to believe that coppers don't lie – it's a credulousness we like to take advantage of – but I didn't feel like deceiving her. For one thing, it could cause difficulties for her, were she to mention it to McGuire, and for another, I found it hard lying to women. It was one of my many flaws.

'We've already requested it from him,' I said. 'It's a routine matter and he's clearing it with his superiors. But in the interests of time, it might prove helpful to our investigations if we could have prior sight of it.'

'I'm afraid you'll just have to wait until the colonel authorises me to give it to you,' she said. 'I'm sorry I can't be more helpful.'

'Not at all,' I said. I walked back and took the chair behind McGuire's desk, so that I was now seated opposite her.

'Is there anything else?' she asked.

I glanced at the framed photographs of the woman and the young soldier on the desk and realised that the woman in the first photograph was younger than I'd initially assumed. She was probably in her early forties, and it was only her demeanour – the tired eyes and baleful expression – that made her look older. As for the young soldier, he wore the pips and insignia of a lieutenant of the Coldstream Guards.

'The woman in this photograph,' I asked. 'Is she the colonel's wife?'

The question seemed to throw her for a moment.

'*Oui*, that is Madame McGuire.'

'And the young man?'

'That is his son, George. He died in the war, at Ypres.'

I reflected on that last statement. It meant there wouldn't even have been a body to bury. Nothing for a mother to lay to rest.

'Captain,' she said, breaking my reverie, 'if there's nothing further, I should get back to my rounds.'

'Of course,' I said. 'Before you do, though, maybe you could arrange for a car to take us back into town?'

She smiled. 'I'll see what I can do.'

Rouvel rose and made for the door, while I got up and walked back to the window and stared out. Behind me, Surrender-not began examining the books on McGuire's shelf

'What do you think, sir?' he asked.

The truth was I didn't know what to think. The similarities with the murdered man in Tangra were difficult to ignore, and yet nothing we'd learned in Barrackpore suggested that Nurse Fernandes's death was anything other than a marital dispute. Was it possible that the two cases were linked – that either George Fernandes or the stranger whom Ruth Fernandes met at the riverside in Rishra had killed both the nurse and the drug lord in Tangra? Such a connection seemed at best fanciful and at worst preposterous.

I continued staring out of the window in the hope of making some sense of it all. Some minutes later an olive-green military staff car drew to a halt outside the front entrance below.

There was a knock at the door and Mathilde Rouvel entered once more.

'Your car is waiting downstairs,' she said.

I thanked her and told her we'd be down in a few moments. After she'd left, I turned to Surrender-not.

'That's odd,' I said.

'What is?' said Surrender-not, looking up from a book he'd taken from the shelf.

'Colonel McGuire's meeting in Calcutta.'

'What about it?'

'He said he was late and that the meeting was extremely important ...'

'Yes?'

'If so, I'm wondering why there was no car waiting for him downstairs.'

'What?'

'I watched him walk out of the building and head off down the street. If he was in such a hurry to get to Calcutta, why didn't he just request a staff car to come here to the hospital? Sister Rouvel managed to organise one for us at the drop of a hat. Look' – I pointed down at the street – 'it's already here.'

Surrender-not pondered the issue. 'Maybe he needed to go somewhere else first?'

'Possibly,' I said. 'Or maybe he just didn't want to talk to us any more.'

THIRTEEN

The journey back took longer than expected on account of the Chitpore Road being clogged by a host of the great unwashed and unshod, all heading south with their placards as if off to a day at the races. I'd intended to stop off at our lodgings for a dose of *kerdū* en route to Lal Bazar, but there was no time for that now and the withdrawal pangs were beginning to bite with a savagery. Instead, I ordered the driver to make straight for police headquarters, and after depositing Surrender-not at his desk to start on the paper-work, I found myself being escorted into Lord Taggart's office by his secretary, an officer called Daniels.

The commissioner was behind his desk, pen in hand and hunched over some papers. 'What have you got for me, Sam?' he said, not deigning to look up as I crossed the expanse between the double doors and his bureau.

'Das, sir. He's not calling off his demonstration and he's not moving it, despite us explaining the seriousness of the situation and the consequences of any action he should decide to take.'

'That's unfortunate,' he said, gesturing with a hand for me to sit. 'Anyway, it appears the matter's out of our hands. The viceroy's ordered out the military. They've imposed a curfew from 6 p.m. tonight.'

To me that sounded like a sure way of adding not so much fuel to the fire as a ton of high explosive. After all, the military weren't exactly known for their judicious crowd-handling techniques.

'You're not serious?'

'Deadly,' he replied. 'Is that all you've got for me?'

'No, sir,' I said, dropping into the chair opposite him. 'I've been up in Rishra.'

'Oh yes?' With his pen, Taggart scored out some typewritten words of the report he was reading and scribbled something in the margin.

'A woman's been murdered. A Goanese nurse returning from work at the military hospital in Barrackpore. You wouldn't happen to know why Banerjee and I were assigned to the case?'

Taggart finally looked up. 'Don't be obtuse, Sam. It's tiring. You were assigned because I ordered you assigned. And I ordered it because the viceroy's key concern now is discrediting Gandhi and Das and all these other Congress hypocrites.' He set down his pen and sighed. 'Look, Sam, I'm not one to condone a murder, especially not one on my own turf, but as such things go, this one could be useful. I want it solved, and solved quickly. It could help get the viceroy off my back.'

Maybe it was the withdrawal symptoms, but I still didn't see what that had to do with me. A more sensible man might have kept quiet, but me – I preferred to give voice to my ignorance.

'You mean you want it tied back to Das and his followers?' I said.

The vein in his temple began to throb. 'Don't be ridiculous. You think I want a whitewash? If I did, I'd hardly have chosen you for the task. I've got plenty of pliant officers who could do a better job of that than you. What I want, Sam, is the truth. I want to be able to tell the viceroy that I've got my best men on the case, and as shocking as it may seem, that just happens to be you and Banerjee.'

'What if it's not Das's supporters?'

He eyed me suspiciously. 'Have you any reason to think it isn't?'

I could hardly tell him that my concerns centred on similarities between the mutilation of the woman's face and that of a corpse hidden in an opium den in Tangra.

'Not really. Though there's a chance this may be a domestic affair. The husband might be involved.'

'Have you any evidence?'

I shook my head. 'It's just a theory.'

He stared at me for a moment. 'She was a non-Bengali, working for the British military and living in Rishra, probably the most Bolshie township east of Moscow,' he said. 'Unless you can prove it was her husband who did her in, I suggest you concentrate your efforts on Congress sympathisers. Now, is there anything else?'

'No, sir.' Nevertheless I made a mental note to ask Surrender-not to contact Sergeant Lamont out in Rishra and get him to confirm George Fernandes's movements at the time his wife had gone missing, and to speak to some of her friends and neighbours. Tongues wagged, in Bengal as much as they did in England, and if Ruth Fernandes *was* carrying on behind her husband's back, the odds were someone would have seen something.

'In that case,' continued Taggart, 'you and Sergeant Banerjee had better make your way down to Howrah Bridge. The viceroy might have ordered the military to handle it, but I want you there to keep an eye on things.'

———

The Strand Road was a study in static, with trucks, cars and omni-buses all marooned like rocks amid a sea of people, a foaming river of brown men dressed in white kurtas, dhotis and Congress caps. For a moment, I thought Das might have heeded our warning and ordered the Congress Volunteers to keep away, but then I saw them, the students and young men, some of them not much more than boys, pigeon-chested and thin-legged, dressed in oversized khaki shirts and shorts and looking to all the world like a Scout troop that had got lost while hiking on Hampstead Heath. These were the boys that had so frightened the readership and editors of the *Englishman* that the viceroy had had no option but to ban them.

The truth was I doubted we had much to fear. These lads were never going to kick us out of India. Indeed I suspected it wouldn't take more than a platoon of the women's army auxiliary corps to strike fear into them, and if Surrender-not's problems with talking to the opposite sex were anything to go by, the ladies probably wouldn't even need to use force. Simply engaging them in conversation would likely see them turn tail and run.

I shook my head at the absurdity of it all, and yet, if it was absurd, I was the only one who seemed to find it so. The Volunteers seemed to be taking themselves seriously, and from the discreetly positioned troops, it appeared the military was too. At street corners stood not the girls of the WAAC, but squads of hard-faced Gurkhas, rifles at the ready, impassively watching the crowds from under their wide-brimmed hats. They were a lurking, menacing presence, like lions stalking their prey, biding their time but ready to strike, ready to turn those white clothes crimson if ordered.

I prayed it wouldn't come to that, for all our sakes. The crowd was large, the largest I'd seen for months, and if it came to bloodshed, there was no guarantee that the only blood spilled would be native, nor that it would be confined to the Strand, or even to Calcutta. Because what the *Englishman*, its readers and the viceroy all failed to grasp was that neither the Congress Party nor its Volunteers were the threat. The actual danger was the dumb, downtrodden millions that made up the real India. For the first time, those poor, illiterate, voiceless masses who made up nine-tenths of the population of this country were on the march, and if driven to anger, I'd no doubt that their sheer numbers could sweep every last Gurkha and Englishman from the face of the land, like Gulliver freeing himself of the shackles of the Lilliputians. In fact, they could do so whenever they chose to. The miracle was that, as yet, they hadn't. Instead they held demonstrations and they prayed. That was fine with me. I was very happy that they preferred to protest rather than revolt – there'd be a hell of a lot of deaths, mine included, if they decided to do otherwise. The question was, why hadn't they? If you believed the talk in the smoke-filled salons of the Bengal Club, it was down to the natural timidity of the native and his inability to stand against the white man, but during the war, I'd seen Indian troops charge headlong at Hun trenches through a lead curtain of machine-gun fire and club the bastards with nothing more than their rifle butts, so I could tell you, timidity didn't come into it.

It was something else, something in the psyche of these people, and though I didn't know what that was, I was damn thankful for it.

Surrender-not and I pushed our way through the crowds. At the front, not far from the mouth of the bridge, a makeshift platform had been erected, bedecked in the Congress colours of red, white and green, and draped with strings of marigolds. Beside it sat a mound of clothes, six feet high and several feet in diameter. On the stage stood a rather fat, bespectacled native, shouting into a heavy metal microphone with wires running down to two large black speakers and to what looked like an oversized car battery. The man, his sweat-covered face contorted in a grimace that could have graced the stage of the Theatre Royal, rattled off his words with the tempo of a Gatling gun, while gesturing bombastically, pointing a stubby finger heavenwards. It was an oratorical style often favoured by those who have precious little to say but are still intent on ramming what they do have down everyone else's throats: a style heavy on sloganeering, designed to whip up the crowd and steamroller debate. The sad fact is, it works.

He thrust a fist into the air and began chanting a rallying cry which the crowd soon took up. Many of them even mimicked his gesture. I wasn't sure what they were saying exactly, but the last two words were clear enough. '*Cholbé nā.*' It meant 'unacceptable', or 'we won't stand for it'. Bengalis used that particular expression a lot. Indeed, if there was one phrase that expressed the recalcitrance that characterised them as a people, it was '*cholbé nā*'. Sometimes it felt as if pretty much everything was unacceptable to them, as though they were defined by their antagonism to every bloody thing. But like the speaker on the stage, you always had the feeling that their rage was theatrical – manufactured for the benefit of those looking on – and it was never much of a surprise to soon find them merrily doing something which only moments earlier they'd decried as *cholbé nā*.

'What's he saying, Sergeant?'

Surrender-not kept his eyes focused on the stage. 'They're pro-testing the military curfew.'

'Would it hurt to be a little more specific?'

He turned to me, his expression darkening. 'He's saying that this latest act by the viceroy shows that he is terrified of the power of the people; that British rule is a yoke around our necks and that anyone who collaborates in the enslavement of his own people is a traitor.'

It had been stupid of me to ask. His vagueness had been a cloak, masking the embarrassment of the truth.

I checked my watch. It was now well after half past five and the sun hung low in the sky, its light reflecting on the river, turning the waters crimson and casting long shadows of a row of soldiers who stood silhouetted on the bank, rifles at the ready. The curfew was due to commence at six. We wouldn't have to wait long to see just how objectionable the protesters found it.

The man onstage fell silent. He dabbed at his forehead with a handkerchief and then continued in a milder, almost reverential tone and suddenly a cheer went up from the crowd.

'He's calling the Deshbandhu to the stage,' said Surrender-not.

Dressed in a white dhoti and shawl and looking every inch the Bengali patrician, Das appeared from behind a screen and slowly mounted the stage. Shaking the fat man's hand, he walked up to the microphone and waited for the applause to abate. Eventually, even the talking stopped and there was silence – something which in Calcutta was akin to a miracle, on a par with the loaves and fishes and water into wine.

Das began speaking softly in Bengali, and Surrender-not commenced a running commentary.

'He's talking about "*swaraj*",' he said.

It was one of Gandhi's favourite words. It translated as self-rule, but the way he and Das used it, it meant commercial independence as much as it did political.

'He's saying that Indians are slaves today ... That our economic slavery is greater than our political slavery ... That India's wealth ends up in the mercantile houses of London and the textile mills of Manchester and Leeds.'

Suddenly Das caught my eye. He smiled, and as though for my benefit, effortlessly switched from Bengali to English.

'From Manchester alone comes sixty crores, six hundred million rupees' worth of cloth every year. Why should we pay six hundred million rupees of India's wealth to the British? If a man spins his own cloth for one or two hours every day, at the end of the year he will find himself with all the necessities for his family.'

With that he reverted back to Bengali, his voice growing louder, his tempo quickening, but his tone was different from the previous speaker. This wasn't sloganeering. This was the speech of a thoughtful man, aimed at challenging one's assumptions rather than steamrollering the listener into agreement.

Ten minutes later it ended to rapturous applause. Das nodded to the crowds and descended from the stage. At the foot of the steps stood his young lieutenant, Subhash Bose, dressed in the uniform of the Volunteers and holding a wooden torch, its top crowned in an oil-soaked cloth. As though choreographed, an onlooker handed Das a lighter. He flicked it open and held the small flame to the rag. The cloth immediately lit up. Taking the torch from Bose, Das walked up to the pile of clothes and touched it to the base.

For a moment nothing happened. Then a tongue of yellow flame emerged, lapping the fabric nearest him, and within minutes, the whole pyre was alight. Orange flames leapt high into the darkening sky, quickly reducing the pile to little more than smoke and ashes.

I half expected the army to move in immediately. A nervous, kinetic tension seemed to pass through the Gurkhas. They looked ready to spring like greyhounds from their traps. The crowd sensed it too, but Das had timed his display with military precision. It was still some minutes before six, and the troops stood their ground, bound by the rules of the curfew. The fact that the demonstration itself was illegal had been conveniently overlooked by all concerned. As usual, the whole thing felt like a game where both parties agreed which rules applied and which could be discounted. Rules, after all, were important. You couldn't play the game without them, and fortunately the Indians seemed to love rules as much as we did. How else could you explain both races' love of cricket, a game so insipid and with rules so arcane that it took five full days to play it properly and which even then, more often than not, ended in a draw? Indeed, at times it felt like the whole non-violent struggle was just some long-drawn-out Test match with us still doggedly at the crease and the Indians bowling all types of odd stuff at us out of the rough.

On the stroke of six, and flanked by a couple of Volunteers, Das walked back onto the stage. He addressed the crowd in Bengali, but this was instruction rather than speech. The Congress Volunteers in the crowd rose and headed towards the approach road to the bridge. There they sat down and linked arms, as a number of white-clad men joined them. If the troops were going to make their move, now was the logical time, and I got the impression that was what Das was expecting, and possibly hoping for. A nervous hush fell over the crowd, a wave of electric anticipation. Agonising seconds ticked by, but the Gurkhas remained rooted where they stood, their faces expressionless. Impassive as rock. I hadn't managed to spot the officer in charge, but whoever he was, I saluted his common sense. This protest of Das's was only significant if we took his bait and chose to make it so. If we ignored his provocations, the crowd would eventually disperse of its own accord. After all, with sunset upon us, the temperature would soon drop like a stone, and cold was the one thing guaranteed to destroy a Bengali's resolve faster than that of a Frenchman in a wine cellar. All we really had to do was sit tight and wait.

Of course, Das knew that as well as I did. I looked over to him and hoped to see at least a flicker of doubt in his eyes. Instead he radiated confidence, like a general surveying developments on a battlefield that were unfolding exactly as planned, and for the first time since I'd met him, I realised I'd underestimated him. Abruptly, his tone changed and he spoke some words in Bengali. The crowd in front of him rose to their feet. And then, slowly, Das began to sing, and within seconds he was joined by hundreds more voices.

'Hell,' said Surrender-not. It wasn't like him to swear. '"Vande Mataram",' he said, '"Hail to the Mother".'

I knew the song – we all did – even if we didn't know the words. It was the unofficial anthem of Free India, and was banned, of course. Singing it was punishable by imprisonment – quite rightly in my opinion, if for no other reason than it sounded terrible. A kind of lamenting dirge that set the hairs on the back of your neck on end.

I thought back to Das's words earlier that day.

'It is our job to provoke a reaction …'

And as provocations went, 'Vande Mataram' was a damn good one.

Ever since 1905, when Lord Curzon had tried and failed to split Bengal in two, the song had resonated as a rallying cry among Bengalis, and had a political significance which was impossible for the military to ignore. The irony was that in the last fifteen years, the only place you'd have heard it sung without fear of punishment was in the ranks of the military, specifically on the battlefields of the Western Front. There the powers that be had been only too happy to turn a deaf ear to Bengali regiments singing it as they'd charged Hun trenches. But that had been a different time and place. Here and now the response was different.

Das had grasped something that I was only now realising. You could ignore provocation only so far. After that, lack of action made you look weak.

Das and Gandhi had grasped something else too. They'd understood the fundamental fragility of our position – that our control of India depended upon force of arms, and that when recourse to violence was your only card, sooner or later you had to play it.

Whether it was the song, the cloth burning, the blatant disregard for the curfew or a combination of all three, the military had been pushed too far. There came a shrill whistle and then the Gurkhas fell upon the crowd, renting the air with the screams of civilians as a hail of blows from their lathis rained down on backs and shoulders.

To one side, flashbulbs popped, betraying the positions of reporters, and a contingent of troops immediately headed towards them. They had to be foreign press. The local English-language papers wouldn't print such photographs, for the simple reason that their readers didn't want to see them. As for the native-language papers, most had been closed down or had their assets seized for contravening the statutes of the Press Act, and those that remained knew better than to risk such reckless action.

Within minutes the troops had reached the foot of the stage where Bose was frantically ordering his volunteers to link arms. The Gurkhas broke through them as if they were no more than a paper chain and climbed the stairs, making for Das and his two assistants. The microphone toppled to the ground sending an ear-splitting shriek from the speakers. Screams went up from the crowd. Around me, troops were busy hauling demonstrators towards the waiting paddy wagons, and up onstage, it looked like Bose and Das, their arms held firmly behind their backs, would soon be joining them.

The Gurkhas began manhandling Das down the stairs. Beside me, Surrender-not moved to intercept them, but I pulled him back. Breathing hard, he turned and stared at me with an anger I'd never seen before.

'We have to do something,' he shouted above the noise.

I placed a restraining hand on his chest. 'There's nothing we can do,' I replied. 'You try to stop them and they'll arrest you too. It'll mean the end of your career – those Gurkhas will probably break your jaw for you too.'

As several soldiers ripped down the red and green bunting from the stage, others hauled Das and Bose to a waiting military van. I watched as the Congress tricolour fell from the stage and was trampled into the dust under the boots of the soldiers and the feet of the fleeing crowd.

'I want you back at Lal Bazar, Sergeant. That's an order,' I said.

'To do what?'

'I don't know. Find out what's happening with Ruth Fernandes's post-mortem.' I turned and began to walk away from the scene.

'What about you?' he asked. 'Aren't you coming?'

'I'll be there as soon as I can,' I said. 'First, though, I need to go to Alipore.'

FOURTEEN

There was a large, red Hispano-Suiza parked at the end of Annie's drive. It wasn't a car you often saw on the streets of Calcutta, partly because it was Spanish, and partly because it cost more than a Rolls-Royce; and while I'd never seen it before, its presence felt as unnerving as discovering a shark in the Serpentine.

I wasn't entirely sure why I was back here. Maybe it was a desire to make sure she was all right, but then again, maybe it was hope that seeing her might cleanse my mind of the sight I'd just witnessed, of Gurkhas falling on unarmed civilians.

The front door had been repainted and workmen were busy traipsing through the house, I assumed putting the finishing touches to the repair of the broken window. Once more Annie's maid, Anju, led me through to the drawing room; she seemed in better spirits than the previous day.

'Whose car is that?' I asked as we traversed the hallway.

'Mr Schmidt, sahib,' she said breathlessly, as though he were the pope.

I didn't like the sound of that.

'German?' I asked.

'No, no, American.' She beamed.

'Even worse.'

She opened the door to the drawing room and ushered me in. At the window stood a tall, blond chap with a moustache on his face and a drink in his hand. He wore khaki trousers with turn-ups and creases that looked sharp enough to slice bread, and a shirt the whiteness of which was matched only by that of his ridiculously perfect teeth.

'Memsahib will be down shortly,' said Anju.

Preceded by his cologne, the man walked over and proferred a manicured hand.

'Schmidt,' he said by way of an answer to a question I hadn't asked. 'Stephen Schmidt. And you are?'

'Wyndham,' I said, warily shaking his hand. 'Captain Wyndham.'

'Pleased to make your acquaintance, Wyndham. Miss Grant's mentioned you.'

'She has?'

'Yep. Said you were a policeman. I'm glad you're here. I wanna know what you're doing about the attack on the lady.'

'You mean the broken window?'

'That's right. I hope you're here with good news.'

'Not exactly.'

Schmidt shook his head as though I'd disappointed him on some fundamental level. Or maybe it was that I'd simply confirmed his low expectations of me.

'You need to catch those responsible and throw the book at them. I want them prosecuted to the full extent of the law.'

The truth was that I'd done very little – actually nothing – about the attack on Annie's house. After she'd turned down my ill-considered offer of posting a constable at her door, I'd had more pressing matters to deal with – not that I was about to tell Schmidt that.

'We're on the case,' I said. 'And rest assured, we shall throw the book at the guilty party. Maybe even two books.'

'Good,' he said, pulling out an engraved silver cigarette case. 'Make sure you do.' He opened it and offered me one.

'What brings you to Calcutta?' I asked, accepting it.

'Business,' he said, extracting a lighter.

'And what business would that be?'

'Tea,' he said with a flourish. 'I supply two-fifths of all the tea consumed in the northern Midwest.'

'Is that a lot?' I asked. 'I'd rather been under the impression that you Americans preferred dumping the stuff in Boston harbour to drinking it.'

'You better believe it.'

'And you plan on staying long?'

The door opened and in walked Annie. She wore a blue silk dress and an ornate diamond-studded silver necklace hung from her neck. It looked like she was preparing to go out for the evening.

'That's a good question,' she said. 'How long *do* you plan on staying, Stephen?'

'For the foreseeable.' He smiled.

That was rather longer than I'd been hoping.

Annie looked from him to me. 'I see you're both getting along.'

'Absolutely,' said Schmidt.

'Like a church on fire,' I said.

'Can I get you a drink, Sam?' she asked. 'Stephen's drinking bourbon.'

'No thank you,' I said stiffly. 'I'm on duty.'

'So what brings you here, Sam?' she said as she walked over to the drinks cabinet and prepared what I assumed was a pink gin. 'Have you caught the vandals who attacked my house?'

'I was just telling Mr Smith here –'

'*Schmidt*,' he corrected me.

'My apologies – Mr Schmidt here that we're working on it. I came round to see that everything was in order.'

'Everything's fine, Sam,' she said, turning and taking a sip of her drink. 'Thank you for your concern.'

'Are you planning on going in to town tonight?' I asked. 'Only, you might want to reschedule. The roads are blocked.'

'Really?' said Schmidt. 'What is it this time?'

'Another protest.'

'Don't these Indians ever get tired of it?'

'They want to be rid of the King of England,' I said. 'I'd have thought that as an American you'd be appreciative of that.'

Schmidt shook his head. 'Not if it means missing a dinner date with Miss Grant here.' He knocked back the last of his bourbon. 'Come now, Annie,' he said. 'If Wyndham's right and the roads are a mess, we should probably leave a little early.'

It wasn't what I'd meant. Instead of 'reschedule' I should have said 'cancel'.

Annie turned to me. 'You don't mind, do you, Sam?'

'I just need a little of your time.' I turned to Schmidt. 'You don't mind if I speak to Miss Grant privately? I need to apprise her of certain developments,' I lied.

Schmidt eyed me dubiously, then looked to Annie.

'We have dinner reservations,' he said.

'I'm sure whatever the captain has to tell me will only take a few minutes,' she replied, before walking towards the door.

'Absolutely,' I said, making to follow her. 'Five at most.'

'Dinner reservations,' I said, when we were out of earshot, back in the hall. 'I hope you're making him take you somewhere expensive.'

'What is it you wanted to tell me?' she said, ignoring the comment.

'There's been an attack,' I said, 'over in Rishra. A Goanese Christian woman was murdered. The commissioner believes Indian radicals might have been responsible.'

She looked at me blankly. 'What has that got to do with me?'

I was asking myself the same question. The truth was, very little, and possibly none at all, but after the attack on her house and the violent dispersal of the crowd at Das's demonstration, I couldn't help but feel a dread that things were spiralling out of control. As an Anglo-Indian, Annie was already a target, and maybe I feared that if the worst happened, I'd fail to save her. Just as I'd failed to save my wife, Sarah.

'Things are turning ugly,' I said. 'Gandhi's proclamation of independence by the end of the year has people from both sides on edge, and this bloody visit by the Prince of Wales is hardly helping matters. I don't want you at risk if the bullets start to fly.'

She touched my arm gently. 'Don't be so melodramatic, Sam.'

'I'm serious,' I said.

She was silent for a moment. With one hand she pulled at the lobe of one her diamond encrusted ears.

'If there's nothing else, Sam, I'd better get back to Stephen.'

'Are you sure about him?' I said.

'What?' she asked.

'Is he *really* a chai-wallah? Everyone knows the Yanks don't know the first thing about tea. My gut tells me he's probably a bootlegger, in town to purchase distillation equipment.'

She looked at me incredulously. 'Not your famous *gut* again, Sam. Stephen's a tea merchant, not some American mobster. You just need to look at him to see he's about as innocent as any man that's ever turned up in Calcutta. In fact, that's one of the things I like about him: he isn't cynical about every bloody thing. He actually enjoys life. Not like you. You see it as some sort of penance, as though you're constantly atoning for the sins of a past life like some bloody Hindu mystic.'

Our voices must have travelled, as suddenly Schmidt was in the hallway.

'Is everything all right?' he asked.

'Perfectly,' Annie replied. 'Captain Wyndham was just leaving.'

'I need to get back to headquarters,' I added for good measure.

'At this time of evening?' he asked.

'I've work to do,' I said. 'The Prince of Wales is arriving in two days.'

Schmidt's eyes lit up. 'You're involved with that?'

'Yes,' I lied. 'The security measures need to be finalised. And more importantly, I need to arrest the vandal who broke Miss Grant's window.'

FIFTEEN

I didn't go back to Lal Bazar. Instead I went home. The events at Annie's house had soured my mood, and besides, I needed a shot of *kerdū* pulp.

The flat was once more in darkness as I entered, but Sandesh, alerted to my presence by the sound of the key in the lock, was already switching on the electric light in the living room.

He wore a troubled expression.

I asked him for a whisky and the *kerdū* juice, and flopped into an armchair.

'Yes, sahib,' he replied, but made no movement in the direction of the drinks cabinet. Instead he remained, hovering awkwardly, a few steps behind me. It didn't take a detective to work out something was wrong.

'What's the matter?'

'The *kerdū* gourds, sahib.'

'What about them?'

'They have expired,' he said nervously.

'What?'

'Two were remaining, sahib, but this afternoon I noticed they are rotten. So I went to market to obtain additional supply, but vegetable seller had none.'

'Did you try somewhere else?' I asked, attempting to hide my rising anxiety.

'I searched in three different markets, sahib. Most items are in short supply today. Many farmers and stallholders are not coming into town or closing early due to the *hartal* at the bridge.'

I felt the perspiration beading on my forehead. 'Can't you cut out the rotten parts and use the rest of what you have?'

Sandesh shook his head. 'I have thrown them out already.'

Our rubbish, like that of all the apartments, ended up in a storage area at the side of the street, and was emptied by the municipal authorities on what seemed an arbitrary and almost capricious basis. For a moment, I considered asking him to retrieve the rotting *kerdū* gourds from the rubbish tip, but that was ridiculous. I might already have lost all respect for myself but I'd be damned if I'd allow my manservant to reach the same conclusion.

'Just bring me the whisky.'

I commended myself on my resolve as he handed me the glass. That's the thing about addiction and denial: a small victory here and there can help to camouflage the bigger defeats. What's more, I knew that in the face of the growing withdrawal pangs that were already wracking my body, my determination would soon falter, evaporating like morning dew on the Deccan.

I downed the whisky and called to Sandesh to bring me another. The clock in the hall chimed a quarter to the hour as a black dog of a mood descended over me. The last forty-eight hours had been quite something. On top of two murders with seemingly no connections, but where the bodies had been mutilated in exactly the same way, I'd also witnessed Das's peaceful demonstration forcibly broken up and the old man carted off by the military to God only knows where. It had been all I could do just to stop Surrender-not from going after them and wrecking his career. To add to it all, Annie was currently off having dinner with some Yank millionaire with a face fit to grace *Time* magazine and a smile worthy of the cover of *Dentistry Weekly*, while I sat here and contemplated salvaging rotten vegetables from the rubbish tip.

If there was such a thing as Christmas cheer in Calcutta, it had singularly failed to find its way to Premchand Boral Street. But then I'd never much been one for the festive spirit. The last Christmas that seemed to stand out in my memory was that of 1913, the year before the war began.

I'd met Sarah a few months earlier, and at that point, I'd had little notion that just over a year later, I'd end up marrying her, but still, I was doing my best to court her. I took her to see Marie Lloyd at the Pavilion and skating on the frozen pond in Victoria Park. That was eight years, and a lifetime, ago.

As with Annie, Sarah too, when I met her, had her fair share of suitors. But they'd never worried me. I was a different man back then, younger, and cocksure. The competition had been different too: intellectuals and political radicals, rather than the millionaires and maharajahs that vied for Annie's affections. The men were worlds apart but, in essence, not that different. Sarah's admirers tried to intimidate you with their intellect, while Annie's used their wealth, and I didn't know which group I despised more.

Sarah died at the fag-end of the war, an early victim of the influenza epidemic that would kill so many. I hadn't been by her bedside; didn't even know she was dead until months later. Rather I was in hospital myself, pumped full of morphine and recuperating from war wounds which, if there truly was a God, would have killed me. Instead I'd survived, continuing to live, when death would have been preferable and more justified.

Maybe Annie was right. Maybe my penance was a life sentence.

It was Sarah's death that had driven me to Calcutta, and it was Annie's presence that had made me stay. And yet Sarah's memory still lived with me and shamed me daily. I hated to think what she'd make of me now: a whisky-soused opium fiend. Would she recognise any part of the man she'd married? The thought burned like a red-hot needle in my temples and I did my best to force it out.

I checked my watch. It was getting late. Where was Surrender-not?

He should have returned from Lal Bazar by now. Part of me suspected he was attempting to find out where the military were taking Das. He might even have tried to accompany them, but that would have been pointless. The military weren't in the habit of letting *any* policemen tag along, let alone a native one.

I got up, grabbed my jacket and headed for the door, more to escape my thoughts than to go looking for the sergeant. I walked down the stairs, out of the building's front door, and sat down on the edge of the veranda. I lit a cigarette and waited for Surrender-not.

The evening air was cool and the street, like some cold-blooded creature, was taking its time coming to life. Only a few lights were on in the bedrooms of the bordellos and the usual stream of punters had dwindled to a trickle, the others possibly suffering from frost-bite of the libido. I smoked the cigarette down to the butt then threw it onto the pavement and made a start on another. It didn't look as though Surrender-not was coming back any time soon. I just hoped he was still at Lal Bazar, working on the mass of paperwork necessitated by our inquiries up in Rishra. He was a conscientious fellow after all – even more so these days, when he seemed to go out of his way to avoid me in the evenings. I didn't blame him. If I could have avoided it, I wouldn't have spent any time with me either.

The door opened behind me, spilling yellow light onto the concrete veranda. I turned to see one of the girls from the brothel next door standing there – a silhouette in a sari.

'*Kee korchho*, Captain, sahib?' she said in that mock-scolding tone women often use with men they can't shout at outright.

I recognised the voice; we'd exchanged pleasantries on a few occasions, but that had been a while back, and for the moment her name escaped me.

'What does it look like I'm doing? I'm sitting here, having a cigarette,' I said, waving the fag at her.

She shook her head. 'You can't smoke here.'

'I bloody can,' I said, taking a drag. Sometimes I wondered what the matter was with these people. What was the point of being masters in their country if an Englishman couldn't even enjoy a cigarette in peace?

'Mr policeman, sahib, you are driving away our customers,' she said, taking a step onto the veranda as though about to shoo me away like a mongrel dog. I remembered her name. *Purnima*. I recalled Surrender-not being quite taken with her, which is to say that, as with all pretty women, he'd found her beguiling, and that was enough to prompt him to spend a few days finding out as much as he could about her – making enquiries of her acquaintances, checking police records, and generally everything short of actually talking to her. It was a pointless exercise of course, but part of me suspected that might just be why he did it.

He'd even told me what the name meant, but I couldn't remember. Probably something to do with the sun or the moon or a goddess. Most women in India seemed to be named after one of that particular trinity.

'What customers?' I said. 'No one's even entered the street since I've been sitting here.'

She came out, sat down beside me and held out her hand for a cigarette. I passed her one.

'Do you blame them?' she said, taking a puff as I held a match to the fag. 'One sahib sitting here on our doorstep. And he is a police-wallah too. They take one look at you and tell the rickshaw-puller to keep walking.'

'They must have phenomenal eyesight to make me out in the dark at that distance. Psychic too, no doubt, if they can tell I'm a policeman. You must have the most accomplished clientele in the city. Which reminds me, soliciting is illegal in Calcutta. I could have you arrested.'

'Please,' she said, rolling her eyes. 'Everyone knows police don't arrest working girls. They wait round the corner for the clients, then threaten to lock them in prison if they don't pay a bribe.'

That much was true. Prostitution, like drug trafficking, fell under the remit of Callaghan's Vice Division, but halting the comfort trade was like holding back the tide – or stopping the non-violence movement. You could arrest every hooker in town tonight and the brothels would be full of new girls by tomorrow. Now and again, the police made a show of conducting raids, mainly for the benefit of the papers, but most of the time Callaghan's men restricted themselves to drugs, and it was the officers from the local thanas who stepped in to fill the void, waiting in alleyways to catch the girls' clients and fleece them as a means of income supplementation.

'Also, if you *did* try to arrest me,' she continued, 'you would have three problems.'

'Three?' I asked.

'Three.' She nodded. 'One: you cannot arrest me only without arresting also all the other girls in the street. It will look like favouritism. Two: everyone knows all the jails are full. You have nowhere to put us.'

'And three?'

'Three,' she said emphatically, 'with all the girls gone from the street, this will become a respectable *para* and the landlord will triple your rent.'

I couldn't fault her logic. Indeed, Bengali women were often a force to be reckoned with. Once they'd got an idea in their heads, there was no dissuading them. My own theory as to why Bengali men spent so much of their time talking politics and agitating against British rule was because it was easier to protest against *our* tyranny than that imposed upon them at home by their women-folk. At the very least, the matter merited further study.

'Now go,' she continued as she stood up. 'Take one of your walks. Go wherever it is you go to half the night.'

I was about to protest, but then I thought, why not? It was still early but it was dark, and I might as well head off and take my chances in Tangra rather than hang around Premchand Boral Street, putting off the punters and smoking till the fags ran out.

I stood up, gave her a nod and headed out into the night.

The nearest tonga rank was a few streets away and I made straight for it. In the early days, I'd avoided it, using tongas from further afield and frequently changing my route, but of late I'd dropped all pretence, the urge for a hit of O trumping any thoughts of precaution. But that was something I was about to regret. As I turned into College Street, a fair-haired, well-built man, English judging by the cut of his suit, stood reading a newspaper under the glow of a lamp post. He looked up as I approached and something in his expression suggested familiarity.

'Excuse me,' he said. 'You wouldn't happen to have a light, would you?'

Instinctively I reached into my pocket for the book of matches, tore one off and struck it. The gentleman held out his hand, but in it was not a cigarette but a revolver. From behind me came the sound of a car drawing to the kerb. I looked round to see a rear door open.

The flame on the cardboard match burned down, singeing my fingers and I threw it to the kerb.

The man gestured towards the car with his gun. 'Get in,' he said.

I considered objecting, but it's tough to argue with a revolver pointed at your stomach. Instead I did as I was told and got into the car, followed by my new friend with the gun. There was another suited gorilla waiting in the back, which made things rather cosy. Up front an Indian driver put his foot down as soon as the door was closed.

I breathed in and tried to keep calm, telling myself that my captors seemed far too polite to be the sort to kidnap me just to put a bullet in my brain. Besides, I reasoned, if my execution was on the cards, whoever had ordered it would have sent natives rather than Englishmen for that particular job. It was cleaner that way.

Cheaper too.

My fears took on a different hue. Wherever they were taking me, I very much doubted it was an opium den. I was already craving a hit and who knew how much longer it would now be before I got one. My new friends didn't seem particularly keen on conversation, so it fell to me to try and break the ice.

'Are we going anywhere nice?'

'You'll see soon enough,' said the one who'd asked me for a light. In truth, I already had an inkling as to where we were heading. I had, after all, met men like these before – military types with necks like tree trunks and a certain muscular presence that was difficult to ignore – the sort favoured by military intelligence to do their donkey work – knocking on doors and sometimes on faces.

The car sped through the Maidan and the thick walls of Fort William loomed in the distance like a bad dream. It was home to the army's Eastern Command and to its intelligence wing, Section H.

The driver was waved quickly through one of the fort's gates and drove on. The place was hardly new to me and, despite the lateness of the hour, I expected I was being taken for a friendly chat with one of Section H's senior officers – a prospect that was as appealing as a tooth extraction. Like Bram Stoker's eponymous vampire, Section H tended to do their best work after dark. But instead of pulling up outside the section's offices, the car sped straight on, its headlights cutting through the darkness, and suddenly I felt the sweat trickle down my back.

Minutes later, we came to a halt outside a squat, oblong building. The gorilla beside me opened the door and got out. When I made no effort to follow him, he bent down and looked at me.

'Come on,' he sighed, and in case I had any thoughts to the contrary, the one still beside me gave me a hefty shove with a palm the size of a tennis racket. I stumbled out, straightened up and took in my surroundings. The building had a steel door and half a dozen slits for windows, three on either side of the entryway. A trickle of cold perspiration ran down the side of my face and onto my neck.

My minder rapped hard on the metallic door and, moments later, an eye-slit slid open. Words were exchanged and then came the sound of bolts being pulled back, before the door slowly opened. The thing was thick, several inches of armour plating that looked like it had been salvaged from the hull of a dreadnought. A concrete stairwell ran down into a dark basement.

'What's down there?' I asked.

A hand pushed me inside. 'You'll see soon enough. You're about to enter the Black Hole of Calcutta,' laughed the voice behind me.

I'd heard the story before. The Black Hole had been the prison where a number of English men and women had suffocated to death. They said the place was still haunted by their souls, but that I knew was nonsense, not because I didn't believe in ghosts, but because *that* prison had been located in the old Fort William: located up near Dalhousie Square and which had been destroyed shortly afterwards.

Sandwiched between the two, I walked down the steep flight of steps, deep into the bowels of the original fort and into history.

The sharp smell of disinfectant clawed at my throat, as the concrete of the upper level gave way to cold stone walls. At the foot of the stairwell was a corridor lit by low-wattage bulbs. We continued along it, past a line of cells before my minder stopped, pushed open a door, stood back and gestured for me to enter.

I assumed I was about to be interrogated, though if they thought I'd be intimidated by the Gothic setting, they were sorely mistaken.

'Let's get this over with,' I said and walked in, then swung round in confusion as I realised the cell was empty. The guard stood there, grinning. He shook his head before slamming the door in my face. Yelling, I threw myself against the cold metal of the cell door.

The observation slit in the door slid open.

'What the hell's going on?' I shouted.

'Major Dawson will see you shortly,' said the voice on the other side. 'In the meantime, pipe down and make yourself at home.'

With that he snapped the slit shut and I heard the sound of boots head back along the corridor.

A wave of fear passed through me. Beating up native prisoners was one thing, but accosting and detaining a police officer was something altogether more serious. Did Section H really have the power to get away with something like that?

I thought about banging on the door again but there was no point. Besides, my body was already aching from the lack of O. The last thing I needed was to add to my own pain through a futile gesture induced by a fit of pique.

I turned round and familiarised myself with my new accommodation. The cell was small and cold and lit by a single bulb encased in a wire-mesh cage high up on one wall. Against another sat a low cot bed with a thin mattress and a threadbare blanket that looked like it dated from the Crimean War.

The city seemed to be spiralling out of control and I was stuck here, cooling my backside in a cell under Fort William. Every minute I spent incarcerated was a minute lost and the trail to whoever had killed Ruth Fernandes and possibly the Chinaman in Tangra grew colder.

I dropped down onto the cot and considered what I was going to say to Dawson when he turned up. Knowing the man, he'd probably derive great delight from keeping me waiting for a while. I just prayed it wouldn't be too long.

SIXTEEN

The minutes creaked by agonisingly slowly as opium cravings tightened their grip on my nerves. The trick was to ignore the gnawing aches by occupying my mind with something constructive. I tried to focus on Ruth Fernandes and the man she'd met before her death, but it was no use. My mind wandered to thoughts of why Dawson was holding me here. Could he know that I'd found Fen Wang's body stuffed in a drawer in the basement of the funeral parlour? Or had his men been involved in some covert activity at Das's demonstration earlier which he thought I might have witnessed? If so, the truth was I'd seen absolutely nothing and I'd be happy to tell him that, even though telling the truth to Dawson wasn't something I did lightly. It went against my instincts but it would be worth it to get out of this cell.

As the time passed and the pain grew, so did a visceral fear. What if Dawson planned to leave me here till morning? What if he wasn't coming at all? I knew from past experience what real withdrawal symptoms were. I'd tried to quit several times before and I'd failed, and the fear of what lay in store if Dawson didn't come soon was as palpable as any pain I was currently feeling.

My watch stopped around midnight and I estimated it was about an hour afterwards that my eyes started watering and my nose began to run. People called it an opium cold. It was the precursor to the real pain. I'd been saving the last cigarette for this moment. I knew that if I left it much later I'd be in too much agony to smoke it. Carefully I took it out from the pack and lit it with shaking hands. Breathing in, I savoured a brief ebbing of the pain and the maelstrom of horrors coursing through my head. However, the respite was short-lived and the pain returned before I'd even finished it. Shivering uncontrollably, I dropped the fag to the floor. The skin on my forearms was pitted with goosebumps – just another symptom of 'going cold turkey'.

I pulled the blanket tight around my shoulders and curled up in an attempt to generate some body heat, but it was no use. The Western Front in December had felt warmer than this. I was freezing to death and yet my clothes and the blanket were drenched in sweat. I felt I was dying, and visions filled my head of Dawson turning up the next morning only to be greeted by my cold corpse. Too weak to crawl to the door, with the last of my strength I yelled for the guard. No one heard or no one cared.

It was then that I found myself doing something I hadn't done since the war. I muttered a prayer.

———

I must have passed into some form of torpor because the next thing I remember, I was being shaken awake by a uniformed sentry. There was a figure standing behind him, but my vision was blurred. Slowly his features came into focus: the slicked-back brown hair, the moustache and the ubiquitous pipe clamped between his jaws.

'Wyndham,' said Major Dawson, 'you look like shit.'

I guessed it was a fair observation. A moment later the smell of pipe tobacco reached my nostrils, my stomach turned and I vomited all over the floor in front of him.

Dawson looked on with a distaste that suggested some of what I'd disgorged had landed on his shoes. I hoped so. After all, it's the little victories that keep you going.

'Get him cleaned up,' he growled to his subordinate, 'then bring him to me.'

———

Ten minutes later, after a bucket of cold water had been thrown in my face, I was led by the blond officer who'd first accosted me in the street over to a nondescript block in the administrative part of the base, dragged up the stairs and deposited on a chair in Dawson's office. The air stank of pipe smoke and it took all of my self-control not to throw up again. I congratulated myself on the achievement. It would have been a shame to vomit in the major's office seeing as he was yet to arrive.

The door behind me opened. Dawson walked in, told his deputy to stand back, and took his seat behind his desk. There was silence for several moments as he made a show of reading a typed sheet of paper that had been left on his desk. Mind games, straight out of an interrogation handbook. If he'd intended it as intimidation, it wasn't working, not because I too had read the handbook, but because I was past caring.

Dawson eventually looked up from the paper.

'So, Wyndham,' he said. 'Apologies for the manner in which you've been brought here, but I have a few questions for you.'

'You know it's an offence to unlawfully detain a police officer,' I said.

He stared at me and sighed. 'I could keep you here all night if I wanted to. All week for that matter and nobody would give a fig. So why don't you just keep your complaints to yourself and afford me some cooperation?'

'What do you want to know?'

'I understand you've been assigned the case of a dead nurse up in Rishra.'

'News travels fast,' I said. Not that that was much of a surprise. Section H had paid informers everywhere. In a city where a man would happily slit his brother's throat for a hundred rupees, their largesse attracted more than a few fair-weather friends. 'Anyway,' I continued, 'what business is it of yours?'

'She was a nurse at a military hospital.'

'But she was a civilian.'

'The woman was a Portuguese national,' he replied. 'The murder of a foreigner, even an Indian one, *is* my business.'

'There's not much to tell you. She was on her way home from her night shift, and someone sliced her open like a hilsa fish.'

'Any suspects?'

I could have told him about her husband, or the shifty-looking native with Assamese features who'd been seen loitering nearby, but I wasn't in the mood to help him.

'Not yet.'

Dawson nodded, then once more scanned the sheet of paper in front of him.

'It's also come to my attention that you've been sniffing around an opium den in Tangra. One that was the scene of a raid by Vice Division a few nights ago.' He paused. 'Anything to say about that?'

'I don't know what you're talking about.'

He looked up. 'Don't play silly buggers with me, Wyndham. You should know by now that I don't take kindly to it. You were there last night, asking questions of a constable.'

I cursed myself. Callaghan had told me that the raid had been carried out at Section H's request. It stood to reason they'd have been keeping the place under watch even after the raid. I should have been more careful.

Dawson continued. 'I want to know what you were doing there.'

'It's a police matter,' I said. 'Nothing to do with you.'

Dawson didn't look convinced. 'A police matter? And all your other trips to Tangra? They were police business too?'

I tried to keep my composure but felt my face betray me.

Dawson gave a bitter laugh. 'That's right, Captain. We know all about your nasty little habit. I've lost track of the number of dens you've frequented. Indeed, you've discovered one or two that even *we* hadn't come across. Please don't tell me that the one raided the other night was your favourite. Now I'll ask you again. What were you doing there last night?'

Dawson's knowledge of my addiction shouldn't have come as a surprise. Part of me had suspected as much ever since I was attacked and almost killed outside a den a few years back. I'd put it down to paranoia but I'd never shaken the feeling that Section H had been behind it. I tried to figure out exactly what lies I could tell him that were plausible enough to get me out of there. The major, though, seemed to misinterpret my silence.

'Don't be difficult, Wyndham. As I've told you, under the emergency powers I can keep you here all night or longer, though by the looks of you, that probably won't be necessary. Just tell me what I want to know and you'll be free to go. I'll even arrange for a car to take you to your destination of choice, whichever stinking opium den that happens to be.'

I tried to concentrate, to come up with a coherent sentence or two, but the pain behind my eyes was excruciating. Dawson picked up a pen and began to write something in the margins of his document. The noise of the nib scratching across the paper's surface seemed amplified a hundredfold, and then a pernicious voice in my head began to whisper:

'*Why not tell him the truth? What have you got to hide?*'

My willpower began to ebb like sand in an egg timer, until the desire to hold out against him seemed nothing more than stubborn recalcitrance. The more I considered it, the more sensible his request seemed. I hadn't mentioned the murder of the Chinaman to anyone because I didn't want to reveal my presence at the opium den, but Dawson already knew about my addiction. What was the harm in telling him everything? We were supposed to be on the same side after all. And as the man said, the sooner I came clean, the sooner I'd get out of here.

'I was there,' I said. 'At the opium den. The night you ordered the raid.'

He laid down his pen and looked up, his face expressionless as a mask. 'Go on.'

'One of the Chinese girls helped me escape, just before Callaghan's men entered.'

'And of all the dens in Calcutta, why did you choose that one?'

'Dumb chance,' I said. 'As you know, I like to visit a variety of places. That night it just happened to be that one.'

I tried to hold his gaze but it felt like my head was about to explode.

'You expect me to believe that?' he said.

'It's the truth.'

'So why go back there last night? If indeed you just chanced to be there and were so fortunate to escape, why the continued interest in the place?'

'Because of the corpse.'

A shadow passed over Dawson's face. 'What corpse might this be?'

Before I could answer, I felt a retching in my throat. I doubled over and vomited on the floor. There was a snarl of disgust from Dawson and almost immediately the hand of my minder grabbed my hair from behind and pulled my head back.

Dawson stood up and leaned across the desk.

'Now listen to me, Wyndham. Tell me about this corpse.'

'A Chinaman,' I said. 'I stumbled across him as I was trying to escape.'

'And what did you do when you found this Chinaman?'

'Nothing. There wasn't anything *to* do. He was dead. I just left him there and ran.'

The major shook his head. 'Wyndham, you know there were no bodies found at the scene.'

'That's what Callaghan told me. But I saw it. That's why I went back.'

'And did you find it?'

I thought about coming clean. They say confession is good for the soul, but really it depends on who your confessor is.

'No,' I said.

He thought for a moment. 'I don't know whether you're lying or you really do believe you saw a body. Either way you're a disgrace. Now here's what you're going to do. You're going to keep me informed about whatever you find out regarding this dead nurse in Rishra and you're going to stop asking any more questions about that opium den in Tangra. If I find out you've gone back there, I'll make sure your life isn't worth living.'

I nodded my assent, though as threats went, it was hardly compelling. I wasn't sure my life was worth living anyway.

Dawson looked to the guard who still held me by the hair.

'Let him go, Allenby.'

Allenby – at least I now knew his assistant's name.

'Get him out of here,' he growled. 'Drop him off in some shitty gullee in Tangra.'

Letting go of my head, Allenby hauled me unceremoniously to my feet and dragged me out. Behind me I heard Dawson's voice.

'And send someone to clean up this mess in here.'

SEVENTEEN

24 December 1921

Dawson's men had followed his orders meticulously, driving to Chinatown and kicking me out into the shittiest alley they could find, which in Tangra was a finely judged affair. From there I'd crawled to the nearest den, onto a cot and into the embrace of the first of a dozen opium pipes. My cravings finally slaked, I'd passed into a stupor which didn't lift until the sun was rising in the east.

Staggering to a main road, I'd hailed a bicycle rickshaw which had taken me to a tonga rank and from there I'd travelled back to town, ordering the driver to drop me off a few streets away from our lodgings, an action that was the flimsiest of fig leaves at the best of times, but was now completely pointless. Something still made me do it, though. Old habits die hard they say, but maybe I was still keeping up the pretence for my own benefit. Even now, part of me still couldn't accept the fact that without the *kerdū* juice I was totally and utterly an opium fiend.

I made my way up the stairs and silently slid the key into the lock. With luck, I'd be able to reach my room without either Sandesh or Surrender-not noticing.

With a muffled click, the lock turned. I pressed down on the handle and pushed open the door, only to find myself face to face with Surrender-not. He looked as though he was about to leave for

Lal Bazar, and for a moment we both simply stood staring at each other. I watched the gamut of emotions play out on his face.

'Dawson's men accosted me,' I said. 'I spent the night at Fort William.' The words sounded feeble, even to me.

The anguish on his face was palpable. I went to move past him, towards the door to my room.

'Sam,' he said quietly. It was rare for him to use my Christian name and it stopped me in my tracks. 'I can smell the *afeem* on you.'

And suddenly a wave of something – guilt or self-loathing possibly, but more a sense of weariness – swept over me. I was tired of it all. Tired of the deception and the constant need to maintain the charade of normality in front of the natives: the need to maintain a stiff upper lip at all bloody times, that unwritten rule that decreed it an indignity to share one's weaknesses with someone because of the colour of their skin, *that* to me was the real white man's burden, not whatever nonsense that fool Kipling might have penned in one his doggerel poems. Forget India, Surrender-not was the closest thing I had to a friend anywhere. If anyone deserved to be taken into my confidence, it was him.

He turned and headed for the front door.

'Wait,' I called after him. It was time to set down the burden. 'I need to talk to you.'

Sandesh was in the living room, making a show of wiping down the coffee table with a rag that smelled of antiseptic. There was little point to the exercise, but wiping down the hard furnishings was part of his daily ritual. What's more, it seemed to make him happy, and neither Surrender-not nor I had ever seen any purpose in curtailing his fun. This morning was different and a stern word from Surrender-not sent him scurrying off to carry on with his chores elsewhere.

I walked over to the drinks cabinet and poured myself a whisky. It might have been seven in the morning but time had lost much of its meaning over the last twenty-four hours, and in any case, I needed a stiff drink to get me through what I was about to do. No Englishman finds it easy discussing his *situation* with anyone, and coming clean to Surrender-not was something I relished as much as losing a limb, but sometimes you reach a point where either you bend with the wind or you break. I knocked back the whisky, poured myself another and turned to find Surrender-not still standing near the door. Walking over to my armchair, I dropped into it and waited for him to take the chair opposite, and with another sip of whisky, I proceeded with the tale of my descent into hell, from my addiction to morphine while recovering from my war wounds, to finding a corpse in an opium den with an oriental knife in its chest, to winding up in a cell in the Black Hole of Calcutta the previous night.

'You must seek help,' he said finally.

'Yes, the thought had occurred,' I replied drily, 'but there's no time at the moment. What matters right now is what Section H are up to. Why their sudden interest in our murder case up in Rishra.'

'You are in no condition to worry about matters like that. The first priority is to obtain a cure for your addic—'

'I give you my word,' I said, 'I'll see to it as soon as we get to the bottom of this case.'

'Your word?'

'Absolutely.'

Surrender-not slowly rubbed the side of his face. He protested some more, but each time I brought him back to the matter of the dead nurse in Rishra.

'It would seem to me,' he said finally, 'that the more pertinent question relates to their interest in your opium den in Tangra, not their curiosity with our case in Rishra.'

'What?'

'They merely want you to keep them abreast of developments up there,' he continued. 'They're happy enough for us to keep investigating, whereas with the opium den, not only was the raid initiated at their behest, they also maintained surveillance on the building thereafter. It would seem likely that your corpse has something to do with it all. Why else would they hide it?'

I stared hard at him. 'Maybe we should go back so you can take a look at it?'

His face dissolved in shock. 'No,' he said vehemently.

'Why not?'

'Because Section H spent half of last night warning you not to. And they're bound to still have it under surveillance.'

'In that case,' I said, 'we'll just have to find a way to outsmart them.'

———

I dispatched Surrender-not to his desk at Lal Bazar and Sandesh to whichever bazaar he needed to go to in order to track down enough *kerdū* gourds to last me at least a week. I wasn't keen on going through the trauma of running out again. Once they'd left, I retreated to my room and collapsed fully clothed onto the bed.

Waking some time later, I showered and shaved and was back out on the street by 10 a.m. Picking up a cup of tea from a stall en route, I headed for the office.

Surrender-not was waiting for me. His face suggested bad news.

'Lord Taggart wants to see us,' he said.

'What about?'

'Das.'

———

We were back in the commissioner's office, seated across the desk from him.

'Surely he's the military's problem,' I said. 'They're the ones who arrested him after all.'

Taggart took off his spectacles and pinched the bridge of his nose.

'It seems he's our problem again. The press have been asking questions and apparently the London papers have picked up on the arrest. There's even a piece in today's *Times* about it. The viceroy and his mandarins in Delhi are worried about the impact on the prince's visit. I take it I don't need to remind you that His Royal Highness arrives in less than twenty-four hours.'

'So they're going to release Das?'

Taggart shook his head. 'Nothing quite so simple. Releasing him would also send the wrong sort of message.'

'What then?'

'He and his aide, this Bose fellow, are to be transferred to the civilian authorities and placed under house arrest. And you two gentlemen' – he gestured across the desk and Surrender-not and me – 'are the ones who are going to fetch them. I want you to take custody of them at Fort William and drive them to Das's home.' He turned to Surrender-not. 'En route, Sergeant, I want you to emphasise to Das that this is his final warning. If he causes any more trouble prior to, or during the prince's visit, he'll be admiring the view out the window of a jail cell in the Andaman Islands.'

'Yes, sir,' mumbled Surrender-not.

I squirmed in my seat.

'With respect, sir,' I said. 'There's the case of the woman murdered in Rishra. Surely we should be focusing on that, not acting as a taxi service for Das.'

'Oh, you're much more than a taxi service, Sam,' said Taggart. 'Think of yourselves as providing a chauffeur service with menaces.'

EIGHTEEN

The morning mist still clung to the trees as we drove through the Maidan towards Fort William. A murder of crows watched warily from their perches as Surrender-not and I sat in silence. I was busy brooding. I'd no desire to see Major Dawson again. The thought of bumping into him so soon after vomiting in his office wasn't something I relished. As for Surrender-not, I suppose he was still coming to terms with everything I'd confessed to him that morning. I expect it's not easy making small talk with a superior officer shortly after they've come clean about being an opium fiend.

To break the tension, I decided to tell him about Annie's new American friend, Stephen Schmidt. Indeed, if there was one thing guaranteed to cheer him up, it was tales of my attempts at reingratiating myself into the lady's affections.

'You met him?'

'Yes.'

'When?'

'Yesterday evening. He was at Annie's house when I got there.'

'I've heard he's extremely wealthy.'

'Where'd you hear that?' I asked.

'Word travels'. He shrugged.

'Judging by his car and his cologne, I wouldn't disagree,' I said.

'What is he like?'

'Like an American.'

Surrender-not was wide-eyed. 'Is he a cowboy?'

'No. He's more of a chai-wallah.'

'A rich chai-wallah,' marvelled Surrender-not. 'That'll be a first.'

'He just sells an awful lot of it,' I said, as the ramparts of Fort William came into view.

Even with our police identification papers, negotiating the checkpoints at the entrance to the fort took longer than it had the previous evening, when I'd been in the company of Dawson's goons. We passed our orders, signed by Lord Taggart, to a flat-faced sentry with the personality of a brick, who took them and disappeared into his guardhouse. After what was probably five minutes but felt longer, he returned and waved us through.

'Head towards St George's barracks,' he said.

'Is that where the demonstrators are being held?' asked Banerjee.

The guard shook his head. 'No, but trust me, you won't fail to spot them.'

We drove past the block containing Section H's office, towards the church of St Peter at the centre of the fort, and on towards St George's barracks. It turned out the sentry had been correct. A short distance from the barracks, an area fenced off with barbed wire had been set up. Within it several hundred natives, some dressed in khaki, most in Congress white, milled around.

Surrender-not ordered the driver to a halt. We got out and walked over to the holding pen. The entrance, nothing more than a gap in the loops of barbed wire, was guarded by a couple of bored-looking Sikhs. I handed the orders to the one with a stripe on his shoulder and explained that we were looking for Das.

He scrutinised the papers then marched off to the barracks, returning minutes later with a boyish-looking ginger-haired officer, who introduced himself as Captain MacKenzie of the Black Watch.

'Rather apt, eh?' he quipped. 'Given I'm tasked with overseeing that lot.' He gestured at the compound with a nod. 'Your man's in there somewhere. As for where exactly, your guess is as good as mine.'

He led us through the gap in the wire and into the throng of natives.

Surrender-not looked uncomfortable. 'What's going to happen to these men?' he asked.

'They'll be processed,' said MacKenzie. 'The ringleaders'll be rooted out and separated from the fellow travellers. We've orders to charge anyone in uniform. As for the others' – he shrugged – 'that's for better paid men than me to decide.'

The air was heavy with the stench of sweat and urine, and around us, men sat on the ground wrapped in grey, military issue blankets, huddled together in groups against the cold. Further in, beneath the relative shelter of the tented roof, lay others, bruised and bandaged, with some receiving medical attention from one of a few overstretched orderlies. A chorus of hacking coughs arose from grizzled and bristled faces. Sanitation consisted of a hastily dug pit at one end of the compound, part of which was being raked over and covered with lime by a number of the detainees under the direction of a British sergeant.

'Das!' called out MacKenzie. 'The officer is looking for C. R. Das!'

Off to one side there was a minor commotion.

'This way,' said MacKenzie, heading towards it like a fisherman alerted to the location of a shoal by eddies in the water.

The knot of Indians melted in front of us, revealing Das, sitting crossed-legged on an army blanket. Around him was gathered a group of younger men, some standing, some on their haunches, and among them stood the bespectacled figure of Das's lieutenant, Subhash Bose.

Das smiled and beckoned to Bose to help him to his feet, then greeted us like long-lost friends.

'Captain Wyndham, Suren,' he said with more good humour than is natural for a man of his age who's just spent a winter's night outside, 'I admit it is a surprise to see you both here, albeit a pleasant one. I hope you have come to tell me that the viceroy has acceded to our demands to quit India.'

'I'm not sure he's making plans to vacate the Viceregal Lodge just yet,' I said. 'At least I haven't received any orders to that effect. For now I'm instructed to take you and Mr Bose to your home.'

'You're freeing us?'

'Not exactly. You're being placed under house arrest.'

'And what of my friends here?' he asked, gesturing to the throng.

'I've no orders pertaining to them.'

Das mulled it over. 'And what if we refuse to go?'

'The matter's not up for debate,' I said. 'Either you come with us or the military will drag you over there in the dead of night and in handcuffs. That would take slightly longer and be less dignified, but the result will be the same.'

'I'm not concerned about my dignity,' he replied.

'Please, *kakū*,' implored Surrender-not, 'another fifteen hours sitting out here will not achieve anything.'

Das looked at Surrender-not, then to his lieutenant, Bose, then to me.

'If you don't mind, I would like to confer with Subhash *babu* for a moment.'

I nodded my assent and he and Bose moved off to one side, conversing quietly in Bengali.

Das returned a few moments later. Bose, however, hung back.

'Very well, gentlemen,' said Das. 'We are at your disposal.'

'What are the terms of my house arrest?' asked Das as we drove back through the gates of the fort. I was seated between him and Bose, with Surrender-not and the driver up front.

'They're quite straightforward,' I said. 'You make no effort to stir up any more trouble prior to or during the Prince of Wales's visit.'

'And what if I refuse to comply?'

It was a good question. In normal circumstances if you broke the law, you went to jail. But Gandhi, Das and their acolytes had subverted the whole game. They *wanted* to be thrown in jail, to show that the threat of a British prison, and by extension, British justice, meant nothing to them. It was as though they viewed incarceration as a moral victory, and so we in turn were placed in the bizarre situation of having to do our damnedest to justify keeping them *out* of prison, without acknowledging the whole thing for the farce it really was. Fortunately, in Das's case, Lord Taggart had already worked out a fall-back position.

'You'll be moved to Darjeeling,' I said. 'I understand you have a house up there too.'

That was the beauty of arresting a man with as many homes as Das. When it came to choosing a place for his incarceration, we were practically spoilt for choice.

'Will I be afforded access to newspapers?' he asked.

'I doubt it,' I said. 'Not that there's much to read in them these days. You won't find anything about yesterday's demonstration, at least not in the English-language papers, and probably very little in the Bengali ones too.'

I omitted mention of the foreign press or the London papers. My job, after all, wasn't to give him an accurate portrayal of the state of play, but rather to dissuade him from any future action which might make the job of the Imperial Police Force – and by extension, my life – any more difficult than it already was.

Das stared out of the window. I'd a fair idea of what he might be thinking. The streets seemed no different from yesterday. The shops were open and the trams were running. Calcutta was going about its business as though his demonstration of the previous evening had never taken place. The truth was that people were tired. Protests, like opium use, suffered from the law of diminishing returns. The more you did it, the less effect it had next time round. Das and his cloth-burning were old news. He and his people had done it many times before and there came a point where people stopped chanting the slogans and began questioning the value of burning garments that could have better kept them warm on a winter's night. As for the arrests, what were a few hundred more when set beside the tens of thousands already in jail?

'Maybe stronger action is required,' Das mused. 'Maybe I should go on hunger strike?'

In the front seat, Surrender-not swivelled round, looking like someone had slapped him.

'Please, *kakū*,' he protested. 'A hunger strike could kill you. And what of *kaki-ma* and your children? You cannot call on them to sacrifice their husband and father.'

Das smiled at him with all the beatific idiocy of a saint looking forward to his day in the colosseum with the lions.

'Nothing worth obtaining is ever achieved without sacrifice, Suren,' he replied.

Most Bengalis have a streak of martyrdom about them, and Das was no exception. It seemed it was up to me to burst his bubble.

'I'd imagine you'd need Gandhi's permission for something like that. And I can't see him allowing his chief lieutenant in Bengal to sign his own death warrant.'

Das came down to earth with a bump as the reality of my words hit him. Surrender-not, meanwhile, looked like a man who'd just avoided being run over by a bus.

There was a coterie of policemen discreetly stationed around Das's house, as discreetly as possible, that is, for armed policemen to be while still maintaining a visible menace.

'What happens now?' asked Das as the car drew to a halt.

'Now, we hand you over to the tender mercies of our colleagues from Bhowanipore thana, and as long as you abide by the conditions of your house arrest, there'll be no need for further action.'

I hoped he'd heed my words. The last thing I wanted to do was to ship the old man off to Darjeeling in December. Calcutta at this time of year was cold enough for any Bengali, but Darjeeling, in the foothills of the Himalayas, would have felt as frigid as the North Pole.

Something told me that was wildly optimistic. As he'd said, the purpose of non-violent non-cooperation was to provoke a reaction, and it was more likely he'd be plotting his next move before he'd even had breakfast.

Das's wife, Basanti Devi, stood as the gate, flanked by the durwan and a young woman in a white sari. Her relief at seeing her husband's face through the car window was palpable.

Das turned to me. 'You must come in for a cup of tea.'

'Another time, perhaps,' I said.

A skinny native constable ran quickly round, opened Das's door, and helped the old man from the car as though he was some VIP arriving at the Dorchester. Das thanked him, patting him on the arm and the constable beamed as though he'd just been blessed by a saint.

And in the expression on the constable's face, I saw the future. This struggle we were engaged in – this battle to keep India British – was one we were destined to lose. If even our own men treated the enemy as saints, then what chance did we stand? It stood to reason that many of the Indians who worked for us, in the police force, the army and the bureaucracy, would have thought as the constable did. They worked for us out of necessity: our cash put food in their bellies, but their hearts were with the other side.

I couldn't blame them. How could I when even describing a man like Das as *the enemy* felt wrong? We'd arrested him for making a speech seeking equality, and thrown him in a makeshift prison camp, open to the elements on one of the coldest nights of the year, and here he was inviting us in for a cup of tea. It was hard to dislike the man, let alone classify him as a mortal foe.

It struck me that was the real problem. To see a man as your enemy, you needed to hate him, and while it was easy to hate a man who fought you with bullets and bombs, it was bloody difficult to hate a man who opposed you by appealing to your own moral compass.

And we British considered ourselves a moral people. What else was the vaunted British sense of fair play but a manifestation of our morality? Gandhi and Das's genius was that they realised that better than we did ourselves. They recognised that when it came down to it, the British and the Indians weren't that different, and the way to beat us was to appeal to our better natures – to make us comprehend the moral incongruity of our position in India.

We could only control India through force of arms, but force was useless against a people who didn't fight back; because you couldn't kill people like that without killing a part of yourself too. That was a dilemma we'd never be able to solve. Indian independence was coming. The Raj was a sick man at death's door and all we were doing was delaying the inevitable. The only question was how long it would take us to realise that and call it a day.

NINETEEN

There was an envelope waiting on my desk at Lal Bazar. It was dated 23 December in florid, feminine handwriting.

I ripped it open and drew out the contents, a few flimsy sheets of paper, closely typed, with the words Barrackpore Military Hospital printed in large block capitals at top, and the name Ruth Fernandes beneath it.

'What is it?' asked Surrender-not.

'Someone's seen fit to send us Nurse Fernandes's personnel file.'

'Who? Colonel McGuire?'

I checked the envelope for any cover note but there was none, but I was quite certain who'd sent it. The date written on the envelope told me everything I needed to know. French handwriting is subtly different to the English variety, especially in the way that certain characters are drawn – the number '1' in particular. The French always write it with a much longer slant at the top.

'I doubt it,' I said, turning over the pages.

'How can you tell?'

'There's no cover note,' I said. 'If it had been sent at McGuire's behest, there would have been one, in fact there's nothing at all with the sender's name on it, which suggests it's been sent surreptitiously. I think this has come from Sister Rouvel, and, if I'm correct, without McGuire's knowledge.'

I sat down and read through the pages. There seemed little in the way of new information. Under her name and address was a short description of her qualifications and pay grade. Set out beneath that was her service history at the hospital. It began in November 1912, shortly after she'd come to Bengal at the behest of her husband, presumably.

She'd been promoted in October 1915 to head of ward. With the war starting in 1914, I imagined the hospital would have seen a large influx of wounded native troops returning for recuperation and rehabilitation the following year. It stood to reason that Fernandes, with her time served in Barrackpore and her previous experience as a nurse in Goa, would have been a natural choice for promotion.

The next entry was succinct. It read simply: *September 1917: Transfer to RAWALPINDI.*

Rawalpindi was a garrison town in the Punjab, over a thousand miles from Bengal, close to the North-West Frontier. By November of the following year though, she was back overseeing her old ward in Barrackpore, a position she retained until her death less than forty-eight hours earlier.

The next page was taken up with annual evaluations of her performance. There was a gap for 1917–18, as was to be expected given that during that time she'd been transferred to Rawalpindi.

I tossed the pages over the desk to Surrender-not and waited for him to read them.

'What do you make of it?' I asked as he finally looked up.

'For the most part there's nothing here.' He shrugged. 'But ...'

'Yes?'

'Why would a staff nurse be transferred from Barrackpore to Rawalpindi?'

'It was wartime,' I said. 'People were moved about all over the place. Things were pretty bad in '17 and a lot of our Indian troops were from the Punjab. Maybe they needed additional nurses to tend to the wounded men sent back there?'

'It's possible.' He shrugged. 'But it's odd that her husband made no mention of it.'

It was a good point. The man had moved his wife and family all the way from Goa to Bengal. And while it was not uncommon in India for a man to leave his family to go off and seek work many hundreds of miles away, it was unheard of for women to do the same. Indeed the chances that George Fernandes had simply let his wife go off to the Punjab for a year were minuscule. Maybe Surrender-not had hit on something. So much of police work consisted of painstakingly poring over documents and most of the time you got precious little for your efforts. More often than not, all you got were more questions. But questions weren't bad. Questions were the loose threads that, if you pulled on them hard enough and followed them for long enough, might just unravel the whole puzzle.

But a reference to Rawalpindi did nothing to progress my theory of a romantic assignation gone wrong. Still, the fact that George Fernandes hadn't mentioned his wife's year-long absence was curious. Just as importantly, it didn't help the theory that her murder was carried out by Congress-supporting vigilantes – the only explanation that seemed to matter to Taggart and the politicians. To them, Ruth Fernandes was more important in death than she'd ever been in life, and the truth, if it didn't fit their preferred narrative, counted for as much as a gob of spit in a downpour.

The Hindus believed that a person's destiny was linked to the positions of heavenly bodies at the instant of birth – that their fates were written in the stars. Ruth Fernandes may have been a Christian, but that hadn't prevented her fate from being sealed the minute she was born. From that moment, three things would always mitigate against her: she was poor; she was a native; and she was a woman. In India, that meant her life counted for little, and, unless it could be made to fit a wider narrative, her death would matter even less.

But her case had landed on my desk, and while it probably didn't matter to her, I'd never been one to give up on lost causes, maybe because I was one myself. I'd keep going as long as there were questions to ask and loose threads to pull; not as a riposte to Surrender-not's father and his belief that we didn't care about the ordinary victims, but because at the end of the day, there was precious little else in my life that seemed noble.

'Any news yet from Sergeant Lamont on the strength of George Fernandes's alibi?' I asked.

'Nothing concrete,' said Surrender-not. 'He left a message saying he'd interviewed the neighbours. They confirm he went around knocking on doors and asking after his wife at around half past eight yesterday morning. That fits in with his story, but it doesn't mean he couldn't have gone out earlier and killed her. Lamont's continuing his inquiries.'

'And where are we with the post-mortem?'

'The body has been transferred to the Medical College mortuary. Dr Lamb has it scheduled for tomorrow.'

'See if you can't persuade him to move it up to this afternoon. Tell him that Taggart wants it made top priority.'

Surrender-not looked at me dubiously. 'What are we hoping to find?'

'I don't know,' I said. 'Maybe Lamb will tell us that her wounds were caused by some oriental ceremonial knife, or something else that connects her to the dead man in the opium den.' Though what that might be was frankly beyond me. The truth was I didn't know what I expected to find, but getting the post-mortem carried out felt like momentum, and in the absence of any clear direction, any momentum felt like progress.

'I suppose we'll know when we see it,' I said.

'There's no chance you're mistaken about the link with the body you found in the opium den?'

I fixed him with a stare. 'There's only one way to find out.'

'We've discussed this, Sam. Going back there would end your career.'

That much was probably true, but it didn't mean we shouldn't do it. Before I could respond, our *peon*, Ram Lal, a stick of a man in a blue shirt and a dhoti as grey as his hair, burst in, clutching a note and panting like a terrier. Surrender-not chided him for entering without first knocking, but there was little point. The old man was in his sixties and the days of learning new tricks were firmly behind him. The odd thing was that there were times when he'd knock fastidiously and then, ignoring calls to enter, wait until someone actually opened the door to let him in. There seemed no rhyme or reason to his behaviour. Ram Lal made his apologies and was about to exit so that he could this time knock and re-enter, when I put a stop to the farce.

'Just give me the chitty,' I said, pointing to the note, crumpled in hand.

'*Hā*, sahib,' he said, placing it on the desk and flattening it out, before nodding several times and backing his way out of the room.

I picked up the chit. It had my name on one side, and on the other was a handwritten note from Lord Taggart. I scanned it quickly and turned to Surrender-not.

'There's been another murder.'

TWENTY

We didn't have far to travel this time. Barely a five-minute drive to an elegant mock-Georgian town house off Park Street. A flight of steps ran from street level up to an open front door, beside which stood the obligatory copper, minding the stable door after the horse had bolted – or, as in this case, been murdered in its bed. This particular horse had been an Englishman called Dunlop, who, according to the note from Taggart, was a scientist of some repute. That was all very good, but I'd never heard of him. Still, I guessed his fame would soon spread. It was rare for an Englishman to be murdered in Calcutta, more so in this fashion, and I'd no doubt the gory details of his death would be plastered all over the front page of the *Englishman* by tomorrow morning.

His bedroom was on the second floor, up a couple of flights of narrow, dimly lit stairs, and guarded by another bobby from the local thana. With a nod, he stood aside and opened the door with an almost military demeanour.

The room itself was spartan. A wardrobe, a writing desk, a watercolour of the Relief of Lucknow on the wall, and a dead man of about fifty, lying atop bloodied sheets on the bed. Dunlop had a grey, angular face and a long, thin nose. As for his eyes, it was impossible to tell as someone had seen fit to pluck them out and carve him up like a Sunday roast. On his chest, the blue pyjamas he wore were despoiled by two stab wounds.

'What do you think?' I asked Surrender-not.

'The same injuries as those inflicted on Ruth Fernandes.'

'But look at the hands. No damaged fingers.'

There came a cough from the hallway and I turned to find a native officer sporting a toothbrush moustache and betel-nut-stained teeth, who introduced himself as Constable Mondol.

'Are you in charge?' I asked.

'Yes, sir. From the Park Street thana.'

'Well, let's have it.'

'We were called to the property by the maidservant, just after eight o'clock this morning,' he said. 'The sahib was found here in this room, as you see him.'

He spoke quietly, as though he felt honoured just being in the home of an Englishman, and that the murder was a minor inconvenience, like a passing rain shower at a garden party.

'Who found him?'

'The memsahib of the house,' he replied, 'Mrs Anthea Dunlop. She came to check on him when he failed to appear for breakfast.'

That spoke of a certain type of relationship. The fact that she came to look for him herself rather than sending the maid suggested that relations between them remained cordial.

'Where is she now?'

'Downstairs, sir. In the parlour. You wish to interview her?'

'We'll get to her in due course,' I said. 'Any idea how the killer gained entry?'

'The roof, probably,' said Mondol. He gestured upwards with one finger, lest I be in some confusion as to where the roof might be. 'The door has been forced. It is likely he left by the same route.'

Too often people in Calcutta spent small fortunes on domestic security, investing in iron bars, thick padlocks and thicker durwans. Yet they forgot about the doors to their roofs, which were often little more than weather-beaten, worm-eaten planks of wood. Because we spent most of our lives on one horizontal plane, too many people neglected to consider the vertical. Not that I was complaining. It was precisely because Callaghan's men had forgotten the roof that I'd been able to make my escape from the opium den three nights back.

I took in the scene once more. Something felt off, like a wrong note in the middle of a piece of music, but what it was evaded me. 'Has anyone tampered with the scene?' I asked.

Mondol shook his head. 'Not since we arrived, and the maid says nothing has been touched since the body was found.'

'Let's go and take a look at the roof,' I said, motioning towards the door.

We followed Mondol out of the room and up the stairs to the roof.

The door had been locked with only a barrel bolt, which actually looked quite sturdy and which was still in place. Unfortunately, the lock keep into which the barrel slotted had been forced from the door jamb. Judging by the state of the wooden door frame, I doubted that forcing the lock would have taken too much effort.

Stepping out onto the roof, I walked over to the ledge at the side of the house. The building was part of a terrace, sandwiched between identical town houses and about one-third of the way along the row of buildings. Only a raised ledge separated each house from its neighbour. Surrender-not appeared behind me and came over.

'You think he came across the other roofs?' he asked.

'Let's find out,' I said, stepping over the ledge and onto the roof of the adjoining building. Surrender-not followed and we crossed two more roofs till we reached the end of the terrace. The ledge there overlooked a sheer drop of three storeys to the street below.

Retracing our steps, we walked to the ledge at the other end of the row. There too we faced an identical drop to the road.

'No obvious route up here,' I said. 'Which means he either obtained access through one of the other houses, or scaled a drainpipe.'

We walked back to the roof of Dunlop's house and over to the gutter at the rear. A lead pipe ran from a hole in the roof down to the ground, converging en route with other pipes from the floors below.

'It's possible,' said Surrender-not as he stared over the edge.

At one time I might have been sceptical. Other than where pipes branched off, there seemed little in the way of hand-holds or other purchase, but in India I'd seen men scale ninety-foot coconut palms with nothing more than their bare limbs and a whispered prayer to the gods. To these people, a drainpipe was about as challenging as a ladder.

'Check the ground at the base of the drainpipe for footprints,' I said. 'And get Mondol to knock on the neighbours' doors, just on the off chance he broke into someone else's place first.'

'Yes, sir.' Surrender-not nodded.

'In the meantime,' I said, 'I'm going to have a word with Mrs Dunlop.'

TWENTY-ONE

Anthea Dunlop was seated on a floral sofa in a parlour that looked like it had been transported from a tea room in the Lake District, complete with a shelf full of mounted china plates and an embroidered Bible verse, framed and mounted on the wall. The woman was staring into space, making no effort to move the few strands of grey hair that had come loose from the severely tied bun and which hung limply at the side of her face.

I negotiated my way around a doily-covered side table and took a seat opposite her. On a sideboard next to her sat a number of framed photographs, including one of a couple in wedding dress.

'Mrs Dunlop?'

She looked up. In her hands she clutched a rosary.

'I'm Captain Wyndham of the Imperial Police Force. I'm sorry for your loss. However, I'm afraid I need to ask you some questions.'

'I've already spoken to the Indian officer,' she replied.

'I'm sure you have,' I said gently, 'but I've been charged with leading the investigation into your husband's death and, if I may, it would be best if I could hear the details from you first-hand.'

She paused, then nodded. 'Of course, Captain.'

'I understand you were the one who found him,' I said. 'I'd be grateful if you could tell me what happened in your own words.'

She began turning the rosary over between her fingers.

'I awoke at around half past six,' she said quietly, 'I dressed and made my way down to breakfast at, well, it must have been around a quarter past seven. The maid has instructions to have everything prepared by seven o'clock. Alastair, my husband, was usually in the dining room before me – he's normally an early riser – but in the run-up to Christmas, he'd secured a week's leave from work, so when I didn't see him, I didn't immediately assume there was anything wrong.'

'Go on,' I said.

'I ate breakfast, and when I'd finished and he still hadn't appeared, I began to worry that he might have taken ill in the night. Calcutta's such an awful place ... so many infections going about, especially at this time of year.'

It was a curious statement to make, but she was right in part – Calcutta really was a God-awful place, but winter wasn't its worst season. You were far more likely to contract something terminal in the monsoon than you were in December. But it was a moot point. Alastair Dunlop hadn't been killed by cholera or dysentery but most likely by a bloody great knife through the chest.

'I went upstairs and knocked on his door,' she said. 'He didn't reply, so I knocked louder and called out to him. It was only when I entered the room and found ...'

She reached for a handkerchief and dabbed at her eyes.

'He was just lying there ... his face ... disfigured ...'

I suddenly regretted having sent Surrender-not out to examine the foot of the drainpipe. He may still have had a problem talking to women his own age, but to the surprise of both of us, we'd discovered that he had a gift for talking to older women, especially the English ones. God only knows what they saw in him, but part of me suspected it was novelty value. A little Indian chap who spoke with a public-school accent – there weren't many of those in the police force. In his absence though, it seemed best just to plough on.

'When was the last time you saw your husband alive, Mrs Dunlop?' I asked, as considerately as it was possible to do of a freshly widowed woman.

'Last night,' she said. 'It must have been around half past nine. We'd returned from dinner at the house of one of my husband's colleagues. That was down in Alipore.'

'What did your husband do?' I asked.

'He was a director at the School of Tropical Medicine.'

'A doctor?'

'He was a scientist,' she replied tersely. 'He'd never taken the Hippocratic oath.'

There was a knock on the door and Surrender-not entered. He smiled at Mrs Dunlop, gave me a nod.

'Come in and take a seat, Sergeant,' I said, gesturing him to the sofa beside her. 'Did you hear anything untoward during the night?' I continued. 'Any unusual noises?'

'Not that I can recall,' she replied hesitantly, 'but I'd taken a sleeping draught – I have done for several years now.' She glanced at the photos on the sideboard and started sobbing.

I looked over meaningfully at Surrender-not.

'May I fetch you a glass of water, Mrs Dunlop?' he asked softly.

She looked up, the streaks of tears running down her dry cheeks. 'Most kind of you to ask, but please don't worry. I'm fine.'

I waited till she'd composed herself.

'Was there anyone else beside you in the house last night?'

'Our maid, Neri, of course, and the cook, Bhakti, but they had both retired to bed by the time Alastair and I had come home. I doubt they'd have heard anything.'

'Have you any idea why someone might wish to harm your husband?' I asked.

'I'm sorry?' Her forehead creased in confusion like a concertina, or was it alarm?

'I'm trying to understand why someone would choose to break into your house in the middle of the night and commit murder.' I pointed to the surroundings. 'Unless you tell me otherwise, this doesn't look like a burglary to me.'

'I don't know if anything has been stolen,' she snapped. 'My husband has been murdered. You'll forgive me for not having carried out an inventory of the contents of the house.'

I decided to temper my questions.

'How long had you been married, Mrs Dunlop?'

'Almost twenty-five years,' she said. 'We met at Oxford. Alastair was doing post-doctoral research into the transmission of airborne diseases and I was studying divinity. Of course, women weren't allowed to graduate in those days, but we were permitted to attend the lectures and sit for the examinations. We were introduced at the home of one of his professors. He took rather a shine to me.'

I scanned the photographs on the sideboard. Other than the one of the happy couple on their wedding day, there didn't appear to be another of Alastair Dunlop.

'Do you have a recent photograph of your husband?' I asked. 'It may help with our inquiries.'

'There may be one in his study,' she said. 'I can take a look for you.'

'That would be very good of you,' I said.

'Is there anything else?'

'We have some questions for your domestic staff, but I may wish to talk to you further.'

A trace of something passed across her face and was gone in an instant.

I watched as she rose, stowed her rosary and walked slowly towards the door, and all the while I wondered what that look had meant.

TWENTY-TWO

The maid knew nothing. That was clear from the start. In our line of work you develop a feel for when someone's lying to you, or at least has the wherewithal to lie to you. In this case, Neri, a peasant girl from some speck of a mud-hut village in the jungle to the south of Calcutta, just didn't fit the bill, and when she pleaded to Surrender-not that the first she'd known of anything amiss was when her mistress came screaming down the stairs this morning, I was inclined to believe her.

She corroborated Mrs Dunlop's account – said she'd offered to go up and call Dunlop for breakfast, but that her memsahib told her not to worry, that she'd go up herself.

The cook, a jolly woman with grey hair and several rolls of fat around her midriff, between her short Indian blouse and the sari tucked in at her waist, had also been helpful – in her own way at least, venturing great detail on her nightly routine and morning in the kitchen, all of which added the sum total of nothing to our inquiry.

That meant our only real source of information would be Mrs Dunlop. Her story of having taken a sleeping draught that had knocked her out seemed a tad too convenient. At the very least, there were other questions I wanted to ask her about her husband. There was no doubt in my mind that the three murders were linked.

Two victims in twenty-four hours with identical wounds might conceivably be called a coincidence, but three in the space of as many days? That was too much.

Then there were the wounds themselves. The missing eyes; the stab marks to the chest – they had to be significant. Were they ritualistic? Bengal had once been home to the *thuggees*, supposedly a cult of Kali-worshipping robbers and murderers. Could these murders be the act of a religious fanatic?

The boys of the fingerprint department had arrived and were making themselves busy in the parlour and the bedroom, so after giving the rest of the house the once-over, along with Surrendernot, I decided to hold court in Dunlop's study.

People leave their imprint on certain places. The parlour, with its chintz and embroidery, had clearly been Mrs Dunlop's territory, but the study was the domain of the dead man.

It was a light, well-sized room, dominated by a solid-looking desk and a bookcase with fewer books that I might have expected of a scientist. Arranged on the walls, in the way a more athletic sort might display sporting trophies, were a plethora of certificates, diplomas and group photographs that Dunlop probably considered necessary to prove his self-worth.

On the desktop sat a few papers weighed down by a hefty green-marble desk lighter, the sight of which made me want to try it out. Sitting down in the leather chair behind the desk, I fished out a Capstan from my pack and pressed down on the heavy brass button atop the lighter, releasing the flame. Taking a puff, I pulled the sheaf of papers from under the makeshift paperweight and scanned them. The first was an invoice from a tailor in the Hogg Market dated 15 December and requesting a payment on account. The second, according to the letterhead, was typed correspondence from some department of the Royal Engineer Corps based in Porton, Wiltshire.

There was a knock at the door and Mrs Dunlop walked in, with Mondol two steps behind her. Her face was ashen, as though the life had been washed out of her, and suggested that the reality of her husband's murder was beginning to sink in. I laid the papers down on the desk, placed my cigarette on the edge of a cut-glass ashtray and stood up.

Mondol handed Surrender-not a blue pill bottle which, from where I stood, looked half empty. Surrender-not gave him a nod and muttered something before the constable turned and left.

'Mrs Dunlop,' I said, gesturing to the chair. 'Take a seat, please. I have a few more questions.'

Anthea Dunlop sat down and placed her hands in her lap. I scanned her face. Her eyes were puffed, but she'd reapplied whatever creams and powders she used to conceal her wrinkles and mask the channels that the tears had forged down her face.

'How long have you been in Calcutta?' I asked.

She thought for a moment. 'It must be four years now,' she said. 'Alastair came out during the war and I joined him six months later.'

'And what brought you to India in the first place?'

She took a handkerchief from her sleeve and dabbed at the corners of her eyes.

'The war,' she said quietly. 'Alastair was called up in 1915 – not as an enlisted man of course, he was far too old for that – but as a biologist, he had certain skills and expertise that the military required. He was posted to Calcutta towards the middle of 1917. He said they were researching a more effective response to malaria.'

'So you came out in early '18?'

'That's correct.'

'Why the delay?'

'I wasn't given any choice,' she said in a tone that suggested she hadn't really cared either way. 'It was wartime. The army could hardly cater for the wives of officers and men accompanying their husbands all over the place. Besides, I had family in England.'

'Your children?'

'My daughter,' she said. 'We'd hoped to go home after the war, but Alastair was offered a position at the School of Tropical Medicine here to continue his research. The irony is we were finally preparing to go home, back to England next month.'

'He'd completed his research here?'

'It wasn't that,' she said. 'The government requested his return.'

'The government?'

'The army at any rate. Alastair said they'd received funding for certain research. They wanted to employ him again.'

'Funding for research into malaria?' I asked.

'That's what he told me.'

There was something odd about that. Why would the military fund research into malaria? And why do it in England rather than here? After all, if there was one thing Calcutta wasn't short of, it was malarial mosquitoes.

'You're sure?' I asked.

A shadow passed over her face.

'I can only tell you what my husband told me.'

She didn't sound wholly convincing. Still, it was eminently plausible that Dunlop had told her he was going back to England to continue research into malaria when in fact the military had other plans for him.

Whatever the case, I wasn't about to get clarity on the matter from Anthea Dunlop. Instead, I changed tack.

'Why did you go to fetch your husband this morning instead of sending the maid?' I asked.

The question caught her unawares.

'I don't know.' She shrugged. 'I think Neri was busy at the time.'

I looked over to Surrender-not who stood close to the door. He shook his head.

'She says she offered to fetch your husband, but you told her not to and went yourself.'

'It's possible,' said Mrs Dunlop. 'I don't recall, exactly.'

She reached into her pocket and drew out her rosary. She gripped the beads tightly, her fingers turning white with the effort.

'Is there something you're not telling us, Mrs Dunlop?' I asked.

The question was met with silence.

Before I could ask anything more, there came the noise of a commotion downstairs. Loud voices were making their presence felt.

I turned to Surrender-not. 'Find out what's going on.'

He headed for the door and opened it to the sound of boots coming up the stairs and a moment later, Allenby, Dawson's blond henchman from the previous night, and two rather large Sikh sepoys filled the doorway.

Grabbing him by the arm, one of them pushed Surrender-not face first up against a wall.

'Let go of him,' I shouted, rising from my seat.

Allenby looked at me as though I was something unpleasant that he'd had the misfortune to step in. Surrender-not's arm was now twisted at an unnatural angle behind his back. As for his face, it was pushed into one of the framed photos that lined the wall.

'I didn't expect to see you again quite so soon, Wyndham,' he said.

'Unhand my officer or I'll release him myself.'

Allenby turned to his man. 'Let him go.'

The Sikh released his grip and Surrender-not let out a breath, before turning and nursing his injured arm.

'What do you want, Allenby?' I asked.

'This investigation has been placed under the aegis of Section H,' he replied. 'It's no longer a police matter. You and your officers are to leave immediately.'

'On whose authority?'

'Do you really need to ask?' he sneered. 'Look, Wyndham, I've got my orders.'

'As do I,' I said. 'I was about to arrest this woman.' It was a lie, but made in the furtherance of a good cause.

Allenby glanced at Mrs Dunlop. 'You're arresting no one, Wyndham.'

I took a moment to assess the situation. Three of them to two of us. God knew where Mondol was, but I doubted he'd be much good in a fight. Not that we were going to fight Allenby and his goons. That was unthinkable. They were British military officers after all, not to mention that the two Sikhs were built like bulls. I caught sight of Surrender-not and for a moment it seemed he was preparing to go another round with the sepoy that had manhandled him. He could be impetuous, but I didn't think he was suicidal.

Allenby turned to his men. 'See these gentlemen out.'

Before they could advance, Surrender-not gave a yell and rushed at the one who'd almost dislocated his arm. It was quite a sight – like a one-man charge of the Light Brigade – and with similar results. He barrelled into the man, I guess hoping to knock him off his feet, but managed merely to bounce off him. The Sikh stared at him, as though unable to quite believe what the little Bengali had just done, and to be fair, I was having trouble believing it myself. For his part, Surrender-not looked like he'd just run head first into a wall. The Sikh regained his wits first and lashed out with a fist the size of a ham hock, sending Surrender-not flying. He landed hard against the wall, before crashing to the floor alongside several of the framed photographs and certificates. The Sikh followed up with a boot to the ribs. Surrender-not doubled over in pain. I stepped between them before the Sikh could do any more damage.

Allenby too barked an order, calling off his attack dog.

'Get out of here, Wyndham,' he said, 'before I have you both arrested.'

Surrender-not was having trouble finding his feet. He scrabbled around slowly among the shards of glass from the shattered frames, as though gathering bits of himself that might have broken and fallen off. I turned and helped him to his feet, and, as he kept one hand held to his ribs, guided him gently towards the door and down the stairs. Out on the street and still holding his side, he walked gingerly towards the car. The driver ran round and opened the door. Surrender-not winced as he climbed in.

'Well, that was interesting,' I said as I got in beside him. 'You do know he could have killed you.'

He shook his head. 'I'm sure he was beginning to tire, sir.'

'Marks for effort though. How are the ribs?'

Surrender-not looked down at his chest, then broke out into a broad smile.

'Fine,' he said, unbuttoning his jacket.

As he did so, something glinted in the light. From beneath it, he slowly drew out a crumpled photograph a little smaller than a sheet of paper.

I looked at him. 'What's that?'

'One of the photographs from Dunlop's wall. I noticed something when that *goonda* had me pinned against it. We really ought to thank him ...'

'What?' I said. 'What did you notice?'

He passed me the print. 'See for yourself.'

I took it and examined it closely. It was another of those group shots, of military men lined up outside a building which looked vaguely familiar. Some standing, the important ones sitting on chairs and a group of natives waiting in the wings. I recognised the building. It was the military hospital at Barrackpore. I stared at the faces, and then I suddenly saw what Surrender-not had. In the centre of the photograph, on a couple of wicker chairs, sat Dunlop and the director of the hospital, Colonel McGuire. Behind them stood a group, including two British officers with white doctor's coats draped over their uniforms. But what really struck me was one of the natives standing on the extreme right of the photograph. A shiver ran down my spine as I saw the face of Ruth Fernandes staring out at me.

TWENTY-THREE

'Bloody hell . . .' I said.

'Now you see why I had to get that photo without Allenby and his men realising,' said Surrender-not. He dabbed at his burst lip with a handkerchief.

'I'm beginning to appreciate that,' I said. 'Still, I'd have felt bad if that Sikh had killed you.'

'Very gracious.' He nodded.

I turned the photograph over. On the reverse, in blue, faded ink, were written the words: *Barrackpore, January 1918.*

'There's our link between Nurse Fernandes and Alastair Dunlop,' said Surrender-not. 'They were both working at Barrackpore Military Hospital in 1918.'

I shook my head. 'That can't be right,' I said. 'If her personnel file's correct, Ruth Fernandes couldn't have been in this photo.'

As the car drove back towards Lal Bazar, I explained it to Surrender-not.

'Rawalpindi,' I said. 'Her file said she'd spent a year there from September 1917. So what's she doing turning up a thousand miles away in a photograph in Barrackpore?'

Surrender-not took a while to respond, possibly because his jaw was beginning to swell up like he'd ingested a mouthful of marbles.

'Maybe the date is wrong?' he mumbled.

'I doubt it,' I said, 'though we could always ask McGuire up at Barrackpore. He may even have a copy of this photograph.'

Surrender-not stared at me. 'I believe Section H just told us in no uncertain terms that we were no longer in charge of this investigation. I doubt they'd take kindly to us going back up there. It's a military cantonment after all.'

'Two of the victims knew each other and Barrackpore is the connection,' I said. 'And given we're not able to question Anthea Dunlop any further, we've no choice but to go back up there.'

'We could always tell Section H what we've discovered and let them deal with it?'

'I don't think they'd be interested. I just told Allenby that we were about to arrest Mrs Dunlop and he didn't even ask why. And anyway, *you* don't want to leave it to Section H any more than I do,' I said. 'That's why you went through that little performance with your turbaned friend back there. You could have pointed out the faces in the photos to Allenby and saved yourself a beating, but you didn't. Besides, I think Allenby's superiors already know of the link between Dunlop and Fernandes. Why else would they eject us quite so unceremoniously from the scene? Whatever's happening here is more serious than a disgruntled native killing a few foreigners, and my gut tells me that Section H already know what's going on. That's why they showed up so quickly – they're trying to keep a lid on it.'

'But how does your dead drug pusher in Tangra fit in?' asked Surrender-not. 'You're sure they're connected?'

'He was butchered in the same way. In fact,' I said as I ordered the driver to stop, 'why don't you see for yourself?'

Thirty minutes later, after stopping off at Premchand Boral Street for a flask of *kerdū* pulp, and amid more protests from Surrender-not as to the inadvisability of upsetting Section H further, we approached the outskirts of Tangra.

'It's lunacy,' he said. 'Trying to gain access to a building that is no doubt still under surveillance and that you've been specifically warned not to go near and from which you've already once been caught exiting. Sheer lunacy.'

'We're not debating the matter,' I said.

The light was fading as the driver pulled to a halt, and the smoke from newly lit fires hung in the greying dusk. Surrender-not and I got out. We'd make the last mile of the journey on foot and under cover of darkness.

We walked, hugging close to the walls of the buildings that abutted a narrow *gullee*. 'How are we supposed to gain access without being spotted?' complained Surrender-not. 'They're bound to have the doors and windows covered.'

'You should have more faith in me, Sergeant,' I said. 'I have a plan.'

'Really?' he said. 'Would you mind telling me what it is?'

'The roof,' I said. 'It's how I got out without being caught by Vice Division when they raided the place a few nights back. And it's how our killer got into Alastair Dunlop's house. I'm hoping our friends from Section H have either forgotten to consider it or are spread too thinly to cover it.'

'And if they *do* have it covered?'

I patted him on his shoulder. 'Then you won't need to worry too much. It'll be pitch black by the time we get there, and I'm a much bigger target than you. Your ability to pass for a stick insect means you'll be perfectly safe. They'll be so busy shooting at me that I doubt they'll even notice you.'

My words must have given him the comfort he needed because the rest of our journey was passed in relative silence. The streets were semi-deserted. It was Christmas Eve and I imagined the God-fearing Chinese of Tangra, converted by Jesuits and Baptists and Lord knows what other competing strains of the true faith, were at home donning their Sunday best and preparing for the midnight services which would herald the Messiah's birthday, leaving the streets to the dogs and the destitute.

'There,' I said, pointing to a mound of refuse piled high against the wall of a squat, brick-built shack. 'That's our staircase.'

The building had a low roof of terracotta tiles resting on bamboo beams and leaned precariously against the side of a taller, two-storey structure. Surrender-not eyed the shack dubiously.

'Are you sure it will take our weight? I doubt the residents would be impressed by the sight of two policemen falling through their roof.'

'It'll be fine,' I said as I began scaling the mound of rubbish. 'Besides, if we do happen to fall through the roof, we'll say we're angels and pass it off as a Christmas miracle.'

The stench from the refuse was almost enough to make me reconsider, but I kept climbing and soon was able to reach for the edge of the roof tiles and pull myself up. I turned and offered a helping hand to Surrender-not whose face suggested he might have stepped in something unsavoury. He clambered up and sat on the ledge beside me. From beneath us came the muffled sound of chatter. The language was indecipherable but the cadences suggested the usual rhythms of family talk rather than the alarm one would expect had they heard the noise of two policemen climbing onto their roof. Slowly we turned and scrabbled our way along the roof to the wall of the adjoining building. This time Surrender-not went first, leaping across the narrow gap and onto a ledge above a barred and shuttered window. I followed and then gave him a leg-up. The sergeant pulled himself over the lip of the roof wall and landed with a thud. For a moment he disappeared from sight, then suddenly his head appeared, bobbing over the parapet as though the fall had disconnected it from his body. He looked down, smiled and leaned over, extending a hand. I grabbed it and began scaling the wall. Suddenly he lurched forward and for a second it felt as though I might have achieved nothing more than to pull the little fellow back down, but he steadied himself against the roof wall and, straining, managed to help me get a hand-hold at the top.

I pulled myself over and we both collapsed onto the flat roof, breathing heavily from the effort.

'Right,' I said eventually, 'break time's over. Let's get moving.'

I stood and made for the far end of the roof, then negotiated the small gap between two adjacent buildings. In the distance I could make out the alcove where I'd hidden from Callaghan's men three nights earlier. Ahead of us was the funeral parlour. If the rooftops were under surveillance, now would be the moment of maximum danger. Crouching low, we crept quietly forward, eventually reaching the ledge that separated it from its neighbour. The door to the stairwell leading down into the building was situated in the centre of the roof. I pointed it out to Surrender-not. He nodded, then put a hand on my wrist.

'Wait here, sir,' he whispered. 'Let me check if the coast is clear.'

'I should be the one to go,' I said.

'But I'm the one who can do the impression of a stick insect.'

With that, he clambered over the ledge and crawled slowly forward towards the door.

At any moment I expected voices to ring out in challenge, or worse still gunshots. I braced myself, but save for the flapping of a pigeon disturbed by our approach, the silence remained blessedly unbroken.

He reached the door and pushed it gently. The wooden panels rattled against the frame. I climbed over the ledge and made my way to him.

'No use,' he said. 'It's locked.'

'We'll just have to find another way in.'

Scrambling to the roof edge, I looked down. To my left, one storey down, was a balcony. It looked deserted, the windows behind it in darkness. Halfway along was a door. I beckoned Surrender-not over.

'See that balcony?' I said. 'That's where you're going.'

He stared at me dubiously.

'I'm going to lower you down and you're going to try that door. I'm hoping that when Callaghan's men finished searching the floor, they didn't have the presence of mind to lock a door merely leading to a balcony. If it's open, make your way inside and up the stairs to the roof and let me in.'

'And what if it's locked?' he asked.

'Then I'll owe you an apology. Now get moving.'

I grabbed his arms and began to lower him slowly over the edge of the wall. His feet scrabbled for purchase against the smooth cement, until finally he was hanging over the balcony. I let go and he dropped to the floor. Somewhere close by a dog barked. Surrender-not froze and I held my breath. Eventually the commotion ceased and I let out a sigh of relief. On the balcony, the sergeant made for the door and turned the handle. I heard a click, then a muffled creaking, and suddenly Surrender-not stuck his head out from under the ledge, beamed a smile and waved.

'Get going,' I urged in a whisper.

He disappeared again, and I made my way back to the door in the middle of the roof and waited. Soon I heard his footsteps on the stone stairs, and then a scraping as he removed from its brackets the wooden bar that held the door closed. I pushed gently and the door swung open.

'The place seems deserted,' said Surrender-not as we descended the stairs to the building's upper storey. I took a moment to get my bearings.

'This way,' I said, setting off along a corridor and then down two flights of stairs to the basement. The air down here was cold but laced with the unmistakable stench of putrefaction. I led Surrender-not to the mortuary room and opened the door. The smell was stronger here. Taking the box of matches from my pocket, I extracted one and struck it against the side. It flickered to life and I walked over to the wall of drawers and pulled out the one that had contained the body of the dead Chinaman. The same scarred and eyeless face stared out at me once more. The match burned down and suddenly the room was plunged back into darkness.

I reached for another and lit it.

'Here,' I said, passing Surrender-not the match. 'Take a look.'

As he examined the corpse, I took out a couple of cigarettes and, with another match, lit them both and passed one to Surrender-not.

'Believe me now?'

The sergeant nodded slowly. 'He's definitely missing his eyes.'

'Look down and you'll see the two stab marks to the chest.' I took a drag of my cigarette. The smoke helped to mask the smell.

'And look,' said Surrender-not, pointing to the victim's left hand. 'He's missing a finger.'

I stared at the hand. The sergeant was right. It was a detail I'd missed. The wound was fresh, and I guessed the digit had been cut off at about the same time the other injuries had been inflicted. It reminded me of Ruth Fernandes's broken finger.

'What's the significance of that?' he wondered.

'Torture, possibly,' I said. 'Maybe the killer wanted information? Maybe he was trying to get them to talk. Whatever the case, well spotted. I shouldn't have missed a detail like that.'

'There's one more thing,' said Surrender-not behind me. 'This man's not Chinese.'

'What?'

'This corpse,' said Surrender-not. 'I think it's Indian.'

The match burned down and he dropped it to the floor. I went to light another but he stopped me and instead reached into his own pocket and pulled out his lighter.

He lit the flame and beckoned me over.

'Here, look,' he said. 'I can see why you'd think the victim was Chinese. The shape of the eye sockets and the cheekbones, but look at the nose and the pallor. The man's Assamese or Nepalese, or possibly Burmese.'

I looked closely at the disfigured corpse. Maybe Surrender-not was correct. The differences still weren't obvious to me: I wasn't exactly firing on all cylinders but I knew better than to question the sergeant on a matter like this. In any case, when I'd first seen the body, I'd been opium-addled. In an opium den, a Chinaman is what I expected to see, and maybe I just assumed that's what he was. When I'd then found him in this room, it had been dark and I hadn't really considered it. All I'd been looking for was a corpse without eyes.

Beside me, Surrender-not was peering closely at the head. He had that curious look on his face. The one he got when his brain was working too fast.

Suddenly he looked up and smiled.

'What is it?' I asked.

'This scar on his face! I've seen it before!'

'Where?'

'In that photograph we stole from Dunlop's study.'

———

It looked like he was right. At least there was a good chance he was. I'd taken out the photograph and laid it flat on my palm. Surrender-not held the flame from his lighter close by. To the left of the shot was a figure, sitting cross-legged on the ground. He looked like a native orderly, in shorts and a khaki shirt. The detail was grainy but there it was, a long scar running down the left side, all the way from the hairline to the chin. What's more if you discounted the eyes, the rest of the face bore a marked resemblance to what was left of the one in the drawer beside us.

I felt nauseous as the ground seemed to shift under my feet.

'He's not a drug lord but a hospital worker.'

'That's our link,' said Surrender-not. 'The three victims knew each other. They're all in this photograph.'

I looked at the photo, examining the faces of Dunlop, Ruth Fernandes and the corpse in the drawer beside me. Surrender-not's theory seemed to make sense. But there were others in the photograph too. What if the killer was going after all of them?

I quickly rescanned the other faces. There, of course, was Colonel McGuire seated next to Alastair Dunlop, Ruth Fernandes and Anthea Dunlop, who'd been spared. But as I looked closely at it, a shiver ran up my spine. There was someone else familiar too, younger and part hidden by shadow in the back row. Mathilde Rouvel.

TWENTY-FOUR

'We need to get to Barrackpore!' I said, closing the drawer and making for the stairs.

I thought about retracing our path across the rooftops, but the clock was ticking, and instead I opted for the direct route: out the front door, and a hell-for-leather sprint to the car. Avoiding the ire of Section H seemed less of a priority now. Three people had been murdered in as many nights, which suggested our killer wasn't keen on wasting time. It was already dark, and for all I knew, his next target might even now be in his sights. As for who that might be, there were no guarantees of course, but given that all three victims so far had been pictured in that photograph in Barrackpore in 1917, the odds suggested the next one was probably staring out from it too. The question was, why hadn't he killed Anthea Dunlop? Had she provided him with the information her husband hadn't? Or was there some other reason?

Of the others still alive, I knew two. We had to decide which to get to first, but that was a matter that could wait till we were en route to Barrackpore.

The car was waiting where we'd left it, and the driver seemed in no mood to linger, stepping out and cranking the engine into life as soon as he saw us turn the corner.

The journey to Barrackpore took an hour – which still proved insufficient time for Surrender-not and I to try and work out what the hell was going on. My initial theories: that both the killing in the opium den was somehow related to drug smuggling, and the murder of Ruth Fernandes was a domestic affair, looked to have been blown out of the water. The first, I realised, had been based solely on the assumption that the dead man in the funeral parlour had been Fen Wang, the drug lord from Shanghai. In turn, that belief had rested on two factors: Callaghan's statement to me that the man they'd been hunting that night was the famed drug baron; and my ridiculous conclusion that because the man in the drawer had Eastern features, he must be Chinese. I cursed myself for having been so sloppy. My assumption as to the man's race was bad enough, but could be forgiven on the grounds that I was groggy from O when I first saw him. What upset me more, though, was the fact that even if he *had* been Chinese, I shouldn't have taken for granted that he was Fen Wang. There were thousands of Chinese in this city after all. But it's hard to resist the siren call of the quick and easy solution. I'd wanted him to be Fen Wang. It fitted my preconceptions of what was going on and I grabbed at it like a drowning man grasping at reeds.

But if the killings weren't linked to a feud over drugs, what were they related to? There were, of course, the victims' wounds – the gouged-out eyes and the same two stab marks to the chest. At first I'd assumed they were meant as a warning, but now I wasn't so sure. Taken together, they seemed almost ritualistic, maybe even religious. At least my conviction that the body in Tangra was somehow linked to the murder of Ruth Fernandes in Rishra had been justified. It was a shame that Alastair Dunlop had had to die to confirm my hypothesis, but that's just the way things go sometimes.

What's more, for the first time we were heading somewhere in anticipation of events rather than chasing after them. The answers, or at least some of them, had to lie in Barrackpore and I was deter-mined to find them.

―――――――

'We'll speak to Nurse Rouvel first,' I said.

Surrender-not seemed surprised by my choice. 'Surely Colonel McGuire would be the logical port of first call, sir?'

'It depends,' I said.

'On what?'

'On whether we want to solve this case or not. McGuire's a mili-tary man. He's not going to tell us anything that hasn't first been cleared through the appropriate channels. And even if, by some miracle, Section H's operatives didn't spot us high-tailing it from the funeral parlour, you can be sure they'll have caught up with us within five minutes of us sitting down with the good colonel. Besides,' I said, 'he'll be off duty by now and tracking him down could take a while. Nurse Rouvel, on the other hand, is more likely to tell us what we need to know. She probably resides in the nurses' quarters and almost certainly has McGuire's address. And anyway,' I added, 'if they're both at imminent risk of being murdered, I think I'd rather save her first.'

―――――――

The nurses' quarters were located in an austere, functional-looking annexe, at some distance removed from the main hospital building. The driver stopped the car and Surrender-not and I jumped out and made for the steps leading up to an open entrance. The night was cold and the chirping of crickets merged with the ticking of the engine as it cooled.

To one side of the lobby, behind a rickety wooden desk, a porter in a faded blue shirt sat reading a native newspaper. I pulled out my warrant card and stuck it between his nose and the newspaper.

He looked up lethargically.

'Yes?'

'Nurse Rouvel's room,' I said. 'Quickly!'

'Second floor,' he said, gesturing with his nose towards a flight of stairs. 'Room 6 ... or 7.'

Surrender-not and I raced for the stairs, taking them two at a time ... for the first flight at least. After that, I just climbed as fast as I still could. Rooms 6 and 7 stood at the far end, facing each other across a narrow, mustard-coloured corridor. We took a door each and knocked, then when nothing happened, we knocked again.

The first to open was number 7. A stout woman in a crumpled cotton dressing gown stared out.

'We're looking for Nurse Rouvel,' I said.

Behind me the door to number 6 opened. 'What are you doing here at this time of night, Captain?' asked a familiar voice. I swivelled round. Mathilde Rouvel stood staring at me as if I was the ghost of Napoleon.

'Miss Rouvel,' I said, 'I need to speak to you.'

The woman from room 7 was still standing in the open doorway and showing no sign of returning to her business.

'Maybe we should discuss this in your room?'

'This is most unusual, Captain,' she remonstrated. She looked tired, the smudge of dark circles around her eyes.

'You're right. Most unusual. That's why we need to speak to you right now. So if we may ... ?' I gestured to the room behind her.

She looked nervous. 'It is against regulations. We are not supposed to have men in our rooms.'

'We're not men,' said Surrender-not, 'we're the police!'

She considered it for a moment.

'Very well, come in.'

I shook my head at Surrender-not's comment, then followed her in.

The room was tiny and furnished with a small table and chair, a wardrobe and a single bed with its mosquito net already hoisted. I checked my watch. It was still not yet 8 p.m.

'I hope we didn't wake you?'

She shook her head. 'Though I was about to retire. My shift starts at five o'clock.'

It suddenly struck me that it didn't take both Surrender-not and me to interview Miss Rouvel.

'Do you have Colonel McGuire's address?' I said.

'You could have asked me that in the corridor.'

'I've a lot more to ask besides that,' I said, 'and time is short, so if you'd be kind enough to answer, we can get on.'

She recited an address and directions which Surrender-not took down in his little notebook.

'Get going, Sergeant,' I said. 'I'll join you as soon as I'm done here.'

Surrender-not nodded and headed for the door.

'There,' she said, once the door had closed. 'Now please tell me what you want.'

Anxiety was etched on her face, though whether it was the prospect of having a strange man in her room or something else that was exercising her was unclear.

I pulled out the photograph that Surrender-not had pilfered from Dunlop's house and pointed to Alastair Dunlop.

'Do you know who this is?'

She stared at me. 'Where did you get this?'

'That's not your concern,' I said. 'Now please identify that man.'

'That is Monsieur Dunlop. He was here during the war, I think.'

'And what did he do here?'

She shrugged, in the manner the French do. She might have been born in India, but in some ways she was as Gallic as a pack of Gauloises. 'You should ask *le directeur*, Colonel McGuire.'

'I'm asking you.'

'And I'm telling you I don't know.' Her tone was firm, but the look in her eyes suggested evasion and I didn't have time for games.

'He's dead,' I said. 'Murdered. In a fashion remarkably similar to your friend Ruth Fernandes' – I tapped the dead nurse's image on the photograph – 'and to this man here.' I tapped the cross-legged figure of the dead man in Tangra. 'All three killed in the same way in the last seventy-two hours. That's one a night. Which means we're due another one ...' I checked my watch for effect ' ... any time now.'

I shoved the photograph towards her.

'You're in there too. So there's a one in five chance that you're going to be next. Not bad odds, but not great either if your life's on the line. Now I'd suggest you afford me some cooperation.'

I watched as my words registered, as she realised the implications; watched as her bravado melted away, till all that was left was a scared young girl.

She stumbled over to the bed and sat down, pulling the mosquito net out of shape. She looked shell-shocked. I fetched the chair from beside the desk and sat down opposite her.

'Miss Rouvel,' I said, 'what was Dunlop doing at the hospital here?'

'Research,' she said, looking at the floor. 'I can't tell you any more than that. They made me sign papers to say I would never talk about it.'

'You need to tell me,' I said. 'Lives may depend upon it.'

She wiped a tear from the corner of one eye. 'I can't. You will have to talk to Colonel McGuire.'

I decided to try a different approach.

I picked up the photograph. 'Who are these people?'

'You want their names?' she asked.

'Yes, but this is a group photograph,' I said. 'What's the group?'

Rouvel moved a strand of hair from her face. 'They were the people assigned to help Dunlop with his work ... apart from *le directeur*, Colonel McGuire, of course. As head of the hospital, he is in all group photographs.'

'And who is this man?' I pointed to the image of the man killed in Tangra.

She looked closely. She seemed to recognise him, but struggled to come up with a name.

'Tamang,' she said finally. 'Prio Tamang. I think he now works for the hospital quartermaster's office, though I have not seen him recently.'

'Why would a quartermaster's assistant be in this photograph?'

She shook her head. 'At that time he was just a hospital orderly. We had a lot of Gurkhas billeted here then. Tamang was Nepalese. I think he was assigned to us because he spoke the language.'

Something jarred.

'Why would Dunlop need a Nepalese speaker for his research?' I asked.

'I told you. I cannot talk about that.'

I turned the photograph over and showed her the words on the reverse. '"Barrackpore, January 1918." Is that correct?'

She nodded slowly. 'If that is what it says, I have no reason to doubt it.'

I flipped the photograph back over and pointed to Ruth Fernandes. 'The problem is, according to Nurse Fernandes's personnel file, she wasn't in Barrackpore in January '18. She wasn't even in Bengal. So how could she be in this photo?'

Rouvel's brow furrowed. 'What do you mean, she wasn't in Bengal? Where else would she be?'

'Rawalpindi.'

The colour drained from Rouvel's face. She gave a bitter laugh. 'How can you hope to stop this killer when there's so much you don't know?'

'Then tell me!' I said, leaning forward and grabbing her arm.

She pulled herself free. 'I can't tell you anything more.' Rising from the bed, she made for the door and opened it wide. 'Now please leave.'

I got up from the chair and followed her.

'The only one who can answer your questions is Colonel McGuire,' she said. 'I suggest you ask him.'

TWENTY-FIVE

I left Mathilde Rouvel with the promise that I'd be back after I'd spoken to McGuire. I told her to pack a bag and make arrangements to spend the night at a friend's place somewhere in the cantonment and said I'd return to escort her over personally, not because I was feeling chivalrous but because I wanted to make sure I knew exactly where she was going.

I walked downstairs in a fog, trying to make sense of the contradictions. Rouvel had known Fernandes during the war. She was adamant that Fernandes had been in Barrackpore in 1917 and 1918, and yet the word 'Rawalpindi' had triggered something in her; a reaction I couldn't quite fathom.

I walked out of the building and into the night, passing a native sepoy, a white coat over his uniform, who stood leaning against the wall, smoking a bidi. The smell of the cheap smouldering cheroot leaf was like balm on my synapses and I couldn't resist stopping to light a cigarette before heading rapidly in the direction of the address for Colonel McGuire which Mathilde Rouvel had provided.

I hadn't gone two hundred yards when I saw Surrender-not coming out of the gloom towards me.

'He's not there,' said the sergeant.

'What do you mean, he's not there?' I asked. 'Where is he then?'

'I don't know, sir. His batman said the colonel had no plans for the evening, but that he received a telephone call about an hour ago. Fifteen minutes later, a car pulled up outside and he and his wife went off.'

'I take it he didn't say where they were going?'

'No, sir. Nor when they'd be back.'

'Did you ask him what the colonel's reaction was to the telephone call?'

'I did, sir. He said it was none of my business. Should we go back and press him on it?'

'McGuire's batman,' I asked. 'British or Indian?'

'Indian.'

I took a pull of my cigarette and thought for a moment. In lieu of anything more useful, part of me was sorely tempted to go and tear a strip off the man, even though he probably had little to tell us. The chance to take out some of my frustrations on someone was hard to resist. But we were on thin ice as it was. Section H had told us to leave well alone. Instead we'd marched straight into the lion's den – onto a military base, looking to question a colonel – and as I knew from the night before, they didn't take particularly kindly to my meddling. I'd little doubt that McGuire's unexpected telephone call and subsequent vanishing act had been orchestrated by them, if not directly, then at least at their behest.

'Leave it,' I said finally. 'I doubt we'll get anything out of the man.'

Surrender-not nodded. 'Did you glean much from Miss Rouvel?'

'A little,' I said. 'The name of the dead man in Tangra, for one. Prio Tamang – Nepalese apparently; an assistant to the hospital quartermaster. During the war, though, he was an orderly. According to Rouvel, he acted as liaison with the wounded Gurkhas who were patients here.'

'Anything else?'

'Just that Dunlop was running some research experiments here in 1917 and that Nurse Fernandes and Nurse Rouvel were on his staff.'

'So Fernandes wasn't in Rawalpindi?'

'Apparently not. Someone must have falsified the details of her personnel file.'

'Who?' he asked. 'And why go to the trouble of falsifying her service record? She was just a nurse. What is it they're trying to conceal?'

'Whatever it is, I think Rouvel knows, but she was too scared to tell me. Seeing as how Colonel McGuire seems to have disappeared for the evening, maybe we should go back and question her again. Come on,' I said, flicking the cigarette butt into the darkness. I turned and began striding back towards the nurses' quarters with Surrender-not half a pace behind.

The porter was still at his seat in the lobby. He looked up as we passed and said something to Surrender-not in Bengali. The sergeant froze in his tracks. Then turned and fired back a response. From the inflexion in his voice, I guessed it was a question. The porter hesitated, then replied, and without warning, Surrender-not took off towards the stairs.

'Come!' he said. 'We have to hurry.'

I ran after him. 'What is it? What's happened?'

'Miss Rouvel,' he panted, between breaths. 'The porter said someone else asked for her room number.'

'When?'

'Two minutes ago.'

'But who?' I said. 'No one passed us.'

Then I remembered. The sepoy in the white coat having a smoke outside. It was dark and I'd paid him scant regard, assuming he was some orderly who was billeted in the building. That had been stupid. The chances of a native sepoy being billeted in the same building as a European woman were zero.

We reached the first-floor landing when there came a scream from the floor above.

'Hell,' I said, casting a glance at Surrender-not as we ran up the second flight.

Doors were already opening in response to the commotion as we made it to Rouvel's floor. At the far end, I saw the head of the short nurse in room 7 sticking out into the hallway, angrily sniffing the air like a mongoose searching out danger. She stared at the doorway directly across from her and suddenly let out a scream of her own.

Time slowed to a crawl as we sprinted along the corridor. Behind me, Surrender-not was shouting at the nurses to get back in their rooms and lock their doors.

Suddenly, a man burst out of Rouvel's room. He was barely five feet tall but carried himself with a purpose and a poise that I realised I'd seen before. Something glinted in his hand – a thick, curved blade. As he turned in my direction, I got a decent look at him, and immediately I had no doubt. The smooth, bronzed, taut skin, the determination in the set of the jaw, the fire in the eyes. The man was a Gurkha.

He saw me and took off in the opposite direction, towards a set of doors at the far end of the corridor.

'Stop! Police!' I shouted, as though that had ever worked. Ahead of me, the man reached the doors and burst through. I made it to Nurse Rouvel's door and peered inside, bracing myself for what I might find. In front of me, Rouvel stood catatonic, rooted to the spot. In her arms she held a suitcase.

'Are you all right?'

She looked at me, and then through me, her eyes not seeming to register what had happened. I grabbed her.

'Mathilde.' Her eyes focused. A spark of recognition.

'I'm all right.'

In the meantime, Surrender-not had run on in pursuit of the attacker, and suddenly I realised I had another problem. If the man really was a trained Gurkha, then Surrender-not wouldn't stand a chance against him. Not at close quarters at least, even with a revolver. I'd heard stories of Gurkhas charging through walls of German machine-gun fire before setting to work on their enemies armed with nothing more than their kukri knives. It was said that their blades could cleave a man's head from his shoulders in one blow.

I turned and ran after him, throwing myself through the doors. The stairwell beyond was in darkness and I groped around, blindly feeling the wall for a light switch as my eyes took their time to adjust. From close by came the sound of footsteps falling rapidly on concrete steps. Then the explosion of a gunshot. I gave up looking for the switch and made for the stairs. From somewhere below came the clang of metal on metal, then a muffled cry.

I reached for my revolver and ran down the first flight, then the second, then stopped dead. In the illumination of the pale light filtering through a window, two bodies were locked together, struggling in the darkness. I raised my gun, then hesitated. There was no clean shot to take.

'Stop!'

The attacker had his arm around Surrender-not's throat, in his hand the kukri, the metal of its blade glinting in the half-light. In his other hand he held Surrender-not's revolver. Slowly he raised it, aiming it at my head.

'Drop the gun,' I said, as calmly as one can when one's heart feels as though it's about to burst through one's chest.

I struggled to bring my breathing under control. Surrender-not too looked like he was having trouble breathing. The man stared at me, then shook his head.

'I don't want to kill your friend.' His voice was thick. Nicotine-coated.

'Then let him go.'

'And then what? You shoot me?' His gun was still pointed squarely at my face.

'No,' I said. 'I won't shoot you if you let him go. On that you have my word.'

'Your word?' He laughed bitterly. 'You are police. Your word means nothing.'

'I'm ex-army,' I said, hoping he at least believed in military honour.

'What regiment?'

'10th Fusiliers.' That wasn't strictly true. I'd spent most of the war in military intelligence, but we wore the uniform and insignia of the fusiliers and now wasn't the time for a clarification.

'I got no quarrel with you,' he said. 'But if you don't do as I say ...' He tightened his grip around Surrender-not's neck. 'Now put down your weapon. Slowly.'

I paused to consider my options and realised I had none.

'Do it now!' There was a nervousness to his voice.

'All right,' I said. With my arms outstretched, and keeping my eyes on him, I slowly bent down and placed my Webley on the floor in front of me.

'Kick it over here.'

I straightened and did as he ordered.

'Good,' he said, bending over and taking Surrender-not with him. Pocketing the pistol in his hand, he picked up mine, then stood back up.

Suddenly he pushed Surrender-not towards me then bolted down the corridor.

The sergeant came flying forwards. 'You all right?' I asked, grabbing him by the shoulders.

'Yes.' He nodded, rubbing his throat with his hand.

'Good. Stay here,' I said, moving past him into the corridor. The Gurkha had almost reached the lobby at the far end.

I set off after him without any thought as to what I'd do if, by some miracle, I managed to catch him. He'd entered the building armed with a knife and now, thanks to Surrender-not and me, he had a pair of police-issue Webleys as well. On the bright side, if the maniac did end up killing me, it would at least save me the trouble of explaining their loss to Lord Taggart.

By the time I made it to the lobby, the Gurkha had fled through the entrance and down the steps, leaving the startled porter in his wake. I followed him out into the night and gave chase, pursuing him round a corner and into an alley heading, I thought, away from the river, realising that, even as I did so, the gap between us was growing by the second. At the end of the alley he turned another corner and I lost him, but I kept on, my legs leaden. My lungs felt as though they were about to explode. I pulled up, breathless. The street was empty. The Gurkha had disappeared.

TWENTY-SIX

I spent the next ten minutes fruitlessly searching for the Gurkha. Trying the locked doors of buildings, pushing against windows, but in the end, I gave up and trudged despondently back towards the nurses' quarters.

My breathing had returned to normal but the exertion of the chase hadn't done me any favours.

Surrender-not was waiting at the steps, a cigarette clutched firmly in his hand, the shock still written on his face.

I walked over to him and for a moment neither of us spoke. There was no need. We both knew what the other was thinking. He was no doubt feeling the guilt of being overpowered, forcing me to bargain for his life and thereby losing what might be our only chance to stop that madman before he killed again. I could have told him he had nothing to feel ashamed about. Some days you got the bull, and some days the bull got you. What mattered was we'd saved Rouvel's life and that we'd both live to fight another day. And at least now we knew what our adversary looked like.

The nurses' quarters were in a state of commotion as we entered. A gaggle of nurses, some in uniform, some in their dressing gowns, had congregated in the lobby, their discordant voices carrying out into the night. A hush gradually descended as they noticed us.

'Where's the porter?' I asked.

'He's gone to alert the authorities,' said a middle-aged nurse – English by the sound of her accent. 'Who are you?'

'We're the authorities,' I said, making for the stairs.

Somewhere close by a siren sounded. The military police would be here soon and I'd no particular wish to be around when they arrived. All I needed was to collect Miss Rouvel and then we could be on our way.

I walked back up to the second floor and along the corridor. Rouvel's door was open and her room empty. There was no sign of her or her suitcase.

'Where is she?' asked Surrender-not behind me.

'Gone,' I said.

———

Not wanting to attract the attention of the military police, we descended via the rear staircase, the one where half an hour earlier we'd unceremoniously handed over our weapons to a five-foot Nepalese with a knife. Some of the rooms on the ground floor were now empty and unlocked, their occupants having chosen to leave their rooms and congregate in the lobby, and we simply exited through the window of one which looked out onto the rear of the building.

'What now?' asked Surrender-not as we hurried towards the car.

I tried to put myself in her position, work out what she might be thinking. Someone had just tried to murder her. Rather than stay and wait for us to return, she'd bolted. Maybe it was because she feared we couldn't protect her, or maybe there was something she didn't want to tell us.

I considered where she might go. The whole of Barrackpore was an army cantonment – as much a military base as it was a town. It was, save for the base at Fort William, probably the most secure location in the whole region.

But the fact was our killer was a military man. Our little altercation with him earlier put that beyond doubt, and rendered Barrackpore about as safe as the beaches of Gallipoli. Rouvel would know that too, and I figured she'd want to get as far from Barrackpore as possible.

'I think she's making a run for it,' I said.

'You think she might be going to join McGuire?'

'No,' I said. 'I think whoever telephoned McGuire had told him of Dunlop's murder. And I think that same someone also sent the car to pick him up. There was no telephone in the nurses' residence. For Rouvel to know where McGuire was, she would have had to have known of his plans to run before we'd arrived. That's unlikely, especially as she'd been unaware of Dunlop's murder. And she's taken her suitcase with her. My guess is McGuire's been taken into protective custody. Rouvel's escape, on the other hand, feels like a flight to safety. I think she's trying to disappear.'

'You think she's making for Calcutta?' he asked.

'Possibly,' I said. 'Or she's making for home.'

Either way, she had a twenty-minute start on us at the most, and she'd no transport. The nearest rickshaw rank still operating at this time of night was a mile away on the main road. I doubted she'd have got far.

For someone without a car, the routes out of Barrackpore were limited to two options: the railway or the river. If she was heading for Calcutta, the obvious choice was a train to Sealdah at the north end of White Town. If, on the other hand, she was heading back home to Chandernagore, the obvious route was a boat across the river to Serampore, from where she could catch a train to take her north to French territory. And the trains would be frequent tonight. It was Christmas Eve and a lot of people would be travelling home for the holiday. Extra trains would be laid on to transport passengers from Calcutta back upcountry.

Whichever direction she was headed in, if she made it onto a train, the chances of me finding her again quickly would be slim, and with McGuire having fled, she was the only one left who could provide the answers I needed.

'We should make for the station,' said Surrender-not.

'You go,' I said, 'and take the car. If she's there, take her into protective custody. Arrest her if you have to. I'll join you as soon as I've searched the ferry ghat down by the river.'

———

With that, we went our separate ways. Surrender-not headed for the car and then to the station. Something in my gut, though, told me that Rouvel would make for the river. It seemed counter-intuitive at first – a boat was slow and dangerous – but in truth, the river was the sensible option. Not only was it the most direct route to Chandernagore, it was easier to reach on foot than the station, and at this time of evening she was unlikely to be stopped. A boat across the river was less risky too. Barrackpore wasn't that big a place and the station was open ground. Waiting there would increase the chances of her being noticed by someone who knew her. The other shore was a different prospect entirely. No one would know her there. She could catch a train from Serampore in complete confidence that no one would recognise her.

I ran towards the riverbank, to the ghat where we'd arrived the day before when we'd taken the boat from Rishra. The more I thought about it, the more convinced I became that this would be Rouvel's escape route.

A low wall overlooked the riverbank. The lights of Rishra and Serampore flickered in the distance, their reflections dancing on the black water. Ahead of me, the ghat was in darkness, save for a solitary light outside a shack on the jetty. The place seemed dead, the air still, the silence broken only by the gentle lapping of the waves against the muddy bank and the sound of my laboured breathing.

I kept running, on towards the deserted bankside, fear growing with each step that I'd made a mistake. Was it possible that she'd headed for the railway or even the road?

The wall ended at a flight of steep stone steps which ran down to a ferrymen's hut and the wooden pier. Below me, a number of small *naukas* had been dragged up and marooned on the mud-bank. Others, like shackled prisoners, were tied pathetically to the pierside. There was no sign that any of the vessels were being made ready for a crossing. I stopped to catch my breath, overcome by fatigue.

I had a choice. Waste more precious minutes descending the steps and searching the shack in the increasingly forlorn hope of finding her, or cutting my losses and heading for the station. I'd made up my mind and was about to turn round when something in the rhythm of the waves lapping against the pier seemed to change. They became irregular, as though disturbed by the wake of a vessel. Leaning against the wall, I peered down into the gloom below. It took several moments to make it out, but there, about a hundred yards out, a small *nauka* was approaching the pier. The vessel had no lights but its solid outline stood silhou-etted against the rippling water, a cadaverous figure leaning on the steering paddle at the rear. Suddenly a figure emerged from the shack below, shoulders and head wrapped in a shawl, and car-rying a suitcase.

I bounded down the stairs, keeping one eye on the treacherous, slime-covered steps and the other on the approaching boat. I reached the pier just as the boat was drawing level and sprinted for the far end. For tense moments, I lost sight of the cowled figure, separated from it by the bulk of the shack. I cleared the edge of the structure. The ferryman had thrown a rope round an iron mooring post and was pulling his boat up to the pier.

The figure in the shawl was speaking. I couldn't make out the words but I knew the voice.

'Miss Rouvel!' I shouted. 'Wait!'

She turned round, and for a moment she hesitated. Then she picked up her case and gingerly stepped into the boat.

'*Chalo*,' she said the boatman, with urgency in her voice and a wad of rupees in her hand.

I pulled out my warrant card and pointed it at the ferryman. 'Stop,' I said. 'This boat isn't going anywhere.'

Behind me came the first stirrings from the shack. The other boatmen, alerted by the commotion, had come out to see what was happening. The last thing I needed was trouble from a shed-load of itinerant ferrymen wondering why I was threatening one of their own. I turned towards them. 'Police business,' I said with as much authority as I could muster. 'Go back inside.'

I jumped onto the boat and steadied myself. Rouvel stood in front of me like a frightened child, holding the suitcase to her breast like a shield.

'I've nothing more to tell you,' she said. 'Please let me go.'

'You tell me what's this is all about and I'll consider it.'

'Don't you see?' she said. 'I don't know. If I did, don't you think I would have left when Ruth Fernandes was killed? Why would I stay in Barrackpore if I thought he would come after me?'

'Who is he?' I said.

'I don't know. I've never seen him before.'

'You're sure?'

'Yes.'

I sensed uncertainty in her voice.

'Maybe he was one of the soldiers who passed through your hospital during the war?' In the belly of the *nauka* sat a small hurricane lamp. I ordered the boatman to light it, and in its dim glow, I pulled out the photograph that showed Dunlop, McGuire, Rouvel, Fernandes and the others lined up outside the hospital in 1917. 'Is he in this photograph?'

She shook her head. 'No.'

'Are you sure?' I asked, looking down at the faces in the picture: British, Indian, Nepalese ... at Rouvel; at Dunlop; at the dead man from the funeral parlour who I now knew was a Nepalese called Prio Tamang; at Anthea Dunlop who'd been spared; and at Ruth Fernandes who was supposedly in Rawalpindi.

'Positive.'

'I need your help, Mathilde,' I said. 'Give me something and I'll let you go. You have my word.'

We stood there for what felt like an eternity. Then she spoke.

'Rawalpindi.'

'What about it?'

She pointed to the photograph. 'You're looking at it.'

And then it hit me. Rawalpindi. I couldn't believe I'd been so stupid.

I thrust the photograph at Rouvel. 'Rawalpindi,' I said. 'It was never the town, was it?'

She swallowed hard but said nothing.

'*This* is Rawalpindi right here, isn't it?' I said, hitting the photograph with the back of my hand. 'These people; Dunlop's work; all of it – Rawalpindi was the code name for his research.'

'Please, I can't tell you anything more,' she pleaded.

'Are people dying because of what Dunlop was researching?'

She shook her head. 'Rawalpindi was evil,' she said, 'but if I tell you, they will arrest me. And you promised to let me go.'

'The police can protect you,' I said. '*I'll* protect you.'

She laughed bitterly. 'Not from these people, Captain. Not from the military. If you want to know about Rawalpindi, you must speak to Colonel McGuire.'

I doubted Section H would let me within a mile of McGuire if they could help it. If I was going to get answers quickly, the only one left to provide them was the poor frightened nurse standing before me.

'Miss Rouvel,' I said gently, 'I may have a solution.'

TWENTY-SEVEN

I stood on the pier and watched the boat cast off into the blackness. I waited until it was almost at mid-river before turning and
heading back towards the stairs to the embankment. With any
luck, Rouvel would be on French soil by sunrise. I'd let her go, not
because she told me everything she knew, or even half of it for that
matter, but because what she did tell me was enough for me to
know she was right. There was no way I could protect her in Calcutta. Not from the military and their attack dogs in Section H;
not given what she knew. It was better that she headed for the relative safety of Chandernagore, outside their jurisdiction.

As I walked back up the steps, the gravity of what she'd told me
began to sink in. It was hard to believe, but the logic of it was
damning. Rawalpindi had never referred to the place in the Punjab but rather a series of experiments, all carried out at Barrackpore
under the aegis of Alastair Dunlop; experiments that had left
some of its subjects dead and others hospitalised – burned and
scarred for life.

But then mustard gas will do that to you.

The Germans had used it first. In July 1917, they'd fired fifty
thousand shells of the stuff at our lines and immediately we knew
that this was something different. Of course, they'd used poison
gas before; so had we, for that matter – chlorine or phosgene agents

mainly, but while they assaulted only the eyes and lungs, this new toxin burned you inside and out.

The lucky ones suffered only the blistering: unbearable, untreatable lesions on the neck, body and limbs. Most victims were blinded. Others slowly suffocated.

At first we'd called it Yperite, after the town of Ypres where it had been used, and because we knew bugger all else about it. Later we'd discover it was a complex concoction of sulphur dichloride and ethylene: a viscous brackenish liquid that smelled of horseradish; and that it was a cytotoxic agent – one that attacked every living cell it touched.

According to Rouvel, the experiments had started in autumn of 1917. Dunlop and his assistants had arrived at Barrackpore and set about establishing their tests to develop a better, more toxic mustard gas of our own.

The military, after the fiasco of the Dardanelles, and believing that Asiatics were hardier to poison gas than white troops, had wanted to develop a weapon that would be effective against all the enemy powers, including the Turks. I'd seen the effects of poison gas during the war. I'd watched men die in agony as the gas seared through their eyes and lungs; seen others cut their own throats when they could no longer stand the pain. Dunlop's task was to calculate the minimum quantity of gas required to produce fatalities. It was wartime after all. Everything was in short supply and there was no sense in wasting the stuff. As for the men, the lab rats on whom the trials were to be inflicted, most had been chosen from the hardiest regiments – the Gurkhas and the Sikhs – and were told that the gas would make them stronger; their subsequent silence bought with the promise of a few paltry rupees.

It all began to make sense. Rawalpindi was the reason why Dunlop, Ruth Fernandes and Prio Tamang were dead. It was the reason why Mathilde Rouvel was running for her life and why the military had presumably whisked Colonel McGuire into protective custody. It also explained Section H's eagerness to know what I was doing at the opium den the night Tamang was killed and their alacrity at preventing me from questioning Anthea Dunlop. Several questions remained, though: who was the Gurkha killing the perpetrators of Rawalpindi? what was his connection to the project? why the ritualistic stab marks and gouging of eyes? and, most importantly, who was next on his list?

I reached the embankment, and in the light of a street lamp, once more pulled out the photograph and examined the faces. In addition to the six people already identified, there were another two white officers, standing directly behind Dunlop. I assumed they were his assistants. My first task had to be to locate them.

Stuffing the photograph back into my jacket pocket, I began to walk in the direction of the station where I expected Surrender-not was still waiting.

———

'No sign of her,' said Surrender-not, descending the steps from the station platform.

'It's all right,' I said. 'I found her.'

The surprise was evident on the sergeant's face.

'Where?'

'Down by the river. At the ghat.'

'And where is she?'

'On her way to Chandernagore,' I said.

'You let her go?'

I gave him a nod. 'We made a deal. She told me what I needed to know, and I let her leave.'

Surrender-not's eyes widened. 'So what did she say?'

'It's a long story, and right now we don't have much time. I'll tell you in the car.'

———

'Revenge,' I said, recounting the details of Rouvel's confession as the Wolseley sped back towards town. 'Our killer appears to have a vendetta against a number of people who were involved in running a series of poison gas experiments on servicemen which were code-named Rawalpindi and carried out here in 1917.'

'You think it's one of the men they experimented on?'

'That would be my guess. In which case, we'd need to see the records of all the test subjects.'

The sergeant mulled it over wordlessly, his forehead furrowed like a ploughed field.

'Don't worry,' I said. 'We're not going to break into the records section at Barrackpore to find them. Section H are as determined to find this chap as we are, and it's about time they did some of the work. Besides, I'm tired.'

Surrender-not winced. 'It's not that, sir.'

'Then what?'

'Why wait so long?'

'What?'

'If the experiments took place in 1917, why does the killer wait almost five years before taking his revenge?'

It was a good question. I stared out at the road and tried to come up with an answer, but instead felt only the growing nausea in my stomach and the aching of my bones. I picked up the bottle of *kerdū* pulp and took a swig.

As usual, my watch had stopped at some point during the fun and games in Barrackpore, but something in the quality of the air told me it was well after midnight. I could have asked Surrender-not, but then we'd once more have got into the whole debate about why I didn't get the damn thing fixed, or, failing that, a new one. The fact was, it was the only possession of my late father's that I'd inherited. It had been with me through the war in France and had never been the same since. The best horologists in Hatton Garden hadn't managed to fix it and there was no way I was about to let some Calcutta watch-wallah mess around with its innards.

I rubbed the fatigue from my eyes as the car entered the environs of College Street. Outside our lodgings on Premchand Boral Street, a long, black saloon loitered with all the menace of an unexploded bomb. It looked like the same one that Section H had used the night before to drop me off in Tangra after I'd spilled my guts in Dawson's office. If I was in line for another journey across town in it, I could only hope that in the meantime they'd had it valeted.

As our Wolseley came to a halt behind it, one of its doors opened and out strode Allenby, the same man who, after asking for a light, had stuck a gun in my ribs the last time. He walked over and waited for me to get out.

'Let me guess,' I said. 'You need another match.'

'That's good,' he replied, a thin sickle of a smile from his slit of a mouth. 'You'll be needing that sense of humour before the night's out.'

I feared I was about to spend another ten hours in a cell under Fort William. I suspected they'd only left me there that long so that, wracked with the pain of opium withdrawal, I'd be more pliable when it came to questioning me. The problem was that now we just didn't have ten hours to spare.

'How about we dispense with the niceties and you just take me to see your organ-grinder?' I said.

He shook his head and ushered me towards the black car.

'*Organ-grinder*,' he said, as though trying the words out in his mouth. 'I suppose Major Dawson is just that, in the figurative sense. Me, on the other hand, well, you could say I'm more the literal type.'

He bent over and pushed me into the car.

Behind me, I heard Surrender-not approach.

'Wait,' he said. 'If you're taking the captain, you're taking me too.'

Allenby straightened and looked at Surrender-not as though appraising a rotten fish.

'Very well,' he said finally. 'If we're going to see the organ-grinder, I suppose the more monkeys the merrier.'

He nodded at the car's rear door. 'Get in.'

The sergeant did just that, and once seated beside me gave me a smile that suggested he considered the whole thing a nice adventure.

Surrender-not and I settled in for the journey to Fort William. However, it wasn't long before I figured something was awry. Instead of carrying on straight along College Street, the car slowed and then turned right into Bow Bazar.

'You do remember the way to Fort William, don't you?' I asked.

Allenby kept his back to me. 'We're not going to Fort William.'

'Then where?'

'Your office.'

Minutes later, flagged through by sentries, the car turned into the courtyard inside Lal Bazar and pulled up close to the block which housed the officers' quarters. The Section H man got out and opened the rear door.

'I thought we were going to see Major Dawson?' I said, exiting the vehicle and stretching my cramping legs.

'We are,' he replied. 'He's here with your boss, Taggart.'

Sweat trickled down my back. That Dawson was here with Taggart in the middle of the night suggested he was making good on his threat. He must have suspected I was getting close to the secret of Rawalpindi and he'd come here to tell the commissioner about my opium habit.

'Come on,' said Allenby, pushing me towards the side entrance. 'We haven't got all night.'

My thoughts raced as we entered the building and made for the stairs up to Taggart's office on the top floor. There was no going back from here. Allegations of drug addiction weren't something you recovered from professionally. I resolved that if this was the end of my career in the Imperial Police Force, or any police force, for that matter, I'd do my damnedest to take Dawson and his friends in the military down with me.

By the time we reached the top of the stairs, my fury had been tempered by cold reality. There was no point in anger – or self-pity for that matter – not when there remained the small matter of a Gurkha still at large and intent on murdering more people.

'Wait outside,' I said to Surrender-not, as we walked down the corridor. 'Whatever happens to me, make sure you tell Taggart about the Gurkha. He needs to be stopped before anyone else gets hurt.'

Lord Taggart's office was at the far end, accessed by a small anteroom in which his secretary sat, but which at this hour was empty. One of the double doors to the commissioner's inner sanctum lay open and light from the office spilled into the anteroom. From inside came the sound of Dawson's voice.

I stopped just short of the threshold and composed myself. Two and a half years I'd been in Calcutta – a pretty good innings by my standards – especially as I'd never expected to last beyond that first month. I wouldn't be too sad to see the back of the place – this accursed city with its abominable climate and ridiculous citizens, both British and Indian – and yet I felt some part of me would be left here, its loss gnawing away at me for the rest of my life. Calcutta could be insidious like that. At least it would draw a line under the fiasco of my relationship with Annie Grant, which had been going on for just as long, and which, judging by the glacial rate of progress achieved during that time, suggested my strategy might have been directed by Field Marshal Haig himself. I'd miss her, no doubt a lot more than she'd miss me, and the thought of that seemed to rouse something in me. Not something noble, but rather the bloody-minded side of my nature. If there was a reason for sticking it out here, it was that when it came to Annie, I realised I wasn't about to admit defeat just yet.

I took a breath, knocked on the open door, and entered.

TWENTY-EIGHT

25 December 1921

Taggart and Dawson were standing beside the windows which lined one side of the office. Judging by the storm that was Taggart's face, whatever Dawson had said had unsettled him, and I feared that storm was about to head my way.

I had some sympathy for the commissioner. He and I went back a long way. We were both wartime veterans of military intelligence, though unlike Dawson, we'd spent our time at the Front, not with our feet up in India. Now Dawson stood next to him, whispering poison into the old man's ear, telling him of my addiction. Years of hard-won trust destroyed in seconds.

Both men turned towards me. Taggart's expression remained grave. Dawson's was inscrutable.

'There you are, Wyndham,' said Taggart. He gestured to one of the two sofas arranged around a small table close by. 'Take a seat, please.'

I walked over, steeling myself for the blow that was about to fall.

'Colonel Dawson here has been apprising me of some rather troubling news,' he said. 'By the way, where's that sergeant of yours?'

'Sir?'

'I understand he accompanied you here. He should hear this too.'

My stomach turned over. It was bad enough having Dawson in the room while the commissioner dragged me over the coals. Did he really need Surrender-not there too?

'He's waiting outside.'

'Sergeant Banerjee,' Taggart called towards the door. 'Come in here, please.'

Surrender-not ventured in, saluted and sat down sheepishly beside me. Taggart sat on the sofa opposite while Dawson continued to prowl around behind him.

'Now,' said Taggart, 'I understand you've both been rather busy tonight.'

'Sir?'

'Up in Barrackpore this evening. Dawson tells me you prevented a woman from being murdered.'

It was impressive how quickly Dawson had learned of that. Still, I wondered what relevance it had.

'We were fortunate.' I nodded. 'We just happened to be in the right place at the wrong time.'

'And you think the attack was linked to the murder of that nurse, Ruth Fernandes?'

'Not just to hers, but to the murder of a scientist named Dunlop last night, and to that of a hospital quartermaster named Prio Tamang four nights ago.'

The mention of Tamang's name evinced a flicker of something in Dawson's eyes.

'We gave chase,' I continued, 'but lost him in the hospital grounds.'

'You saw his face?' asked Dawson.

'Yes.'

'What did he look like?'

'Like a Gurkha.'

'How old?'

'I don't know,' I said, rubbing the back of my neck. 'In his for-ties, I think. You never can tell with orientals ... at least *I* can't. And it was dark.'

'How did you know he'd decided to attack this nurse, Rouvel?' asked Taggart.

Confusion gave way to relief as it began to dawn on me that maybe I wasn't here because of my drug habit after all. I pulled the photograph from my pocket and held it out towards him.

'I think he wants to kill the people in this photograph – most of them, at any rate. He seems to have spared one. And I think this man's his next target.' I pointed to the figure of Colonel McGuire.

'What makes you say that?' asked Dawson.

'I think you know,' I said. 'I assume it was you who ordered him taken into protective custody.' I turned to Lord Taggart and pre-pared to deliver my bombshell. 'It's to do with something that happened during the war, sir. A series of tests code-named Rawal-pindi. Mustard gas experiments carried out on unsuspecting native troops. I think our man may have been one of those on whom the gas was tested. He's exacting his revenge on the people who took part in his torment.' I turned back to Dawson. 'You need to go through the records of all the men who were test subjects at the facility. Find out which of them it is.'

I waited as the words sank in. Taggart and Dawson exchanged a glance, then Dawson came over and sat down beside the com-missioner.

'Tell him,' said Taggart.

Dawson gave an almost imperceptible nod in response.

'The commissioner knows all about Rawalpindi,' he said, 'including some details that you don't yet know. It's true that cer-tain experiments were carried out under Dunlop's aegis. As for the records, my men have already started going through them, but so far nothing useful has come to light.'

'There's more,' said Taggart tersely.

Dawson hesitated. 'Several shipments of mustard gas arrived from Britain in 1917, but not all of the stocks were used in the tests. The remainder was kept under guard in the arsenal at Barrackpore. Recently, an order was received for them to be transferred back to Britain. As part of that transfer, the remaining stocks were moved to Fort William to be made ready for the journey back home.'

He paused and shifted awkwardly in his seat.

'Tell him,' said Taggart once again, this time more forcefully.

Dawson coughed. The colour seemed to drain from his face.

'It appears that during that transfer to Fort William two weeks ago, several canisters of the gas went missing ...'

The words hit me with the force of a howitzer blast and for a moment I sat there, mute. Until now I'd assumed we were dealing with an insane Gurkha armed only with a kukri knife. Now it seemed he might have an arsenal of poison gas too. I felt the bile rising in my stomach. I'd watched poison gas decimate regiments of battle-hardened troops, and now Dawson was telling me that such a weapon might have fallen into the hands of a madman hell-bent on revenge.

'How?' I asked. 'Surely they must have been under the tightest security for the transfer?'

'They were,' said Dawson. 'We have no idea how they were stolen. All we know is that 126 canisters left Barrackpore and 123 were checked into stores at Fort William. That was when Section H was called in. Our investigations focused on the staff overseeing the transfer. We eliminated the British officers at both Barrackpore and Fort William and our suspicions fell upon the quartermaster's assistant, Tamang. We believed he might be trying to sell them, either to the Russians – both the Reds and the Whites have their agents in Calcutta looking for whatever they can use in their civil war – or worse, to one of our home-grown terrorist groups.

'Four nights ago, one of our operatives trailed him to an opium den in Tangra. Believing he was meeting his contact, possibly to receive his pay-off, our man called for additional support. Unfortunately, our units have been stretched by Gandhi's wearisome agitation and weren't in place to mount a raid in time. So we called in the assistance of your Vice Division. They got there in time to find Tamang's body, but not his contact. At that point, we feared the trail had gone cold and that we might never recover the canisters. But then your nurse was killed in Rishra and Dunlop was murdered in his bed.'

'How difficult would it be for him to deploy the gas?' I asked.

'It would be relatively straightforward,' said Dawson. 'The canisters each have a small rubberised sealed aperture under a screwed-down lid. A resourceful military man could figure out a way of decanting the gas into smaller, home-made bombs, or ...'

'Or what?'

'We've no way of knowing what else he's smuggled out. He may have explosive detonators.' He clasped his hands together. 'We need to stop him before he sets off those canisters. Our one hope is that he goes after McGuire and the remaining members of that photograph before he does so.'

I shook my head, scarcely able to comprehend what Dawson was saying.

'Twelve hours ago you didn't want us anywhere near this case. Now, you're suddenly spilling everything?'

Dawson looked queasy. 'We're out of options,' he said quietly. 'We have to stop him before he uses those canisters, and you and your sergeant are the only ones who can positively identify him.'

I turned to Taggart. 'And you knew about this?'

'The wartime tests, yes. The theft of the gas canisters, no.'

Beside me, Surrender-not stirred. 'If he has the gas,' he asked, 'why hasn't he used it already?'

Dawson checked his watch. 'Prince Edward, the Prince of Wales, arrives at Howrah in four hours. In less than twelve hours he'll be attending a reception at the racecourse followed by a garden party at Government House. Half of white Calcutta will turn out to greet him ...'

His voice trailed off, as though he was unable to bring himself to finish the thought. I didn't blame him. A man with a grudge against the British was on the loose with several shells' worth of mustard gas. The consequences of him carrying out a gas attack on civilians didn't bear thinking about.

'Cancel the prince's engagements.'

'Impossible,' said Taggart. 'Can you imagine the uproar if we were to admit that the heir to the throne of the empire isn't safe in the premier city of the Raj? The Congress Party would have a field day and the international press would chalk it up as a victory for Gandhi and Das. It would kick new life into their failing non-cooperation movement.'

'Then claim he's sick,' I said.

Dawson shook his head. 'Again, it would be taken as a sign of weakness. He was in perfect health yesterday in Benares but falls ill the moment he gets to Calcutta? The Indians would claim it was a fiction. They'd say the Prince of Wales was too scared to show his face in the city. Besides, the risk isn't to the prince – we can protect him, both at the town hall and the garden party at Government House. It's the crowds coming to the town hall that are the problem.'

'And not just the whites,' added Lord Taggart sombrely. 'I expect Das will have cajoled his Congress-wallahs to come out in force to protest the visit. They'll be there too.'

'No doubt,' said Dawson. 'Our sources believe he's planning a gathering on the Maidan followed by a march to the town hall.'

Taggart turned to me. 'You need to go and speak to Das. Remind him he's under house arrest. Tell him if he attempts to leave the premises he'll be arrested and brought to Lal Bazar. And double the guard on his house. His non-cooperation movement is nearly dead. If we can get through the prince's visit, the odds are it'll collapse under the weight of its own expectations. Once you've done that, head to Fort William. For the next twenty-four hours, I'm placing both you and Surrender-not under Dawson's command.'

I made to protest, but the commissioner silenced me with a wave of his hand. 'There'll be no discussion of the matter, Captain. You're on remarkably thin ice as it is.'

I sat back on the sofa.

'That's better,' he continued. 'The major has a plan which we hope will smoke out your Gurkha friend.'

From the inside breast pocket of his uniform, Dawson extracted his pipe, taking several moments to light it with a match, and then puffed gently as the tobacco gradually began to smoulder.

'We're going to use Colonel McGuire as bait,' he said.

TWENTY-NINE

From Taggart's office I headed for the car with Dawson's words reverberating round my skull. As plans went, it was audacious, which was just another way of saying it was desperate. But with only hours to go before the largest gathering of British residents that Calcutta had seen since the king-emperor's visit a decade ago, and a madman armed with enough mustard gas to cause carnage, it was time to consider even the longest of shots.

So Taggart had already known about Rawalpindi. That was a shock, though in hindsight it shouldn't have been. Wasn't it another example of the hypocrisy that Indians accused us of – setting ourselves up as 'protectors' in their land while treating them little better than serfs? Sometimes I didn't blame them for wanting to see the back of us. As for Taggart, he had a habit of knowing more than he let on. He'd been a senior officer in military intelligence during the war, so he could have known of Rawalpindi from the day it had been conceived. Now, though, he was no longer part of the military but the chief of police in Bengal. That meant his dealings with the military, especially with their intelligence arm, often boiled down to a struggle for influence over the policing of the city. In the past he'd used me as a useful instrument to dig into places where Section H might prefer he didn't go, and I feared that may be it was the same this time. It was possible he'd suspected something from the moment Nurse Fernandes's body was found up in Rishra, but judging from the expression on his face, I got the feeling he was telling the truth when he claimed that the theft of the mustard gas had come as news to him too.

Taggart had ordered us to head home and get what rest we could. At seven in the morning, we were to report to Das's house to urge him to call off his march – which no doubt he would refuse to do. Something told me that act would trigger events which would spiral out of control. But that was a matter for the morning. Right now, all I wanted to do was get to my bed.

Beside me, Surrender-not was tight-lipped. I guessed the shock had passed and the realisation that he'd cheated death by a whisker earlier was beginning to sink in.

'Are you all right, Sergeant?' I asked.

He gave a curt nod and turned once more to stare out at the empty streets.

We continued in silence for some minutes more before he piped up.

'We could have captured him tonight,' he said. 'It is my fault he escaped. And now who knows how many more may die because of my mistake.'

'Nonsense,' I said. 'You did everything you could. And you heard Dawson's plan. We'll catch him yet.'

'Do you think the plan will work?' he asked. His tone suggested he needed reassurance that his earlier error could be put right, and in such a situation it was beholden on me to give him not my honest opinion, but rather the answer he needed.

'I'm sure it will. The man's obviously mad. You just need to see how he's carved up his victims to know that. I doubt he'll be able to resist passing up the opportunity to kill McGuire, even if he suspects it's a trap.'

Surrender-not pondered my words in silence.

'You're wrong, you know,' he said finally. 'He's not mad. If he was, he'd have killed both of us tonight. But he didn't.'

I turned to face him. 'What are you implying?' I asked.

Surrender-not looked out at the streets once more. 'He has a plan and he intends to stick to it. A man like that doesn't make mistakes. We should pray that he only wishes to kill McGuire and not thousands of innocent civilians.'

———

By the time the car drew up outside our lodgings, even the prostitutes of Premchand Boral Street had called it a night. I staggered up the stairs with limbs like lead, opened the front door and switched on the electric light in the hallway. Surrender-not walked past me and headed for his room. From the living room came the stirrings of our manservant Sandesh, and moments later he padded barefoot into the corridor.

'*Kerdū*, sahib?'

I replied with a nod, then went through the living room and out onto the veranda while he went off to prepare the juice. The moon bathed the veranda in its pale light, and a thin breeze was blowing from the direction of the river. I sat down on one of the wicker chairs. It had been a long night, one that had seen some of the pieces fall into place. I'd discovered the link between the murders of Alastair Dunlop, Ruth Fernandes and the dead man in Tangra – Prio Tamang; we'd foiled the attempted murder of Mathilde Rouvel, looked our killer in the eye and learned the secret of Operation Rawalpindi. It would have been a good night had it stopped there, but then had come Dawson's bombshell about the missing mustard gas and suddenly things were far worse than I'd feared.

And there was still the matter of the killer's identity. I'd seen enough to know that he was a Gurkha, possibly still serving in the military. The problem was, there were thousands of Gurkhas in the army; tens of thousands if you included those who'd fought in the war and were now demobbed. The chances of Dawson's men identifying him before time ran out were slim. Yet as Sandesh appeared on the veranda with my *kerdū* pulp, there was one other question that vexed me, the one Surrender-not had raised about the timing.

The tests had taken place in 1917. Why had our attacker waited over four years before seeking his revenge? Maybe it was tied somehow to the movement of the remaining mustard gas stocks from Barrackpore to Fort William, but I didn't see how. I was missing something. It was there, amorphous and just beyond my grasp. Whatever it was, I realised I wasn't going to figure it out by staring into the middle of the night. Instead I took the glass of *kerdū* from Sandesh, drank it down and headed for bed.

I shuffled along the corridor and into my darkened room. I didn't bother with the lights as I knew the layout precisely. Kicking off my shoes, I removed my socks, unbuttoned my shirt and trousers and, letting them lie where they fell, made straight for the bed. I untucked one side of the mosquito net, lifted it and climbed in. One of the constants of Calcutta life was the interminable battle against mosquitoes. Someone had decided it was a good idea to build the city over a swamp, and that had sealed Calcutta's fate. It was the ideal breeding ground for all sorts of objectionable creatures, but the malaria-carrying mosquitoes were the worst. Everyone in the city, from the lieutenant governor to the lowliest rickshaw-wallah, was at their mercy, and every night, part of Sandesh's routine was to hoist the mosquito nets over our beds, then lower and stow them away each morning.

I carefully tucked the net back between the mattress and the bed frame and made myself comfortable. There was a certain sense of inviolability that came with being inside of the net, as though it were a shield from all that Calcutta could throw at you. I closed my eyes.

A moment later, I sat bolt upright.

Reaching for the side of the net, I wrenched it up, hauled myself off the bed and made for the light switch. Turning it on, I grabbed my shirt and trousers back off the floor and quickly put them on again, then headed for the door.

I hurried along the hallway and banged on Surrender-not's door, then without waiting for a reply, I barged into his room and switched on the light.

'Get up!' I said.

Surrender-not sat up in his bed and groggily rubbed the sleep from his face.

'Get dressed. We need to question Mrs Dunlop again.'

He seemed incredulous. 'Now?'

'It has to be now,' I said. 'There's no more time.'

'Why?'

'The mosquito net,' I said breathlessly. 'If Dunlop had been murdered in his bed, and nobody had touched the scene of the crime, why was there no mosquito net over his bed?'

Surrender-not stared at me through the thin white mesh of his own mosquito net.

'Ten minutes,' I said. 'I'll meet you in the hallway. First, though, I need to make a couple of telephone calls.'

THIRTY

The first call had been to the transport pool at Lal Bazar, requesting that a car be sent to us immediately. The second was to the Park Street thana, ordering them to send officers back to the Dunlop residence at Park Street. I asked that Constable Mondol, who'd been there earlier in the day, be present. Constables generally lived in police force accommodation provided near or next to their thanas, and the good thing about India was that native officers didn't tend to question an order issued by a sahib, even if that meant being roused from their beds in the middle of the night.

The boys from the Park Street thana had reached the Dunlop house before we arrived, and we were let in by a young constable who escorted us up the stairs.

It hadn't taken Mondol's men long to find traces of something amiss, and soon we were standing once more at the entrance to Dunlop's study.

Mondol himself was kneeling on the floor. He looked up and grinned, then pointed to a brownish stain between on the tassels of a rug that covered much of the floor.

'There,' he said, almost triumphantly.

'That could be anything,' said Surrender-not sternly.

Mondol bent down, lifted a corner of the rug and pulled it back. The varnish on the floorboards was thin and in certain places had worn through. In one such spot, not much larger than the palm of a hand, the boards were partly stained.

I walked over and knelt down beside him, then ran my finger over it.

'Someone's tried to clean up,' I said.

I got to my feet, then addressed Mondol. 'Bring Mrs Dunlop in here. Then search this place from top to bottom.'

His brow creased. 'For what, sir?'

'For whatever was used to clean up,' barked Surrender-not. 'Rags or cloths or sheets stained with blood. Check the refuse. Check the fireplaces.'

The constable nodded and turned on his heel.

It appeared Dunlop might have been killed right here in his study. I took the seat behind the dead man's desk and stared at the photographs on the wall. Those that Surrender-not had dragged down with him as part of his dying swan routine, and which had not been damaged, had been replaced, and the floor swept of shattered glass. Still, there were several empty spaces where photographs had previously hung, their absence made conspicuous by the discoloured outlines of their frames on the wall.

The door creaked open and, accompanied by a constable, Anthea Dunlop entered, looking like thunder, wrapped in a dressing gown.

'What's the meaning of this, Captain? I take it you realise it's the middle of the night. Your behaviour is tantamount to harassment. Rest assured, I shall be lodging a complaint with your superiors in the morning.'

'Forgive me, Mrs Dunlop,' I said, 'but what we have to discuss can't wait till morning.'

She eyed me suspiciously. 'I was rather given to understand that you weren't supposed to be discussing *anything* further with me.' She gestured to Surrender-not who stood next to the door. 'I'm sure your assistant hasn't forgotten.'

'I doubt our friends in the military are going to object this time,' I replied, directing her to the chair opposite. 'In fact they seem to be positively keen to encourage our investigations. You have a telephone, I believe. We can call them if you wish?'

She stood there, raging silently, and for a moment I felt she was actually considering it, but then she thought better of it and sat down.

'What do you wish to know?'

'For a start, Mrs Dunlop,' I said, 'how about you tell me why you lied to us?'

'Excuse me?'

I looked her in the eye. 'Your husband wasn't killed in his bed, was he?'

There was a flicker, something in the eyes. Just as there had been the first time I'd questioned her. It wasn't fear, exactly, but something else. Was it defiance? I watched as her hand went to the pocket of her dressing gown, then came back up empty. Maybe she was searching for her rosary. It didn't look like she needed a handkerchief.

She sighed bitterly. 'Why would you say that?'

'Because it's true,' I said. 'Because I doubt his research into malaria went as far as sleeping without a mosquito net. I think you know who killed your husband. I think you're covering for them. What I don't know is why.'

It was a statement calculated to shock, but there was no alternative – I didn't have time for niceties – and to be honest, I was too tired to care. Given she was a recently widowed woman one might have expected the waterworks to start, but Anthea Dunlop didn't shed a tear. Instead, she looked up at me.

'I don't know what you mean, Captain. I've told you already, I'd taken a sleeping draught. I found Alastair lying in his room in the morning.'

It was the wrong answer. Or maybe she just said it in the wrong way. Whatever the case, she was lying. She was asking me to believe that a murderer entered her home, found her husband, brought him in here, killed him, cleaned up the mess and placed a rug over the one area where the traces of blood couldn't be removed, then left without her or anyone else in the house noticing. Even for Calcutta, the story stank. Not for a moment did I consider she'd killed her husband herself, but that didn't mean she was innocent.

'Is someone threatening you?' I asked. 'Is that why you're shielding them? If so, we can protect you.' It was the second time that night I'd offered police protection to a woman. Mathilde Rouvel hadn't believed I could protect her. This time the reaction was different. Anthea Dunlop obviously didn't think she needed protection.

'I've told you, Captain. I don't know what you're talking about.'

Her tone was casual; almost flippant. It certainly wasn't the tenor of a woman trying desperately to convince me of the truth of her story.

And then it struck me. She believed her husband's death was justified. She was a religious woman, a devout Catholic with a clearly defined sense of right and wrong. Maybe her husband had done something she couldn't condone. It was clear she felt no guilt over his murder, but from her expression it seemed lying to me was proving a little harder. Suddenly I understood that earlier flicker in her eyes. She *wanted* to tell me – to explain why her husband had to die and why she'd been right to protect his killer.

All I had to do was ask the right question.

'Mustard gas,' I said.

She looked at me in horror. 'What?'

'When did you find out your husband wasn't researching a cure for malaria but was working on creating a more toxic strain of mustard gas for the military?'

'I didn't –'

'Did you know before you even left England? At the very least, you must have realised the nature of his work when you came out here and took up your position as a nurse at the hospital in Barrackpore. It must have been difficult, a God-fearing woman such as yourself, having to live in the same house as a man who was developing weapons of mass murder.'

'I didn't know,' she said forcefully. There were tears and anger in her eyes. 'He told me he was working on a countermeasure. And I'd believed him until ...'

'Until what?'

'Until Colonel McGuire told me the truth.'

'McGuire?' I asked. 'The director of the hospital? Why would he tell you?'

'Grief,' she said. 'It was the end of 1917. His son had been wounded at Passchendaele. The boy had been burned terribly in a gas attack and died in hospital a week later. And here he was, in charge of a facility where they were running a mustard gas research programme. The irony wasn't lost on him. He took it stoically at first, but there was one occasion, I had cause to go to his office and he was drunk. He wasn't making much sense, kept roaring on about the wrath of the Lord. He saw it as God's punishment for his role in facilitating evil.

'Of course I confronted Alastair about it. He told me he had no choice in the matter, that he was working for the good of king and country. I made him promise me he'd stop once the war was over. And he did. He took the position at the School of Tropical Medicine.'

She wiped the tears from her eyes.

'Then that letter arrived from London, recalling him to Porton Down to continue his research. I begged him to turn it down, but he refused. He never saw the evil in what he was doing, only the scientific challenge: the goal of perfecting ever more effective poisons. It was when he accepted the post that I realised he was no longer the man I'd married. I don't know that I would have done anything about it if that man hadn't showed up about a month ago.'

'Who?' I asked.

She fell silent.

'I don't know what hold this man has over you,' I said, 'but you should know that we suspect he has acquired a substantial quantity of poison gas and that he intends to use it on innocent civilians. Our only hope of stopping him rests with you telling me everything you know.'

I watched the struggle play out in her eyes.

'Mrs Dunlop,' I said gently, 'this man is about to murder countless people. You have a chance to atone for your husband's work. You can help me stop him.'

She wiped a tear from the corner of her eye.

'Gurung,' she said. 'His name is Lacchiman Gurung. He's a rifleman in one of the Gurkha regiments.'

'Do you know which one?'

'No.'

I looked over at Surrender-not, who already had his notepad out and was scribbling down the details. 'Get on the telephone to Dawson. Tell him the man we're looking for is Rifleman Lacchiman Gurung.'

'Immediately, sir,' he said, making for the door.

I turned back to Anthea Dunlop. 'Why did he come to you a month ago? Was he one of the subjects your husband carried out his tests on?'

She shook her head. 'No, but he was the father of one of them. His son, Bahadur, was only fifteen when he signed up. Bobby, we called him. He was a tiny boy, even for a Nepalese. I expect they'd have rejected him if it hadn't been wartime. He was recruited for the tests by Prio – Prio Tamang, that is. Tamang was a hospital orderly but he also acted as an unofficial gallah-wallah, one of those men who go round the Nepalese hill villages and sign up boys for the army.' She smiled to herself. 'I suppose none of this would have occurred if Bobby hadn't been quite so tiny.'

'What happened?' I asked.

'The tests,' she said. 'Alastair's tests. He'd told me that part of developing a countermeasure meant exposing the subjects to small amounts of gas. He said they weren't harmful and that when lethal concentrations *were* used, the men were given gas masks. The accident occurred on one of the high-concentration trials. The gas masks were army issue, you see, and Bobby's head was too little for even the smallest size to fit. During the trial, his mask slipped.'

She paused and looked past me.

'I remember they brought him in to the infirmary. We'd seen injuries before, but nothing like this. Both his eyes were burned through and his breathing was ragged. He survived for almost three days in agony, before he finally passed away.

'During that time, I looked after him as though he were my own son. Afterwards, I felt I had a duty to write to his family. His father was stationed on the Western Front, and I sent him a letter, telling him his son was at peace. I expect the censors took their black pencils to it, but at least some of what I wrote made it to Lacchiman. He wrote back, thanking me for my kindness towards his son and that was an end of it. At least it was, until a month ago when he turned up at my door. He told me his regiment had just been posted to Calcutta and that he wanted to thank me personally for what I'd done for his son. He was a shy man, ill at ease, but polite to a fault. It became apparent that he had no real idea how his son had died.'

'And you set him right?' I asked.

She stared at me. 'Every parent has a right to know how their child died, Captain. Not to tell him would have been a crime – before God if not the law.'

'How did he take the news?'

'Stoically. Would you expect a native to react any other way when given such news by a memsahib? To do otherwise would no doubt have been shameful to him.'

'Well, his subsequent actions seem to have been rather less stoic,' I said. 'He's already murdered three people, including your husband.'

'Alastair deserved his fate,' she said. 'My husband wanted to create more weapons, better weapons. Ones that would kill more sons. And all because it was a scientific challenge.'

'What happened after Gurung left?'

'About a fortnight ago, he came back to the house. He told me he'd met the man who'd recruited his son for the tests – I assumed that was Prio Tamang – and that after plying him with drink, Tamang had told him the names of those responsible for the tests. He told me he knew what my husband had done during the war, and that he was going to seek revenge. I told him only God should seek retribution. Of course, he quoted the Bible, *"Eye for eye, tooth for tooth, hand for hand, foot for foot"* – it seems to be a verse most popular with heathens – and I, in turn, told him of Our Lord's response, *"Whosoever shall smite thee on thy right cheek, turn to him the other also."* I thought I had convinced him.' She turned away. 'Obviously, I was wrong.'

That was an understatement. In my experience, turning the other cheek wasn't a philosophy the Gurkhas put much stock in. They were far more likely to follow the doctrine that if someone were to smite you on the right cheek, the best thing to do would be to smash them in the face so hard that they'd never entertain the thought of trying to smite you ever again. Less a case of *an eye for an eye* and more of *you take my eye, I'll take your whole head.* Indeed, that tempered, homicidal rage was one of the reasons we prized them so highly as soldiers.

Yet something in the words still struck home.

An eye for an eye.

'What did you tell Gurung about the injuries sustained by his son?'

Anthea Dunlop looked away.

'Mrs Dunlop,' I said forcefully, 'what injuries did Bahadur Gurung sustain and what exactly did you tell his father?'

She looked up. There were tears in her eyes. 'I told him the truth!'

'That Bahadur Gurung was blinded by the gas?'

She nodded.

'Did it also affect his lungs?'

'It was the damage to his lungs that finally killed him,' she said.

'And you told all this to his father, didn't you? That's why he marked your husband and his other victims with the same wounds. Eye for eye. Lung for lung.'

The woman didn't reply. She didn't need to.

Yet I imagined that for a man like Gurung, the gassing of his son by the British military, an institution he'd probably venerated and served since he'd been old enough to join, would be the ultimate act of betrayal. For such a sin, the slaying of those directly responsible might not be enough.

I pictured the scene: Gurung tracking down Prio Tamang, the man responsible for recruiting his son for Rawalpindi; getting Tamang drunk, hoping to find out details of the persons responsible for his son's death; then discovering that Prio Tamang was now no longer just a recruiter of innocent Nepalese village boys, these days he's assistant quartermaster at Barrackpore. During their conversation, Tamang boasts about the transfer of the remaining mustard gas stocks from Barrackpore to Fort William, and Gurung realises that here is a way of exacting the sort of revenge that would be fitting. He bribes Tamang to 'lose' some of the mustard gas canisters en route to Fort William. Tamang delivers them to Gurung, but instead of the expected pay-off at the opium den in Tangra, the Gurkha murders him – the first in the sequence of revenge killings that would then include Ruth Fernandes, Alastair Dunlop, Mathilde Rouvel and Colonel McGuire, before the ultimate act of retribution, the gassing of massed civilians in Calcutta on Christmas Day.

'And that was the last time you saw him?' I asked. 'Until last night?'

'Yes,' she said, recovering some of her composure. 'He broke in some time after midnight. I was in bed and Alastair was in here, working.' There was a bitterness to her tone. 'All he did was work. Lacchiman must have known that the servants' quarters were on the ground floor, for he came in through the roof. He entered my bedroom first.'

'You didn't scream?'

'I would have, but he clamped his hand over my mouth before I realised what was happening. He said he wasn't going to harm me. That he was here to ask my husband some questions.'

'And you told him Alastair was in his study?'

'Yes.'

'Then what happened?'

'He bound and gagged me, then left the room. I heard him cross the landing to the study. I heard Alastair call out once, but that was it. I assumed Gurung had threatened him with a gun. The next thing I remember is Gurung returning to the room. He looked like the Devil ... or maybe one of Our Lord's avenging angels. They do say that Satan is nothing more than one of God's fallen angels, don't they? He bent down and started to untie me. I asked him what he'd done. He didn't reply.'

The door opened and Surrender-not walked in. He gave me a nod, then returned to his place beside me.

I pulled the photograph from my pocket, flattened it out on the desk and pointed out her own image. 'He's after those involved with Operation Rawalpindi,' I said, 'even the nurses who cared for the injured and the dying. So why didn't he kill you?'

Once more she stared at the wall. 'Would you believe me if I said I'd asked him to? I too have lost children, I've contemplated taking my own life more than once, but of course self-harm is a sin for which there is no absolution. Had he killed me, he would have been doing me a service, but he refused. He said he didn't want my death on his conscience.'

'And yet, he's prepared to poison innocent civilians?'

'*You* say he's prepared to do so,' she said. 'I've seen no evidence of that. So far, he's only killed those whom he sees as responsible for his son's death.'

Her point might have been well made, had it not been for the fact that the man had stolen several canisters of mustard gas. Her defence of him triggered something else in my head.

'Did you ask Gurung to kill your husband?'

'No,' she replied flatly, 'but I didn't try to stop him. My husband was creating weapons more poisonous than those which killed Bahadur Gurung. If you knew someone whose purpose was to sow death, wouldn't you try to stop them, Captain?'

I stared at her. 'That's exactly what I'm trying to do, Mrs Dunlop.'

THIRTY-ONE

Five o'clock. Christmas morning. It was supposed to be a day of joy; of hope and rebirth. Maybe it was. We now had the name of our killer – Lacchiman Gurung – and with that came the hope, however slender, of stopping him before he killed again.

To the east, the sky was beginning to lighten. We walked back down the steps from Anthea Dunlop's residence to the car. Our driver sat dozing in his seat, his head resting against the glass, and it took a rap on his window from Surrender-not to jolt him from his slumber.

'Fort William. *Chalo!*' I said as we got in.

'What did Dawson say when you telephoned him?' I asked Surrender-not.

'He said he'd alert the relevant authorities and commence a search among all military units in and around the city.' Surrender-not smiled. 'He was most grateful for the information. He even went as far as to say "thank you".'

'And you thought we wouldn't live to see the day,' I said. 'If we're lucky, Dawson's men will track him down and arrest him before long and that'll be an end to it.' But even as I said the words, I doubted that capturing Rifleman Gurung was going to be quite that easy. For a start, nothing in Calcutta was ever easy; and for another thing, the man we were chasing just happened to be a battle-hardened Gurkha.

'He had some news of his own,' Surrender-not continued. 'The two other English doctors in the photograph – Dunlop's assistants; they both returned to England after the war. If Gurung is going after them, he's going to need to make a boat trip.'

That left McGuire as the sole British member of the photograph so far unvisited by the Gurkha. The possibilities for murder were narrowing and I felt happier on that journey than I had done two hours earlier. I now knew my enemy, by name and by face, and more importantly, I understood his motive. There was still the imminent danger of him launching a gas attack that would lead to mass casualties, but we now stood a better chance of stopping him than we had done previously, even if the odds were still stacked against us.

The car sped westwards towards the river, across the Maidan along Outram Road, with the parade ground and Victoria Memorial to our left. Fort William loomed like a behemoth in the half-light. A bright-eyed sentry waved us briskly through the Chowringhee Gate and soon we pulled up outside the block that was home to Section H.

Dawson's office was a frosted-glass and wood cubicle at the far end of a larger room on the second floor. Despite the hour, the place seemed as frenzied as Bow Bazar during the festival of the goddess Durga, with scores of uniformed men and women busy at their desks, on telephones, or rushing, paper-laden, from one room to another. Among the commotion, I spotted the familiar face of Marjorie Braithwaite, Dawson's secretary.

Marjorie was a formidable-looking woman with a permanent scowl, the no-nonsense temperament of a headmistress and a reputation for being the most trustworthy secretary in Calcutta – all indispensable qualities for a woman who was assistant to one of the most feared secret policemen in India. The mere sound of her voice was known to put the fear of God into subordinates, to the extent that I suspected she'd attended at least some of the interrogation training courses that Section H officers were sent on. Surrender-not was terrified of her, but I quite liked her, and though her loyalty was always to her boss, she seemed to have a weary tolerance for me.

We made our way to her desk.

'Marjorie,' I said, 'we're here to see Torquemada. It's urgent.'

She shook her head and sighed. 'Go through, Captain Wyndham. He's expecting you.'

I thanked her and headed for Dawson's office.

'And, Captain,' she called. 'You shouldn't call him that. He doesn't like it and I'd hate to see him pull out your fingernails on account of a little joke.'

I gave her a smile and knocked on the major's door.

Dawson was seated behind his desk, his pipe clamped between his jaws and the telephone held to one ear. Less than forty-eight hours ago, he'd interrogated me in here and I'd vomited on his floor. Now he was rather less hostile, though I'd have been a fool to think that this was anything more than a truce: a pause in hostilities while we faced a more pressing foe. He gestured with a nod of his head towards the two chairs that faced him across the desk.

'Any news?' I said as he replaced the receiver.

He puffed vigorously on his pipe, sending a cloud of smoke ceilingward.

'Rifleman Lacchiman Guring,' he said, tapping a thin buff-coloured file on the desk in front of him. 'Private, first class, of the 4th Regiment, the Prince of Wales Own Gurkhas. Age forty-two. Enlisted in 1897, saw active service on the Afghan border, then in France and Palestine during the war. A career soldier, he turned down the offer of demobilisation in 1920. Most recently, posted with his regiment to Calcutta last month, to this very base.'

'Have you arrested him?'

Dawson took another puff on his pipe. His eyes were bloodshot.

'Not yet. He went AWOL just over a week ago. At about the same time that the stocks of gas went missing.'

'Any idea where he might be holed up?'

'We're checking for any known relatives he may have in the area and putting the word out among our operatives in the native parts of town. We'll spot him if he surfaces.'

It was hollow bravado. Like me, Dawson was too long in the tooth to believe his own rhetoric. Gurung had gone to ground. The only way we'd catch him now was to pre-empt him: figure out where he was going, then get there first.

'Your plan to use McGuire,' I said. 'Is that still on the cards?'

Dawson rubbed his forehead. 'It has to be,' he said. 'There's a Christmas fair in the grounds of Barrackpore cantonment in a few hours. Most personnel are being given the morning off in honour of the Prince of Wales's visit. Colonel McGuire is going to spend his morning at the fair, being as conspicuous as possible.'

'You think that'll flush Gurung out?'

'I hope so.'

'Why don't you just go ahead and paint a target on McGuire's back?'

'Believe me, I would do if I thought it would help.' He removed the pipe from his mouth. 'By the way, how did Mrs Dunlop know his name?'

'Because she'd met him twice before. His son was a victim of the Rawalpindi experiments – she nursed him in the days before his death. He'd lost his sight and his lungs were burned. The father is out for revenge.'

'Let's hope, then,' said Dawson, 'that his desire for vengeance leads him to take chances going after McGuire.'

———

Twenty minutes later, having swallowed a cupful of black coffee in a nearby barracks mess hall, Surrender-not and I were back in the car, stuck somewhere along the Strand Road. In anticipation of the Prince of Wales's imminent arrival, the quickest route back into town – along Red Road and up past Government House – had been closed and the traffic diverted along the riverfront. In the distance, the bridge across to Howrah was shrouded in early-morning mist. Dawn had broken, and with it, the city began waking to Christmas Day. The road was already choked, the carts of traders carrying fresh produce, jostling for entry into the city. This morning, though, the traffic was joined by another sort of crowd. White-clad, placard-carrying protesters streamed towards the shoreline, trying, presumably, to make for Howrah station.

Ahead of us, the traffic was stalled, the demonstrators corralled by a military ring of steel, holding them back from the bridge and the boulevards into town beyond. At the river ghats too, long queues had formed as soldiers restricted access to the ferry piers, questioning anyone who looked like they might be out to cause trouble.

'So much for the Prince of Wales's low-key entry to the city,' said Surrender-not.

It wasn't exactly a surprise. In India, even the best-kept secrets have a habit of slipping out and, as usual, the problem lay with the Indians themselves. It was a pity the country couldn't function without them, not the bureaucracy, or the railways, or the forces of law and order; and wherever you had Indians in the system, whether it was a lowly *peon* or a fat *babu* pen-pusher, you had the risk that information would leak to the opponents of the Raj. People talked, and all it would have taken would have been a Congress-sympathising stationmaster's assistant in Benares or Patna, or somewhere else along the route, to realise that the VIP on the special train passing through the station was His Royal Highness the Prince of Wales, and get a message to the local party cadre, and the news would reach Calcutta hours before the prince did.

A fleet of vehicles appeared on far side of the bridge: an olive-green armoured car led the way across, followed by two black saloons, one a Rolls, the other possibly a Crossley – it was hard to tell at this distance – both with their roofs up, with another military car bringing up the rear. After the cortège came a busload of what I presumed were the royal retinue, then another carrying the gentlemen of the press and a lorry with the newsreel technicians from Pathé who travelled with the circus.

The vehicles made their way briskly across the bridge, then past the gaggle of protesters and the stalled traffic on the bankside, before speeding off along Harrison Road. Surrender-not craned his neck, hoping to catch a glimpse of the prince, but it was pointless. At this distance, all that could be said was that Prince Edward could have been any one of several pale smudges in the rear of the Rolls that flew past.

'Looks like it could be a while before they reopen the road,' he said, settling down again. 'We're wasting time sitting here.'

'Agreed.' I nodded, then tapped the driver on the shoulder. 'We'll walk from here.'

Our destination was the domed structure of Government House. In the days when Calcutta had been the capital of the Raj, Government House had been the seat from which the viceroy administered this nation of several hundred million souls. Power might have shifted to Delhi, but the building itself was still among the grandest in the country, and, as such, was deemed a fitting residence for the visiting prince.

On Dawson's orders, we were to liaise with the prince's attachés and the military officers coordinating security during his stay.

We were met on the steps of the building by a tall India Office mandarin in spectacles, morning suit, cravat and pinstriped trousers, who introduced himself as Beaumont and who led us, in businesslike fashion, along marbled corridors.

'The first time you speak to the prince, you are to address him as "Your Royal Highness",' he said, explaining protocol. 'Thereafter you may call him "sir".'

'That all seems straightforward.' I nodded.

We reached the East Wing, where he transferred us to the care of a familiar face – Dawson's man, Allenby.

'His Royal Highness will be at the briefing,' said Allenby, leading us up a flight of stairs. 'It's senior officers only, so your sergeant is going to have to remain outside.'

I turned to Surrender-not. 'Is that all right with you, Sergeant?'

'I suppose so, sir.'

'Good man,' I said. 'God forbid the prince should meet an actual Indian on his tour of the country.'

Allenby shot me an acid glance.

'Does he know of the threat yet?' I asked.

'No,' said Allenby, as we reached the top and began walking along a carpeted corridor. 'And I'll thank you not to mention it to him, either.'

'Don't you think he should be told?'

'Told what, exactly? We've received no threats against him in particular. And Calcutta's hardly Sarajevo.'

Geographically, at least, he was correct, but as for the threat, no one had considered Sarajevo particularly dangerous till the heir to the throne of one of the largest empires in Europe had been murdered there.

Depositing Surrender-not in an anteroom, we entered a large room dominated by a chandelier and a painting of the defeat of Tipu Sultan at the Battle of Mysore. French windows opened onto a balcony and offered what might generally be considered a pleasing aspect, but in a building like this, most aspects were likely to be pleasing.

In the centre of the room, seated on a chesterfield while those around him stood, was the prince. He sat with a drink in one hand and the other arm draped over the back of the sofa. He'd grown up in the five years since I'd last seen him. Now he was no longer a boy pretending to be an adult, but a man, relaxed in demeanour and with the looks and charm of a matinee idol.

Allenby bowed, then made the introductions. 'Your Royal Highness, may I introduce Captain Wyndham of the Imperial Police Force? He will be acting as our liaison with the civilian authorities.'

The prince rose. 'How do you do, Captain,' he said, shaking my hand.

'Your Royal Highness,' I said. 'We met once before, sir, back in France in '17. You were visiting the troops.'

'Really?' he said. 'You'll forgive me if I don't recall. I met a lot of men on those tours. I only hope the visits did some good.'

'I'm sure they did,' I lied.

The prince turned to one of his aides, an equerry in a naval officer's uniform. 'Archie here was just explaining for the umpteenth time the itinerary for today.'

The aide winced. 'Sir, it's imperative that things pass off smoothly,' he said, as though explaining an unpleasant fact to a recalcitrant child.

'I'm sure they'll pass off perfectly,' said the prince. 'They loved me in Lucknow, didn't they?'

'With respect, sir,' said the equerry, 'Lucknow isn't Calcutta.'

'Come now, Archie. Ever since we started this tour, everyone's been saying how awful things are in Calcutta, but it's Christmas. How bad can it be? Besides, there'll be plenty of troops to make sure things don't get out of hand.' He turned to one of the military officers, a stout chap with grey hair and clipped moustache. 'Isn't that so, General?'

'We'll keep things tight, sir,' the officer replied. 'We shall leave Government House at a quarter past noon precisely and follow an indirect route to the town hall, forgoing the open-top carriage for a closed limousine, and arriving at Esplanade Row approximately fifteen minutes later.'

'The town hall fronts directly onto the road, and is flanked by taller buildings on both sides,' I said. 'His Royal Highness would have to walk from the car, and up the steps. While I'm sure security precautions have been taken, he would still be exposed for a few minutes. It might be preferable for the convoy to stop at the rear of the building. It would be easier to protect.'

A hush descended over the gathering. Archie, the prince's equerry, gave an embarrassed cough. The silence was broken by the prince himself.

'I'm the bloody Prince of Wales, for goodness' sake,' he said. 'I'm certainly not going to skulk in through the back door, Captain, no matter what the risk.'

It might not have been the safest option, but I certainly couldn't fault his bravery. Indeed, in his position, I'd have probably felt the same.

'Very good, sir,' I said.

Beside me, Allenby piped up.

'The captain makes a useful point, however. There is a march planned by some Congress hotheads at the same time as your speech at the town hall. The roads may become choked. Should they do so, we shall have a car waiting at the back of the hall to bring you back here at the end of the function.'

It looked as though the prince was about to raise another objection, but then seemed to think better of it.

'Your Royal Highness will be greeted on the steps of the town hall, by a flower-bearer,' said Archie, 'and then by the mayor and assorted local dignitaries. The mayor will lead you inside. Your speech is scheduled to commence at 1 p.m. and should last approximately thirty minutes, followed by photographs for the press. The whole thing should be over by 2 p.m., so that we return here by half past two, in time for the reception on the lawns at 3 p.m.'

'When does that finish?' asked the prince.

'At 5 p.m., sir,' said Archie, 'followed at 8 p.m. by the dinner in your honour hosted by the Bengal Chamber of Commerce.'

'Another dinner?' said the prince. 'Can't we cancel it? Say I'm ill or something?'

'Commerce is the city's lifeblood, sir,' said the equerry. 'Some of the most influential men in the country will be there.'

'But it's Christmas Day, for goodness' sake,' the prince remonstrated. 'Can't I even have that one evening to myself?'

'It's the last official event of the tour, sir,' said Archie. 'Tomorrow you have the Boxing Day races, and the following day we set sail for home.'

Talk of the turf club seemed to mollify the prince.

'What's the going like out here? I don't suppose it's any good?'

'I think you'll be pleasantly surprised, sir,' piped up another of the generals. 'Some of the maharajahs have very fine stables.'

The meeting broke up with the arrival of a turbaned manservant in red-and-gold livery, who announced that the prince's breakfast was waiting. The officers began to file out, and I was about to join them when the prince called out to me.

'One moment, Captain.'

I turned. 'Yes, sir?'

'Where was it in France that we met?'

'Ypres, sir,' I said, making sure to pronounce the name properly. During the war, all us Tommies had pronounced it 'Wipers', like the contraptions on a car's windscreen.

'We took some terrible losses at Ypres,' he said thoughtfully. 'I assume you lost some friends.'

'I did, sir,' I said, though I could have added that by then I had very few friends left to lose.

———

I rejoined Surrender-not in the anteroom.

'Come on,' I said. 'We need to head north.'

'Where to?' he asked.

'Barrackpore.'

We made our way back down the stairs and along the corridor.

'So what was the prince like?' asked Surrender-not as we emerged out into daylight.

'Not as bad as I expected,' I said.

'That's high praise, coming from you, sir. Just as well. I suppose he'll be king-emperor one day.'

'That depends.'

'On what?'

'On whether he makes it through the day.'

THIRTY-TWO

Colonel McGuire's bungalow sat on the edge of Barrackpore, an innocuous whitewashed house no different to those on either side of it, with green shutters framing the windows and potted begonias on the veranda. To the rear, a garden sloped gently down to the riverbank, and to the front, a path bisected pristine lawns. It was, in some ways, the epitome of the dream of British India: neat, ordered and, servants aside, devoid of natives.

McGuire was seated on a sofa in a drawing room that appeared to have been furnished from the flora of a Burmese jungle, with heavy furniture and floorboards made of dark, varnished teak. Next to him sat a woman in a Harris-tweed skirt and sensible shoes. Middle-aged, with straight, greying hair and the bronzed skin that told of an English life lived too long in the sun, she seemed in some distress, intermittently dabbing at her eyes with a handkerchief. Beside them sat a Section H man, one of their thicker-set officers to be sure, the type usually more useful with his fists than his wits, and whether he was there for McGuire's protection or to stop him making a beeline for the exit and the first steamer back to Britain, was debatable. From the look on the colonel's pallid face and the dark patches under the armpits of his shirt, you might have got decent odds on the latter.

Across from them sat Dawson, who in contrast seemed a study in composure, that is until we walked in, at which point he began to look as though afflicted by the onset of severe indigestion. It was the welcome he normally reserved for me but it was still a surprise, because I thought he might actually want us here.

He appeared to be in two minds about whether to deal with us or finish his conversation with McGuire first. In the end, he decided bolstering McGuire's collapsing confidence was the more pressing concern.

'You'll be under constant surveillance,' said Dawson. 'Our men will be stationed among the crowds. At no time will one be more than a few feet away from you. The risk to you will be negligible.' He neglected to mention the gas, but then, why would he? McGuire would not know of its theft and there was no need to worry him further.

Dawson's tone implied that the matter was not up for debate. Of course, McGuire, though a doctor, was also a military officer, so I supposed debate had never been an issue. Whatever he might have thought of the plan, McGuire was a soldier honour-bound to obey orders.

He swallowed and reached for his wife's hand.

'If you'll excuse me for a moment,' said Dawson. Leaving the McGuires with their minder, he ushered Surrender-not and me into the hallway.

'You're no longer needed here, Wyndham,' he said, herding us towards the front door.

I stopped and turned towards him.

'So you've caught him, have you?' I said. 'Because the look on McGuire's face would suggest otherwise.'

Dawson reached into his pocket, extracted a sheet of paper and unfolded it. 'No, we haven't caught him, *yet*, but after you furnished us with his name and regiment, we brought in some of his senior officers and had this sketch prepared. It's been distributed to all our people and to the guards at the entrances to the base.'

I looked at the drawing, sniffed, then handed it to Surrender-not. In truth, it wasn't a bad likeness, but I wasn't about to tell Dawson that.

'What do you think, Sergeant?' I asked.

Surrender-not made a show of examining the picture. 'This could be anyone,' he said. 'Any Gurkha, at least.'

'Exactly,' I said, taking the sheet from him and tossing it back to Dawson. 'Good luck finding him with that. I'm guessing you got some English sketch artist to knock it up – someone who probably couldn't tell the difference between a Nepalese and a Chinaman. With respect, Major, this cantonment is the size of a small town. If Gurung decides to show up here, you'll need more than a few Section H officers and sentries armed with a hashed scribble of a portrait to stop him. You need men who've seen him recently, and close up, and unless I'm mistaken, Sergeant Banerjee and I are the only such witnesses you've got.'

A pained expression came over Dawson's face not dissimilar from the one he'd worn just after I'd vomited in his office a few nights earlier.

'Don't try to be clever, Wyndham,' he said. 'It doesn't suit you. You might be able to identify Gurung, but he's seen you too. If he catches sight of you or your sergeant here before you spot him, he'll make a run for it and we'll have lost him. This is our last chance to stop him before … who knows what happens. I don't want you ruining it.'

Then it dawned on me.

'All those fine words you just spouted to McGuire and his wife about there being no real danger – it's hogwash, isn't it? You know the only way you're going to stop Gurung is if you catch him in the physical act of attacking McGuire. You don't really care if the colonel lives or dies, just so long as you catch Gurung.'

Dawson's face darkened. 'McGuire's a serving officer. He knows what that entails, and yes, I'd gladly sacrifice him if it means we stop Gurung from using the mustard gas he's stolen.'

'And what if he uses the gas here?' I asked. 'In Barrackpore?'

'If we can't stop him using it, then I'd much rather he used it here than on the crowds in central Calcutta. This is a military cantonment. Most of the people at the fair will be soldiers or their families, there are gas masks aplenty and, most importantly, the fair is on open ground. The chances are, most would escape without serious injury. But I fear Gurung is smart enough to know that too. The casualties accruing from him unleashing the gas on five hundred people in an open space pale in comparison to releasing it in streets jammed with fifty times that number.'

It seemed heartless, even by Dawson's standards.

'You're willing to sacrifice all these people?' I asked.

'For the greater good?' he replied. 'Wouldn't you?'

Suddenly Surrender-not piped up. 'If I may, Major Dawson. I expect you will be commanding operations from somewhere.'

Dawson fixed him with a stare. 'What's that got to do with anything?'

'I-I assume,' stammered Surrender-not, 'that it is probably somewhere which affords a view of the fair?'

'It's on the top floor of the admin block overlooking the sports fields.'

'Maybe, the captain and I could join you there?'

The major took his time considering it. I suspected he wasn't used to Indians utilising independent thought, at least not Indians on our side.

'Give us a couple of pairs of binoculars and let us sit on the roof,' I said. 'We'll be out of sight and still have a good chance of spotting him before he gets close to McGuire.'

'Very well,' he said finally. 'You'd better come with me.'

An airy tune emanated from a mechanical Verbeeck fairground organ and floated up to our perch on the roof of the cantonment's administration block, its artificial cheerfulness feeling as out of place as the contraption itself, which would have been more at home on the promenade in Brighton than in the middle of Bengal.

Indeed, it brought back memories of a few stolen days spent with Sarah on furlough in Eastbourne. It must have been July '16 or maybe August. In those few days, life had seemed more real, more urgent than it had ever done before, or since. The days were etched in my mind, painted with an intensity that still burned bright.

We'd been married the year before, and a fortnight later, I'd gone to war. Those days in Eastbourne were as close to the joys of newly wedded bliss that we ever got to share, the joys that, until the war, most husbands and wives probably took for granted. We looked forward to the day when the fighting would end and we could be husband and wife, but it never turned out that way, and the anger I felt at her loss had never subsided. The memories were bitter-sweet now and I forced them from my mind as I peered through a pair of field glasses down at the fairground attractions that had been set up on the sports fields below.

I'd said it half in jest, but Dawson had taken the suggestion seriously, and rather than have us in his command post on the second floor, he'd placed Surrender-not and me on the roof of the admin building with one set of binoculars between us. That last act of pettiness was a statement – on a base this size, it shouldn't have been beyond the wit of man to find another pair – but I guessed it was his way of showing who was in charge. I didn't argue. After the previous night's run-in with Rifleman Gurung, the whole affair had become personal, for both me and Surrender-not, and it was enough of a victory that we were sitting on this roof, still actively involved in the case.

As the morning warmed up, the crowds below began to grow. Servicemen – British, Indian and a fair few Nepalese – together with wives and children, ambled between the stalls and the rides. I focused in on McGuire. He and his wife had stopped to take in the routine of a monkey dressed in a red waistcoat, dancing in time to a tune played on a *shenai* by his owner, an emaciated-looking native with mahogany skin and a pencil moustache and who wore a waist-coat matching his monkey's. Around the animal's neck was tied a wire rope, the other end of which was held by the thin man and which glinted in the sunlight. McGuire looked nervous, his eyes searching the faces of the crowd around him.

'Anything?' asked Surrender-not beside me.

'Nothing yet.'

I shifted the focus from McGuire onto the crowd around him, looking not just for Gurung, but also seeing if I could spot Section H's operatives. Dawson had told us there were four of them down there, and in the twenty minutes or so since we'd taken up our station, I was fairly certain I'd spotted at least a couple of them. One, a native, was standing not ten feet away from the medical director, and though he looked to be watching the same monkey routine, his gaze kept shifting to McGuire.

Another, an Englishman, stood further away, ostensibly buying a sherbet from a sugar-cane seller. The vendor, in a vest and lungi, was passing stalks of cane through a wringer similar to the type used to wash clothes, turning a large wheel and collecting the juice in a vessel at its foot. Once again it was his focus on the good doctor, rather than the sherbet seller, that betrayed him.

I was less certain about the third, but my eye fell on another native, a large Sikh loitering by the path leading from the fields towards the riverbank. While he wasn't looking at McGuire, it was his size and seeming disinterest in any of the amusements which aroused my suspicion.

I passed the binoculars to Surrender-not.

'Take a look,' I said. 'See if you can spot anyone who might be Gurung.'

———

The best part of an hour later, he was still looking. The sun was overhead now and the temperature, while pleasant at ground level, was starting to feel uncomfortable on the roof. The crowds below us had grown and, around some of the stalls, the throng was such that bodies jostled to get past each other.

I held out a hand. 'My turn,' I said.

Surrender-not lowered the field glasses and passed them to me.

'McGuire's over there, by the shooting gallery,' he said, pointing out a booth to the left.

I picked up the binoculars and trained them on the stall in question. McGuire had picked up one of the toy-like rifles and was trying his luck, aiming at a row of tin figures. I watched as he aimed, then squeezed the trigger. He was too far away for us to hear the crack of the rifle going off and it felt a bit like watching a silent picture on one of those Mutoscope machines you find on the promenade at seafronts. One of the targets fell and McGuire reloaded, then took aim at the next. Once more he pulled the trigger and a moment later another of the tin targets fell. I had to hand it to him. These games tended to be rigged – the gunsights slightly off or the rifling of the barrel skewed so that the bullet travelled out at a less than straight angle – but McGuire seemed to have compensated for that. He wasn't a bad shot for a doctor. Beside him the stallholder grimaced as McGuire reloaded and prepared for another round. As he did so, a young native boy walked up to him and pulled at his tunic. For a moment, McGuire looked as though he'd been struck by lightning. Then he lowered his rifle and turned towards the boy.

'Hello,' I said. 'Something's happening.'

The child looked to be around ten or eleven, and from his stick-thin frame and ragged clothing, it appeared he might be part of the travelling fair rather than the offspring of anyone at the cantonment. He handed a slip of paper to McGuire, then ran off, disappearing back into the crowd. McGuire unfolded the note, scanned it, then looked around forlornly for the boy. Crumpling the paper into a ball, he pocketed it and then began moving quickly through the crowd as though searching for something.

'What's going on?' asked Surrender-not.

'A boy just handed McGuire a note; and now the colonel's looking for something ... or someone.'

Down below, McGuire's minders had noticed the change of behaviour too. Two of them left their stations and began following him as he weaved his way through the crowds. Another – a short native in a white shirt and khaki trousers that I hadn't noticed earlier – also broke cover, all three of them tracking McGuire at such a close distance that if Gurung *was* in the vicinity, he was sure to have realised that McGuire was being tailed.

Suddenly, McGuire stopped in his tracks. He turned then headed straight towards the building on whose roof we were perched.

'What's he up to?' I asked, passing the binoculars to Surrender-not and pointing out McGuire.

'Maybe he's coming to see Major Dawson?' the sergeant ventured. 'It could be that Dawson sent him that note. Maybe there's been a development?'

Down below, the Section H operatives were now close enough for me to see their faces clearly. All three had slowed and were keeping their distance, obviously relieved that McGuire was heading to what looked like a rendezvous with their boss, Dawson.

I waited a few minutes, just to see if he'd reappear, then stood up and stretched my aching limbs. 'Stay here,' I said. 'Keep an eye on the crowd for Gurung. I'm going down to see what McGuire has to tell Dawson.'

I ran across the roof and down the stairs to the second floor. It took me a few minutes to locate the room where Dawson had set up his base of operations, longer than it should have, given the trail of pipe tobacco left in the air. Dawson was silhouetted, standing with his back to the window, with his face in shadow, berating two of his men – one of whom I recognised as one of the doctor's tails.

'Where's McGuire?' I asked.

'Gone,' said Dawson.

'What? Didn't he come up here?'

'Look around, Wyndham,' said Dawson acidly, 'do you see him here?'

'Didn't you send him that note? The one that urchin delivered?'

'Of course not. Why the hell would I send a bloody carnival-wallah's child?'

'So, you've lost him? But he came in here. I saw him.'

'So did my bloody officers,' said Dawson. 'They all just stood outside and chatted among themselves like a chapter of the Women's Institute. I've got them searching the building now, but ...'

As the initial shock passed, I began to think through the chain of events.

'You won't find him,' I said. 'It's an old trick. He's walked in the front door and straight out the back. Get your men searching the cantonment. He can't have gone far.'

Dawson stared at me, his animosity tempered by the knowledge that I was probably right. He nodded to one of his officers who quickly left the room to carry out the order.

'So where's he going?' said Dawson, turning to me.

'No idea.' I shrugged. 'But it doesn't take a genius to figure out it has something to do with the note that child passed to him.'

Whatever had been in it had spooked McGuire. So much so that he'd spent the next few minutes trying to find the child who'd delivered it. But then a thought struck me.

'Maybe he wasn't looking for the boy.'

'What?' asked Dawson, but I was already halfway to the door and making for the stairs.

With Dawson a few paces behind me, I raced back up the stairs and flung open the door to the roof. At the sound of the commotion, Surrender-not lowered the binoculars and turned to face me.

'McGuire's wife!' I shouted. 'Can you see her?'

Surrender-not picked up the glasses and quickly scanned the crowd. As the seconds ticked by, a black dread began to well up in the pit of my stomach, and after the longest minute of nothing, I knew.

'The house,' I said. 'He's making for the house.'

Seconds later, all three of us were racing down the stairs, out of the building and into the sunlight. Dawson was shouting something to his men but Surrender-not and I ignored him and headed for McGuire's bungalow. We were there within five minutes. In the distance I could hear a siren wailing. The sensible thing to do would have been to wait for Dawson's men, but there was no time. I pulled out my revolver and, with Surrender-not behind me, made for the steps up to the front door.

THIRTY-THREE

The door had been forced. It swayed slightly in the gentle December breeze, splinters hanging from the area where the lock met the door jamb. Silently I pushed it open with the toe of my shoe and waited in anticipation of gunshots. None came. Just a dead silence broken only by the distant wailing of the siren. Even the birds seemed mute.

The splintered door told me my fears had been correct. Gurung was here and by now he no doubt had McGuire. I ran through the probable sequence of events in my head. Gurung had been at the fair. He'd realised McGuire was being watched – actually, a man like that would have assumed from the outset that the director would be under surveillance. So he'd hatched a plan. Instead of going after McGuire, he'd get the man to come to him. And for that he needed Mrs McGuire. At some point, she and McGuire must have parted company. McGuire's minders would have kept focus on him and not his wife, and it wouldn't have taken much for Gurung to isolate her and force her, probably at knifepoint, to do his bidding. He'd have brought her back here, then paid the urchin to deliver his note to McGuire. And McGuire would have felt he had no choice but to comply with whatever Gurung had ordered in that note.

Revolver drawn, I inched my way inside with Surrender-not a step behind. The hallway was unlit, shrouded in shadow, and as my eyes adjusted to the gloom, I made out the doors to the drawing room and the dining room and the passage that most likely led to the bedrooms.

There were two ways to do this, slowly and methodically, or to go in with guns blazing. It had now been about twenty minutes since McGuire had walked through the admin building and given us all the slip. Assuming Gurung had told him to come here, and that he'd come directly, he would probably have arrived here no more than ten minutes ago. It wasn't a difficult decision. Ten minutes – it could be a blink of an eye or a lifetime. It was more than long enough to kill a man, yet not much time to pluck his eyes out and ceremonially carve him up. McGuire might already be dead, but there was a chance – a good one – that Gurung was still here.

Instinctively, I made for the first door, the one to the drawing room, kicked it open and dived in. The room was silent but for the ticking of a clock. Behind me, Surrender-not was already heading down the hall and making for the next door. He didn't have a gun – it took a lot of paperwork and questions asked before a native officer received a replacement – so it was either damn brave of him or remarkably foolish. Gurung could be waiting behind it, ready to welcome him with a chestful of lead. Not that Surrender-not seemed to care. I steeled myself for the sound of gunfire, but once again, none came. Sometimes I didn't give that boy enough credit. I breathed once more and backed out into the hallway.

'Empty,' said Surrender-not.

'The bedrooms,' I said. 'He left Dunlop's body lying on a bed. Maybe he's doing the same here?'

We moved fast, through the hallway, to the rear of the house. From somewhere close by came a thud, the sound of furniture toppling over.

'That one,' said Surrender-not pointing to a door.

'Brace yourself,' I said, taking a deep breath before turning the handle and pushing open the door.

At first the room looked empty. But then, between the bed and the dressing table, Surrender-not spotted the leg of the upturned chair. He ran in and I followed. On the floor, gagged and tied to the chair, lay Mrs McGuire. I helped Surrender-not right it. He untied the gag around her mouth and let it fall to the floor.

'Are you all right, Mrs McGuire?' he asked.

The woman seemed to be in shock.

I placed my hands on her shoulders. 'Mrs McGuire.'

At the sound of my voice she looked up at me and tried to focus. 'Do you know where your husband is?'

Again, she said nothing, just shook her head.

I left Surrender-not to untie her and headed back into the hall. Frantically, I made my way along it, kicking open every door and, each time, being met with nothing but an empty room.

Behind me came the sound of voices and boots running up the front steps. Major Dawson's men had arrived. I walked quickly back to the front hall. Soldiers were already searching the rooms off it.

'Tell me he's here,' said the major, red-faced. In different circumstances I might have enjoyed his discomfort, but not now. Not today.

'We haven't found him,' I said. 'Though the wife was tied up in one of the bedrooms.'

Dawson let fly a string of expletives. 'How the hell did we lose him?' he exclaimed, his voice reverberating off the walls.

'Mrs McGuire can tell us what happened, but my guess is Gurung targeted her. He would have realised that McGuire would be under surveillance, but there was a chance that his wife wouldn't be. He grabbed her, then sent McGuire a note, forcing him to come back here.'

'So where are they?' asked Dawson as his men continued their search.

'Gone,' I said.

'Gone? Gone where?'

'Who knows?' I shrugged.

'Well, they can't have got far,' he said. 'They're probably still in the cantonment somewhere.'

'You could try locking down the base,' I said, 'but I expect Gurung's done his homework. He'll know how to slip in and out of this place without getting caught. Besides, there's a bloody great river at the foot of the garden. If he had access to a boat, he could be halfway to Calcutta by now.'

Dawson reached into his pocket and fumbled for his pipe. 'We can't just wait here and do nothing,' he said. 'I'm going to order the complete shutdown of the base and a watch on the river.'

It was the right thing to do, of course, but it was a bit late to be shutting the stable door. Our horse hadn't just bolted, he'd taken the prize filly with him and was now off to set fire to the farm.

'Do what you need to,' I said, 'but if you really want to avert a catastrophe, cancel the prince's engagements today.'

Dawson sighed. 'You know that's not going to happen. The viceroy's hands are tied.'

'Then you'd better pray that Gurung decides that carving up McGuire is vengeance enough for the death of his son. If he could enter a cantonment like Barrackpore with impunity, what chance have we got of stopping him if he decides to murder innocent civilians in the middle of White Town? Not just British. Indians too.'

The major's face darkened. 'Let *me* worry about the British,' he said. '*You* just focus on keeping the Indians off the street.'

THIRTY-FOUR

The car sped towards Bhowanipore and Das's house. Surrender-not and I sat in the rear, licking our wounds. Twice now we'd had the opportunity to catch Gurung and twice we'd come away with nothing, and I was too much of a fatalist to think we might get a third chance. Dawson should have been as concerned as I was. The only sensible course of action would be to cancel the Prince of Wales's engagements, to stop the immediate risk to thousands of civilians and buy us time to apprehend the Gurkha, but that wasn't going to happen. As Lord Taggart had told me earlier, any cancellation would be seen as a victory for the forces arrayed against us, the forces of Gandhi and Das and chaos. And so as the minutes ticked away, instead of redoubling our efforts to find Gurung, here we were dashing across town in the hope that we could convince our opponents to cancel their plans. It felt like a fool's errand, but we had no choice.

Beside me, Surrender-not had that look on his face – the one that told me his brain was overheating, probably trying to untangle some Gordian knot that it had tied itself into.

'What?' I asked.

'Sir?'

'What's bothering you this time?'

He pondered the question before replying.

'McGuire,' he said. 'Why did Gurung abduct him? Why not kill him on the spot?'

'Maybe he didn't have time,' I said. 'He wants his victims to bear the same scars as his dead son, remember, and he had no idea how long it'd be before we worked out where McGuire might have gone.'

'That would suggest he'll kill McGuire as soon as he gets the time to do so.'

'Probably.'

'And yet, on each of the previous occasions he's waited before killing his victim: we know he asked questions of Dunlop before he murdered him, and the wounds to the hands of Ruth Fernandes and Prio Tamang suggested they were tortured for information. Maybe he'll do the same with McGuire?'

'It's possible,' I said. 'McGuire was in charge of the facility. He was the top of the tree after all, but we can't count on that. In the meantime, we'd be better served if you put McGuire out of your mind and worked out how to convince Das to call off his demonstration.'

'Yes, sir,' he said. 'What if Das refuses to comply?'

'In that case,' I brooded, 'he's going to end the day either back in jail or dead, alongside many of his devoted followers.'

Das's manservant opened the door tentatively and greeted us with a look that suggested he'd have been happier opening it to a gang of dacoits come to rob the place. Not that there was much chance of that, what with the armed police stationed around the entrances to the property.

We were shown into the same overlarge drawing room with its mirrors and portraits and waited while the servant went to fetch his master. Neither Surrender-not nor I felt like sitting. With Rifleman Gurung still on the loose, the last place we wanted to be was in the salon of an overpaid lawyer with a martyr complex, taking tea and explaining to him the finer points of mustard gas exposure and the need for him to call off his demonstrations.

The door opened and Das walked in, with his wife and his lieutenant Subhash Bose in attendance. Basanti Das was wearing a khaki sari, almost as though she were a female member of the Congress Volunteers.

Das placed his palms together in *pranam*.

'Please,' he said, gesturing to a sofa.

I took up his invitation – there seemed no point in making things more difficult than they needed to be – and Surrender-not did likewise. Das and his wife took a seat on the sofa opposite while Bose perched himself on its armrest. As he did so, a gilded clock on the mantelpiece chimed softly.

'Would you care for some tea?' asked Mrs Das.

But now wasn't the time for the niceties.

'There's a matter of some urgency which we need to discuss,' I said, declining the offer.

'Of course,' said Das. 'Please continue.'

'We understand you have called for a gathering on the Maidan for three o'clock this afternoon.'

Das said nothing.

'I'm here to tell you, in the strongest terms, to call off the demonstration and that if you do not, you'll be in breach of the terms of your house arrest and will be returned to prison.'

Das removed his spectacles and wiped them on the folds of his dhoti.

'You do not think that as citizens of the empire Indians should turn out to greet the Prince of Wales, our future king-emperor?' he asked.

It was a typically Bengali response – neither a yes nor a no, but an opening salvo in a game of words that I was not in the mood to indulge.

'Mr Das,' I said, 'we have received credible intelligence that an attack is planned on the crowds greeting the prince later today, an attack that could result in significant loss of life. If you do not call off your protests, the consequences could be catastrophic.'

'It's true, *kakū*,' said Surrender-not. 'The captain and I have seen the evidence. It's not a trick.'

Das listened carefully, then exchanged a look with Bose, before turning back to face us. He steepled the fingers of both hands.

'Please tell me more about this intelligence you've received.'

'I'm not at liberty to divulge that,' I said.

'How very convenient,' snorted Bose from his perch. 'If we march, our supporters will be in imminent danger; however, you cannot inform us of what shape that danger may take. One might even think you wanted to keep us off the streets, because if you arrest us, you've nowhere left to put us. Thank heavens we have Surendranath's assurance that all is above board.'

I felt Surrender-not tense beside me. He was about to respond when Mrs Das interjected.

'This attack of which you speak, would it not affect the British crowds too? In such circumstances, I take it you have already cancelled the prince's plans and informed the attendees?'

'I don't believe such action has yet been taken,' I said, 'though increased security measures are being implemented.'

Das feigned surprise. 'I must profess, it is unusual for your authorities to care so much for the safety of Indian protesters while at the same time disregarding the risks to Calcutta's British citizens, let alone to the prince himself.'

'That's not something I can comment on,' I said. 'All I can tell you is that the threat is real and that the consequences could be grave. If you do not call off the march, I am ordered to take you, and your assistant here, back into custody.'

Das thought for a moment. 'I shall not lie to you, Captain. I am aware of the protests planned for this afternoon and I approve of them. But you are mistaken to think that I have the power to stop them, even if I wished to.'

'Again,' I said, 'I would remind you that you are under house arrest. Should you leave the confines of this property, you will be detained immediately.'

'You have a dozen men stationed outside, checking all vehicles that come and go from the house. How exactly do you expect me to leave its confines?'

It would have been a fair question had I not already stood by impotently as another Indian evaded our security forces little more than an hour earlier.

'Please, Das *kaku*,' said Surrender-not. 'Nothing good can come of this. The agitation has been going on too long and people are tired.'

Das took his wife's hand and sighed. 'We shall see, Suren. Maybe you are right. Or maybe we shall surprise you. Either way, my course is set. I must follow the path which Gandhi-ji has laid out for me.'

With that he and his wife rose. Beside them, Bose followed suit.

All three accompanied us back to the front steps. I turned to Das at the gate.

'You're sure you want to do this?'

'What choice do I have, Captain? We are all allotted our roles by the Almighty.'

'If people die today,' I said, 'it'll be on your head.'

He looked at me. In the week since I'd met him, he seemed to have aged a decade.

'If what you say is true, I would ask only that you let me march and die with them.'

'If I may –' said Surrender-not.

'Please don't,' said Das. For the first time, the old man seemed to lose his composure. 'Enough has been said already. Maybe if you'd spent less time talking to me and more to your own kith and kin, you'd know that your father intends to march with the protesters today.'

THIRTY-FIVE

The Dases and Bose retreated inside as the Wolseley drew up. Surrender-not just stood there in shock.

'You need to speak to your father,' I said. 'Convince him to stay away. We can telephone from here.'

'It would be futile,' he said eventually. 'You saw how Das reacted. My father's response will be no different.'

I slammed my palm against the bonnet of the car. We were under orders not to mention anything about the threat of mustard gas, to Das or anyone else. But family was family and it wouldn't be the first time we'd disobeyed a direct command.

'You need to tell him about the specific threat. Tell him about the gas.'

Surrender-not shook his head. 'It's too late,' he said. 'The protest on the Maidan begins in less than an hour. If my father *is* planning on going, he has probably left already.'

'Still ...' I said.

'I know,' he said. 'I must try.'

Das's front door was still open and Surrender-not headed back inside.

I lit a cigarette and tried to ignore the cramps wracking my limbs. My thoughts turned to Gurung. He was out there, probably no more than a few miles away, plotting his final act of revenge on an unsuspecting populace. No, not plotting. A man of Gurung's background and ability would have finalised his plans long ago. All that remained was for him to execute it. As for McGuire, the bile rose in my gut as I thought about his fate. I hoped Gurung had killed him quickly, even if his previous murders suggested otherwise. At the same time, there was the nagging, accusatory voice at the back of my head questioning my own actions. Once McGuire had received that note, I should have been quicker to realise that something was wrong. Why hadn't we been watching McGuire's wife?

Surrender-not emerged from the house and back into the sunshine. His face told me everything I needed to know. His father was en route to the demonstration on the Maidan.

'Get in,' I said, flicking away the butt of my cigarette. 'I told Taggart I'd report back to him at Lal Bazar, but that doesn't mean you need to be there. We'll drop you off at the Maidan – see if you can find your father.'

———

The roads were choked, as they always seemed to be these days, and the car crawled through the congested streets north towards the Maidan. I spent most of the journey talking, trying to divert Surrender-not's attention from thoughts of his father. Nevertheless, the boy still spent much of it staring out the window doing his impression of a Carmelite nun.

The crowds were converging on the flat open ground of the Maidan, and it was clear that this demonstration was on a different scale to those of recent months, with thousands of white-clad natives drifting in from the north and from the ferry ghats on the river to the west. While some seemed in high spirits, talking and singing as they went, most were silent, their nerves etched on their faces.

Government troops, ferried in by the lorry-load, looked on war-ily from their positions around the fringes of the park but made no effort to interfere. Indeed, with the numbers arriving, short of opening fire, it wasn't clear what they might do to intervene even if they wanted to.

Surrender-not ordered the driver to stop close to the junction where Chowringhee met Outram Road.

'Good luck,' I said as he got out, before telling the driver to make for Premchand Boral Street. I needed a top-up of *kerdū* pulp before heading on to Lal Bazar.

———

Lord Taggart's face had taken on the pallor and portent of a mon-soon cloud. The usual stolid calm was gone. Now he paced his office with all the urgency and uncertainty of an expectant father as I summarised this morning's debacle. Of course he already knew that we'd lost Gurung, and McGuire too – Major Dawson had told him as much, he said, in a brief thirty-second telephone call – but it was left to me to give him the detail.

'What now?' he asked.

In the five years that I'd known him, it was the first time I'd seen him lost for direction and it was disconcerting for both of us. Taggart was a thinker, a chess player who had a knack of thinking several steps ahead and of seeing the sense in the whole canvas while others saw only the confusion in the centre, but faced with Gurung and his mustard gas, he was as blind as the rest of us.

I told him what I said to Dawson earlier. 'Cancel the prince's itinerary.'

'You know I can't do that.'

'The only other option is to disperse the protesters, using force if necessary.'

He stopped pacing and turned towards me. The conflict playing out in his head was etched on his face.

'Very well,' he said quietly. 'I suppose we're out of time. I'll inform the viceroy's people that we need to break up the crowd. I'll tell them I take full responsibility'

It was a brave act, one which we both knew would cost him his job. With the world's press in the city, the pictures of unarmed protesters being manhandled by the authorities would be in the papers and newsreels across the world by Boxing Day. It was a scene that London and Delhi wanted to avoid at all costs and whoever authorised it would pay dearly. It was the right thing to do, and yet ...

'Wait,' I said. 'I've seen the crowds. They're too large. We don't have the manpower to shift them. It'll take the military to move them. That means getting Dawson to do it.'

Taggart walked back to his desk and sank into his chair. He composed himself, then picked up the telephone.

'I'll speak to him,' said Taggart.

I breathed a sigh of relief. Whatever Gurung was planning, dispersing the crowds might at least put a spanner in the works. The sight of soldiers manhandling the protesters would make uncomfortable viewing but it was far better than the alternative of stretcher-bearers carting off gassed civilians.

Taggart dialled the switchboard and asked to be connected to Fort William. There was a click as the operator attempted the connection and then the commissioner asked to be put through to Dawson. I waited as the major's extension rang. And then, just as Dawson answered, a terrible thought struck me. Suddenly the picture swam before my eyes – of an explosion and panicked soldiers firing on a crowd engulfed in a smog of thick, choking gas. A vision of hell.

Before he could speak, I made for Taggart's desk and pressed down the lever on the telephone, cutting the connection. Taggart looked up at me in anger.

'What are you playing at, Sam?'

'We can't disperse the crowd,' I said.

'But you just –'

'Gurung will have thought of that. He'd know that we'd need to use force to shift Das's protesters. What better time to set off his mustard gas than when the world's press are watching our troops manhandle unarmed demonstrators? The soldiers will think they're under attack. Some might even start shooting and we'll have a bloodbath on our hands. Even if no shots are fired, it'll look like we released the gas.'

Taggart slowly returned the receiver to its cradle as the full horror sunk in. He leaned forward and rested his head in his hands. When he finally spoke, it was with the voice of a broken man.

'What do we do?'

My throat felt dry.

'We have to think like Gurung.' I checked my watch. 'In less than an hour, the Prince of Wales is scheduled to commence his speech at the town hall. The Congress-wallahs gathering on the Maidan will make their way there to protest. The time of maximum danger will be when the prince has finished his speech and the attendees at the town hall are about to leave, coming into proximity with the protesters. If I were Gurung, that's when I'd set off the gas. We need to take whatever precautions we can.'

'You really think he'll seek to kill Indians too?'

'Remember, Gurung's not Indian,' I said. 'He's Nepalese, and the Gurkhas have never had problems when it's come to killing natives. The massacre in Amritsar in '19 is proof enough of that. I doubt he'll care about Indian casualties any more than he would British ones.'

The thought seemed to galvanise the commissioner. 'The area inside the town hall gates has been checked and double-checked for explosives of any kind,' he said. 'As for the prince, he'll be leaving by the rear entrance and taken straight to Government House. The route is circuitous and closely guarded and there'll be decoy vehicles too.'

'That leaves the streets outside the town hall where the protesters' march will finish. I'm guessing Gurung will try to conceal himself within the crowd.'

'I'll issue instructions to both our men and Dawson's to stop and check the identity of any man who looks even vaguely Nepalese.'

I signalled my assent. I didn't particularly like it, but we were out of options.

'I'll get down to the town hall,' I said. My instincts told me that one way or another, things would end there.

THIRTY-SIX

The town hall was the quintessential Calcutta building, a white-washed, neoclassical structure complete with Doric columns, shuttered windows and a faded grandeur that mirrored the city's own decline from capital city to provincial outpost. If set apart from its surroundings, it might have been described as a handsome building, imposing even, but bordered as it was by the magnificent High Court and little more than a stone's throw away from Government House, it felt rather underwhelming: a plain old maid sitting between more beautiful sisters.

Exactly fifty years ago, at a time when the town hall had been the judiciary's temporary home, one of the judges had been assassinated on its steps by a puritanical Mohammedan. I prayed we'd make it through the day without adding to that number

Esplanade Row was thick with bodies: on the steps of the town hall stood a column of kilted soldiers of the Black Watch, while a solid line of khaki-clad sepoys and white-uniformed officers of the Calcutta police kept back the crowds and checked the credentials of the hundreds of British residents who'd turned out in honour of their prince. Dressed in their Sunday best and with many of them carrying Union Jacks, they pushed forward, those with tickets jostling to enter the building, those without lining the route or craning at the open windows in the hope of catching a glimpse of the man whose picture had, for the last fortnight, seemed to smile from the front page of every English newspaper printed in the city.

There was something of a strange euphoria among the white crowd. For a year now, *their* Calcutta, predictable, orderly, hierarchical, appeared to have been overrun by forces outside their control, the streets seized by brown men who seemed to have forgotten their place. Today, however, their prince and future king-emperor was in town and these people felt as though they were in command again. In the face of vicissitude, many no doubt hoped that this rich, effete man, who knew nothing of them or their lives, could turn the clock back to the glory days when Calcutta was great and those with brown skin knew who was top dog.

Their fears were real, and understandable. The problem was, I doubted that the man they'd come to see could do anything about it.

Even now, the peril they so feared, the little brown men in their white caps and homespun clothes, were gathering in their thousands on the Maidan, getting ready to march up Red Road to confront them.

I was about to head towards them when a carriage drew up at the military cordon. The lacquered door opened and out stepped the American, Schmidt. He turned and, offering a hand, helped Annie from the cab.

I cursed to myself. Then walked over to them. The Yank saw me coming and flashed me a smile with those ridiculously white teeth.

'Look who it is, Miss Grant,' he said. 'It's your friend Mr Wyndham.'

Annie looked at me like I was a dose of the clap.

'You come to meet the prince too, Wyndham?' said the American. He held out his hand which I ignored.

'Annie,' I said, 'this place isn't safe. You need to leave.'

Annie rolled her eyes. 'The Prince of Wales is coming here, Sam. This is probably the safest place in Calcutta.'

'It's not,' I said. 'And you need to go. Now!'

'Don't worry, Wyndham,' said Schmidt. 'I'll look after her. Make sure she doesn't come to harm. You can trust me on that.'

I contemplated doing the decent thing and punching him in the face, but this wasn't the time. Besides, I couldn't have afforded to pay for his dental bills. Instead I ignored him.

'I'm serious, Annie,' I said. 'Go home. Take George Washington with you if you have to, but please go.'

It looked like she was considering it. Beside her, the American was shaking his head. She turned to him.

'Maybe we should listen to Sam?'

At that moment, a roar went up from the crowd as a row of red-liveried Bengal Lancers appeared, followed by an open carriage topped with a gold silk canopy and pulled by four horses. Behind it came another carriage, this one without a canopy, and another phalanx of the Lancers.

'Listen, honey,' said Schmidt, 'I'm not going home till I meet the prince.'

The cordon of soldiers parted to allow the procession to pass, then closed ranks once more. The carriage came to a halt at the foot of the stairs and Prince Edward, in a medal-laden white dress uniform and pith helmet topped with enough ostrich feathers to fill half a dozen pillows, descended to cheers and a garland of flowers from a girl of about six.

Out from the town hall filed a line of dignitaries, with the lieutenant governor at their head. Flanked by a couple of senior military men, the prince made his way up the stairs, shaking hands with the VIPs.

'It looks like we're staying, Sam,' said Annie.

The thought of so many innocents being gassed was unconscionable. That Annie might be one of them was more than I could stomach. I thought about physically carrying her out of there, but I doubted she'd have appreciated it. Schmidt, too, might have tried to intervene, and while that didn't bother me, getting into a brawl in front of the Prince of Wales and a kilted detachment of the Black Watch seemed counterproductive. Even in uniform, it took a particularly determined Scotsman to knowingly avoid a fight. The only hope I had of averting disaster was to find Gurung.

'If you won't leave,' I said, 'promise me one thing. Stay inside the town hall until the crowds have dispersed. At the first sign of trouble, find a place to hide and stay there. I'll come back for you.'

I didn't wait for a reply – she'd only have accused me of being melodramatic again. Instead I turned and ran towards the perimeter of sepoys, then headed for the Maidan.

The crowds had grown twentyfold since I'd dropped off Surrender-not and the Maidan was now a sea of white, roaring with the sound of ten thousand voices. The soldiers were still there, looking on warily, but the futility of the task was clear. Trying to stop these men marching on the town hall was like trying to hold back the tide. You could do it, for a while, but in the end, you were going to drown. Close by stood a group of men in rolled-up shirtsleeves who had the look of sharks waiting for a feeding frenzy, and it didn't take the flashbulbs and cameras on tripods to tell me that these were the gentlemen of the international press corps.

As on the evening when Das had held his protest beside Howrah Bridge, a stage, bedecked with tricolours and a bank of tannoys, had been erected at one end. At present it was empty, though music was issuing from the loudspeakers, and while I didn't understand the words, the strident, martial melodies suggested songs meant to stiffen the resolve.

Finding Surrender-not in this melee would have proved difficult, had we not decided beforehand that it might be more efficient for him to try and find me. I was, after all, a white face in a sea of brown ones, and though it was hard finding a needle in a haystack, it was infinitesimally harder locating one particular blade of hay out of a whole bale.

We'd agreed that I'd return by half past two and that I'd wait for him close to the stage. I made my way through the throng of men – and they were almost all men – towards the music, eliciting some curious looks on the way. It was hard to take in the good-naturedness of it all. Once more the sense of absurdity hit me: these men, born into bondage, seemed to bear no personal ill will towards me, a representative of the authority that made them second-class citizens in their own land. Indeed, I'd felt less safe walking down the Whitechapel Road of a Friday night in London than I did here.

I reached the foot of the stage and searched the sea of faces for Surrender-not, and, a few minutes later, was relieved to see him emerge from the crowd and make his way over.

'Did you find your father?' I asked.

'Yes,' he replied, deadpan. 'He's here with my eldest brother.'

'The one who doesn't like you?'

'Neither of them likes me these days.'

'I take it you didn't manage to convince them to leave.'

Surrender-not gave a curt shake of the head.

'Did you tell them about the gas?'

'Yes. They didn't believe me. They asked where an Indian terror-ist would obtain such a weapon and why he would use it in an area crowded with Indians.'

'You did your best,' I said and tried to mask the hollowness of my reassurance by offering him a cigarette. He took it and I lit his, and one for myself.

'I hope your meeting with Lord Taggart was more fruitful,' he said, taking a pull.

'What do you think?' I said. 'Cancelling the prince's reception at the town hall is out of the question. Taggart considered breaking up the little party here by force, but I stopped him.'

Surrender-not looked at me curiously. 'Why?'

'Because it would be the perfect opportunity for Gurung to set off his mustard gas and blame us.'

'So our only hope is to find him in this crowd?'

I took a drag of my cigarette and didn't bother to reply.

Several vehicles drew up on the road bordering the Maidan. The first was an open-topped car driven by an Indian and with three khaki-clad men of the Congress Volunteers seated in the rear. It was followed by a larger car, a black one with a fixed roof and curtained windows. An old lorry carrying a group of Volunteers brought up the rear. The vehicles mounted the pavement before making their way across the grass towards the assembled crowd, stopping close to the stage.

The three passengers exited the lead vehicle, two heading for the stage, the other for the larger car with the curtained windows. Of the two heading for the stage, one was eminently familiar. There was no mistaking the bespectacled boyish features of Das's assistant, Subhash Bose.

'What the hell's he doing here?' I asked. 'How'd he manage to get past our guards?'

'You think the men of the Bhowanipore thana are impervious to bribes?' asked Surrender-not.

I looked to the troops gathered nearby. Their commanding officer, a young man with a tanned face and a lieutenant's pips on his shoulders, looked as nervous as I felt. Bose was under the same rules of house arrest as Das, and his presence here could mean only one thing.

The Congress Volunteers disembarked from their lorry and formed a line to the stairs leading up to the stage. The rear door of the black car opened and out stepped Das, dressed in a spotless white dhoti and chador. It was one thing for the officers to turn a blind eye to Bose slipping out from house arrest, quite another for them to let Das go too. That could cost them their livelihoods and earn a charge of dereliction of duty into the bargain. I doubted any of them would have been stupid enough to let that happen. It begged the question: how had the old man given his minders the slip? When I thought about it, though, I realised it mightn't have been too hard. His home was the size of a city block with almost as many entrances and exits. It probably had a cellar too, and like the funeral parlour in Tangra, it was possible that it connected to other cellars. Das could have walked out right under the feet of his jailers.

At the side of the field, the young lieutenant seemed unsure what to do, and his indecision appeared to be infecting his men. I'd hoped against hope that the passenger was someone else, but part of me knew it would be Das, and suddenly I realised that I'd known from the start – from the minute Taggart had called me into his office four days ago – that it would come to this. That it would fall to Surrender-not and me to arrest him. It was a scenario I'd wanted to avoid; not for my sake, but for Surrender-not's. That he might have to arrest a man revered throughout Bengal, a man he referred to as *uncle*, would be a test I wasn't sure he was up to.

Das made for the stairs, shielded by the line of Volunteers. In the distance, the lieutenant still dithered.

'Get out of here,' I said to Surrender-not. 'I need to stop this before things get out of hand.'

He didn't respond. Just stood there rooted like a statue.

'I have to get Das off that stage before our army friends there do something rash. You can't be any part of this. Now get going!' I said it with a force and an urgency I hoped would shake him out of his vacillation.

Surrender-not shook his head slowly, as though in a trance, 'I can't, Sam. Not while Gurung is still out there.'

I didn't have time to debate it with him. Instead I uttered a few choice words then told him to wait there as I pushed my way through the line of khaki and up the stairs. Das was now centre stage, standing at a microphone while Bose remained at the foot of the stairs. As I reached the platform, a chorus of jeers went up from the crowd as though I were the villain in some ridiculous pantomime. Das looked at me and smiled.

'I am sorry, Captain Wyndham,' he said. 'I realise I must have caused you much aggravation. I hope you understand that my actions are dictated by moral necessity rather than any wish to create difficulties for you.'

I could have told him that my actions too were dictated by moral necessity, the necessity to avert a potential bloodbath that might well leave him and his non-violent followers to suffer the most violent of deaths, but there was no point.

'Mr Das,' I said, 'I am arresting you for breach of the terms of your house arrest. I cannot allow you to address the crowd.'

The microphone in front of Das picked up and amplified my voice and suddenly the jeering grew louder.

Das looked to Bose, then back to me. 'If you arrest me, someone else will take my place,' he said theatrically, to cheers from the crowd.

'I'll arrest anyone who addresses this crowd,' I said.

By now, the lieutenant and his troops had reached the stage, and accompanied by two of his men, he began climbing the steps.

'Take this man into custody,' I said. 'Make sure you get him out of here safely.'

The lieutenant probably had no idea who I was, but he seemed happy, even relieved, to follow my orders.

Das held out his arms, like a prisoner waiting to be shackled. The noise of the crowd grew louder.

'No handcuffs,' I said to the lieutenant.

Amid a cacophony of heckles from the ranks of his supporters, Das was led down the steps and towards the soldiers. I returned to where Surrender-not stood waiting. As they passed the black car, Das said something to one of his guards and the procession stopped. The door opened and a diminutive figure in a white sari stepped out.

'Basanti Devi,' gasped Surrender-not.

'What's she doing here?'

I watched as she bent down and touched her husband's feet, then rose, adjusted the *aanchal* of her sari so that it covered the back of her head, and slowly climbed the stairs to the stage, past the young lieutenant who stood there dumbstruck.

'Bloody hell,' said Surrender-not.

'What?' I asked

'She's going to speak,' he said anxiously, 'and you've just told the crowd we'll arrest anyone who addresses them. If the army arrest her, we're finished.'

A wave of nausea passed through me as the full implication of the sergeant's words hit home and I realised that Das had played me for a fool. Our taking his wife into custody was what he was banking on. Arresting him was one thing, but arresting his wife, a high-caste woman, and carting her off to jail was quite another. I couldn't recall the last time a woman of high standing had been arrested in Calcutta. The crowd would be outraged, and, thanks to our friends in the press, word would spread across the city and the province and then the whole country. It was the sort of insult that was almost guaranteed to rekindle the flagging support for Gandhi's non-cooperation movement. I felt like I'd been punched in the stomach.

By the time I regained my wits it was too late to stop her. Basanti Das had reached the microphone and a hush fell over the crowd. She began to speak in Bengali, her voice, amplified by the speakers, seemed to quiver at first but then she found her rhythm.

'What's she saying?' I asked.

'She's telling them that Das has been arrested and that she intends to lead the march in his place. If she is arrested, they are to continue to the town hall and carry out a burning of foreign cloth.'

A cheer went up from the throng, prompting the lieutenant to issue the order for her arrest. Two soldiers hurried back onto the stage and arrested her.

For a minute confusion reigned. The crowd hurled insults at the soldiers, some of whom looked like they were still in their teens. I watched as they in turn gripped their rifles tighter, scared of what the protesters might do. Just as it looked like things might turn nasty, Bose climbed to the stage and calmed the crowd.

'He's telling them to remember Das's words,' said Surrender-not, without waiting for me to ask. 'They are soldiers of peace. There must be no violence. He's telling them to march on the town hall.'

The crowd began to move like some great beast newly awakened and, with the Volunteers to the fore, headed in the direction of Red Road and the town hall.

THIRTY-SEVEN

Surrender-not and I went with them, weaving in and out of the crowd, frantically searching for anyone who bore even the slightest resemblance to Gurung. There was, of course, the possibility that the Gurkha had disguised himself, changed his features in some way, but Surrender-not thought that unlikely. He thought there was something about the way Gurung had carried himself, the way he'd talked when we'd encountered him the night before, that suggested he might find donning a physical disguise beneath his dignity. I pointed out that he'd disguised himself as a hospital porter to gain access to Nurse Rouvel's dormitory and, more importantly, that in this instance, dignity would surely take second place to the desire to complete the mission he'd set himself.

The arrest of Basanti Das had achieved the impact that her husband had no doubt been hoping for. Riled by her arrest, the crowd marched along Red Road shouting their slogans with a vigour I hadn't seen since the early months of the non-cooperation campaign.

The forward ranks of the Congress Volunteers reached Esplanade Row as the clocks struck four. The winter sun was already low in the sky as they and the thousands behind them reached the perimeter established by steel-helmeted troops blocking off access to the town hall.

For the next five minutes there was a tense stand-off, with the Volunteers showing the same resolve and regimentation as the soldiers set against them. Behind them the crowds continued to shout their slogans of 'British out' and 'Long live Gandhi-ji' at a level that must have been clearly audible to the Prince of Wales and his audience through the open windows of the town hall.

Those few hundred British and Anglo-Indians that hadn't managed to make it into the hall, and had settled for listening to the prince from the lawns, were now torn between the speech being given inside and the uproar in the street. The young hotheads among them chose to confront the Indians.

'The crowd is getting restless,' Surrender-not shouted to me above the cacophony of voices. 'At this rate there'll be blood on the streets even before Gurung's involvement.'

He was right. Without Das to instil order, things were starting to spiral out of control.

'Bose,' I said. 'Where is he?'

'In the back of a police van on Red Road,' said Surrender-not, gesturing over his shoulder. 'They detained him as he came off the stage.'

'Well, go and bloody un-detain him and bring him here,' I shouted. 'And hurry.'

Surrender-not nodded and turned to fight his way back through the crowd. The weight of protesters now pressing against the front ranks was growing ever more intense and I realised the futility of the hope that I might spot Gurung in the melee. As it was, the density of the crowd meant that I couldn't see anyone other than the five or six faces immediately around me. Gurung could have been standing two feet away and I wouldn't have seen him. I needed a vantage point from where I'd be able to survey the throng.

Fighting my way through to the military cordon, I showed my warrant card to one of the soldiers and negotiated ingress to the ring of steel. I ran to the town hall and up its steps. It wasn't much altitude but it was the best I could find.

I turned and looked out over the sea of faces. If Gurung set off his mustard gas now, it would trigger a chain of events that couldn't be stopped. Panic would set in and the crowd would stampede in all directions, including into the cordon of soldiers. They, in turn, would see the surge of bodies as an attack and open fire and only the Devil knew where things would go from there.

From inside came the strains of the band striking up and soon the sound of hundreds of voices singing 'God Save the King' floated out. It meant the prince's speech was over. He'd probably spend some minutes glad-handing selected dignitaries before exiting by the back door and being whisked off to Government House.

The door behind me opened and Dawson walked out. He looked as though someone had hit him about the face with a damp rag.

'What have you to report, Wyndham?'

'Nothing good,' I said. 'Das tried to speak to the protesters on the Maidan. We arrested him.'

'Das? How did he get out of his house?'

'That's irrelevant now,' I said. 'What matters is he brought his wife with him. When we arrested him, she tried to speak in his place. Your men arrested her too. The crowd didn't like it. I doubt the rest of India will either when it's in the papers tomorrow.'

Dawson cursed. 'The viceroy'll be furious.'

'Believe me,' I said, 'if that's the worst news you have to give him today, then we'll all be lucky.'

'Gurung?' he asked.

I shook my head. 'No sign of him.'

The moment of maximum danger was fast approaching. When the prince left and his audience exited the building, no more than five feet from the crowds of protesters. It would be the moment of maximum vulnerability. The moment of maximum confusion. All at once I felt impotent, paralysed by the fear that I was about to fail: not just in my duty to protect the hundreds, maybe thousands of people of this city, both British and Indian, who were about to die; but more importantly, to Surrender-not, and to his father and brother; and especially to Annie. That would be a failure for which there could be no atonement or redemption.

As more protesters arrived, the pressure on the front ranks was growing intolerable and the discipline of the Congress Volunteers looked to be wavering. The line broke, and I had a vision of soldiers firing at the onrushing crowd, of white homespun turning crimson. But instead of a surge of protesters, it was Surrender-not and Bose who appeared through the gap. The Volunteers fought to close the breach behind them and, for the moment, their line held.

I left Dawson on the steps and ran down to negotiate safe passage for Surrender-not and Bose through the few feet of no-man's-land between the Volunteers and the army and over to our side.

'You need to tell your people to disperse,' I shouted to Bose. 'You've made your point. You've protested under the prince's nose. Now tell them to go home. The soldiers aren't going to budge and they'll respond with force if you push them much further.'

'You heard Basanti Devi,' he replied. 'The demonstration will not end until we have carried out the burning of foreign cloth.'

I shook my head in disbelief. 'You can't be serious. We're minutes away from a riot and you want to burn cloth?'

'There will be no rioting,' he said calmly. 'At least not from our side.'

'Get on with it, then,' I said. 'Burn your damn cloth and end this.'

Surrender-not accompanied him back through the cordon and to his own men while I returned to my position atop the town hall steps, still hoping against hope that I'd been wrong, and that with the kidnapping and slaying of McGuire, Gurung's thirst for revenge had been slaked.

Below me, Bose issued a command and, moments later, from out of the throng appeared two Volunteers carrying a crate and a bullhorn. They placed the crate at Bose's feet. He climbed atop it and, taking the megaphone, began to address the crowd. Within seconds the shouts had died as the mass of men struggled to hear what he was saying.

He spoke in Bengali, but there was something in the tone and tempo of his voice, the clipped syllables, that made me think he was rushing his speech, and given that Bengalis weren't exactly known for brevity, I got the impression that, despite his bravado, he too might have been afraid that things were close to spiralling out of control.

But slowly the crowd began to respond to his words. Some turned and shouted his instructions to others further back, and gradually the pressure at the front began to lessen. Within minutes, the Volunteers managed to clear a gap ten feet wide between the protesters and Dawson's troops.

Bose issued more orders, and from the crowd, a line of men appeared. They walked solemnly to the centre of the clearing and, one by one, began to throw garments onto the ground: one a shirt, another a coat, a third a scarf and so on until the pile of discarded foreign cloth had reached head height. As Das had done a few days earlier, Bose took a lit torch and set it at the base of the pile.

Behind me, the doors to the town hall opened and the invitees to the prince's reception began to file out. I turned and urged them back into the building, and after certain initial remonstration from some of the congregation, they decided to heed my instructions, no doubt aided in their decision by the sight of several thousand

Indians setting fire to a pile of clothes a yard away and me reaching for my revolver.

Golden flames began to rise from the mound of discarded material, illuminating the darkening sky, and soon the pile was completely engulfed in fire, sending a column of thick black smoke into the air.

It was then that the explosion occurred.

THIRTY-EIGHT

It sounded like a firecracker going off or a car backfiring. The shock caused those closest to scream, and then white smoke began to rise. It was coming from somewhere not far from the front of the crowd, only a few yards from the ranks of Congress Volunteers. Instinctively, the men in the immediate vicinity began to scatter.

I turned to Dawson. 'You need to get the prince out of here,' I shouted. He nodded and set off inside, while I started to cajole and corral the people on the lawns back up the stairs and into the town hall.

I heard what I thought was the sound of an engine starting. Whatever else happened, at least the Prince of Wales would soon be within the safety of Government House.

The smoke drifted slowly in our direction, engulfing the ashes of the bonfire that Bose had lit. Surrender-not was down there. I grabbed a handkerchief from my pocket, covered my mouth and nose, and ran down the stairs towards the line of soldiers. But then came the sound of a second explosion, followed by another in quick succession, and I saw a plume of white smoke rise from the direction of Government Place. Three explosions. Three canisters of gas. Gurung had shown his hand, and yet if he was hoping to catch the prince in an explosion, he'd failed. His Highness's car couldn't have reached Government Place yet.

The street was now shrouded in a white mist. Panic was setting in over the crowd as I broke through the cordon and headed for where I thought I'd last seen Surrender-not and Bose standing. As I rushed forward my eyes began to sting, but through the smoke I thought I could make out Surrender-not. He and Bose were still on their feet, directing the Volunteers to disperse the crowd. It was then that I realised something wasn't right.

Surrender-not, Bose, the Volunteers – they should all have been suffering from the symptoms of mustard gas exposure by now, but they didn't seem to be having any trouble breathing. My eyes too. While they *were* stinging from the smoke, they weren't burning.

I dropped the handkerchief from my mouth and inhaled.

Smoke. Ordinary smoke.

Surrender-not saw me and came over. He too looked bewildered.

'Something's happened to the gas,' he said. 'It's a miracle!'

The problem was I didn't believe in miracles.

'He's set off smoke bombs,' I said, 'not mustard gas.'

The crowd, too, startled by the noise of the explosions, was beginning to realise that the smoke was benign.

Surrender-not broke into a broad smile.

'We should have known he wouldn't murder innocent civilians,' he said. 'It should have been obvious after he spared my life last night. His revenge was complete with McGuire.'

I afforded myself a sigh of relief, but I wasn't yet convinced. It didn't make any sense.

Why set off smoke bombs when you had mustard gas, and why steal mustard gas if you weren't going to use it?

'If he's finished, why the smoke bombs?'

'What?' said Surrender-not.

'If he's had his revenge, why not just disappear? Why set off the smoke bombs? No,' I said. 'He wouldn't do that without a reason.

He's always been three steps ahead of us. This is no different. It *has* to be part of his plan.'

'But what is his plan?'

I worked through the facts. An explosion here, then two outside Government House, yet nothing but harmless smoke.

And then it struck me.

'The prince.'

Surrender-not stared at me blankly.

'He doesn't want revenge on the crowd. He's after the Prince of Wales. That's why he set off the other two smoke bombs. He's blocking off the route to Government House. Dawson and his men will be forced to change their plan. He's herding the prince to a place where he can kill him.'

'But how can he know where Dawson will take the prince?'

'It's obvious, isn't it? He'll take him to the safest place in Calcutta. He'll take him to Fort William.'

Surrender-not blinked. 'Gurung'll never get past the security.'

'He got in and out of Barrackpore easily enough.'

'That was a sprawling cantonment. This is Fort William.'

'And Fort William is where his regiment is currently stationed,' I said. 'It's where he went AWOL from last week.'

That seemed to convince him.

'We'll need transport,' he said, looking around. The routes towards Red Road and Government House were still cordoned off and jammed with bodies. 'The High Court,' he continued, setting off down Esplanade Row. 'There's bound to be a car or two there.'

'How can you be sure?' I asked, following him at a run.

He shouted over his shoulder. 'Have you ever known a judge to walk anywhere?'

Ten minutes later, with the aid of some rough words and gratuitous waving of my revolver, we had convinced a frightened-looking court officer to lend us one of the honourable judges' cars, and were now flying along the strand towards Fort William. I drove while Surrender-not stared out of the window.

'How did he set off the two devices on Government Row?' he asked.

'The same way he set off the one among the protesters. Some sort of pull-ring igniter on a home-made device, I expect. They're quite straightforward. All you really need is some potassium nitrate, some sugar and a glass bottle.'

'No,' said Surrender-not, 'I meant they were set off some distance apart but went off at the same time.'

I looked over at him. 'Are you suggesting he's getting help?'

'I'm not suggesting anything,' he said. 'I just don't understand it.'

'It's possible he rigged up some sort of timing mechanism on one of them; waited for it to go off and then let off the other device. The bigger issue now is how he plans to get the mustard gas inside the fort.'

Surrender-not looked at me. 'What if it's been there all along?'

'What?'

'Consider it,' he said. 'The whole stock of mustard gas was transferred from Barrackpore to Fort William in advance of it being shipped back to England. Prio Tamang, the first victim, was involved in the shipment. He would have told Gurung about its arrival. The records show that all stocks left Barrackpore but the stocktake at Fort William showed three canisters missing. Gurung was stationed at Fort William the night they arrived. Instead of smuggling them out, he could have simply hidden the three canisters somewhere on the base.'

My head spun at the sheer simplicity of it. While Dawson instituted a city-wide search, maybe the stolen canisters had been under his nose all along, inside his own base and mere yards from where he was sitting.

———

The fort's Calcutta Gate was barred by a red-and-white-striped boom gate and a troop of nervy-looking sepoys. A soldier scrutinised our papers with a thoroughness that, at another time, might have been almost admirable, while another two inspected the vehicle and two more stood watch with rifles at the ready.

'What is the purpose of your visit?' asked the guard, bending down to make sure that both Surrender-not and I were who our papers claimed we were.

Telling the truth was out of the question. Explaining that we were here in an attempt to stop the imminent assassination of the Prince of Wales in a mustard gas attack was just the sort of response guaranteed to ensure we would be held here at gunpoint until some officer could be found to deal with the matter, and we didn't have the time for that. Nevertheless, a blatant lie could easily be checked and might cost us even more dearly. What was needed was something banal.

'We're here to see Miss Braithwaite, secretary to Major Dawson,' I said. Of course, no such meeting existed, but I felt sure that Marjorie Braithwaite would confirm my story when the guards inevitably phoned her to check. For the Prince of Wales's sake if not mine, I just prayed she was at her desk.

The sepoy asking the questions disappeared into the guardhouse. Through the doorway I watched as he picked up the telephone receiver and spoke to the operator. Precious seconds ticked by.

'I don't think this is going to work,' whispered Surrender-not.

'That's hardly the spirit,' I muttered. 'And you better pray that it does, because short of scaling the walls, I can't think of any other way to get in.'

The guard replaced the receiver and called over to one of his colleagues.

'Keep calm,' I said to Surrender-not as the second sentry entered the guardhouse. A brief conversation ensued before both men returned. The first guard bent over to speak to me while the other walked over to the boom gate. 'Miss Braithwaite says you are to proceed to Admin Block 6.'

I didn't need telling twice, and before the boom had even been half raised, I gunned the car past it, then under the thick brick arch of the Calcutta Gate and into Fort William.

THIRTY-NINE

The activity at the base spoke volumes: a doubling of the guard; platoons of sepoys deploying to defensive positions; and lorry-loads of troops mobilising in a haze of exhaust smoke. We ignored them all and headed for Admin Block 6.

'They're putting the fort under lockdown,' I said. 'Dawson must have brought the prince back here.'

'Looks like we arrived just in time,' said Surrender-not. 'Two minutes later and we might not have made it through the gate.'

I slammed on the brakes outside Section H's office and jumped out. The entrance was barred by a gorilla in uniform, holding a rifle with a nasty-looking bayonet affixed to it.

'We've been ordered to report to Major Dawson,' I said, shoving my warrant card in his face. 'It's critical we speak to him.'

He shook a tree trunk of a neck. 'Not possible, sir. We have orders. No one in or out.'

I didn't have time to discuss the matter civilly.

'Listen to me, son,' I said. 'I don't know if you've ever seen Major Dawson in one of his rages, but believe me, it's not a pretty sight. He's expecting to hear from me in the next five minutes, and if he doesn't he's going to be furious, and he's going to want to know why. Now unless you'd like to spend the rest of your military service cleaning latrines, I suggest you let me and my colleague pass.'

Once I'd explained it to him, it didn't take him long to realise the wisdom of acceding to my wishes. He stood aside and, with a nod of his head, gestured to the stairwell inside, but by then, Surrender-not and I were already past him.

Taking the stairs two at a time, we made it to the second floor and along the corridor to the large office that housed Section H. Dawson was inside, pipe in hand, surrounded by three of his men and poring over a map laid out on a desk.

'Where's the prince?'

Dawson looked up. 'Wyndham?' he said in exasperation. 'You're like the proverbial bad penny –' but before he could continue, an explosion rattled the windows of the room.

I rushed to the window as an air-raid siren began to wail. A plume of greyish smoke was rising from a building nearby and soon came the sort of screams that I'd last heard on a battlefield in France.

Dawson was beside me.

'Mustard gas,' I said. 'The devices he set off in town were smoke bombs. These are the real thing. Gurung's after the prince.'

Dawson's pipe fell to the floor. He shook his head, unwilling, or unable, to accept the facts.

'But how? How did he get in?'

'There's no time for that,' I said. 'Right now we need to get to the prince.'

———

'He's in the senior officers' apartments. One of the buildings near the St George's Gate,' said Dawson as we raced down the stairs and out of the building. I jumped into the car as Dawson made for the passenger seat.

'We'll need gas masks,' I said, as Surrender-not and Dawson's man, Allenby, sat in the rear.

Dawson pointed the way. 'The stores are located near St Patrick's Chapel.'

It didn't take long to confirm that this was the real thing. The scene resembled a battleground. A squad of men in gas masks stretchered one poor sepoy, his eyes covered with makeshift bandages and his shirt open to the navel, revealing the most horrendous purple burns. Writhing in paroxysms of pain, his cries carried over to us till they were drowned by distance and the droning of the siren. We passed others, the walking wounded, being led away by their comrades towards a line of trucks which then sped off, I presumed to the fort's infirmary.

A mass of troops jostled outside the equipment store as a harassed-looking lieutenant tried to impose some order. Beside him, a sergeant and his men were busy setting up a distribution system. Dawson and Allenby jumped out and made for the head of the queue, returning with five gas masks – one for each of us, and one for the prince. As they hopped back in there was a second explosion. I looked to Dawson.

He handed me a gas mask. 'That came from the direction of the officers' quarters,' he said.

'Gurung's figured out where the prince is,' I said.

The good news, if there was any, was that he was only a few minutes ahead of us. I put on the gas mask and pointed the car in the direction of the explosion.

We drove into white mist, a thick fog of poisonous gas, past men, some already burned, fleeing the other way.

It was difficult to communicate with the gas masks on, and I relied on Dawson pointing out the direction he wanted me to take. He held up a hand and ordered me to stop outside a nondescript three-storey building. We got out and ran towards the entrance. Two men lay prostrate at the open doorway. Surrender-not bent down beside one of them and checked for a pulse, then touched a hand to the chest of one of them. He looked up, then raised a hand with bloodstained fingers.

The guards had been shot. I drew my revolver, as did Dawson and Allenby. Surrender-not picked up the rifle of one of the dead sentries and followed us in. Not much of the gas had penetrated past the doorway, and once through the hallway, Dawson removed his mask.

'How did he manage to shoot the sentries?' he asked. 'They'd been warned not to let any Gurkhas near the building.'

'He'd have been wearing a gas mask,' I said. 'They wouldn't have known he was a Gurkha.'

Dawson shook his head. 'They were *my* men. They would have challenged him as soon as he approached.'

'The inquest can wait,' I said. 'Now, where's the prince?'

'Top floor,' he said, pointing to the stairs.

A shot rang out and the plasterwork behind my head exploded into a hail of splinters. The shot had come from the top of the stairs.

The four of us scattered, taking what cover we could. Another shot rang out and I tried to locate the gunman.

'It looks like we've found our man,' I shouted to Dawson. 'Is there another way up?'

'Two more stairwells,' he said. 'One at either end of the building.'

'You and Allenby take one of them. Get up there and secure the prince's quarters,' I said. 'We'll deal with Gurung.'

The Section H men rushed off along the corridor and I turned to Surrender-not. The sergeant had taken shelter behind a doorway. 'You think you can keep him occupied?'

Surrender-not's response took the form of a shot fired up the stairs towards the first-floor landing.

'Good,' I said, as Gurung let off another volley in reply. I prepared to rise from my crouched position. 'Get ready to give me some covering fire.'

Surrender-not shot back at him. 'Where are you going?'

'I'm going to outflank him,' I said. 'Ready?'

Surrender-not nodded, then fired two shots. I sprinted from my position to the corridor which would take me to the stairwell at the opposite end of the building from the one Dawson and Allenby had made for. Gurung saw me and fired, the bullet crashing into the wall behind me.

I made it to the corridor and ran. Doors on either side lay open, the rooms deserted. Behind me came the sound of more gunfire. I reached the door at the end and burst through to the stairwell, then raced up to the first floor.

I gently pushed open the door on the landing, which I hoped led to a corridor that would take me back to the central stairwell where Gurung was holding out. Peering round, I spotted him, rifle in hand, lying flat on his stomach and taking potshots at Surrender-not downstairs.

I crept slowly into the corridor with my gun drawn, and hoping that Gurung was too occupied to notice, I made it to the first open door. I entered the room, and from the relative safety of the doorway stuck my head back out into the corridor. Gurung, still prostrate, was no more than thirty yards away.

Taking a breath, I raised my revolver and stepped out into the corridor.

'Drop your gun, Gurung!' I shouted.

The Gurkha swivelled round, and in one fluid motion turned onto his side and pointed his rifle at me. I fired before he could pull the trigger, hitting him in the leg. Stunned, he cried out in pain, then regained his composure and fired back at me. I ducked back into the doorway as he fired another shot, splintering the door jamb. But before he could do much else, a shot rang out from the lower floor.

I leaned into the corridor and fired, hitting nothing but air. Leaving a smeared trail of blood behind him, Gurung was dragging himself across the floor, making for one of the rooms. I fired another shot. This one found its mark, hitting him in the chest. The rifle fell from his grasp. I walked up and, with my revolver trained on his head, kicked his weapon away. He was still alive – just. Over the sound of his ragged breathing, I called out to Surrender-not who came running up the stairs.

'See what you can do for him,' I said. 'I'm going to find Dawson.'

Two shots rang out on the second floor, then another.

Surrender-not and I turned to each other in horror.

Gurung tried to speak. 'You're too late,' he rasped, then coughed blood.

The stairwell began to spin and a black dread began to form in the pit of my stomach. If Gurung was here, why the gunshots upstairs?

'Stay here,' I shouted as I made once more for the stairs. 'And keep him alive!'

The second-floor landing looked like a battlefield. Three men, all in uniform, lay dead. Two had had their throats slit. The third lay face down, his back despoiled by multiple stab wounds. Stepping over the bodies, I headed in the direction from which the gunshots had come. It wasn't hard to find the prince's room. Two sentries lay dead on the floor and beside them sat Allenby with a hole in his head.

Inside the room, someone was talking. It wasn't a conversation, just a rambling monologue.

With my revolver raised, I stepped into the open doorway. Dawson was lying wounded and unconscious on a sofa, but that was the least of my worries. In front of me stood a uniformed British officer holding a gun to the head of the kneeling prince. His cheeks were wet and it looked like he was trying to explain something to his prisoner. The prince though didn't seem to be listening. His face glistened with sweat and he looked shell-shocked: like a man unable to grasp what was happening to him.

Involuntarily I took a step back as I realised I recognised the officer. I'd seen him that morning, mainly through a pair of binoculars.

'McGuire?' I said, not quite believing what I was seeing.

He snapped out of his soliloquy and turned towards me, his eyes red and half mad.

'Don't come any closer, Wyndham. I'm warning you, I'll kill him.'

I didn't doubt his sincerity.

'Put the gun down, Colonel,' I said calmly. 'We can sort this out.'

He gave an odd laugh. 'It's a tad late for that, don't you think?'

'Why are you doing this?'

'The same reason as Gurung – poison gas took my son as it did his. I watched his son die in agony – in my hospital – burned beyond recognition. Killed by experiments carried out under my watch. I've relived that death a thousand times since. Have you ever seen a boy die from mustard gas exposure, Wyndham? My own boy must have suffered the same way. Someone has to pay for that.'

'You've had your revenge,' I said. 'Dunlop, and the others, they're all dead. No one else needs to die.'

'Revenge? Do you know what it is to lose a son? Do you think the king does? Of course not!' He shook the prince by the scruff of his neck. 'This little bastard didn't even go to the Front. He was too precious to risk! But it was OK for my boy to serve and to die. And in whose name do you think butchers like Dunlop create their wretched weapons? It's all done for king and country! Well, the king's going to feel *my* pain – a father's pain.'

The man was unhinged; destroyed by his grief. He wasn't going to release the prince. Not while he had an ounce of strength left in his body. I tightened the grip on my revolver. Wrapped my finger round the trigger.

He noticed the tensing of my arms and took a step to one side, revealing a metal cylinder with an improvised trigger mechanism at one end attached to a cord. It was the final missing canister.

I'd spend a long time reliving his next actions, analysing them to see if there was something I could have done, but the truth is, he had a gun to the head of the Prince of Wales and I didn't stand a chance. In one swift motion he pulled on the cord, then swung his revolver from the prince's head to his own and fired. The cylinder ruptured with a crack as McGuire's lifeless body hit the floor. A wisp of yellowish smoke began to seep out, infiltrating the room.

Instinctively I rushed forward. Wrenching a heavy curtain from its hooks, I threw it over the canister, then grabbed the prince who was doubled over, coughing, and hauled him out of the room.

'Are you all right, Your Highness?' I asked.

The prince continued to cough, but looked up and nodded.

Leaving him there, I took a deep breath and ran back in, this time to rescue Dawson. My lungs began to ache as I dragged the wounded spymaster into the hallway before turning and shutting the door.

The major had lost a lot of blood. 'Help me get him down the stairs,' I said to the prince, and between us, we carried him down to the first-floor landing where Surrender-not was still seeing to Gurung's wounds.

The next few minutes passed in a blur and my memory became a mere tableau of images: helping the Prince of Wales with his gas mask; putting on my own; driving him to the nearest checkpoint; sending a detachment of men in gas masks and a medical unit back to the officers' quarters. An hour later it was all over bar the shouting.

Surrender-not and I were held for questioning. Not in the dungeon Dawson had placed me in two days earlier, but in a nice, walnut-panelled office with thick carpets and a picture of the king-emperor on the wall. Surrender-not was held in a waiting room while a very pleasant chap called Smith with neatly parted hair and a well-pressed suit questioned me rather affably for longer than seemed necessary, given that we were on the same side. A debrief he called it, not that there was much I could tell him, seeing as I was still trying to make sense of it myself. I told them that the best person to ask would be Rifleman Lacchiman Gurung, who, the last time I'd seen him, was still alive, and who, according to Surrender-not, had been taken under guard to the infirmary five minutes after Major Dawson. In the end, the debrief became more of a warning. A message delivered in no uncertain terms that Surrender-not and I weren't to discuss what had transpired with anyone, not even each other.

'Is there anything we can do for you, Captain?' asked Smith, bringing our conversation to an end.

'I'd like to question Rifleman Gurung as soon as possible,' I said. 'He's wanted in connection with a series of murders in Calcutta and Barrackpore.'

Smith did his best not to laugh in my face, which was nice of him, then stood up and walked to the door. 'I'm afraid that's not going to be possible, Captain,' he said, opening it. It was my cue to leave. 'All those matters will be dealt with by Section H.'

FORTY

They shot Gurung at 6 a.m. on 31 December. A firing squad at Fort William on the coldest day of the year, though as a man of the mountains, I doubt he'd have felt the chill. I wasn't there of course. Neither was Surrender-not, but Dawson was, and it was he who told me. It wasn't that we were now fast friends – far from it. He just saw it as a repayment for me returning for him after I'd got the prince out of harm's way. You'd think saving a man's life might incline him to reconsider his views about you, but I got the feeling that in Dawson's case, saving his life only made him resent me more. Not that I cared. To me it didn't matter if it was Dawson, Kaiser Wilhelm or even the Devil himself who'd been lying wounded in the room. I'd have gone back for anyone, because you don't leave a man to the gas. Still, when he sent over a bottle of twenty-five-year-old Glenfarclas to my office by way of a thank-you, I wasn't about to turn it down. The silver lining to having a secret policeman as your enemy is that he tends to know all about you, even your favourite whisky. I even invited him round to join me for a glass but he declined.

Instead we'd met early one morning on a bench beside the reflecting pool at the Victoria Memorial. The location was his choice. It was the sort of innocuous rendezvous point spymasters love, not that there was anything clandestine about our meeting, but I suppose old habits die hard.

He was already there when I arrived. In civvies, with a cane at his side and his pipe stuck in his mouth. On his lap was a small brown packet of peanuts. He took one, shelled it, and threw the two reddish nuts within onto the grass where a small flock of birds had gathered in expectation.

'How's the leg?' I asked, taking a seat next to him.

He shelled another couple, dropping the detritus at his feet. 'Bloody awful. Doctor says I might be left with a permanent limp.'

'Look on the bright side,' I said.

'Yes, I know. It's better than being dead.'

'I was going to say that cane gives you a certain gravitas. Spymasters need that.'

He looked over and scowled.

'You wanted to see me?' I said.

He removed the pipe from his lips and placed it on the bench between us.

'We interrogated Gurung. He was more than happy to tell us everything. On being posted to Calcutta, he went to see Anthea Dunlop to thank her for her earlier kindness towards his son. She told him how his boy really died and how her husband was being recalled to England to continue his work.

'Odd lady, Mrs Dunlop. We questioned her too of course, but it was difficult to get much out of her other than the wrath of God. She believed her husband was doing the Devil's work and needed to be stopped. She was the one who introduced Gurung to Colonel McGuire. It appears the doctor never recovered from the loss of his son to the gas at Passchendaele. Saw it as some sort of divine punishment for the experiments that were going on at his facility. When he found out that the government had recalled Dunlop to Porton Down to restart his work, the man snapped.'

Dawson shelled another nut and once more threw the contents to the birds.

'According to Gurung,' he continued, 'he was happy just to kill Dunlop and those others he held directly responsible for his son's death. It was McGuire's idea to go after the Prince of Wales. The man seems to have been driven mad by grief. They staged his abduction at Barrackpore as it was the only way McGuire could get clear of my men. Then they infiltrated the crowd outside the town hall and Government House and set off their smoke bombs, surmising we'd mistake it for a gas attack and take the prince to Fort William.'

'But what about McGuire's assistant, Nurse Rouvel?' I asked. 'Why did Gurung try to kill her?'

Dawson shook his head. 'Gurung hadn't gone there to kill Rouvel. He'd gone to deliver a message to McGuire but by then the doctor was in the protective custody of my men. He'd hoped to persuade Rouvel to deliver it, but when he arrived at her door she just started screaming as though the sky was falling in.'

'That would have been my fault,' I said. 'I'd spoken to her no more than ten minutes earlier. Told her that someone might try and kill her that night.'

Dawson shelled another nut. This time, though, he offered the contents to me.

'No thanks,' I said.

'Suit yourself.'

He shrugged and popped the two nuts into his mouth.

'I hear you've decided to take a leave of absence,' he said.

'It's good to see nothing gets past you,' I said, 'even when you're supposed to be recovering.'

'Going anywhere nice?'

I was off to a Buddhist monastery near a place called Jatinga, in Assam, where, according to Dr Chatterjee, the monks helped you cleanse your body of opium. But I was sure he already knew that. And unless you considered withdrawal sweats, vomiting and close examination of one's own stools to be pleasant experiences, *nice* it certainly wouldn't be.

'Assam,' I said.

'Bit cold this time of year, no?'

'I suppose so.'

———

I left him with his pipe and his starlings and began walking back through the grounds towards the taxi rank on Chowringhee. I had a few things to do before catching the train to Darjeeling at noon. Not that there was much chance of the thing leaving on time. A new round of strikes by signalmen had reduced the railway time-table to a work of fiction. Indeed, all across Bengal the natives had, with renewed vigour, embarked on making the lives of us British as miserable as possible. It was Basanti Das's fault. Actually it was my fault for letting them arrest her that day on the Maidan. As Surrender-not had foreseen, sticking her in a jail cell had been a huge political error. It had shocked the locals in the way that some-one throwing Queen Victoria in prison might have shocked the English, and though the military released her soon afterwards, the damage had been done.

As for the Prince of Wales, once the initial impact had worn off, he seemed to view the whole thing as some extraordinary adven-ture, and it took all the persuasive powers of the viceroy, the India Office and, according to Dawson, a telegram from his father, the king, to convince him to keep his mouth shut about the whole affair. He'd spent Boxing Day at the races, then boarded a ship for Southampton and the press reported the whole trip a great success, with the exuberant natives even letting off firecrackers and smoke bombs in their appreciation of the prince, as though it was some sort of bloody custom. Of the gas attack on Fort William, there was nothing save for an official dispatch, recording an accident that had occurred during the transportation of some toxic chemicals, which had resulted in the deaths of several men and officers, and injuries to some others. Everything else was swept away and forgotten about.

———

From the memorial I took a cab, not north towards home, but south, to Alipore. Ordering the taxi-wallah to stop outside the gates to Annie's house, I alighted, paid him and, after a few words with the durwan, started on the not inconsiderable walk up the curved driveway.

At a distance, the house looked serene, and, set among the palm-fringed rolling lawns, it seemed a world away from the turmoil that gripped streets only a few miles distant. I turned the bend and was grateful to see no sign of the monstrous Hispano-Suiza that had been parked outside on my last visit.

As I approached the end of the driveway, the front door opened and out stepped Annie's maid, Anju, dressed in a faded orange sari and carrying a jute bag. She turned to shut the door then slipped on a pair of sandals which sat nearby on the veranda.

'Morning, Anju,' I said.

The maid spun round in surprise. 'Captain Wyndham, sahib,' she said, quickly adjusting the *aanchal* of her sari so that it covered her head.

'Off somewhere nice?' I asked.

'To the market, only,' she said, proffering the jute bag as corroboration.

'Is her ladyship at home?'

'Memsahib is home, sir.' She nodded. 'But she is not expecting visitors.'

'I was in the area,' I said. 'I thought I'd drop by.'

Anju left me in the drawing room, with its brocade sofas and Hindu sculptures, while she set off to inform her mistress. I was much too nervy to sit down, and ignoring the sofa, I walked over to the window and gazed out onto the lawns, yet again mentally rehearsing what I'd come to say.

In the distance, two mynah birds were playing under a coconut palm. They were clever birds, mynahs. Some saw them as a nuisance and there'd been a cull a few years earlier, but the mynahs had learned to spot the traps set out for them and began avoiding them. Rumour had it they'd taught their offspring how to avoid them too.

The door opened behind me and I turned to see Annie enter the room, wrapped in a pink silk dressing gown. She seemed surprised to see me, but, I thought, not altogether annoyed.

'Don't tell me you've caught them,' she said incredulously.

'Who?'

'The vandals who smashed my window, of course. That *is* why you're here at this hour, isn't it?'

I confess I'd forgotten about her damn window. I considered spinning her a line – *we're almost there, following up every lead*, et cetera – but then stopped myself. There was, I realised, no point in it.

'We're not going to catch them, Annie,' I said. 'With all that's going on in the city, I'm afraid your broken window doesn't really qualify as top priority.'

She smiled. 'I didn't think so. So what *does* bring you out here so early?'

Now was the time to tell her, but suddenly I'd lost the courage to do so. Instead I stalled.

'I came to ask you if you'd reconsidered my advice about leaving the city for a while.'

'Sam,' she sighed, 'we've been through this.'

'You've seen what it's like out there. The demonstrations are multiplying, things are getting worse. I'm not asking you to emigrate, just take a holiday. Go away for a few weeks till things calm down.'

A smile played across her lips.

'As it happens, Stephen Schmidt *has* asked me to accompany him to London. He's leaving next week. He has some business there apparently.'

'I was thinking somewhere in the opposite direction might be better. Somewhere south. It'd be warmer.'

Abruptly the memory of our last conversation entered my mind. It had been on the steps of the town hall, just as Gurung and McGuire had set off their smoke bombs. At the time, I'd assumed they were mustard gas. I recalled the terror and the helplessness I'd felt at the thought that I'd been unable to protect her. I realised then that I could never forgive myself if she remained and something happened to her.

'Sorry,' I said. 'That was petty of me. Schmidt isn't such a bad egg. Lord knows he can't be any worse than half the chinless wonders you seem to surround yourself with these days. You should take him up on his offer.'

She stared at me.

'Was that an apology, Sam? Are you feeling all right? What's more: a positive word for another man. I never thought I'd see the day.'

'What can I say?' I shrugged. 'He must have won me over with that smile of his.'

She laughed, despite herself. 'You really are trying to get rid of me, aren't you, Sam?'

'I'm thinking of your best interests,' I said. And it was true. For too long I'd told myself that her best interests were whatever mine happened to be. The truth was nothing of the sort.

'Well, Captain Wyndham,' she said, 'I'll tell you what I told Mr Schmidt. Calcutta's my home and I don't plan on leaving it any time soon.'

Despite my fine words, I couldn't help but feel my stomach leap.

'Besides,' she continued, 'who in their right mind would want to go to London in January?'

It was a good question.

'So you see, Captain, you better *had* catch whoever broke my windows because I'm not going anywhere.'

'Yes, *ma'am*,' I said. 'About the investigation, though – there may be a slight hiatus. I'm going away for a few weeks.'

'Really?' she said. 'You're taking a holiday? Now I *know* there's something wrong with you.'

I took a breath and steeled myself.

'It's not a holiday,' I said. 'I'm going to an ashram up in Assam somewhere. I'm going to get cleaned up ...'

She seemed perplexed for a moment, but then the penny dropped. I waited for her reaction. Her reply, when it came, was a surprise. She smiled, then shook her head, and it felt as though a weight had been lifted from both our shoulders.

'You know it won't be easy, Sam,' she said, walking over and taking my hand. 'They say *afeem* is one of the hardest addictions to overcome.'

I could have told her I'd already figured that out for myself, but sometimes it pays to keep my mouth shut.

'But rest assured,' she continued, 'I'll still be here when you get back.'

We said our farewells and I left her there, framed by the twin statues of Lord Shiva.

Two hours later I was walking across the concourse of Sealdah station. My suitcase, containing a generous three-day supply of *kerdū* pulp, was on the head of a red-shirted porter whom Surrender-not had sent off ahead to scout out my platform.

The days since Das's arrest had been difficult for the young sergeant. He was now, more than ever, an outcaste among his own kind, and as anger at the treatment of Basanti Das grew, so had Surrender-not's doubts about continuing as an officer in His Majesty's Imperial Police Force. I'd given him the same advice I'd given Annie: go away. Take a holiday from Calcutta. The difference was, he'd accepted it.

In two days he was off to Dacca, in East Bengal, to stay with an aunt. Dacca was far enough from the hothouse of Calcutta for him to have a chance of putting some perspective on things. And if a rapprochement with his family was to be engineered, the intercession of his father's sister would be a good start.

'You're sure you have everything?' he asked, sounding like a mother packing her child off to school.

'Yes,' I said, taking my case from the porter.

'Well ... good luck, Sam,' he said and stretched out a hand.

'And to you, too,' I said, shaking it. 'And Suren—'

'Yes, I know,' he said. 'I shall consider my options most carefully.'

'I was going to tell you not to talk to any of the working girls in the flat downstairs,' I said. 'I wouldn't want them taking advantage of you tonight. Without me there to protect you, goodness knows what they'll have you doing.'

'Yes, Sam.'

'Well, get going, young man,' I said. 'You know I can't stand long goodbyes. Get back and make sure Sandesh isn't loafing about.'

With that I left him and boarded in search of my compartment.

The train pulled out of the station only forty minutes late, which, I felt, constituted another triumph for the British Empire, and as we headed north through the Bengal countryside and I began to doze, my thoughts returned to Annie, standing there between the twin statues of Lord Shiva dancing his celestial dance. The destroyer and the creator. Destruction and rebirth.

Maybe there was something to Hindu mysticism after all.

AUTHOR'S NOTE

While fictionalised, many of the events and characters in the book are grounded in real history.

Gandhi did call for non-violent, non-cooperation with the aim of independence by the end of 1921, and amid the turmoil, the British government really did send Prince Edward, later King Edward VIII, who married Mrs Wallis Simpson and then abdicated, on a goodwill tour. Chitta Ranjan Das was indeed Gandhi's chief lieutenant in Bengal, and Subhash Bose, a man who would later go on to be a nationalist hero, had recently returned from England and become Das's deputy.

Das's wife, Basanti Devi, did speak to a rally in place of her husband and was duly arrested by the authorities, thereby re-energising the flagging non-cooperation movement.

Porton Down has, for over a hundred years, been the home of the UK Ministry of Defence's science and technology laboratory. Their scientists, as they were later to do with British and Australian troops, did carry out biological tests, including mustard gas experiments, on unsuspecting Indian troops, though these experiments took place mostly during the 1930s rather than during the First World War. The clandestine tests were carried out at a facility in the city of Rawalpindi, now in Pakistan.

Anyone interested in reading more on the subject could do no better than to start by tracking down a copy of *Gassed: British Chemical Warfare Experiments on Humans at Porton Down* by the journalist Rob Evans.

ACKNOWLEDGEMENTS

There are so many people without whom this novel wouldn't have seen the light of day, and I thank them all for their contributions, both large and small.

I'm indebted, in particular, to the fantastic team at Harvill Secker: to my editor, Jade Chandler, for helping turn a shed into a greenhouse; to Anna Redman for her tireless work over almost four years; to Sophie Painter for her fantastic marketing campaigns and to Kris Potter for his wonderful artwork. I must also thank Katherine Fry for her eagle eyes. I'm also grateful to Jane Kirby, Monique Corless, Sam Coates and Penny Liechti in the rights team for helping Sam and Surrender-not travel across continents. Thanks too, to Liz Foley, Rachel Cugnoni, Richard Cable, Bethan Jones, Alex Russell, Tom Drake-Lee and the wider team at Vintage for all their support, and to my agent, Sam Copeland, and the team at Rogers, Coleridge and White for all their hard work.

A special thank you is due to Christina Ellicott at Vintage and to all the staff at Waterstones for being such great supporters of the books and giving the first in the series, *A Rising Man*, such a wonderful start.

A debt of gratitude is owed to Vaseem Khan, Ayisha Malik, Alex Caan, AA Dhand and Imran Mahmood, all fantastic authors and known collectively as Team Dishoom, for their support and for the esoteric Twitter conversations.

Thanks of course, to all those good friends who let me borrow their names without worrying about what I'd do with them: to Darren Callaghan, Scott Lamont, Mathilde Rouvel, Alastair Dunlop and Iain McGuire.

Thanks too, to Darren Sharma for all the free lunches and the half a dozen emails which appear without fail in my inbox each morning; to the staff at the Idea Store Canary Wharf for offering me sanctuary; and to my partners at Houghton Street Capital, Hash, Alok and Neeraj, for putting up with my diva-esque tendencies and questionable work ethic. These are unlikely to change any time soon.

Thank you to Jonny Flint for bringing some sort of order to the chaos that is the Mukherjee house; to my boys, Milan and Aran, the source of so much of that chaos; and finally of course, thank you to my wife, Sonal, who puts up with so much and asks for so little. I'm blessed to be with you.